Lincoln Peirce

BiG NATE

MR. POPULARITY

D0089697

HARPER
An Imprint of HarperCollinsPublishers

Big Nate: Mr. Popularity
Copyright © 2014 by United Feature Syndicate, Inc.
All rights reserved. Printed in the United States of America.
No part of this book may be used or reproduced in any manner whatsoever without
written permission except in the case of brief quotations embodied in critical
articles and reviews. For information address HarperCollins Children's Books, a
division of HarperCollins Publishers, 195 Broadway, New York, NY 10007.
www.harpercollinschildrens.com
www.bignatebooks.com

Go to www.bignate.com to read the *Big Nate* comic strip.

Library of Congress Control Number: 2013956489
ISBN 978-0-06-208700-3 (pbk.)

Typography by Andrea Vandergrift
20 21 22   CG / LSCC   20 19 18 17 16 15
❖
First Edition

More

BiG
NATE

adventures from

Lincoln Peirce

Novels:

BIG NATE: IN A CLASS BY HIMSELF

BIG NATE STRIKES AGAIN

BIG NATE ON A ROLL

BIG NATE GOES FOR BROKE

BIG NATE FLIPS OUT

BIG NATE: IN THE ZONE

Activity Books:

BIG NATE BOREDOM BUSTER

BIG NATE FUN BLASTER

BIG NATE DOODLEPALOOZA

Comic Compilations:

BIG NATE: WHAT COULD POSSIBLY GO WRONG?

BIG NATE: HERE GOES NOTHING

BIG NATE: GENIUS MODE

BIG NATE FROM THE TOP

BIG NATE OUT LOUD

BIG NATE AND FRIENDS

BIG NATE MAKES THE GRADE

BIG NATE: GAME ON!

BIG NATE: I CAN'T TAKE IT!

BIG NATE: GREAT MINDS THINK ALIKE

SIR STORYTIME

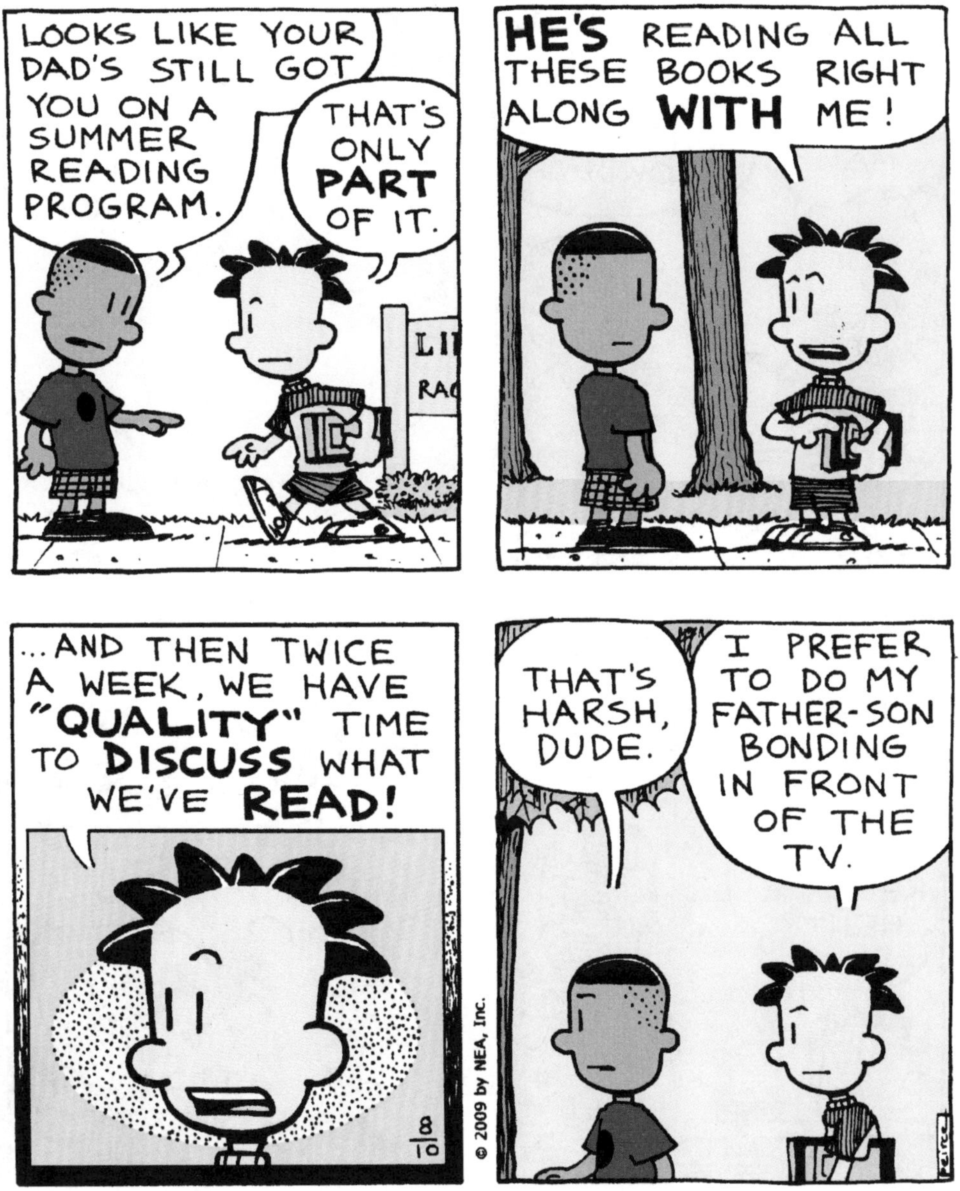
LOOKS LIKE YOUR DAD'S STILL GOT YOU ON A SUMMER READING PROGRAM.
THAT'S ONLY **PART** OF IT.
HE'S READING ALL THESE BOOKS RIGHT ALONG **WITH** ME!
...AND THEN TWICE A WEEK, WE HAVE "**QUALITY**" TIME TO **DISCUSS** WHAT WE'VE **READ**!
© 2009 by NEA, Inc.
THAT'S HARSH, DUDE.
I PREFER TO DO MY FATHER-SON BONDING IN FRONT OF THE TV.

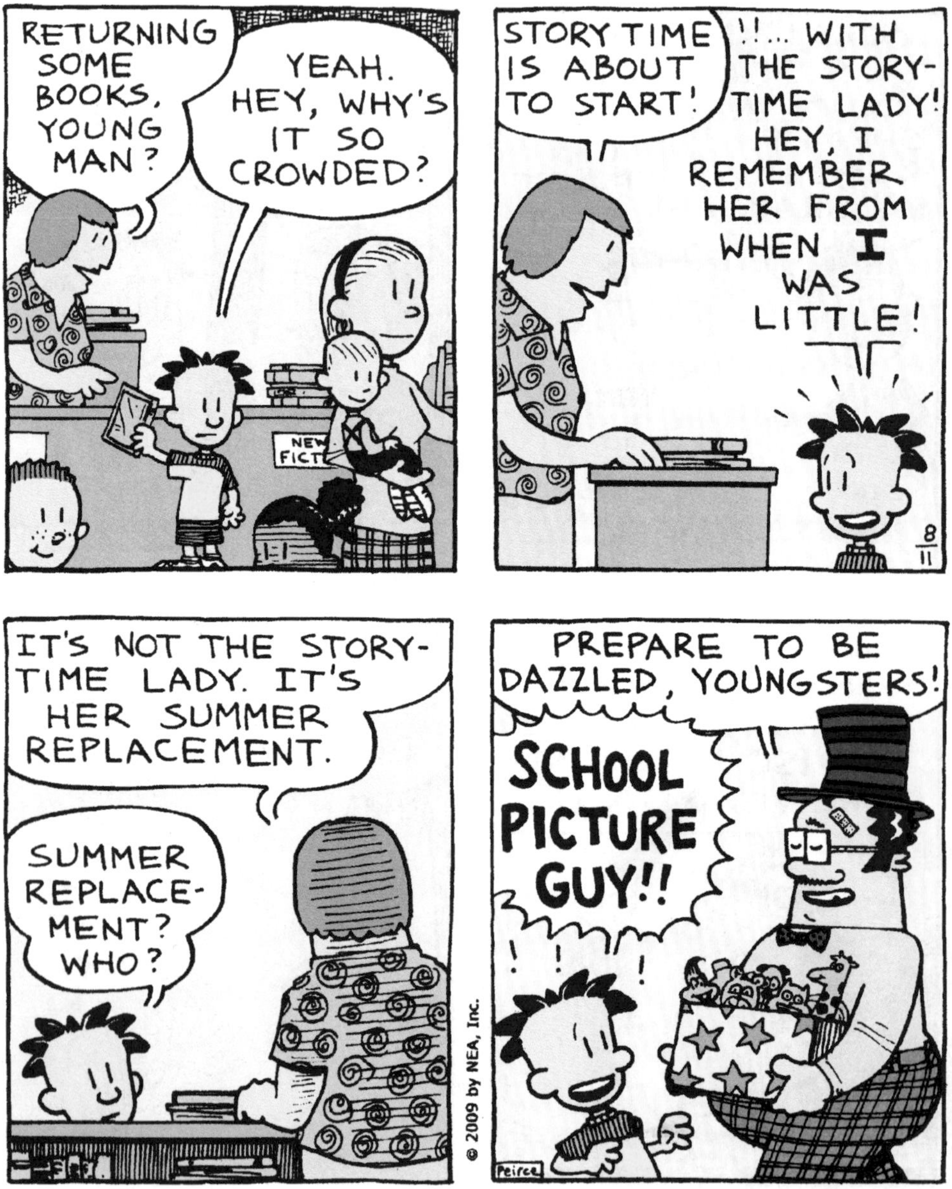
RETURNING SOME BOOKS, YOUNG MAN?
YEAH. HEY, WHY'S IT SO CROWDED?
NEW FICT
STORY TIME IS ABOUT TO START!
!!... WITH THE STORY-TIME LADY! HEY, I REMEMBER HER FROM WHEN I WAS LITTLE!
8/11
IT'S NOT THE STORY-TIME LADY. IT'S HER SUMMER REPLACEMENT.
SUMMER REPLACE-MENT? WHO?
PREPARE TO BE DAZZLED, YOUNGSTERS!
SCHOOL PICTURE GUY!!
! ! !
Peirce
© 2009 by NEA, Inc.

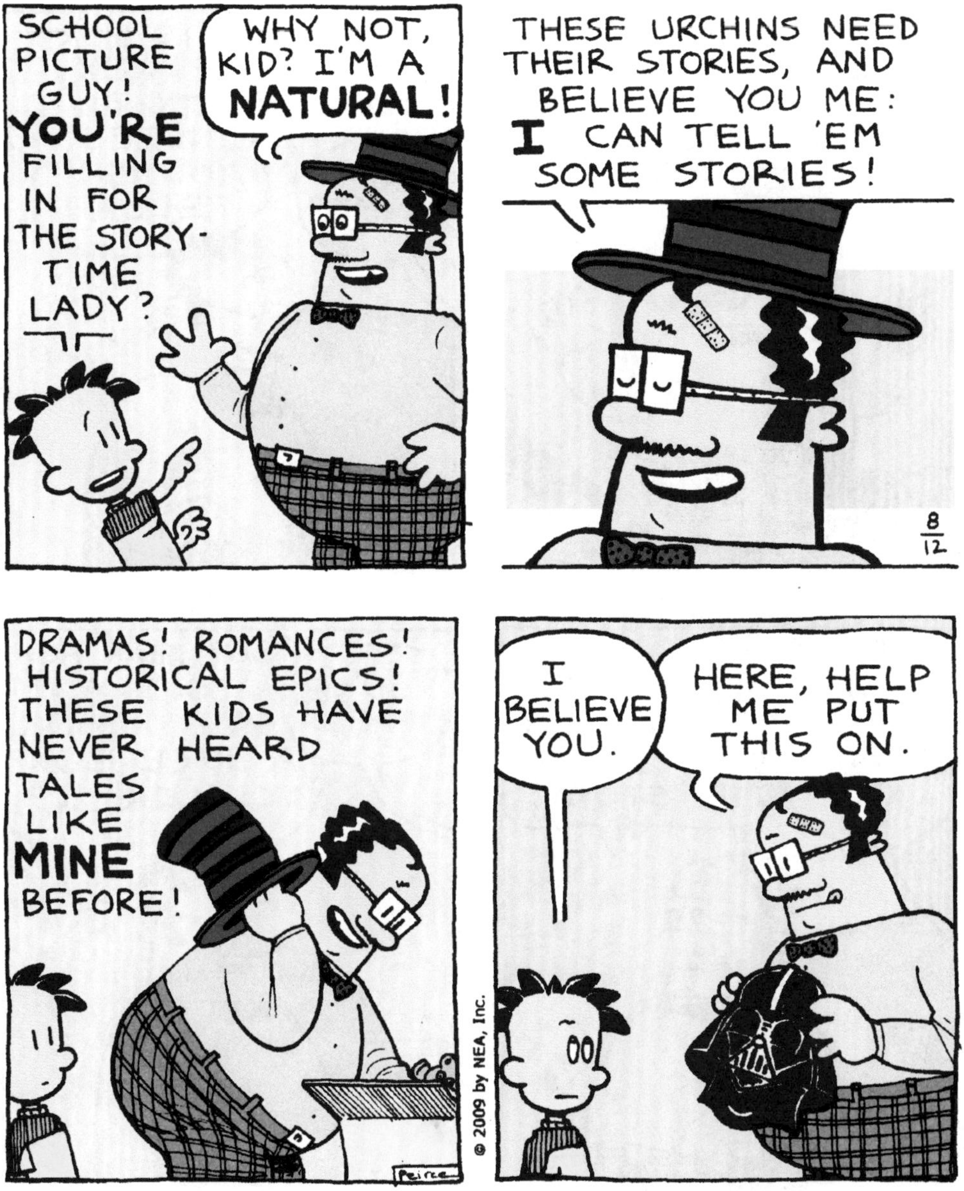
SCHOOL PICTURE GUY! YOU'RE FILLING IN FOR THE STORY-TIME LADY?
WHY NOT, KID? I'M A NATURAL!
THESE URCHINS NEED THEIR STORIES, AND BELIEVE YOU ME: I CAN TELL 'EM SOME STORIES!
8/12
DRAMAS! ROMANCES! HISTORICAL EPICS! THESE KIDS HAVE NEVER HEARD TALES LIKE MINE BEFORE!
Peirce
I BELIEVE YOU.
HERE, HELP ME PUT THIS ON.

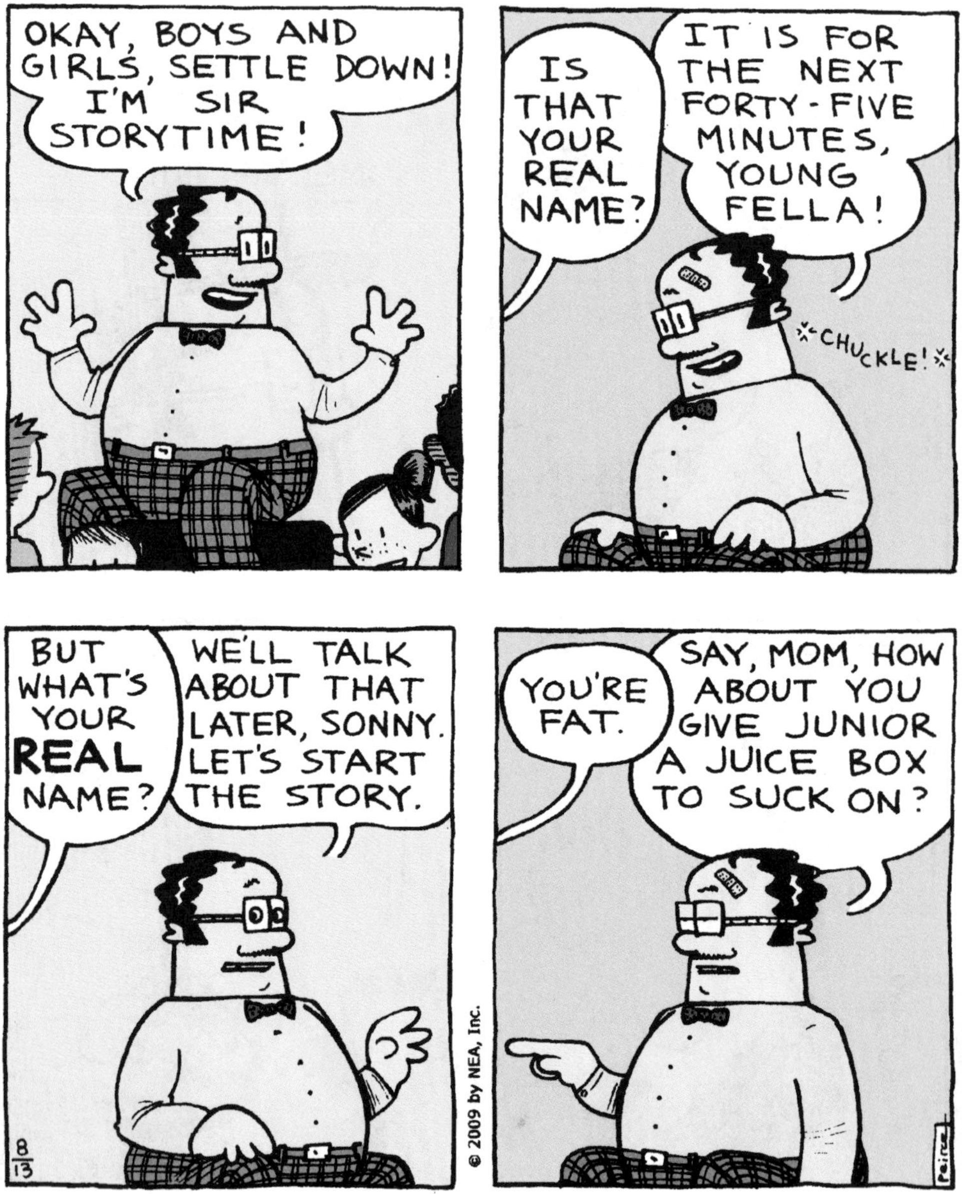
OKAY, BOYS AND GIRLS, SETTLE DOWN! I'M SIR STORYTIME!
IS THAT YOUR REAL NAME?
IT IS FOR THE NEXT FORTY-FIVE MINUTES, YOUNG FELLA!
CHUCKLE!
BUT WHAT'S YOUR **REAL** NAME?
WE'LL TALK ABOUT THAT LATER, SONNY. LET'S START THE STORY.
YOU'RE FAT.
SAY, MOM, HOW ABOUT YOU GIVE JUNIOR A JUICE BOX TO SUCK ON?
8/13
Peirce

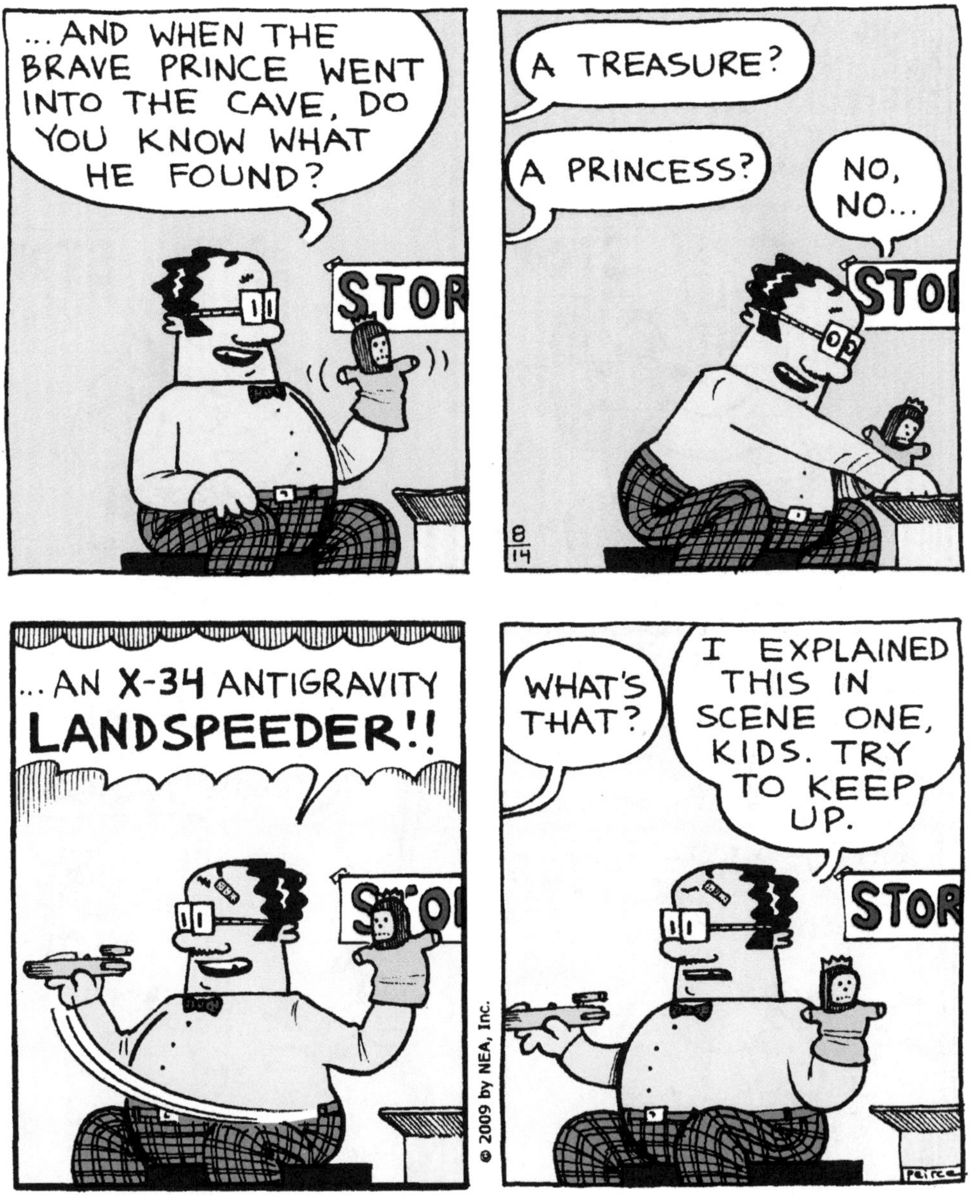
...AND WHEN THE BRAVE PRINCE WENT INTO THE CAVE, DO YOU KNOW WHAT HE FOUND?
STOR
A TREASURE?
A PRINCESS?
NO, NO...
STOR
8/14
...AN X-34 ANTIGRAVITY LANDSPEEDER!!
WHAT'S THAT?
I EXPLAINED THIS IN SCENE ONE, KIDS. TRY TO KEEP UP.
STOR
© 2009 by NEA, Inc.
PEIRCE

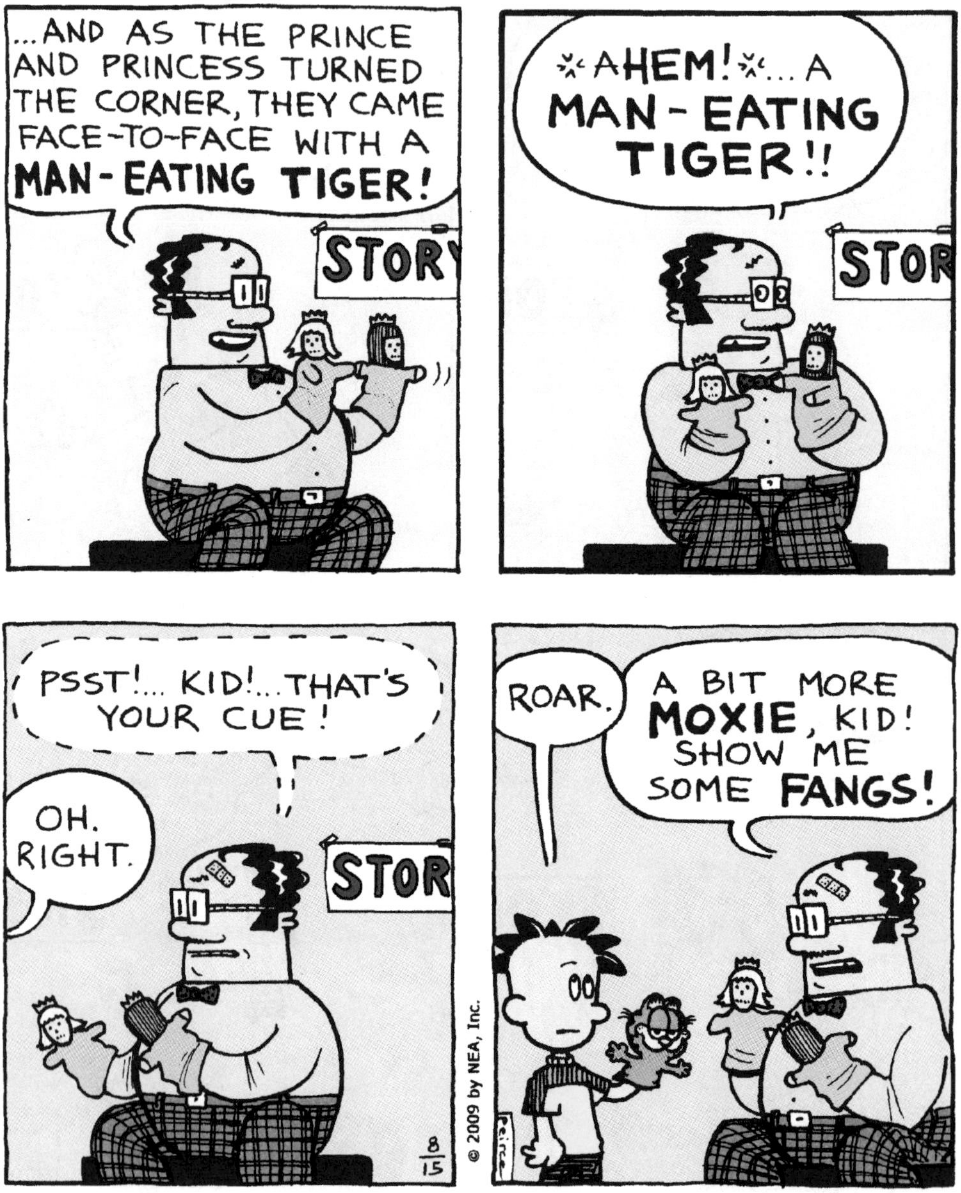

...AND AS THE PRINCE AND PRINCESS TURNED THE CORNER, THEY CAME FACE-TO-FACE WITH A MAN-EATING TIGER!
STORY
AHEM!... A MAN-EATING TIGER!!
STOR
PSST!... KID!... THAT'S YOUR CUE!
OH. RIGHT.
STOR
8
15
© 2009 by NEA, Inc.
ROAR.
A BIT MORE MOXIE, KID! SHOW ME SOME FANGS!

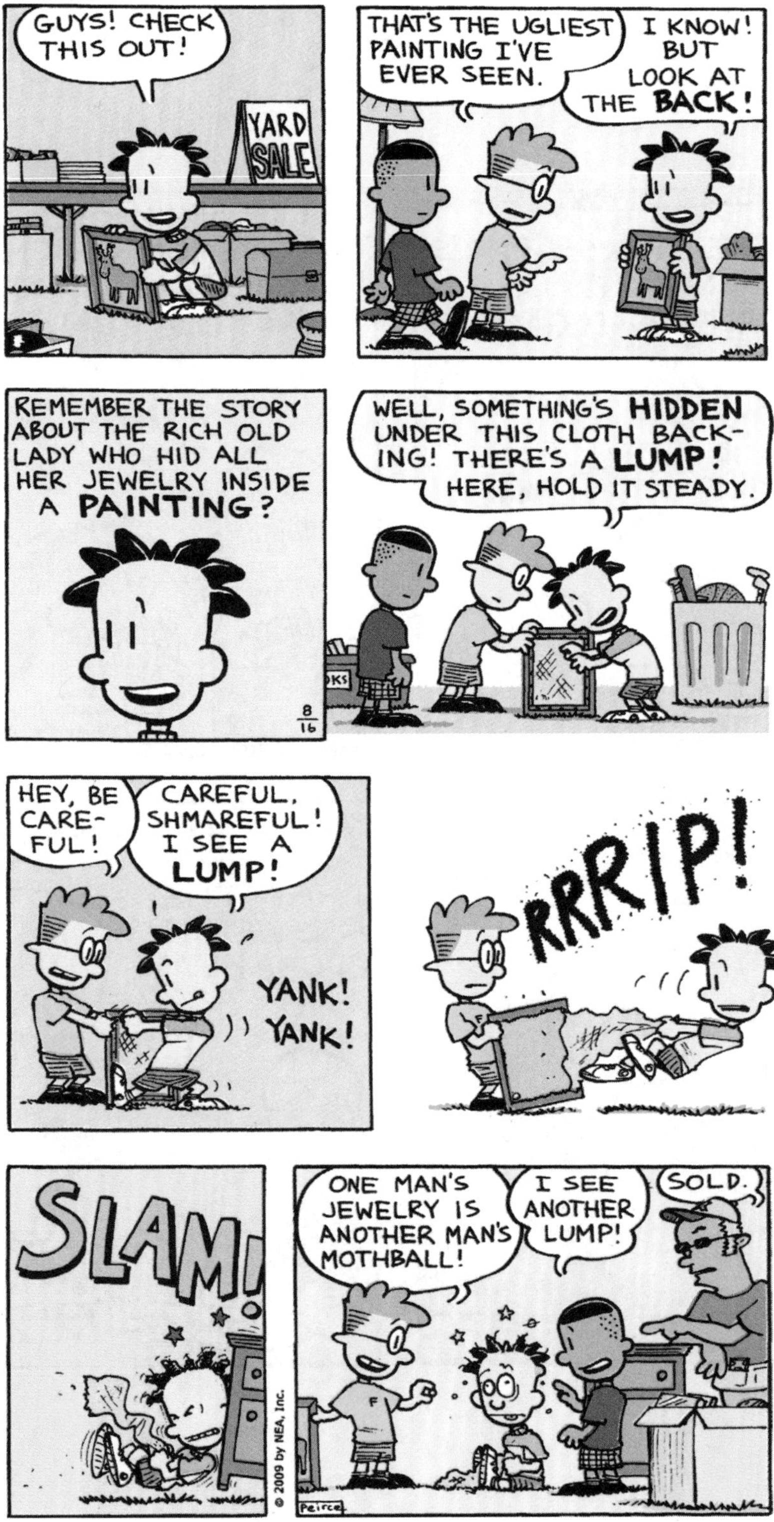
GUYS! CHECK THIS OUT!
YARD SALE
THAT'S THE UGLIEST PAINTING I'VE EVER SEEN.
I KNOW! BUT LOOK AT THE **BACK**!
REMEMBER THE STORY ABOUT THE RICH OLD LADY WHO HID ALL HER JEWELRY INSIDE A **PAINTING**?
WELL, SOMETHING'S **HIDDEN** UNDER THIS CLOTH BACK-ING! THERE'S A **LUMP**! HERE, HOLD IT STEADY.
8/16
HEY, BE CARE-FUL!
CAREFUL, SHMAREFUL! I SEE A **LUMP**!
YANK! YANK!
RRRIP!
SLAM!
© 2009 by NEA, Inc.
ONE MAN'S JEWELRY IS ANOTHER MAN'S MOTHBALL!
I SEE ANOTHER LUMP!
SOLD.
Peirce

WHEN OPPORTUNITY KNOCKS ...

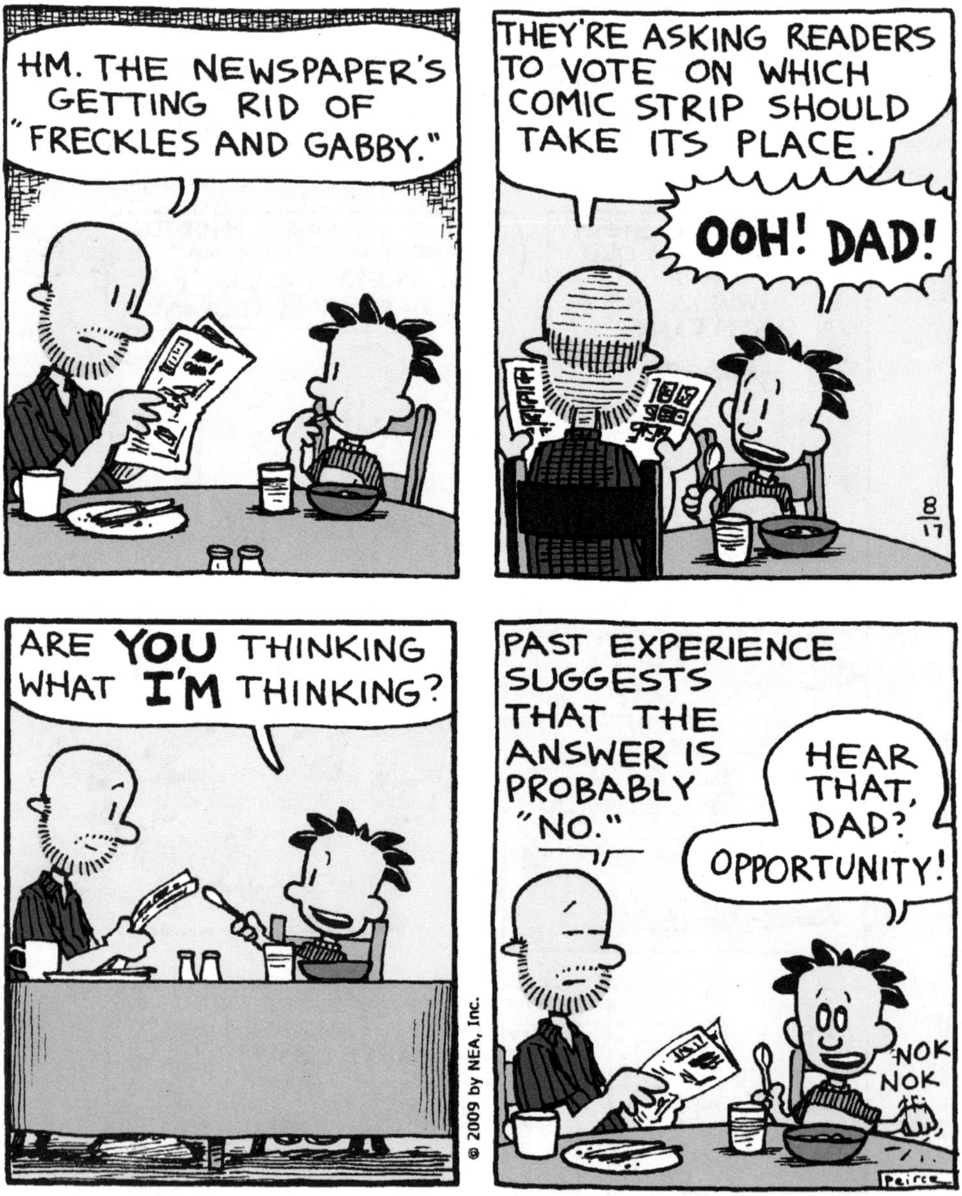
HM. THE NEWSPAPER'S GETTING RID OF "FRECKLES AND GABBY."
THEY'RE ASKING READERS TO VOTE ON WHICH COMIC STRIP SHOULD TAKE ITS PLACE.
OOH! DAD!
8/17
ARE YOU THINKING WHAT I'M THINKING?
PAST EXPERIENCE SUGGESTS THAT THE ANSWER IS PROBABLY "NO."
HEAR THAT, DAD? OPPORTUNITY!
NOK NOK
peirce

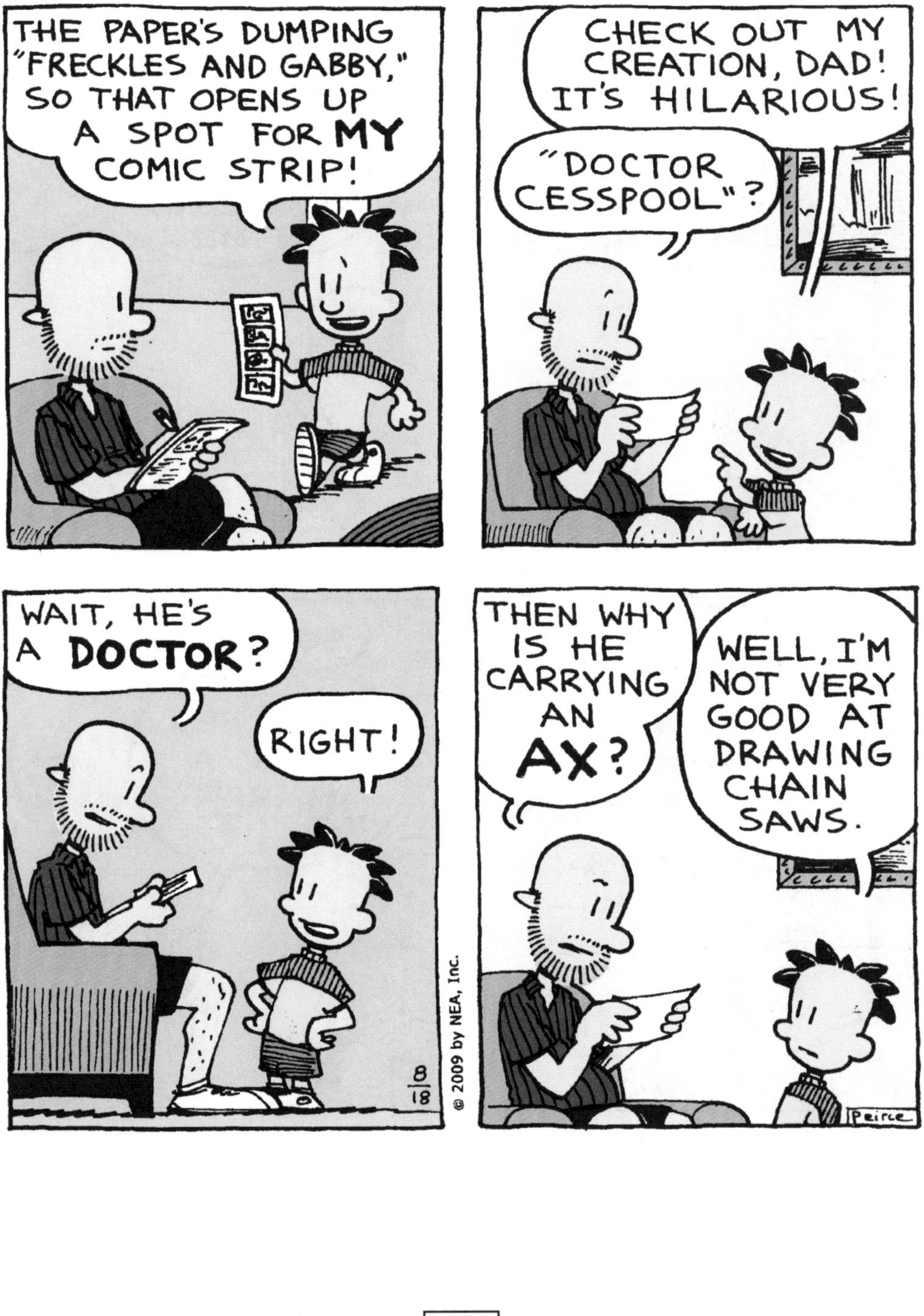
THE PAPER'S DUMPING "FRECKLES AND GABBY," SO THAT OPENS UP A SPOT FOR **MY** COMIC STRIP!
CHECK OUT MY CREATION, DAD! IT'S HILARIOUS!
"DOCTOR CESSPOOL"?
WAIT, HE'S A **DOCTOR**?
RIGHT!
8/18
© 2009 by NEA, Inc.
THEN WHY IS HE CARRYING AN **AX**?
WELL, I'M NOT VERY GOOD AT DRAWING CHAIN SAWS.
Peirce

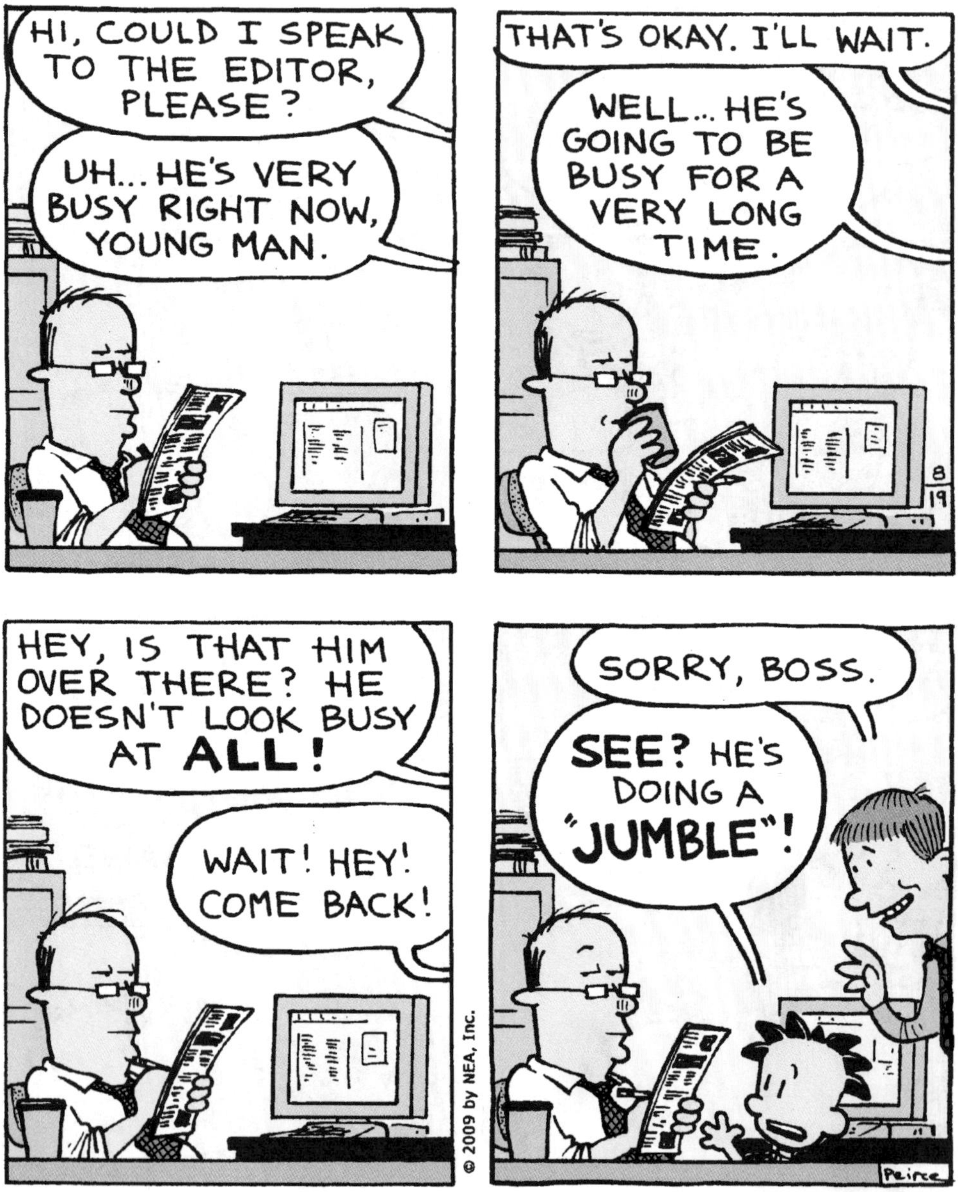
HI, COULD I SPEAK TO THE EDITOR, PLEASE?
UH... HE'S VERY BUSY RIGHT NOW, YOUNG MAN.
THAT'S OKAY. I'LL WAIT.
WELL... HE'S GOING TO BE BUSY FOR A VERY LONG TIME.
8 19
HEY, IS THAT HIM OVER THERE? HE DOESN'T LOOK BUSY AT ALL!
WAIT! HEY! COME BACK!
SORRY, BOSS.
SEE? HE'S DOING A "JUMBLE"!
PEIRCE

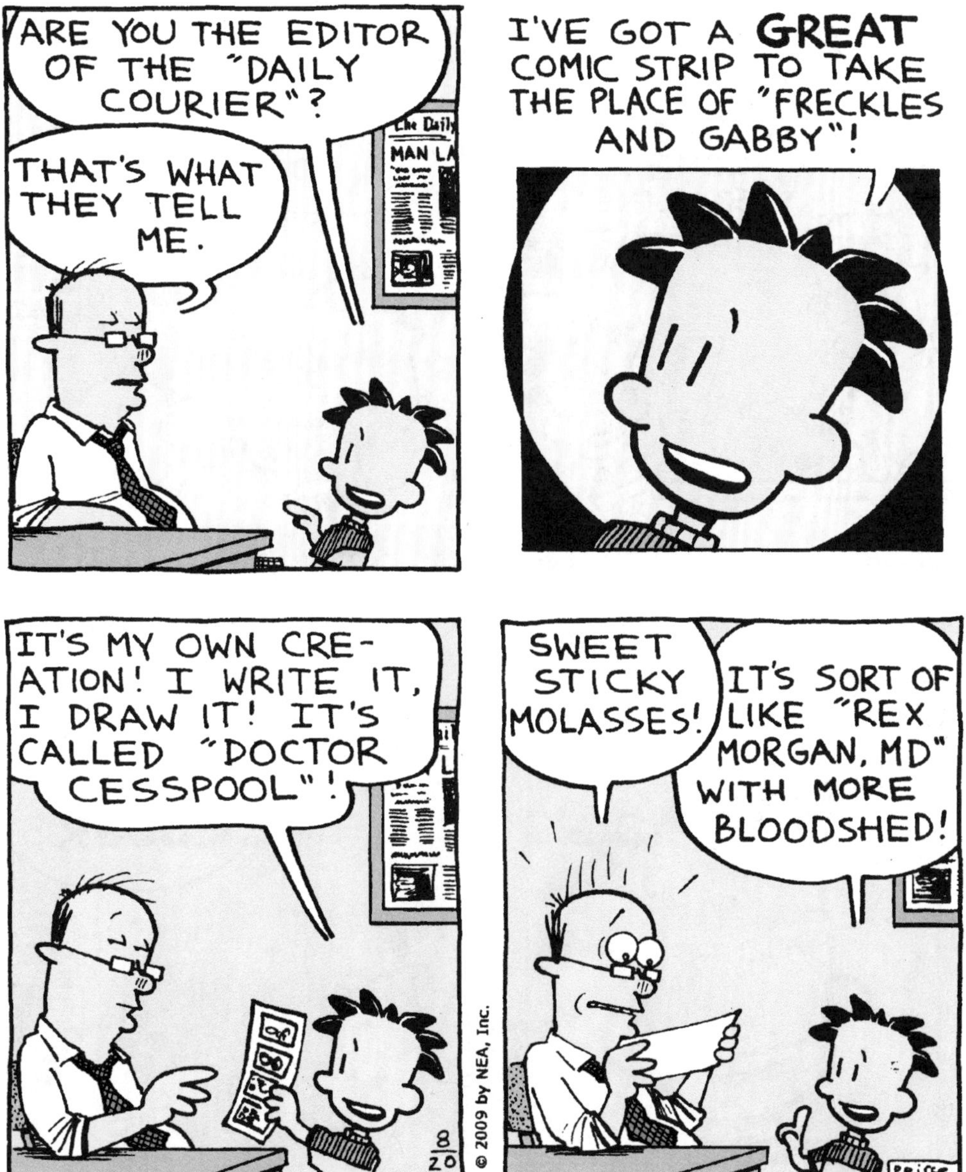
ARE YOU THE EDITOR OF THE "DAILY COURIER"?
THAT'S WHAT THEY TELL ME.
I'VE GOT A GREAT COMIC STRIP TO TAKE THE PLACE OF "FRECKLES AND GABBY"!
IT'S MY OWN CRE-ATION! I WRITE IT, I DRAW IT! IT'S CALLED "DOCTOR CESSPOOL"!
8/20
© 2009 by NEA, Inc.
SWEET STICKY MOLASSES!
IT'S SORT OF LIKE "REX MORGAN, MD" WITH MORE BLOODSHED!
peirce

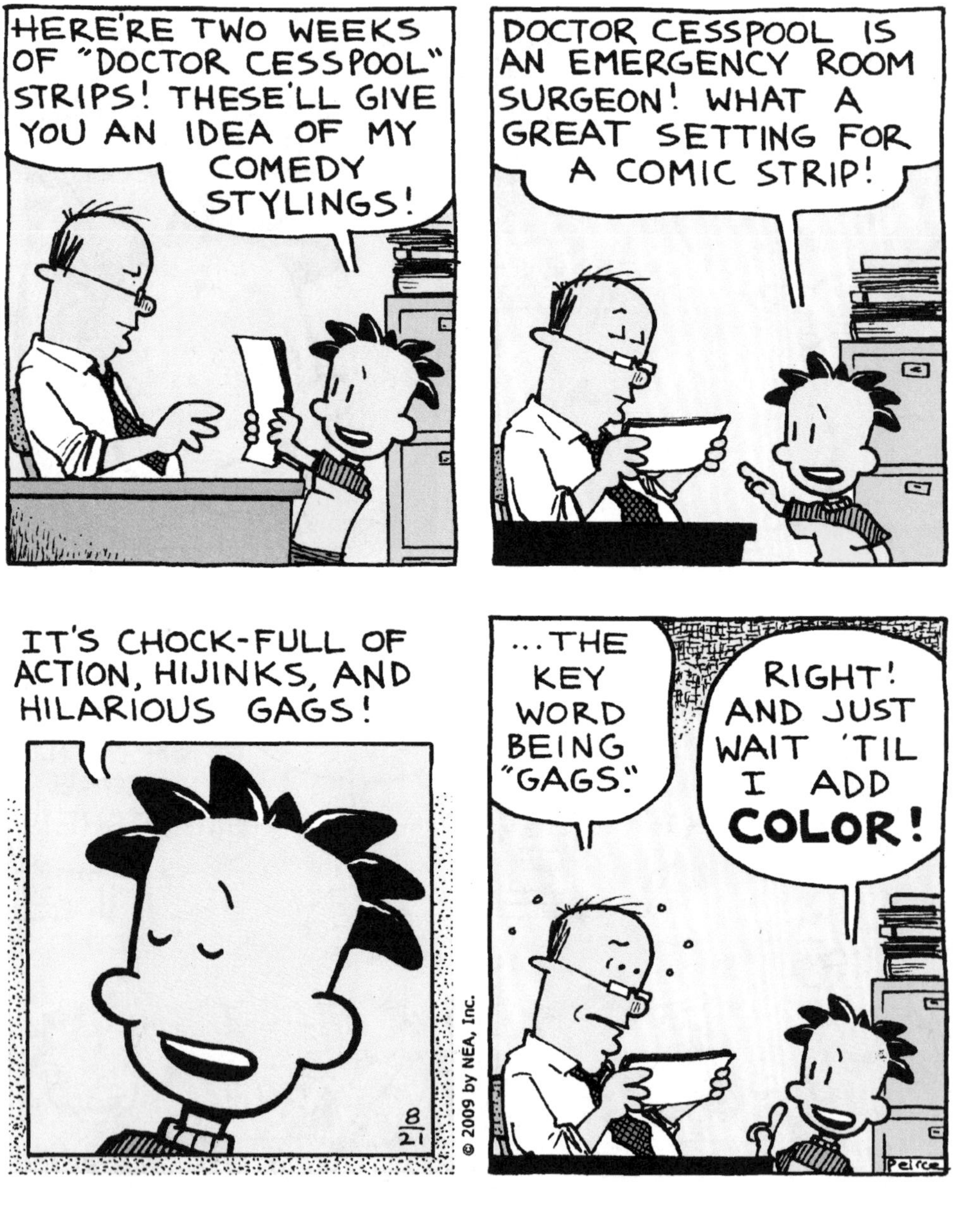
HERE'RE TWO WEEKS OF "DOCTOR CESSPOOL" STRIPS! THESE'LL GIVE YOU AN IDEA OF MY COMEDY STYLINGS!
DOCTOR CESSPOOL IS AN EMERGENCY ROOM SURGEON! WHAT A GREAT SETTING FOR A COMIC STRIP!
IT'S CHOCK-FULL OF ACTION, HIJINKS, AND HILARIOUS GAGS!
...THE KEY WORD BEING "GAGS."
RIGHT! AND JUST WAIT 'TIL I ADD COLOR!
8/21
© 2009 by NEA, Inc.
Peirce

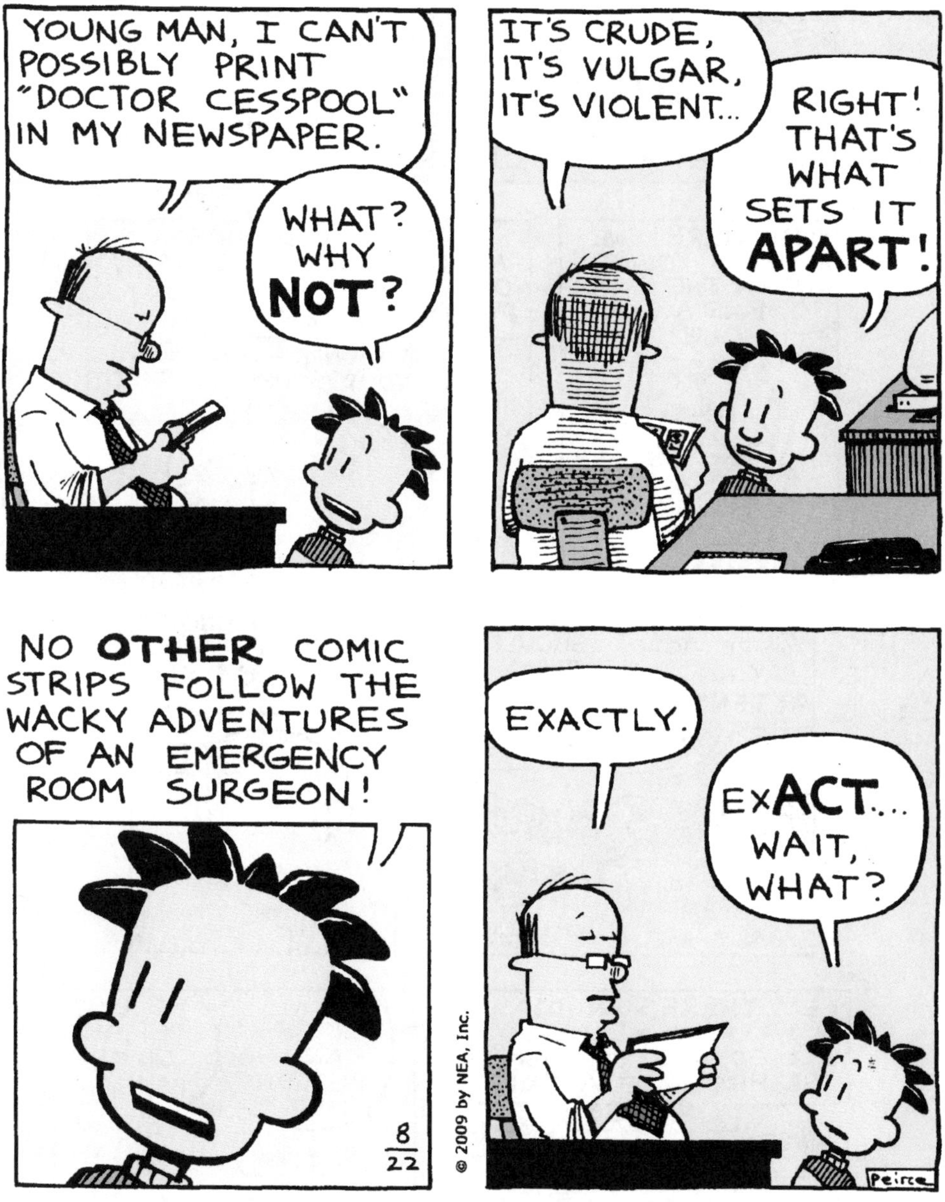
YOUNG MAN, I CAN'T POSSIBLY PRINT "DOCTOR CESSPOOL" IN MY NEWSPAPER.
WHAT? WHY **NOT**?
IT'S CRUDE, IT'S VULGAR, IT'S VIOLENT...
RIGHT! THAT'S WHAT SETS IT **APART**!
NO **OTHER** COMIC STRIPS FOLLOW THE WACKY ADVENTURES OF AN EMERGENCY ROOM SURGEON!
8/22
© 2009 by NEA, Inc.
EXACTLY.
ExACT... WAIT, WHAT?
Peirce

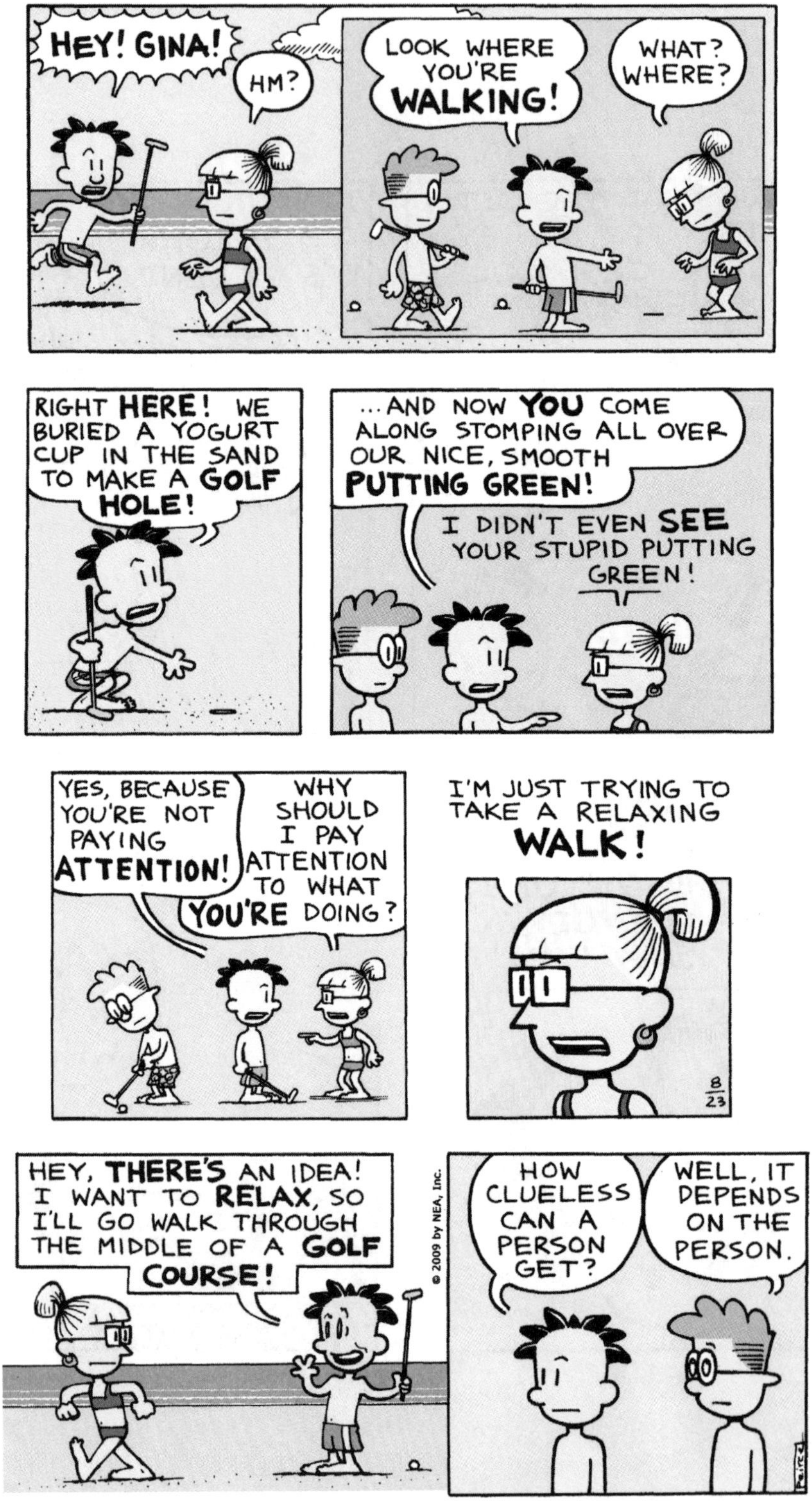
HEY! GINA!
HM?
LOOK WHERE YOU'RE WALKING!
WHAT? WHERE?
RIGHT HERE! WE BURIED A YOGURT CUP IN THE SAND TO MAKE A GOLF HOLE!
...AND NOW YOU COME ALONG STOMPING ALL OVER OUR NICE, SMOOTH PUTTING GREEN!
I DIDN'T EVEN SEE YOUR STUPID PUTTING GREEN!
YES, BECAUSE YOU'RE NOT PAYING ATTENTION!
WHY SHOULD I PAY ATTENTION TO WHAT YOU'RE DOING?
I'M JUST TRYING TO TAKE A RELAXING WALK!
8/23
HEY, THERE'S AN IDEA! I WANT TO RELAX, SO I'LL GO WALK THROUGH THE MIDDLE OF A GOLF COURSE!
© 2009 by NEA, Inc.
HOW CLUELESS CAN A PERSON GET?
WELL, IT DEPENDS ON THE PERSON.
Peirce

SHOP 'TIL YOU DROP

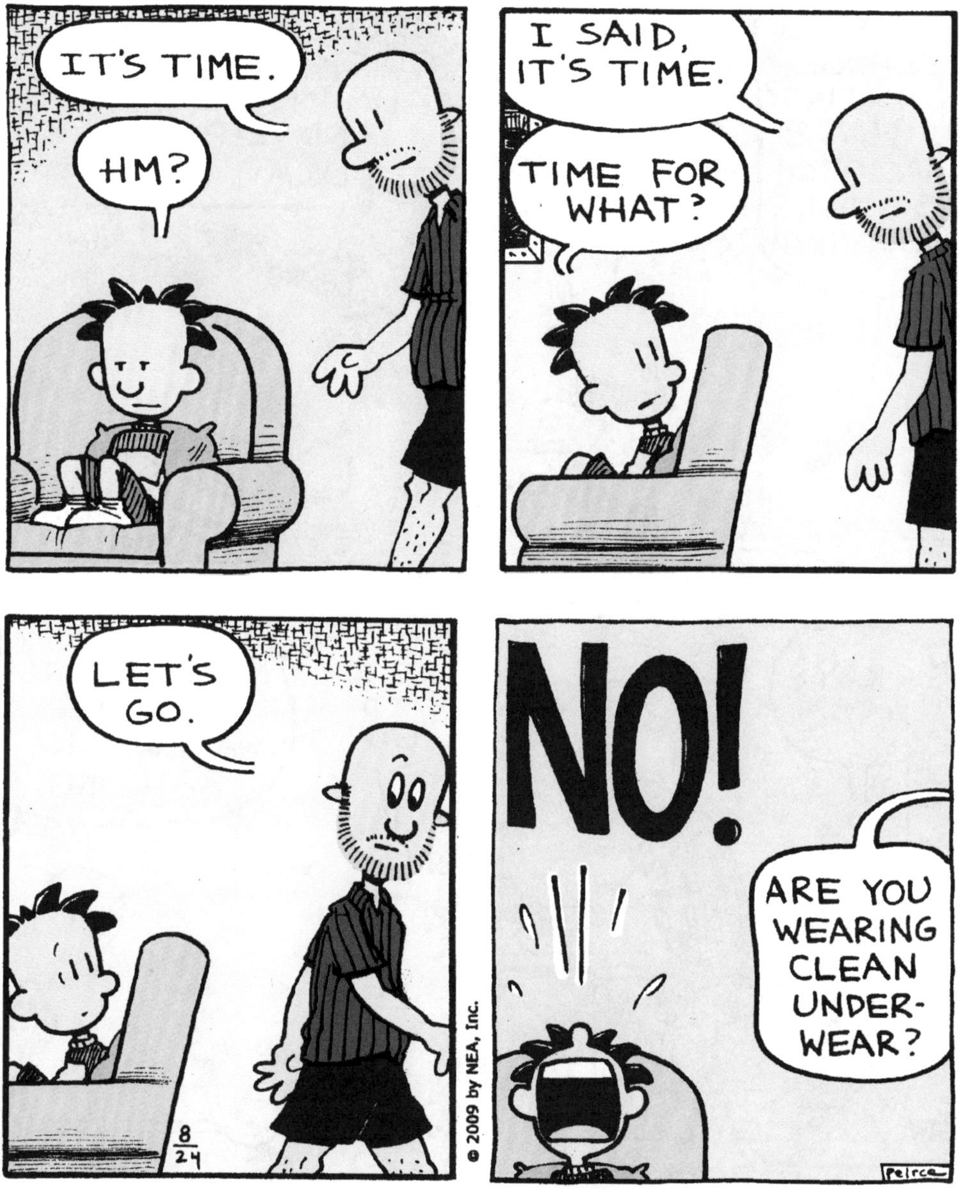
IT'S TIME.
HM?
I SAID, IT'S TIME.
TIME FOR WHAT?
LET'S GO.
8/24
© 2009 by NEA, Inc.
NO!
ARE YOU WEARING CLEAN UNDER-WEAR?
peirce

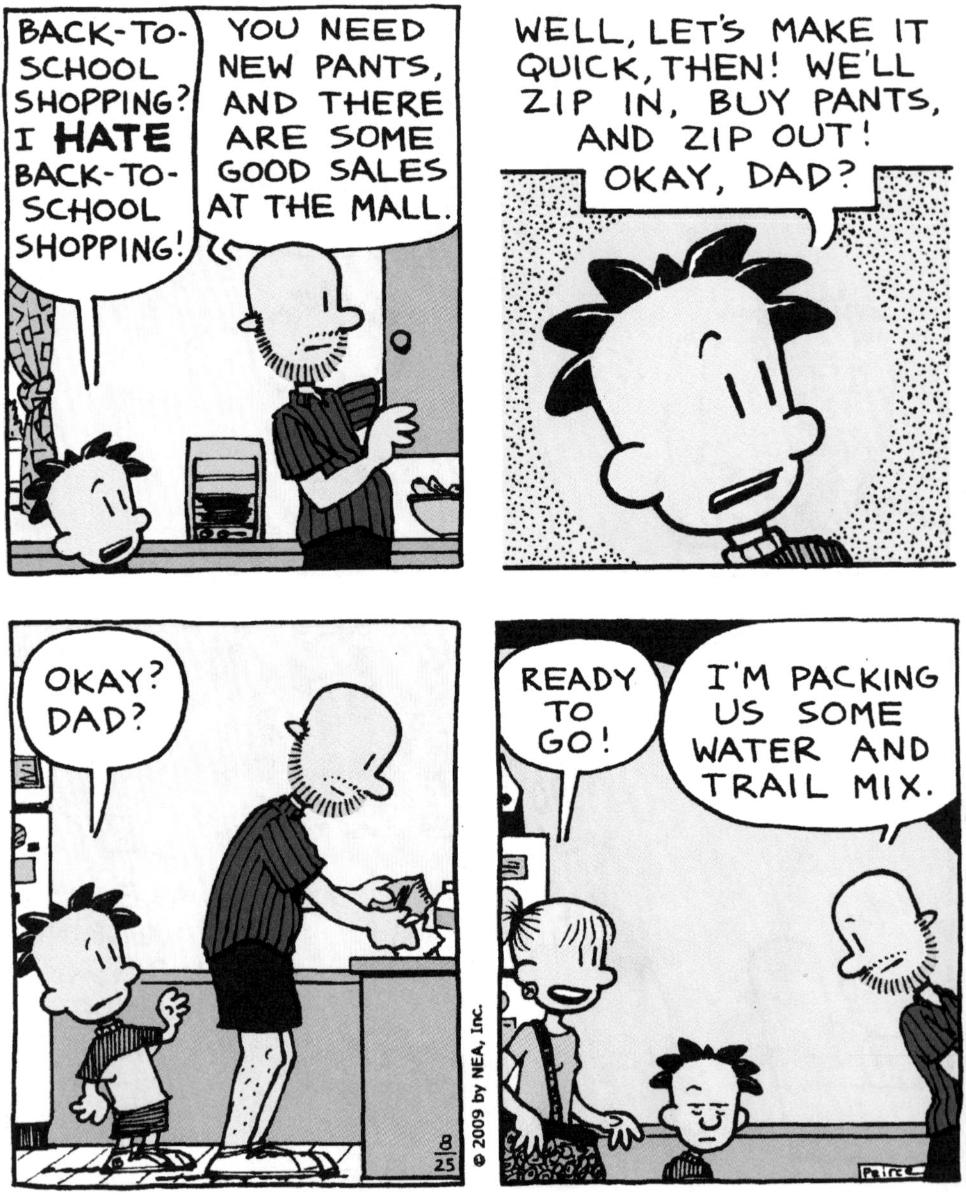
BACK-TO-SCHOOL SHOPPING? I HATE BACK-TO-SCHOOL SHOPPING!
YOU NEED NEW PANTS, AND THERE ARE SOME GOOD SALES AT THE MALL.
WELL, LET'S MAKE IT QUICK, THEN! WE'LL ZIP IN, BUY PANTS, AND ZIP OUT! OKAY, DAD?
OKAY? DAD?
8/25
© 2009 by NEA, Inc.
READY TO GO!
I'M PACKING US SOME WATER AND TRAIL MIX.
PEIRCE

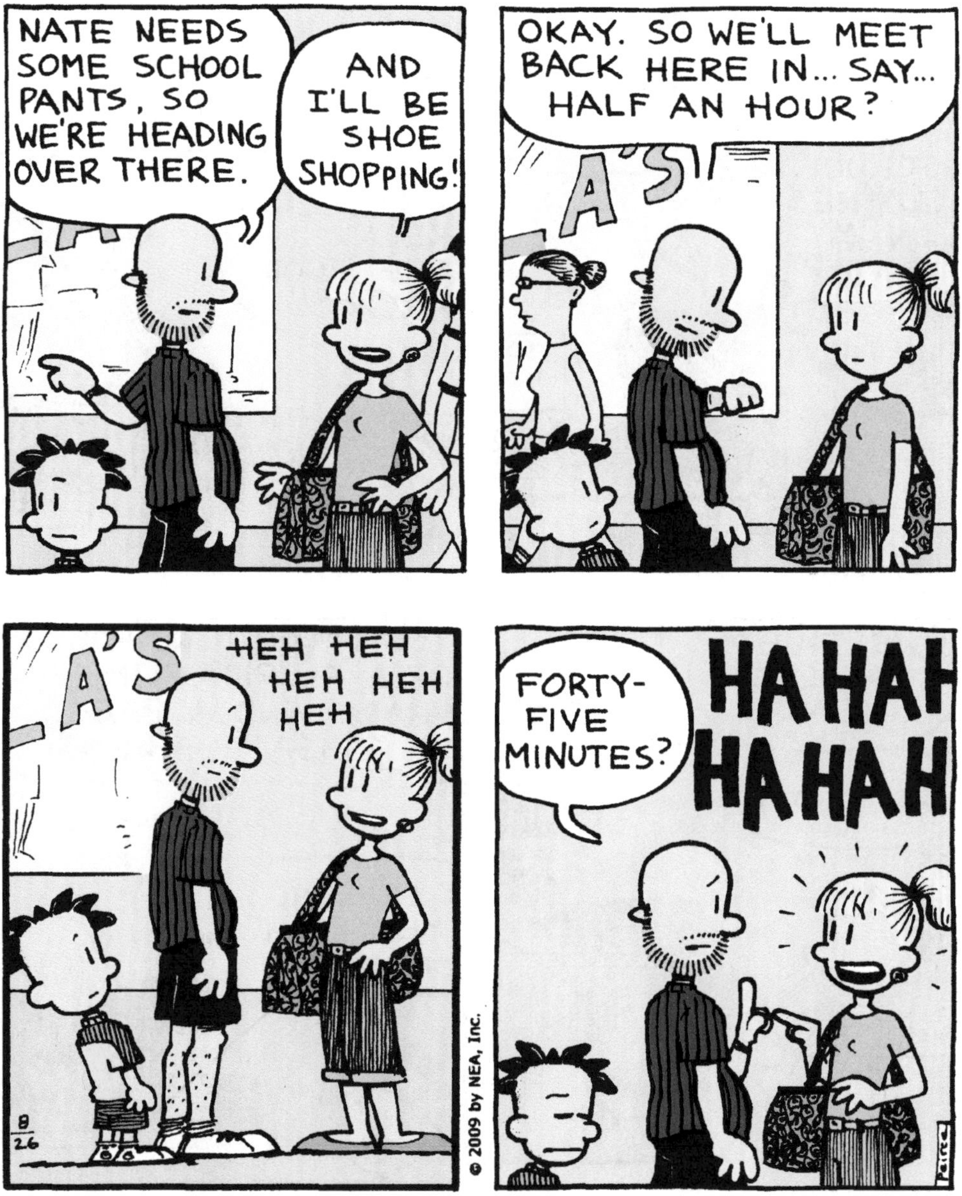
NATE NEEDS SOME SCHOOL PANTS, SO WE'RE HEADING OVER THERE.
AND I'LL BE SHOE SHOPPING!
OKAY. SO WE'LL MEET BACK HERE IN... SAY... HALF AN HOUR?
HEH HEH HEH HEH HEH
FORTY-FIVE MINUTES?
HAHAH HAHAH
© 2009 by NEA, Inc.

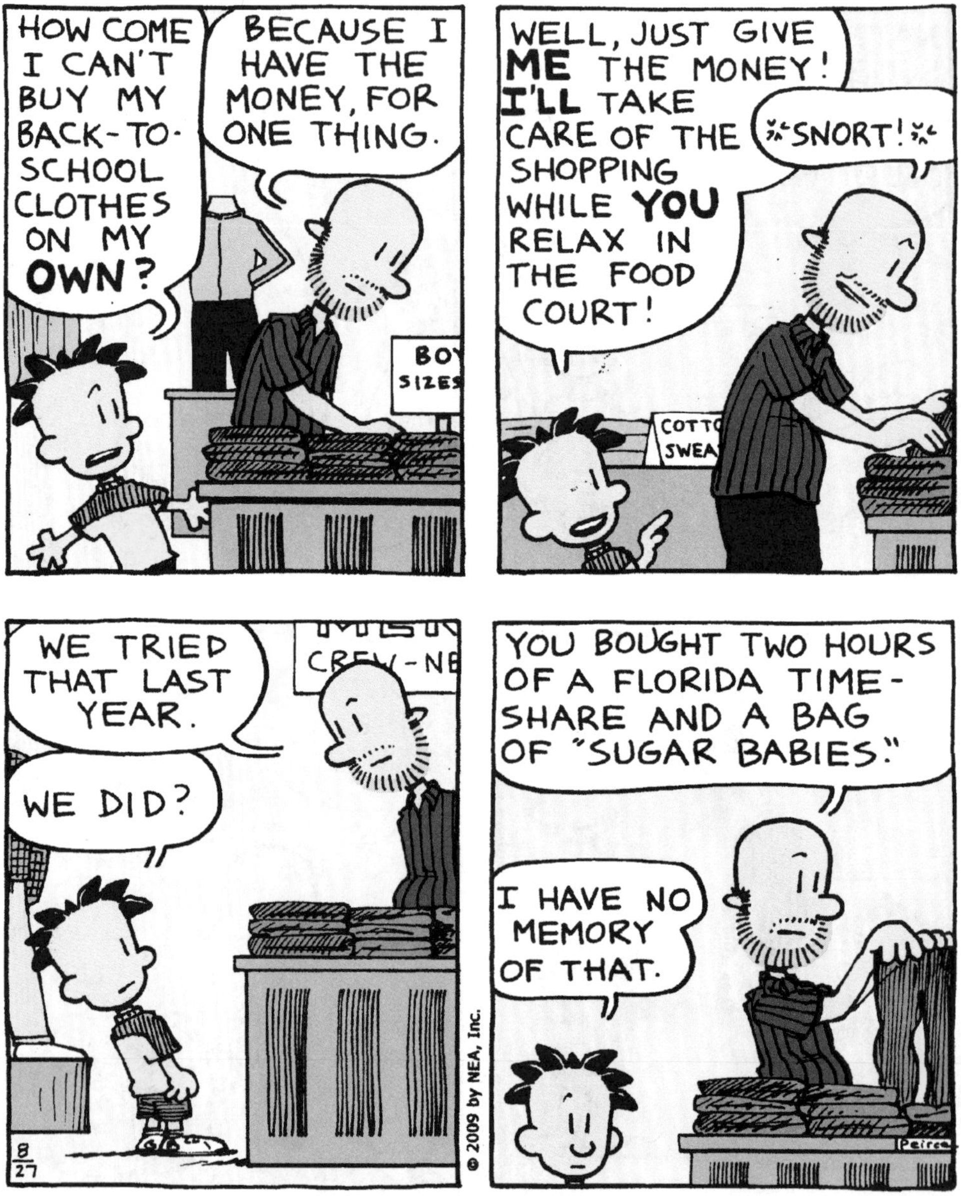
HOW COME I CAN'T BUY MY BACK-TO-SCHOOL CLOTHES ON MY OWN?
BECAUSE I HAVE THE MONEY, FOR ONE THING.
BOY SIZES
WELL, JUST GIVE ME THE MONEY! I'LL TAKE CARE OF THE SHOPPING WHILE YOU RELAX IN THE FOOD COURT!
SNORT!
WE TRIED THAT LAST YEAR.
WE DID?
YOU BOUGHT TWO HOURS OF A FLORIDA TIME-SHARE AND A BAG OF "SUGAR BABIES."
I HAVE NO MEMORY OF THAT.
8/27
© 2009 by NEA, Inc.
Peirce

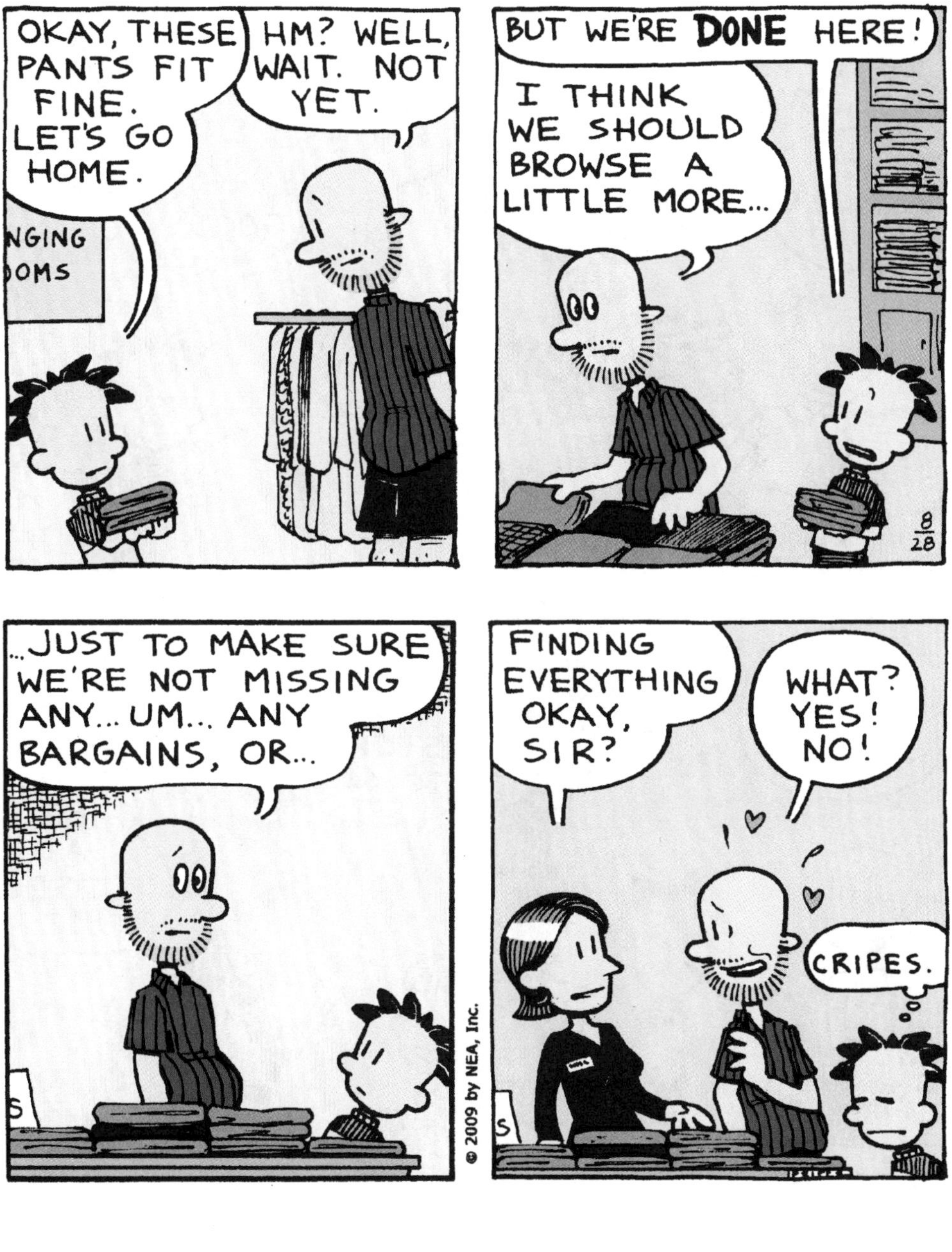
OKAY, THESE PANTS FIT FINE. LET'S GO HOME.
HM? WELL, WAIT. NOT YET.
NGING
OOMS
BUT WE'RE **DONE** HERE!
I THINK WE SHOULD BROWSE A LITTLE MORE...
8/28
...JUST TO MAKE SURE WE'RE NOT MISSING ANY... UM... ANY BARGAINS, OR...
© 2009 by NEA, Inc.
FINDING EVERYTHING OKAY, SIR?
WHAT? YES! NO!
CRIPES.

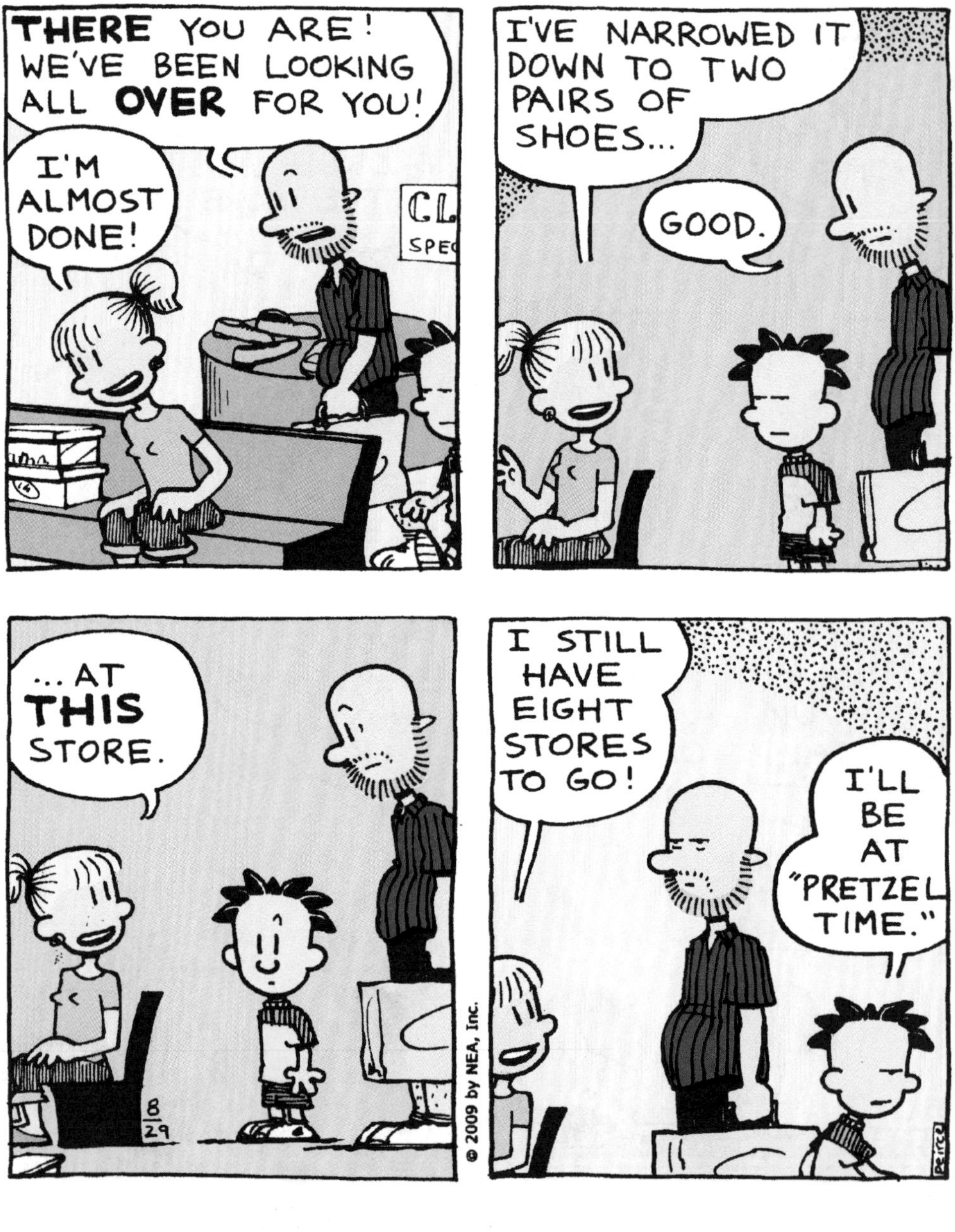
THERE YOU ARE! WE'VE BEEN LOOKING ALL OVER FOR YOU!
I'M ALMOST DONE!
I'VE NARROWED IT DOWN TO TWO PAIRS OF SHOES...
GOOD.
...AT THIS STORE.
8/29
© 2009 by NEA, Inc.
I STILL HAVE EIGHT STORES TO GO!
I'LL BE AT "PRETZEL TIME."

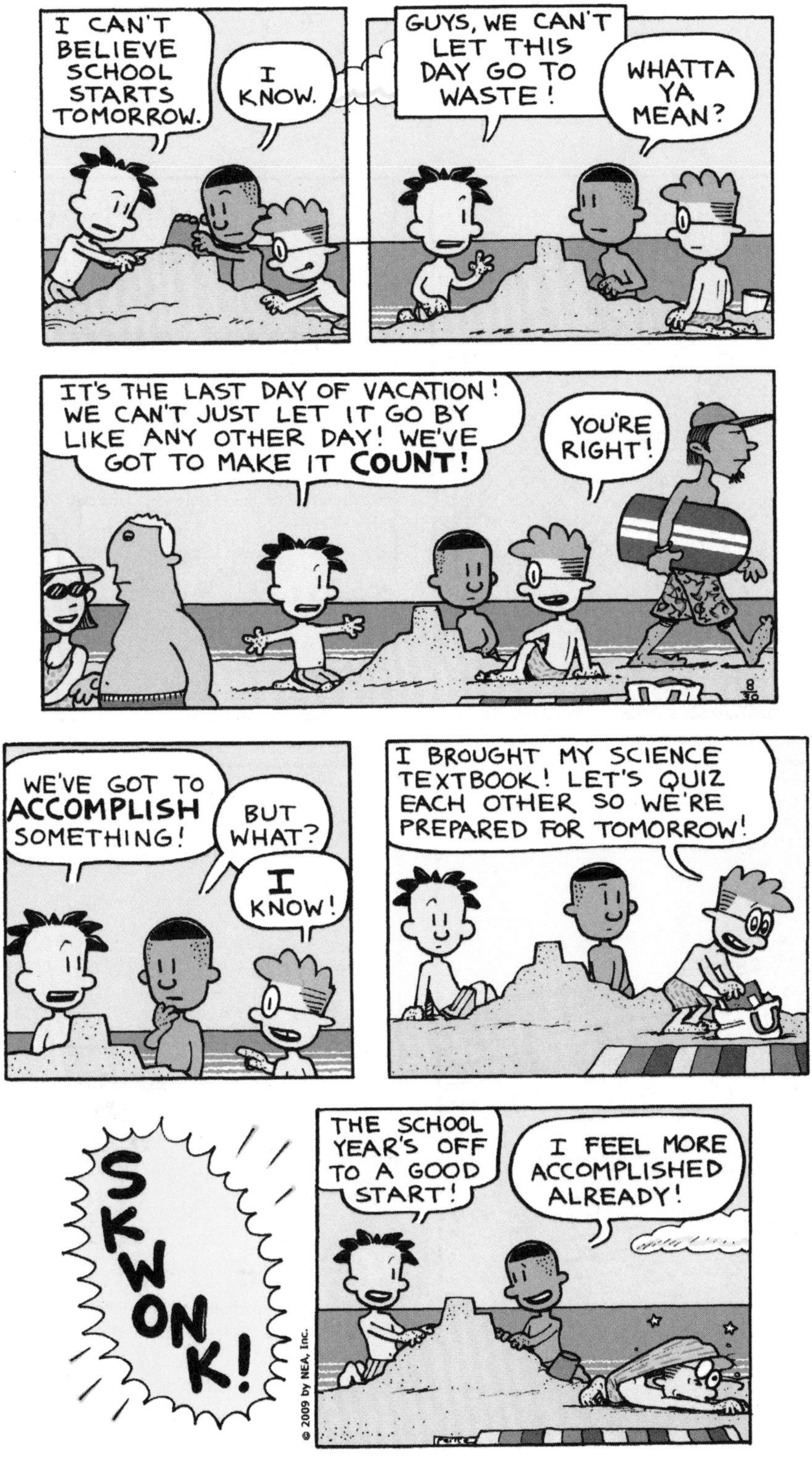
I CAN'T BELIEVE SCHOOL STARTS TOMORROW.
I KNOW.
GUYS, WE CAN'T LET THIS DAY GO TO WASTE!
WHATTA YA MEAN?
IT'S THE LAST DAY OF VACATION! WE CAN'T JUST LET IT GO BY LIKE ANY OTHER DAY! WE'VE GOT TO MAKE IT COUNT!
YOU'RE RIGHT!
WE'VE GOT TO ACCOMPLISH SOMETHING!
BUT WHAT?
I KNOW!
I BROUGHT MY SCIENCE TEXTBOOK! LET'S QUIZ EACH OTHER SO WE'RE PREPARED FOR TOMORROW!
SKWONK!
THE SCHOOL YEAR'S OFF TO A GOOD START!
I FEEL MORE ACCOMPLISHED ALREADY!
© 2009 by NEA, Inc.

LEARNING ≠ FUN

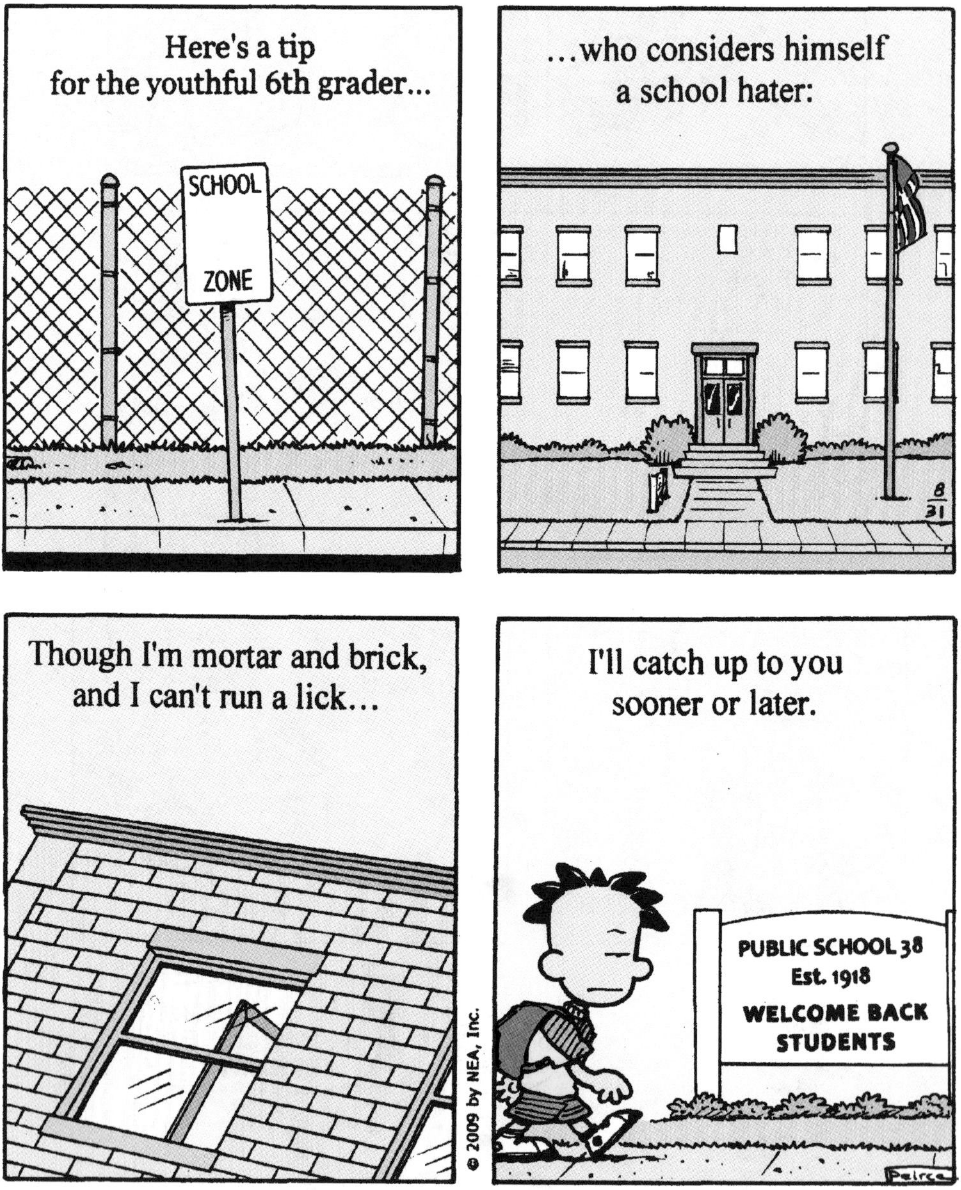

Here's a tip for the youthful 6th grader...
SCHOOL
ZONE
...who considers himself a school hater:
8/31
Though I'm mortar and brick, and I can't run a lick...
© 2009 by NEA, Inc.
I'll catch up to you sooner or later.
PUBLIC SCHOOL 38
Est. 1918
WELCOME BACK
STUDENTS
Peirce

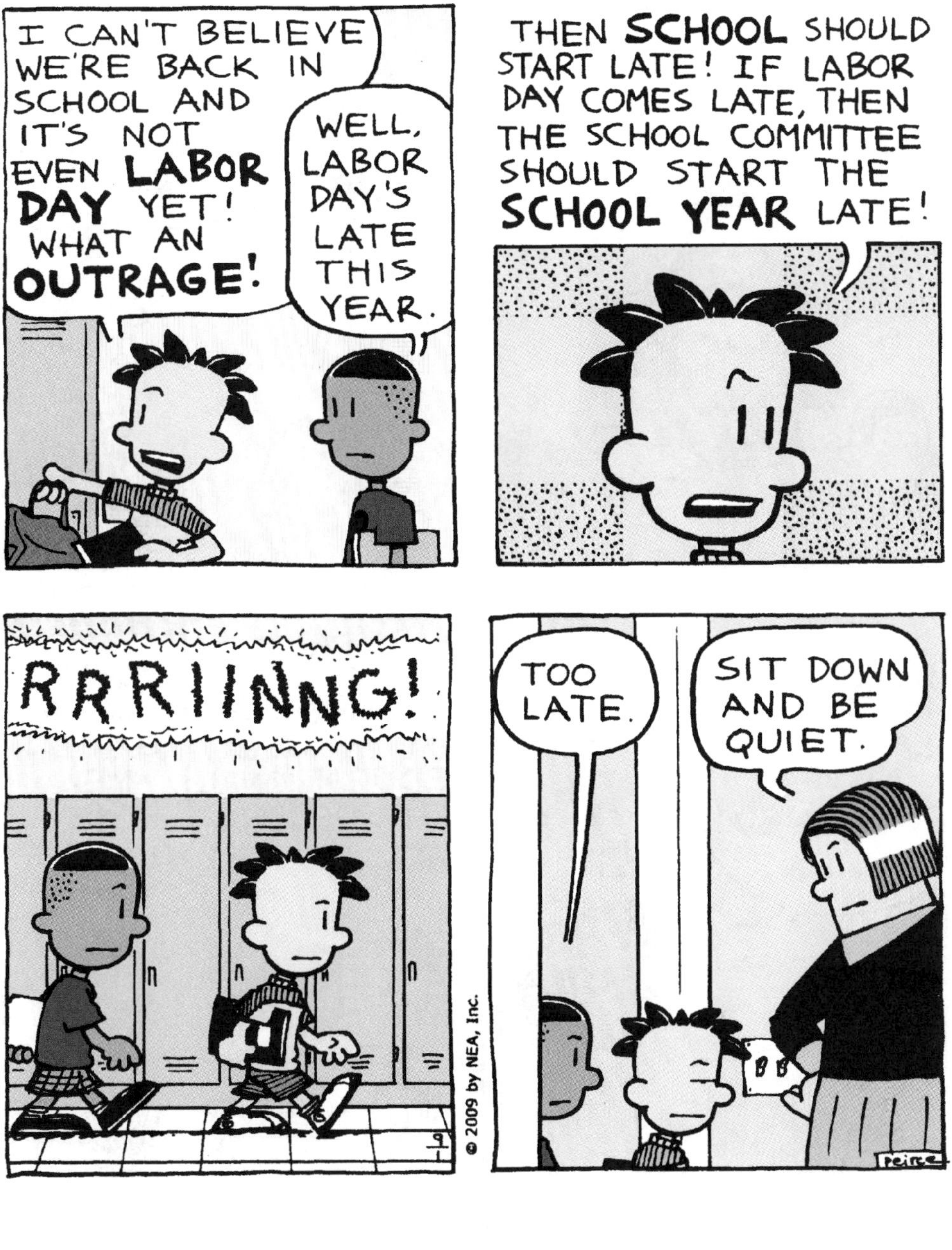
I CAN'T BELIEVE WE'RE BACK IN SCHOOL AND IT'S NOT EVEN LABOR DAY YET! WHAT AN OUTRAGE!
WELL, LABOR DAY'S LATE THIS YEAR.
THEN SCHOOL SHOULD START LATE! IF LABOR DAY COMES LATE, THEN THE SCHOOL COMMITTEE SHOULD START THE SCHOOL YEAR LATE!
RRRIINNG!
© 2009 by NEA, Inc.
TOO LATE.
SIT DOWN AND BE QUIET.

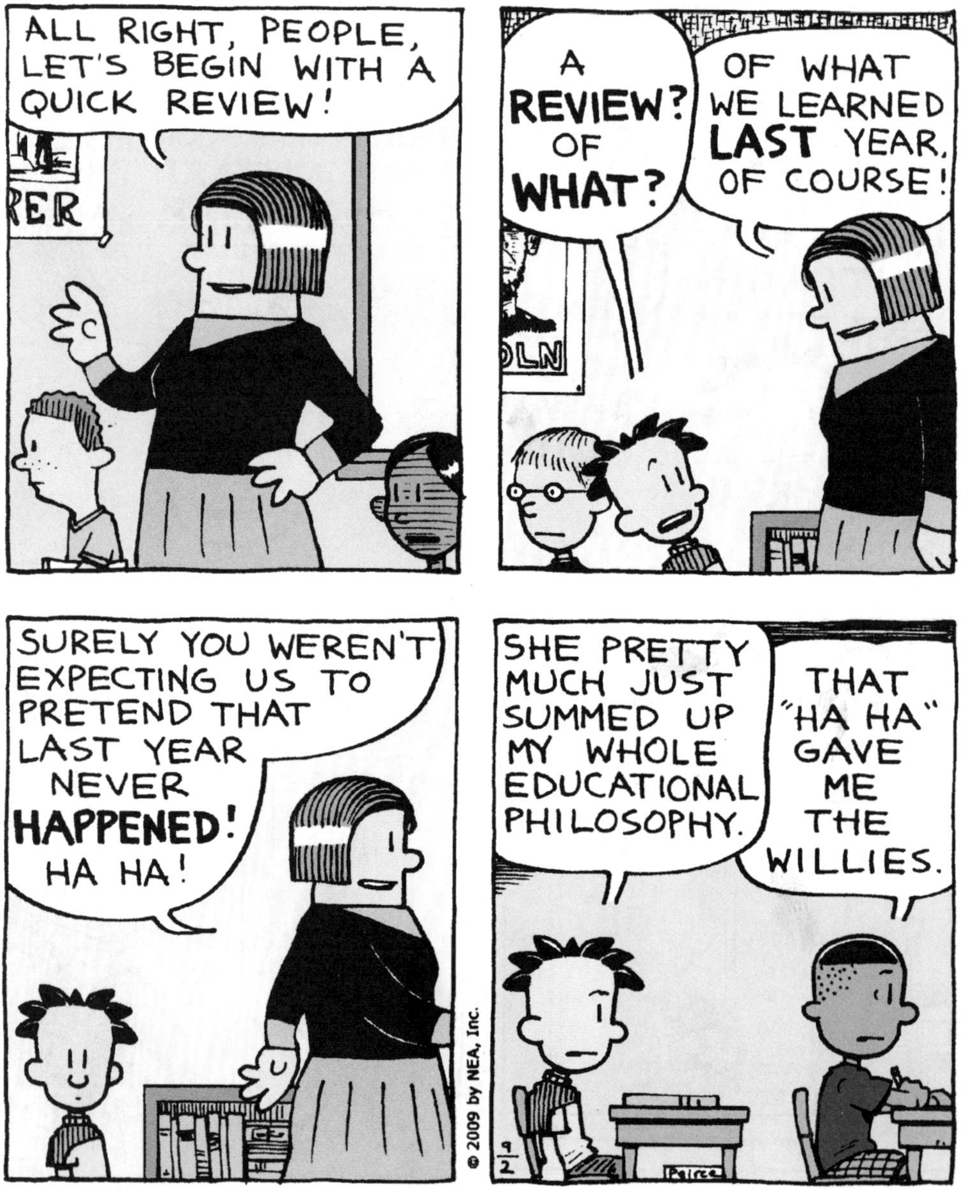
ALL RIGHT, PEOPLE, LET'S BEGIN WITH A QUICK REVIEW!
ER
A **REVIEW?** OF **WHAT?**
OF WHAT WE LEARNED **LAST** YEAR, OF COURSE!
OLN
SURELY YOU WEREN'T EXPECTING US TO PRETEND THAT LAST YEAR NEVER **HAPPENED!** HA HA!
© 2009 by NEA, Inc.
9/2
SHE PRETTY MUCH JUST SUMMED UP MY WHOLE EDUCATIONAL PHILOSOPHY.
THAT "HA HA" GAVE ME THE WILLIES.
Peirce

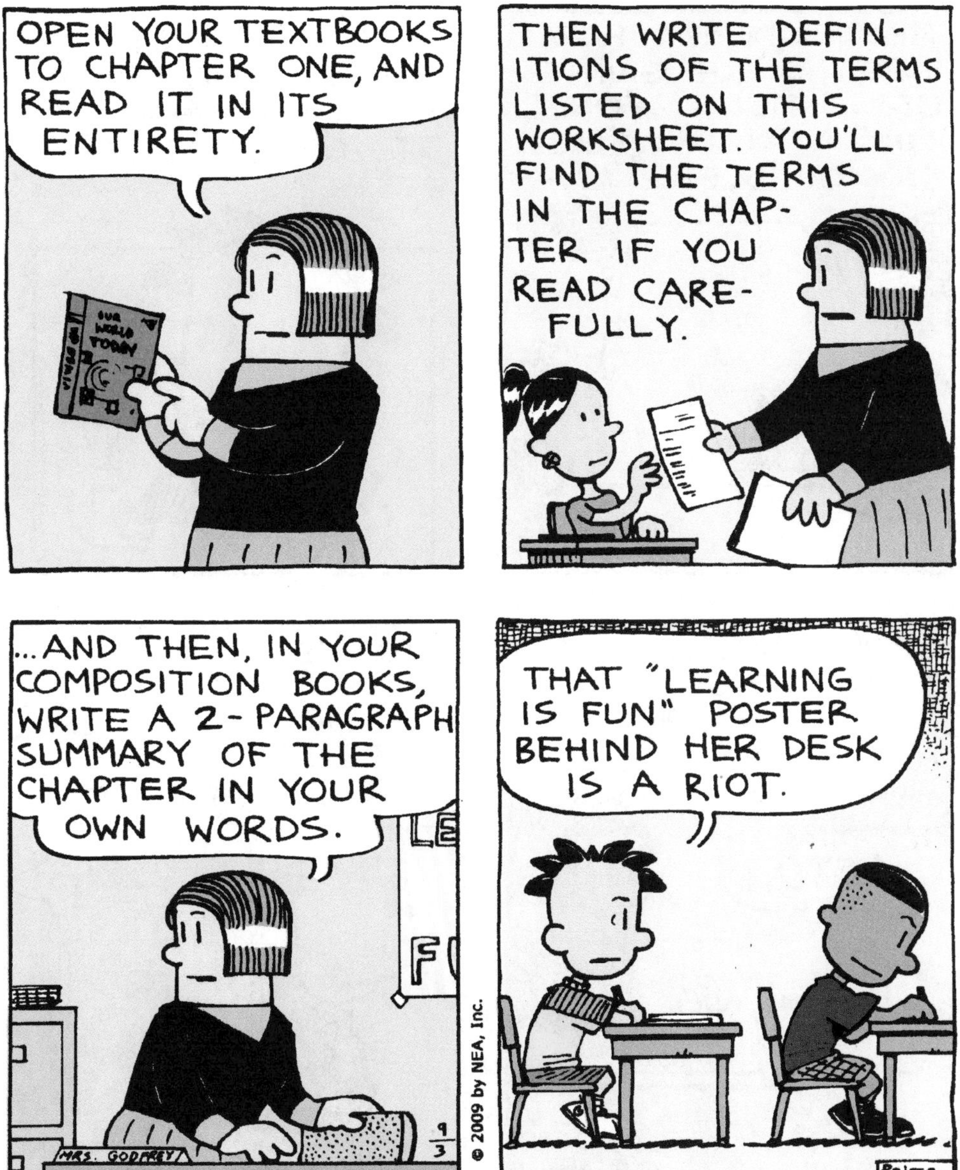
OPEN YOUR TEXTBOOKS TO CHAPTER ONE, AND READ IT IN ITS ENTIRETY.
THEN WRITE DEFINITIONS OF THE TERMS LISTED ON THIS WORKSHEET. YOU'LL FIND THE TERMS IN THE CHAPTER IF YOU READ CAREFULLY.
...AND THEN, IN YOUR COMPOSITION BOOKS, WRITE A 2-PARAGRAPH SUMMARY OF THE CHAPTER IN YOUR OWN WORDS.
MRS. GODFREY
© 2009 by NEA, Inc.
THAT "LEARNING IS FUN" POSTER BEHIND HER DESK IS A RIOT.
Peirce

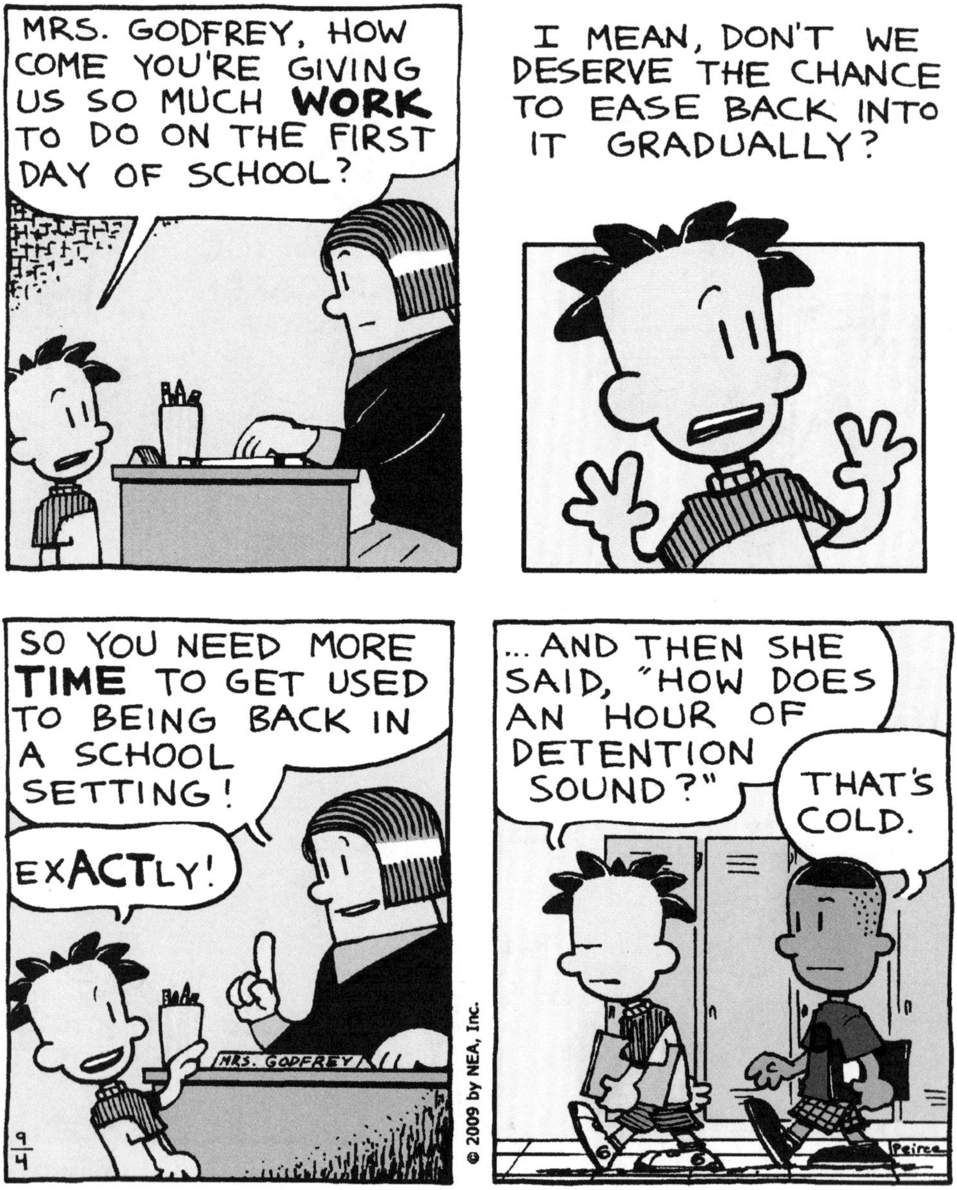
MRS. GODFREY, HOW COME YOU'RE GIVING US SO MUCH WORK TO DO ON THE FIRST DAY OF SCHOOL?
I MEAN, DON'T WE DESERVE THE CHANCE TO EASE BACK INTO IT GRADUALLY?
SO YOU NEED MORE TIME TO GET USED TO BEING BACK IN A SCHOOL SETTING!
EXACTLY!
MRS. GODFREY
9/4
© 2009 by NEA, Inc.
...AND THEN SHE SAID, "HOW DOES AN HOUR OF DETENTION SOUND?"
THAT'S COLD.
Peirce

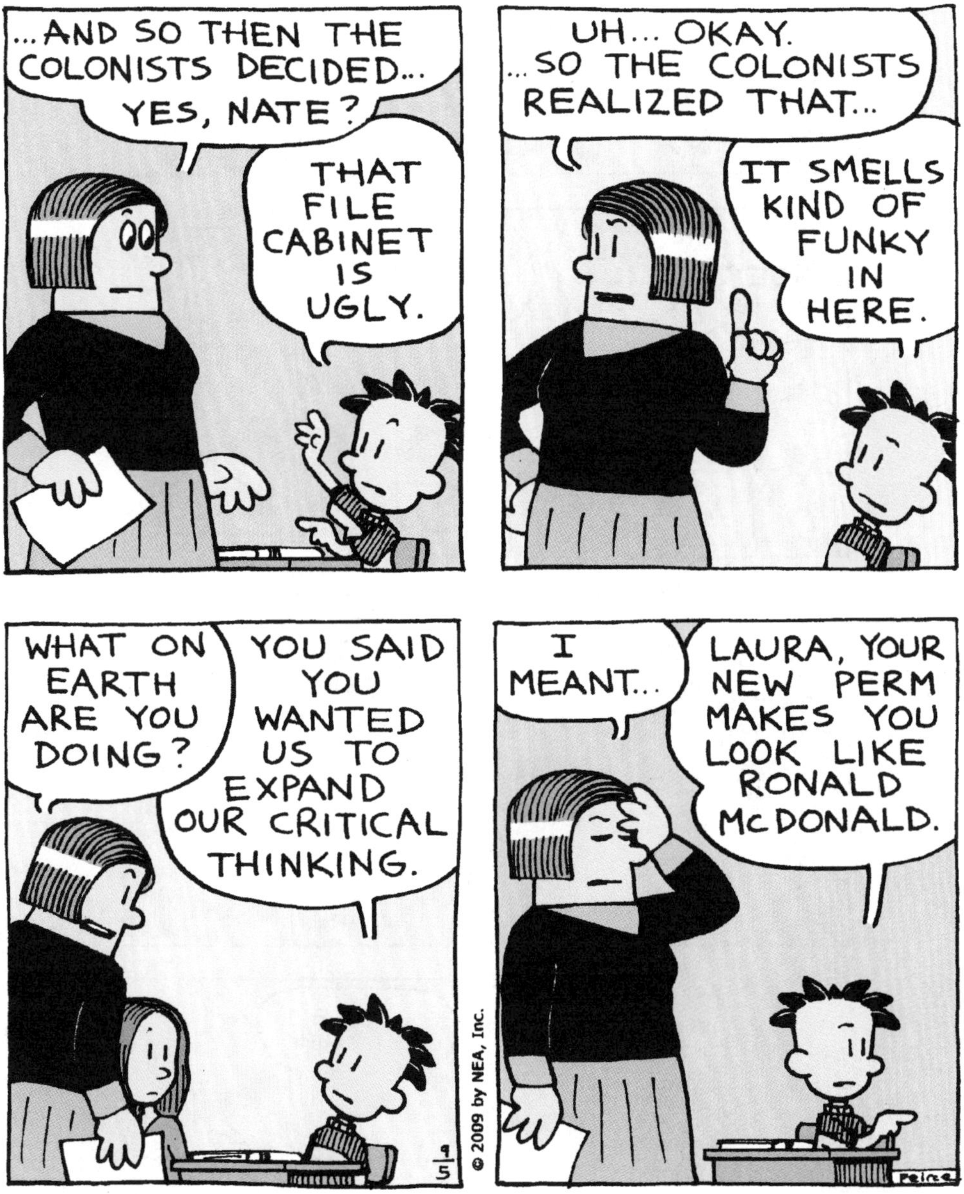
...AND SO THEN THE COLONISTS DECIDED... YES, NATE?
THAT FILE CABINET IS UGLY.
UH... OKAY. ...SO THE COLONISTS REALIZED THAT...
IT SMELLS KIND OF FUNKY IN HERE.
WHAT ON EARTH ARE YOU DOING?
YOU SAID YOU WANTED US TO EXPAND OUR CRITICAL THINKING.
I MEANT...
LAURA, YOUR NEW PERM MAKES YOU LOOK LIKE RONALD McDONALD.
9/5
© 2009 by NEA, Inc.
PEIRCE

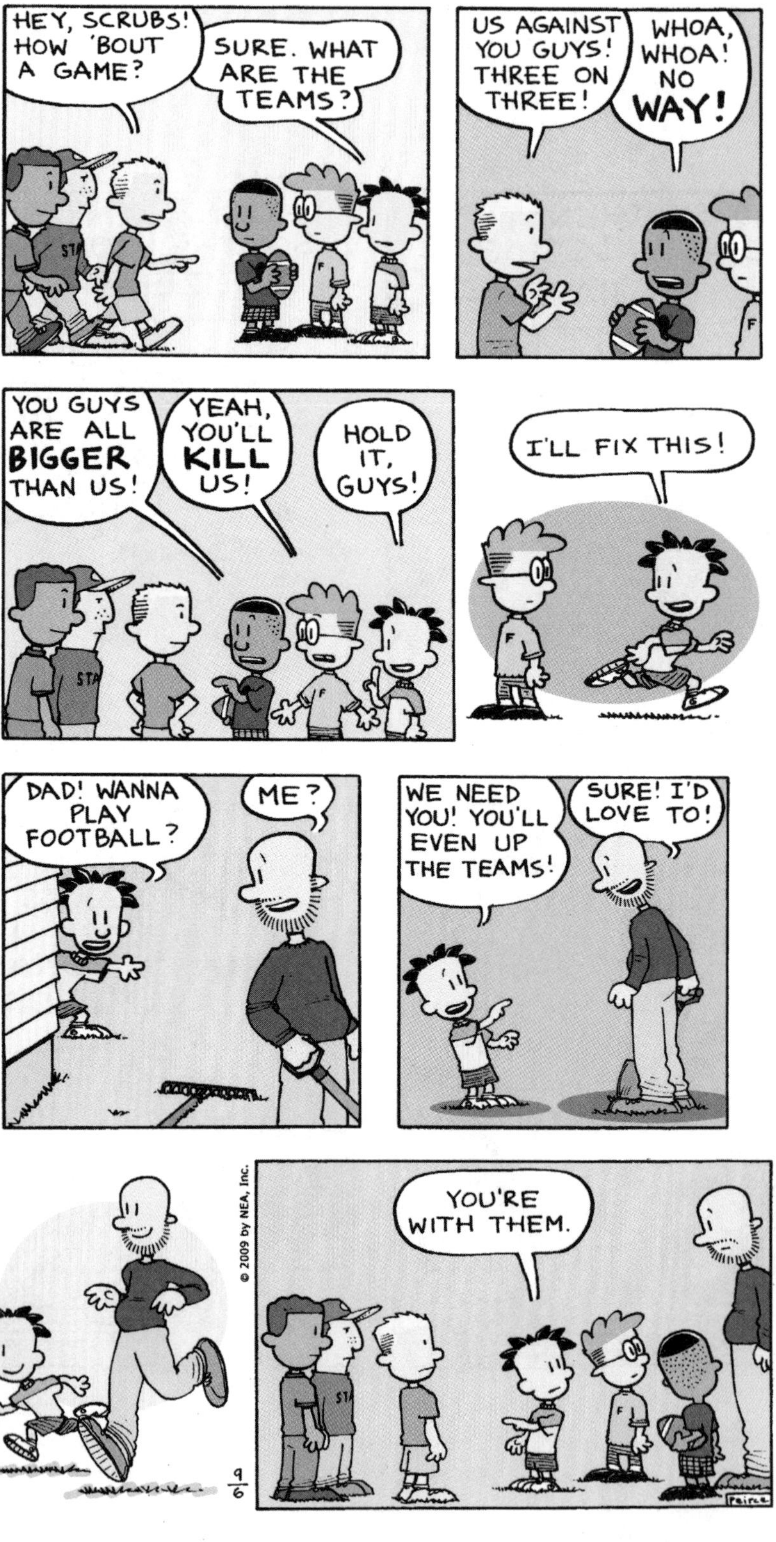
HEY, SCRUBS! HOW 'BOUT A GAME?
SURE. WHAT ARE THE TEAMS?
US AGAINST YOU GUYS! THREE ON THREE!
WHOA, WHOA! NO WAY!
YOU GUYS ARE ALL BIGGER THAN US!
YEAH, YOU'LL KILL US!
HOLD IT, GUYS!
I'LL FIX THIS!
DAD! WANNA PLAY FOOTBALL?
ME?
WE NEED YOU! YOU'LL EVEN UP THE TEAMS!
SURE! I'D LOVE TO!
© 2009 by NEA, Inc.
9/6
YOU'RE WITH THEM.
PEIRCE

GOOD SUB, BAD SUB

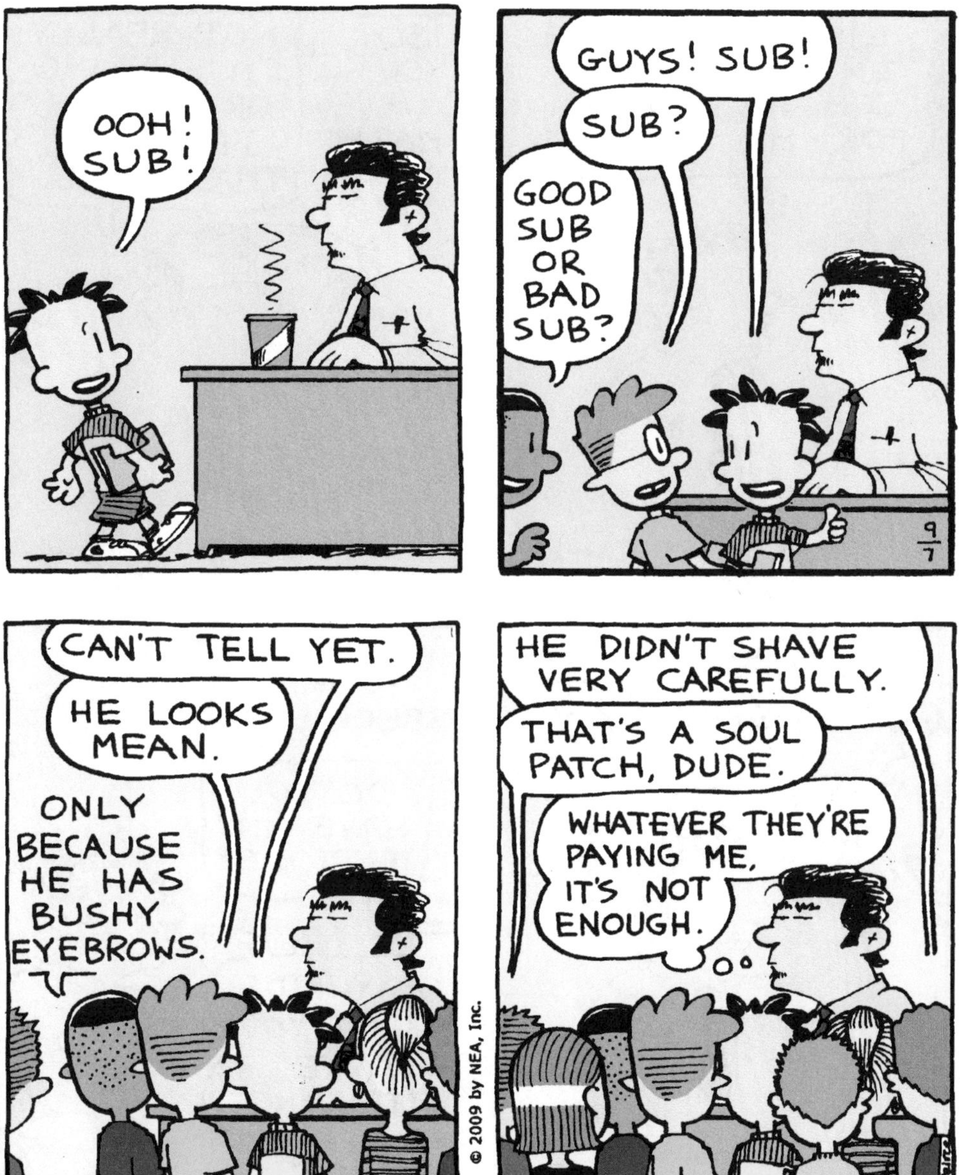
OOH! SUB!
GUYS! SUB!
SUB?
GOOD SUB OR BAD SUB?
CAN'T TELL YET.
HE LOOKS MEAN.
ONLY BECAUSE HE HAS BUSHY EYEBROWS.
© 2009 by NEA, Inc.
HE DIDN'T SHAVE VERY CAREFULLY.
THAT'S A SOUL PATCH, DUDE.
WHATEVER THEY'RE PAYING ME, IT'S NOT ENOUGH.

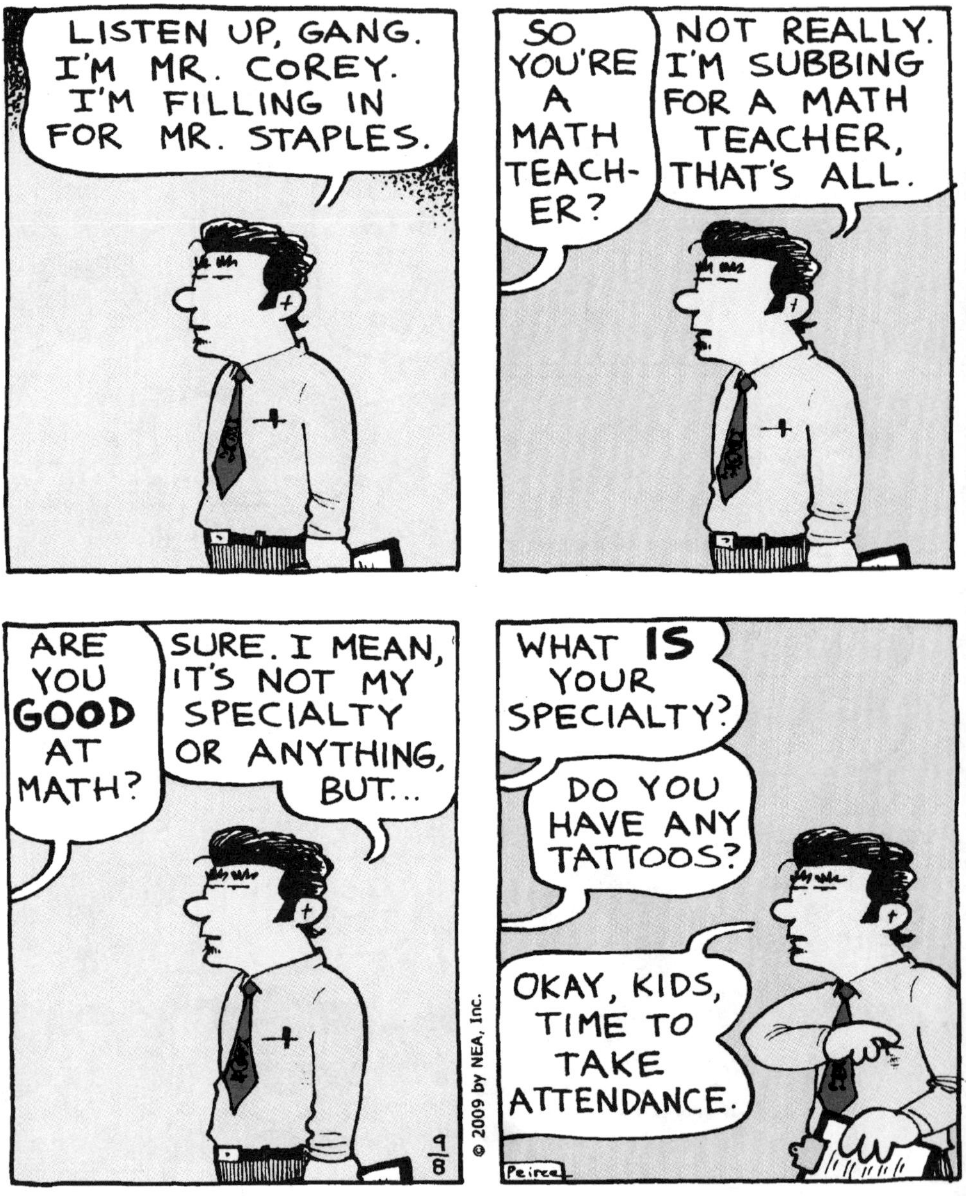
LISTEN UP, GANG. I'M MR. COREY. I'M FILLING IN FOR MR. STAPLES.
SO YOU'RE A MATH TEACH-ER?
NOT REALLY. I'M SUBBING FOR A MATH TEACHER, THAT'S ALL.
ARE YOU **GOOD** AT MATH?
SURE. I MEAN, IT'S NOT MY SPECIALTY OR ANYTHING, BUT...
9/8
WHAT **IS** YOUR SPECIALTY?
DO YOU HAVE ANY TATTOOS?
OKAY, KIDS, TIME TO TAKE ATTENDANCE.
Peirce

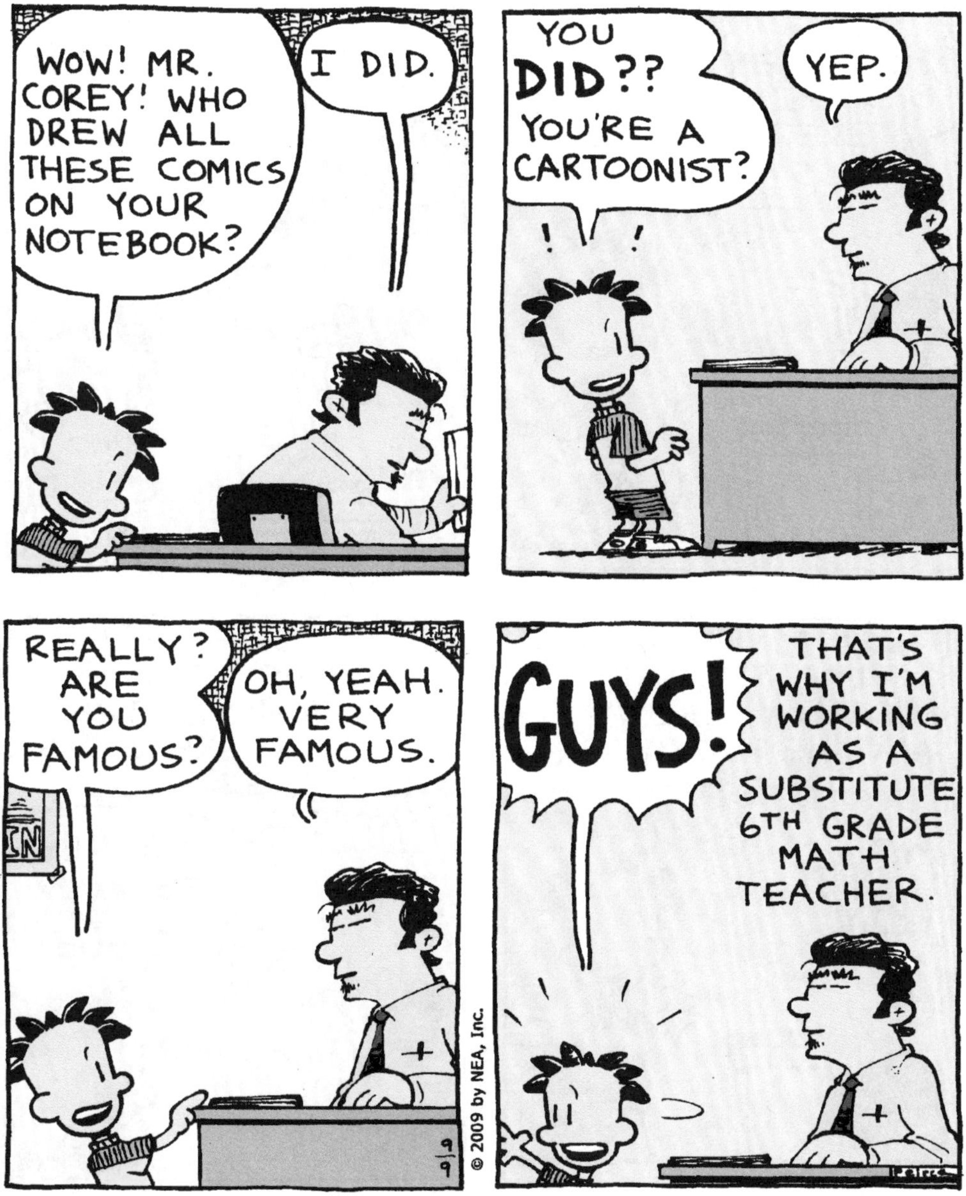
WOW! MR. COREY! WHO DREW ALL THESE COMICS ON YOUR NOTEBOOK?
I DID.
YOU DID?? YOU'RE A CARTOONIST?
YEP.
REALLY? ARE YOU FAMOUS?
OH, YEAH. VERY FAMOUS.
GUYS!
THAT'S WHY I'M WORKING AS A SUBSTITUTE 6TH GRADE MATH TEACHER.
© 2009 by NEA, Inc.

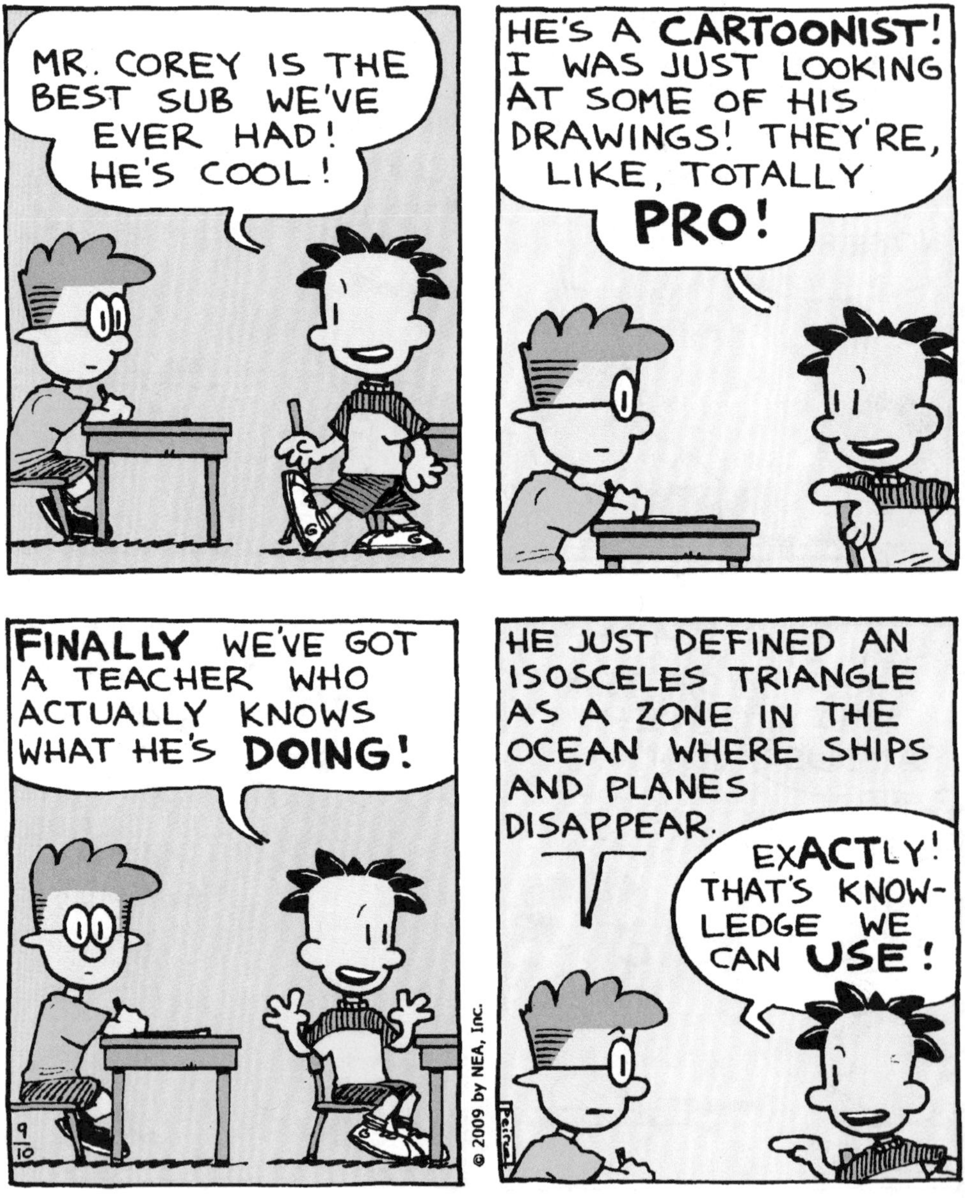
MR. COREY IS THE BEST SUB WE'VE EVER HAD! HE'S COOL!
HE'S A **CARTOONIST**! I WAS JUST LOOKING AT SOME OF HIS DRAWINGS! THEY'RE, LIKE, TOTALLY **PRO**!
FINALLY WE'VE GOT A TEACHER WHO ACTUALLY KNOWS WHAT HE'S **DOING**!
9/10
© 2009 by NEA, Inc.
HE JUST DEFINED AN ISOSCELES TRIANGLE AS A ZONE IN THE OCEAN WHERE SHIPS AND PLANES DISAPPEAR.
EX**ACT**LY! THAT'S KNOW-LEDGE WE CAN **USE**!
Peirce

I WISH YOU COULD BE OUR TEACHER **PERMANENTLY**, MR. COREY.

THAT'S KIND OF YOU TO SAY.

YOU'RE **WAY** BETTER THAN MR. STAPLES!

OH, I DOUBT THAT.

IT'S **TRUE!** HE CAN'T DRAW AWESOME CARTOONS LIKE **YOU** CAN! HE CAN'T DRAW **ANYTHING!**

9/11

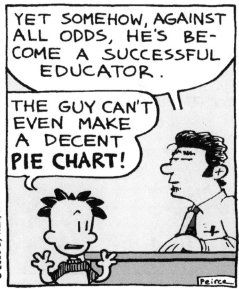

YET SOMEHOW, AGAINST ALL ODDS, HE'S BECOME A SUCCESSFUL EDUCATOR.

THE GUY CAN'T EVEN MAKE A DECENT **PIE CHART!**

Peirce

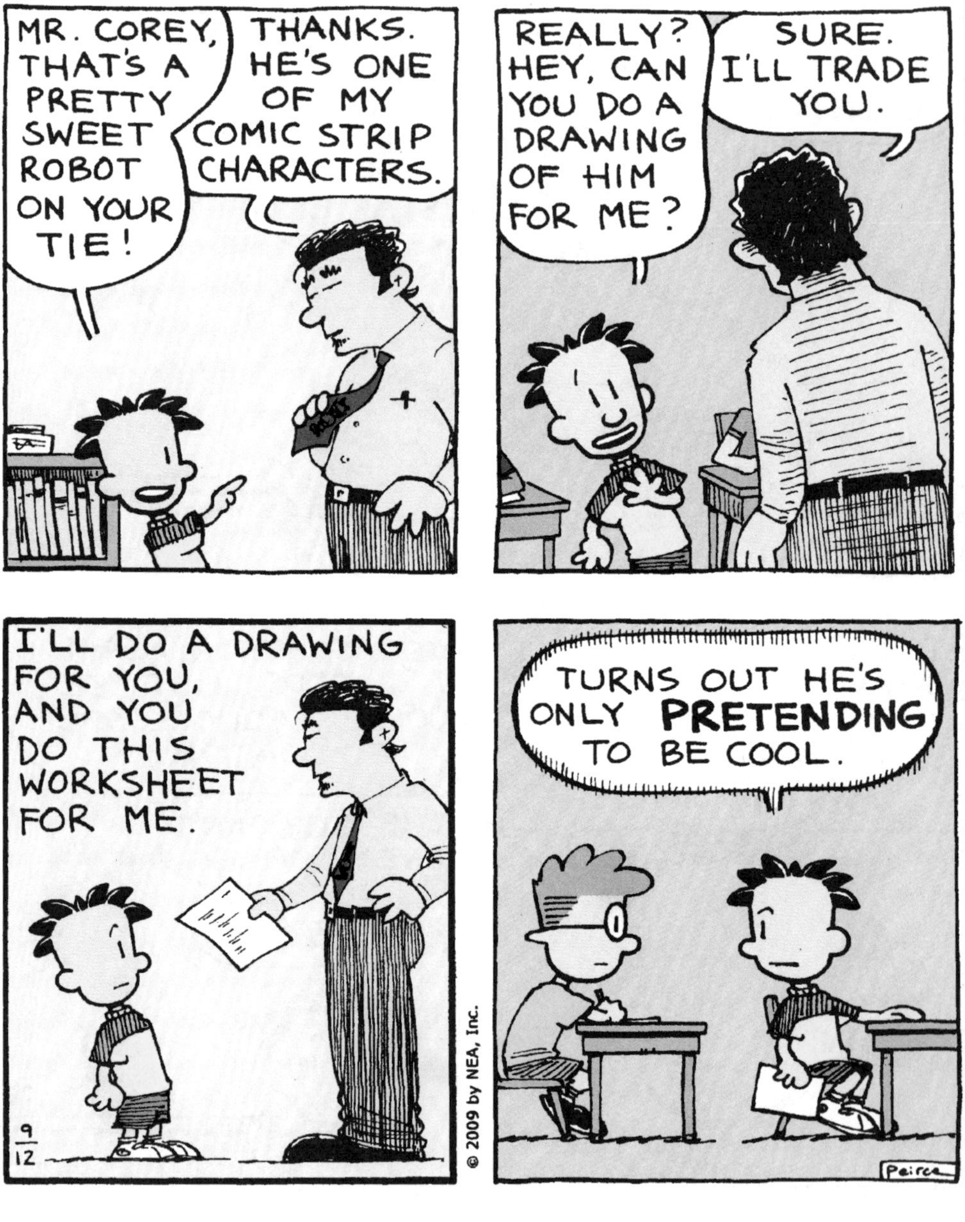
MR. COREY, THAT'S A PRETTY SWEET ROBOT ON YOUR TIE!
THANKS. HE'S ONE OF MY COMIC STRIP CHARACTERS.
REALLY? HEY, CAN YOU DO A DRAWING OF HIM FOR ME?
SURE. I'LL TRADE YOU.
I'LL DO A DRAWING FOR YOU, AND YOU DO THIS WORKSHEET FOR ME.
9/12
© 2009 by NEA, Inc.
TURNS OUT HE'S ONLY **PRETENDING** TO BE COOL.
Peirce

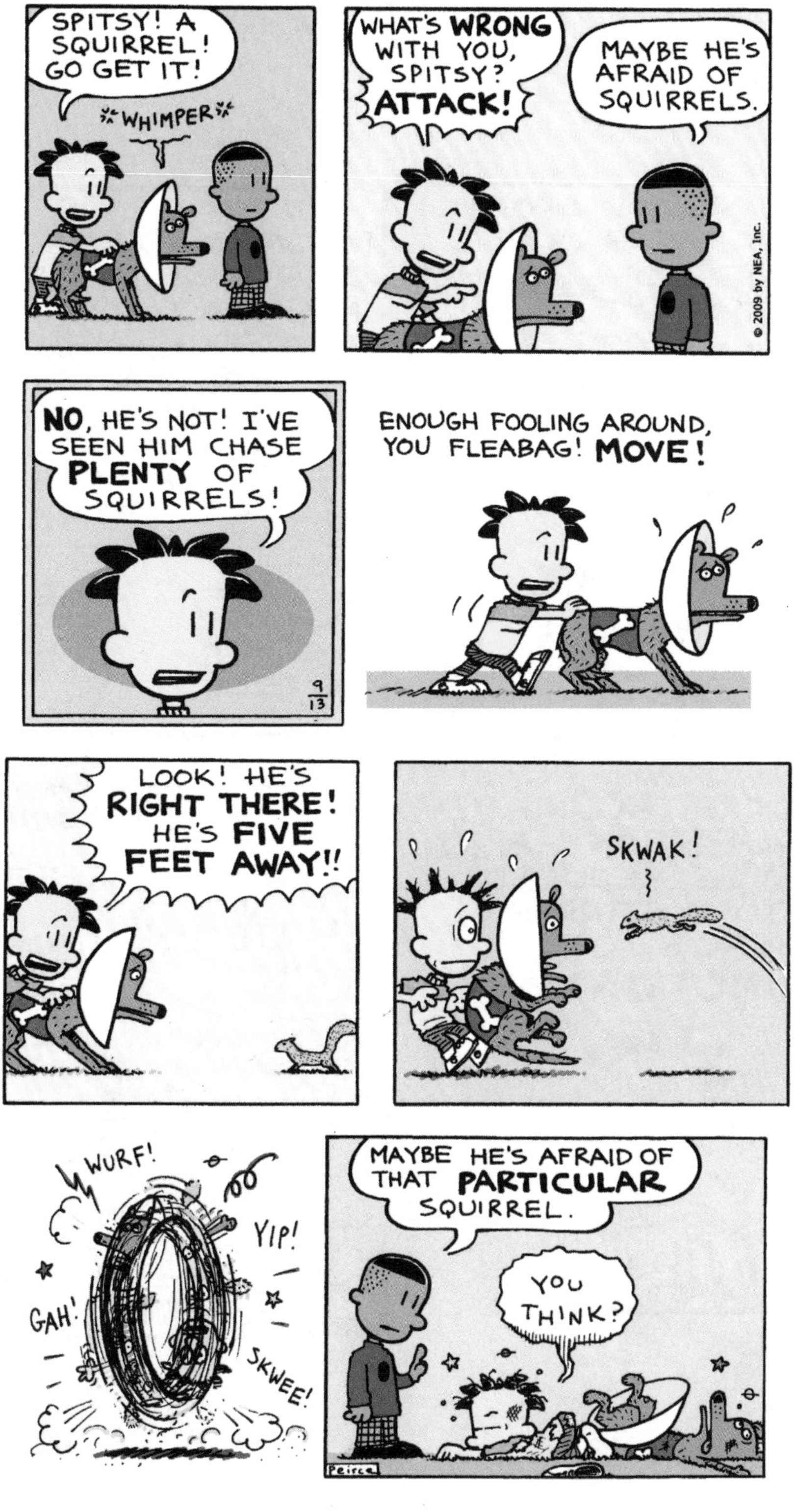
SPITSY! A SQUIRREL! GO GET IT!
WHIMPER
WHAT'S WRONG WITH YOU, SPITSY? ATTACK!
MAYBE HE'S AFRAID OF SQUIRRELS.
© 2009 by NEA, Inc.
NO, HE'S NOT! I'VE SEEN HIM CHASE PLENTY OF SQUIRRELS!
9/13
ENOUGH FOOLING AROUND, YOU FLEABAG! MOVE!
LOOK! HE'S RIGHT THERE! HE'S FIVE FEET AWAY!!
SKWAK!
WURF!
YIP!
GAH!
SKWEE!
MAYBE HE'S AFRAID OF THAT PARTICULAR SQUIRREL.
YOU THINK?
Peirce

ZEROING IN

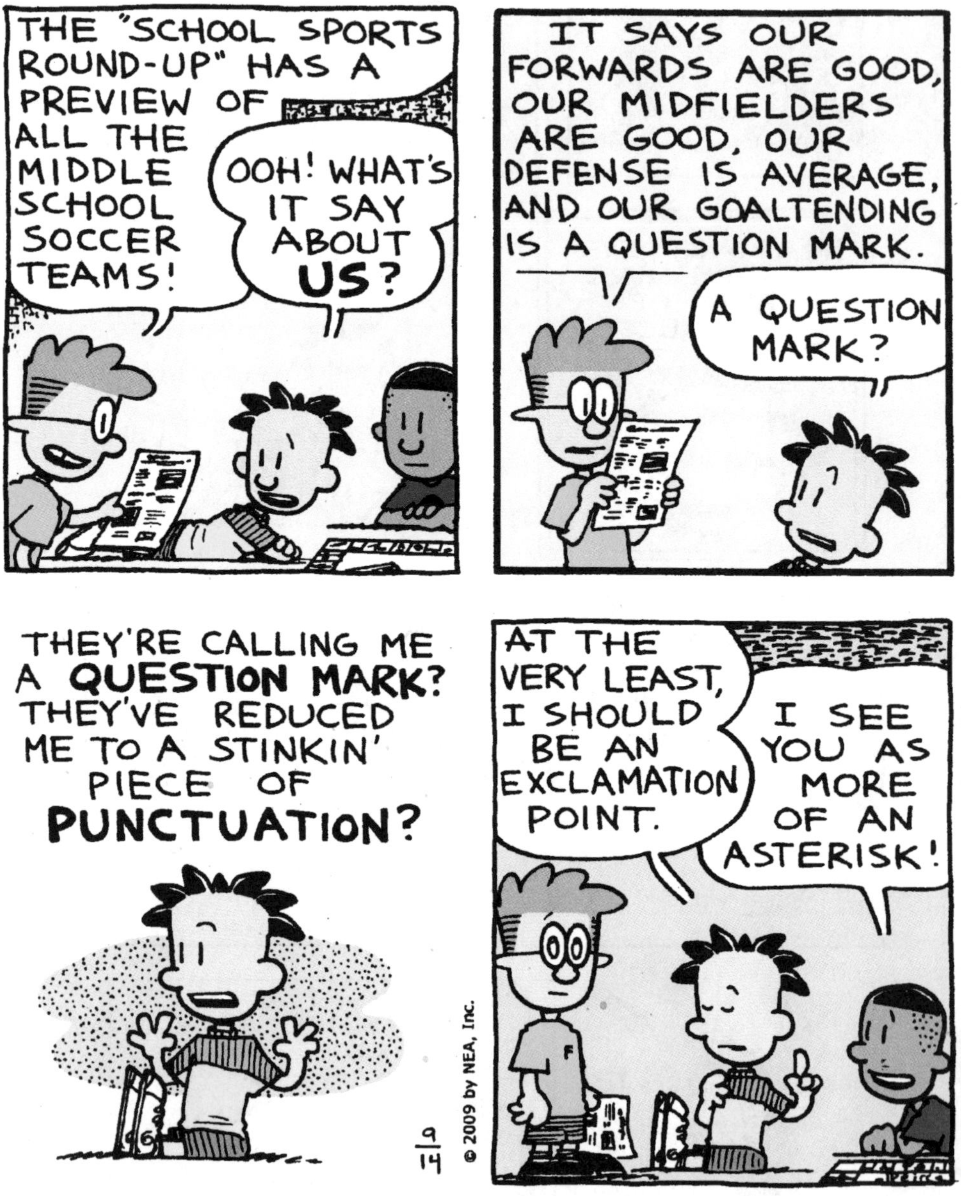

THE "SCHOOL SPORTS ROUND-UP" HAS A PREVIEW OF ALL THE MIDDLE SCHOOL SOCCER TEAMS!
OOH! WHAT'S IT SAY ABOUT **US**?
IT SAYS OUR FORWARDS ARE GOOD, OUR MIDFIELDERS ARE GOOD, OUR DEFENSE IS AVERAGE, AND OUR GOALTENDING IS A QUESTION MARK.
A QUESTION MARK?
THEY'RE CALLING ME A **QUESTION MARK**? THEY'VE REDUCED ME TO A STINKIN' PIECE OF **PUNCTUATION**?
9/14
© 2009 by NEA, Inc.
AT THE VERY LEAST, I SHOULD BE AN EXCLAMATION POINT.
I SEE YOU AS MORE OF AN ASTERISK!

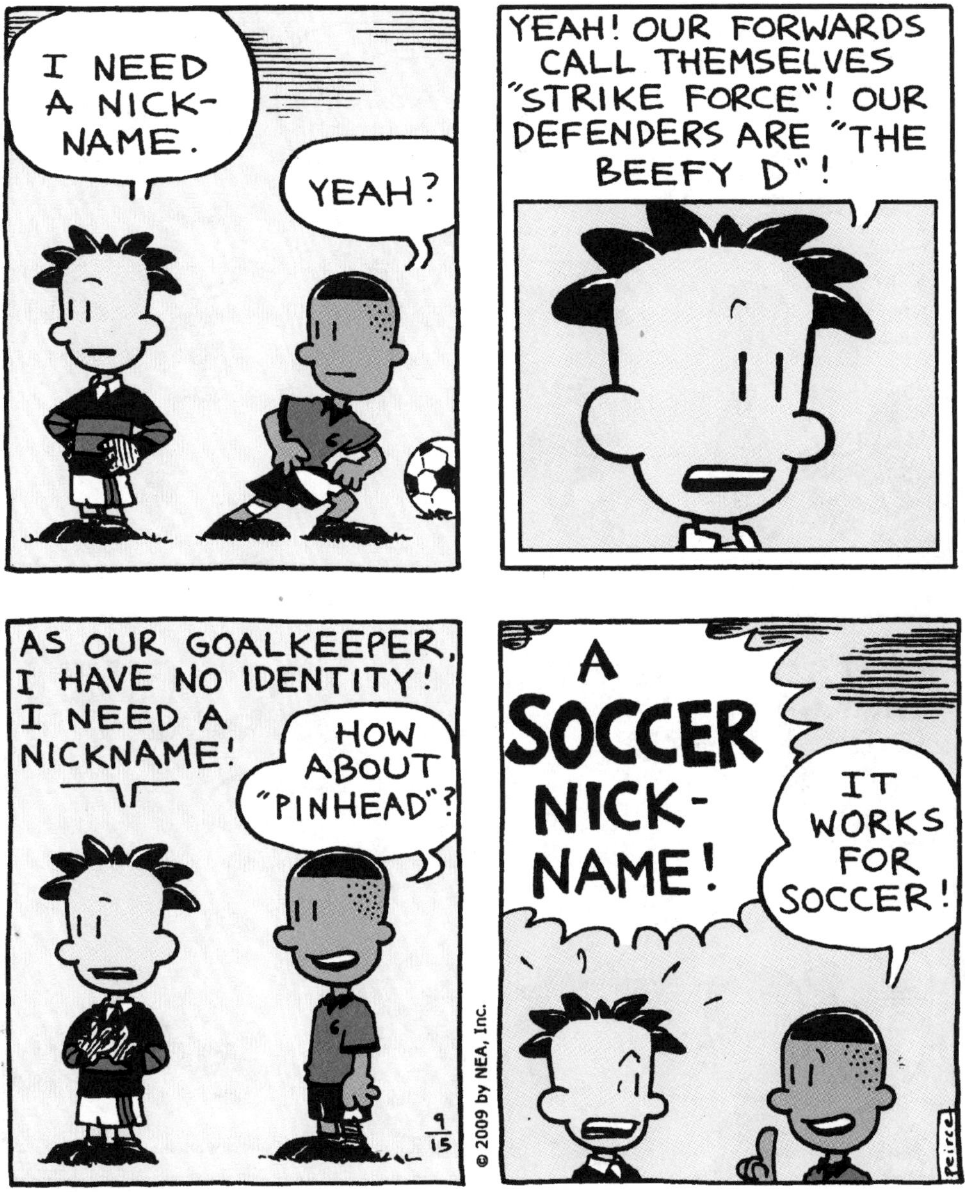
I NEED A NICK-NAME.
YEAH?
YEAH! OUR FORWARDS CALL THEMSELVES "STRIKE FORCE"! OUR DEFENDERS ARE "THE BEEFY D"!
AS OUR GOALKEEPER, I HAVE NO IDENTITY! I NEED A NICKNAME!
HOW ABOUT "PINHEAD"?
9/15
© 2009 by NEA, Inc.
A SOCCER NICK-NAME!
IT WORKS FOR SOCCER!
peirce

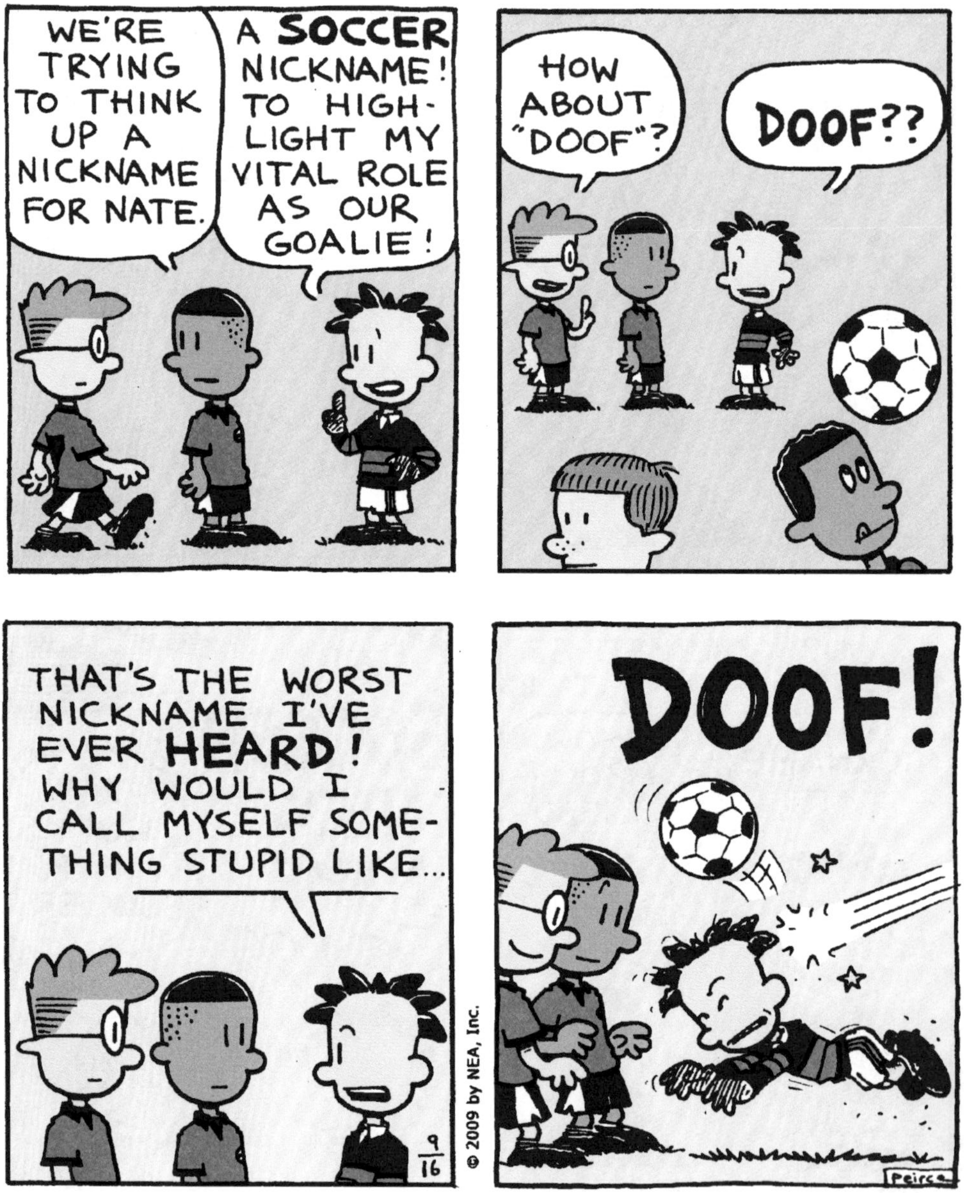
WE'RE TRYING TO THINK UP A NICKNAME FOR NATE.
A **SOCCER** NICKNAME! TO HIGH-LIGHT MY VITAL ROLE AS OUR GOALIE!
HOW ABOUT "DOOF"?
DOOF??
THAT'S THE WORST NICKNAME I'VE EVER **HEARD**! WHY WOULD I CALL MYSELF SOME-THING STUPID LIKE...
9/16
DOOF!
Peirce

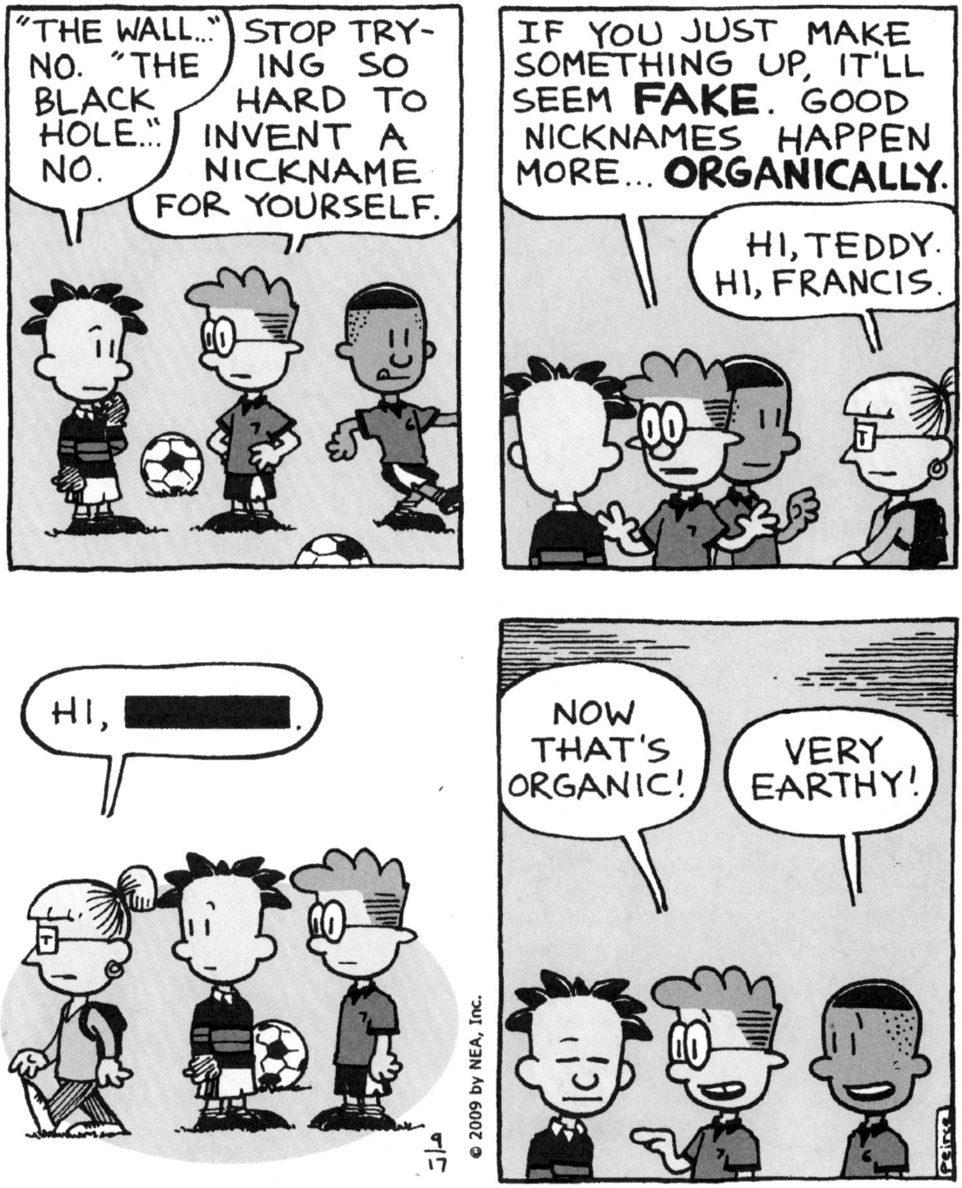
"THE WALL..." NO. "THE BLACK HOLE..." NO.
STOP TRYING SO HARD TO INVENT A NICKNAME FOR YOURSELF.
IF YOU JUST MAKE SOMETHING UP, IT'LL SEEM **FAKE**. GOOD NICKNAMES HAPPEN MORE... **ORGANICALLY**.
HI, TEDDY. HI, FRANCIS.
HI, [redacted].
NOW THAT'S ORGANIC!
VERY EARTHY!

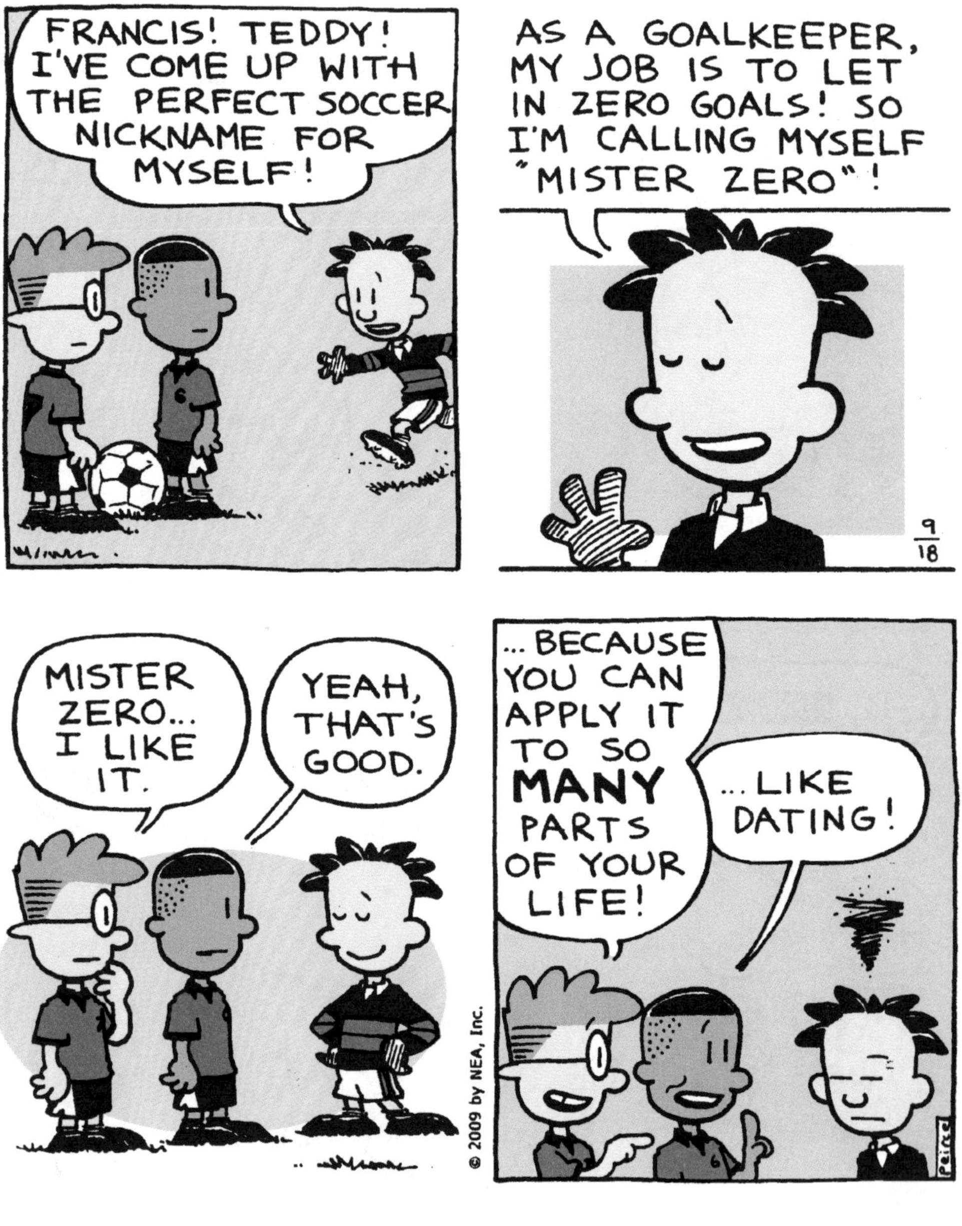
FRANCIS! TEDDY! I'VE COME UP WITH THE PERFECT SOCCER NICKNAME FOR MYSELF!
AS A GOALKEEPER, MY JOB IS TO LET IN ZERO GOALS! SO I'M CALLING MYSELF "MISTER ZERO"!
9/18
MISTER ZERO... I LIKE IT.
YEAH, THAT'S GOOD.
© 2009 by NEA, Inc.
...BECAUSE YOU CAN APPLY IT TO SO **MANY** PARTS OF YOUR LIFE!
...LIKE DATING!
Peirce

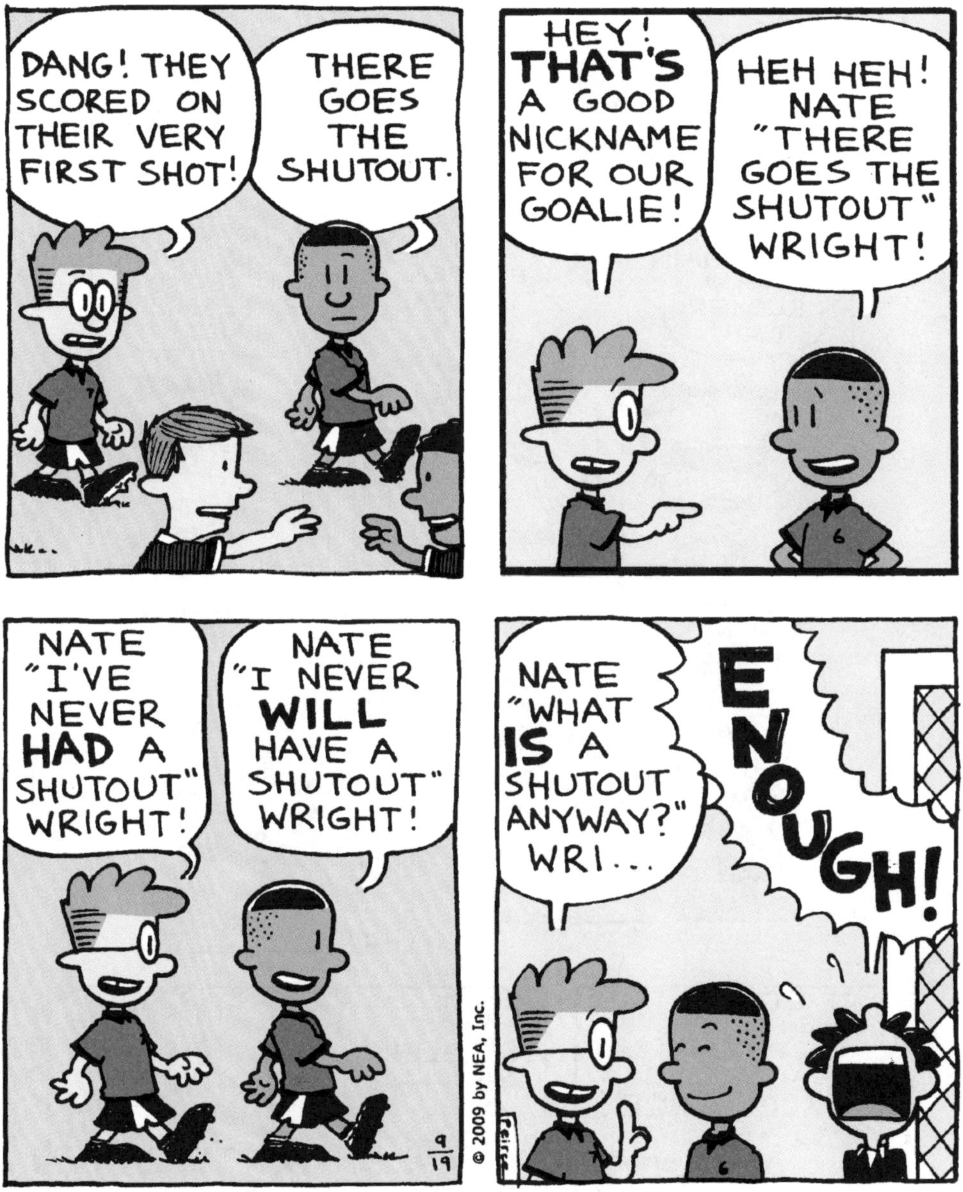
DANG! THEY SCORED ON THEIR VERY FIRST SHOT!
THERE GOES THE SHUTOUT.
HEY! THAT'S A GOOD NICKNAME FOR OUR GOALIE!
HEH HEH! NATE "THERE GOES THE SHUTOUT" WRIGHT!
NATE "I'VE NEVER HAD A SHUTOUT" WRIGHT!
NATE "I NEVER WILL HAVE A SHUTOUT" WRIGHT!
NATE "WHAT IS A SHUTOUT ANYWAY?" WRI...
ENOUGH!

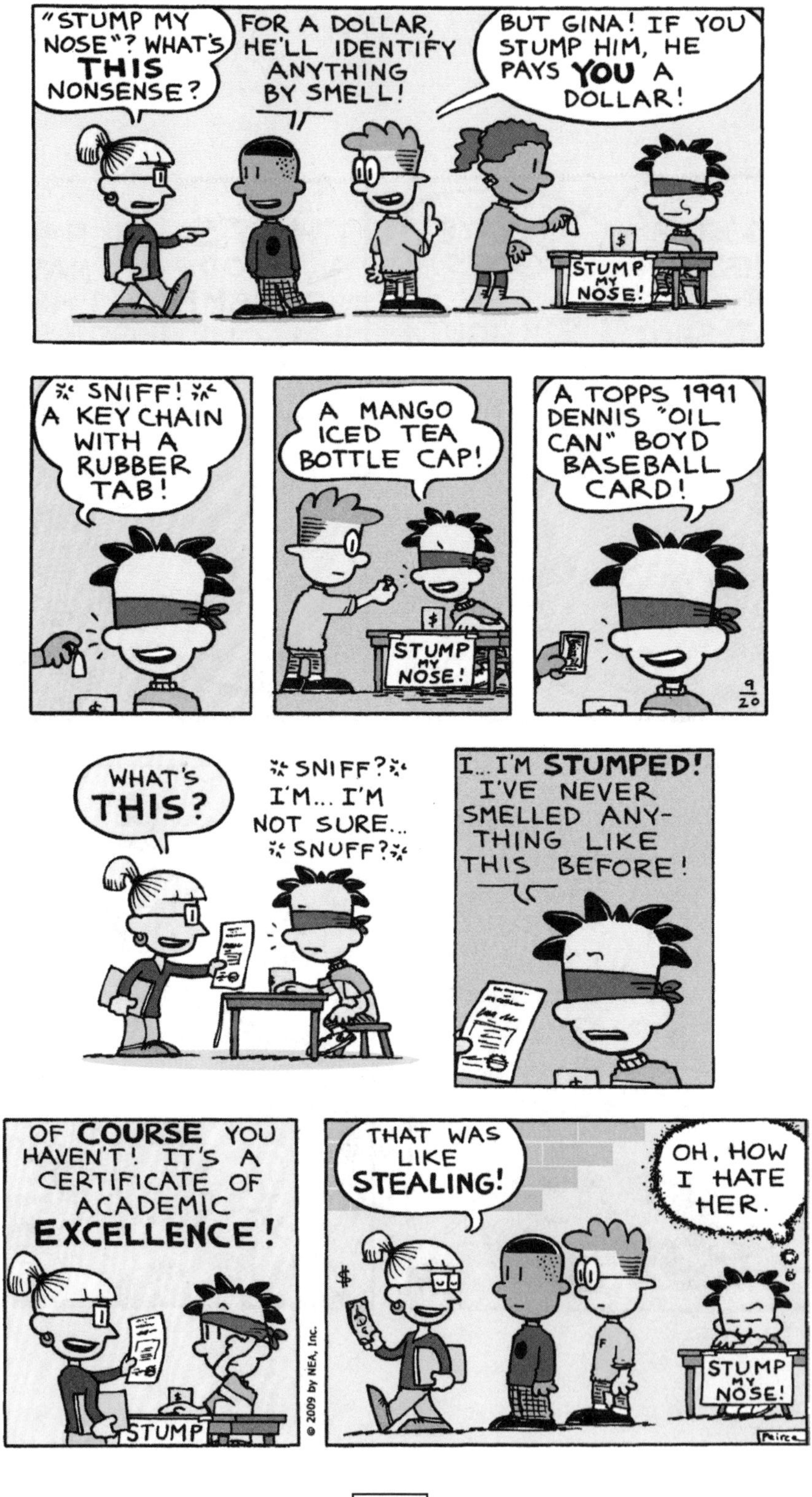
"STUMP MY NOSE"? WHAT'S THIS NONSENSE?
FOR A DOLLAR, HE'LL IDENTIFY ANYTHING BY SMELL!
BUT GINA! IF YOU STUMP HIM, HE PAYS YOU A DOLLAR!
STUMP MY NOSE!
SNIFF! A KEY CHAIN WITH A RUBBER TAB!
A MANGO ICED TEA BOTTLE CAP!
STUMP MY NOSE!
A TOPPS 1991 DENNIS "OIL CAN" BOYD BASEBALL CARD!
9/20
WHAT'S THIS?
SNIFF? I'M... I'M NOT SURE... SNUFF?
I... I'M STUMPED! I'VE NEVER SMELLED ANYTHING LIKE THIS BEFORE!
OF COURSE YOU HAVEN'T! IT'S A CERTIFICATE OF ACADEMIC EXCELLENCE!
STUMP
© 2009 by NEA, Inc.
THAT WAS LIKE STEALING!
OH, HOW I HATE HER.
STUMP MY NOSE!
Peirce

MR. POPULARITY

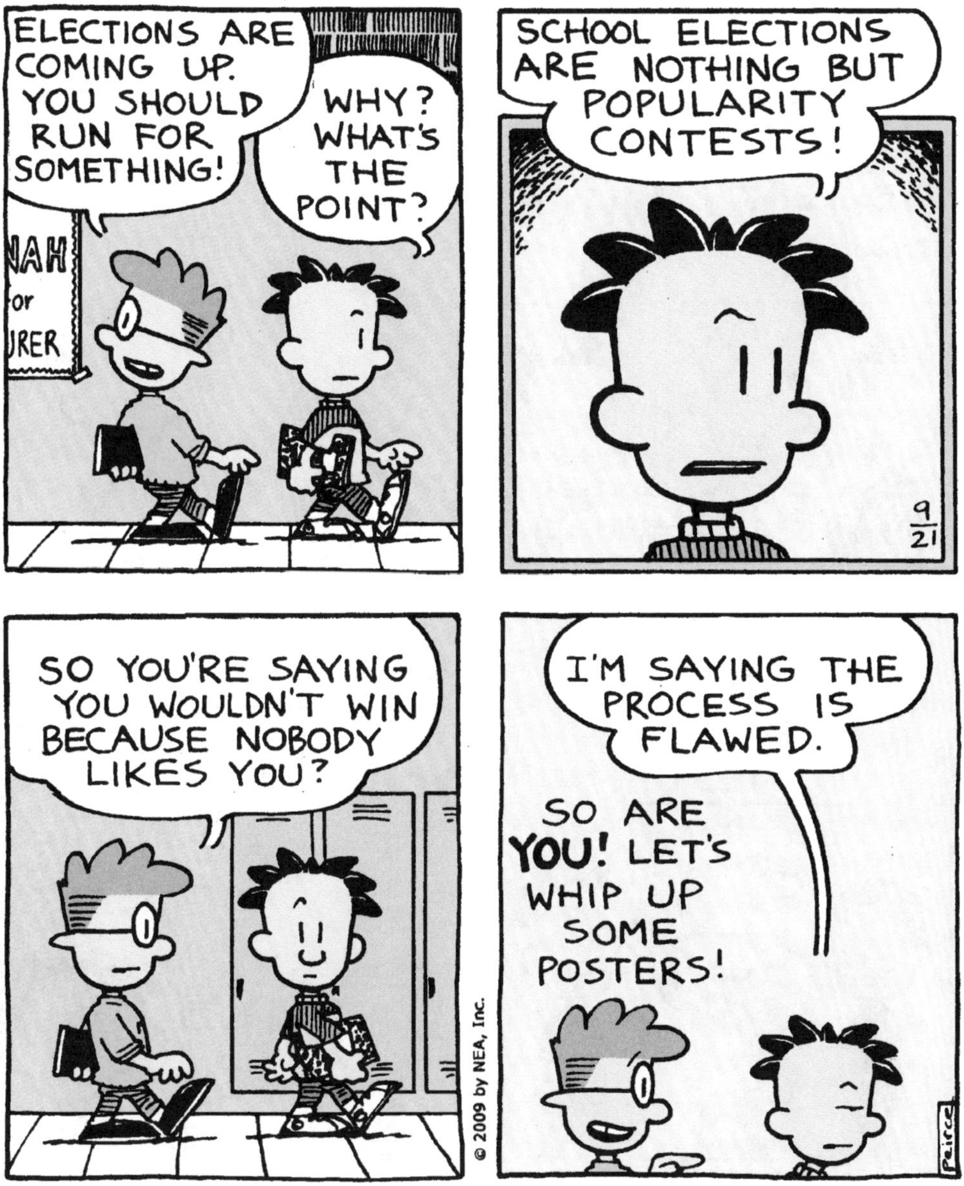
ELECTIONS ARE COMING UP. YOU SHOULD RUN FOR SOMETHING!
WHY? WHAT'S THE POINT?
NAH
for
URER
SCHOOL ELECTIONS ARE NOTHING BUT POPULARITY CONTESTS!
9/21
SO YOU'RE SAYING YOU WOULDN'T WIN BECAUSE NOBODY LIKES YOU?
I'M SAYING THE PROCESS IS FLAWED.
SO ARE **YOU!** LET'S WHIP UP SOME POSTERS!
Peirce

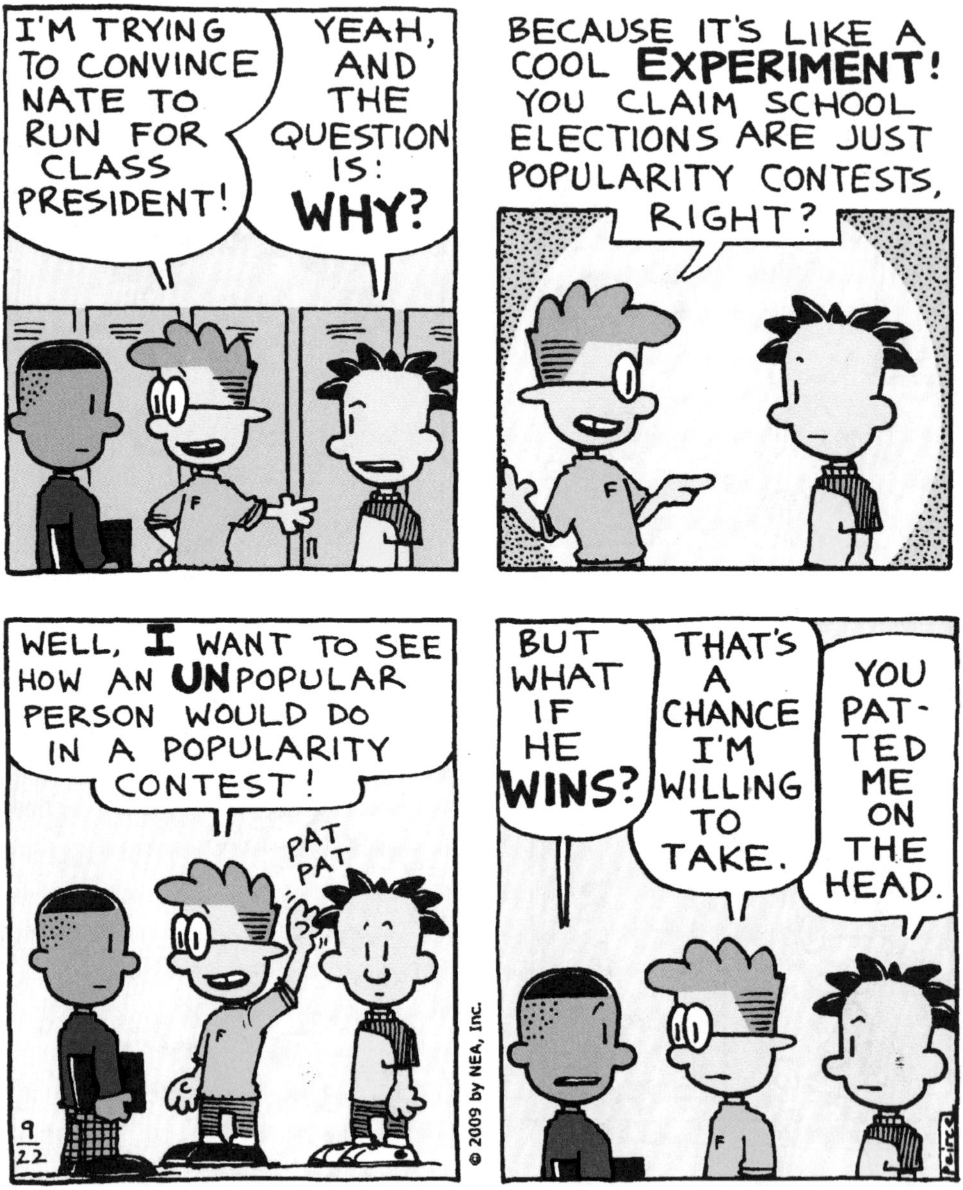
I'M TRYING TO CONVINCE NATE TO RUN FOR CLASS PRESIDENT!
YEAH, AND THE QUESTION IS: WHY?
BECAUSE IT'S LIKE A COOL EXPERIMENT! YOU CLAIM SCHOOL ELECTIONS ARE JUST POPULARITY CONTESTS, RIGHT?
WELL, I WANT TO SEE HOW AN UNPOPULAR PERSON WOULD DO IN A POPULARITY CONTEST!
PAT PAT
BUT WHAT IF HE WINS?
THAT'S A CHANCE I'M WILLING TO TAKE.
YOU PATTED ME ON THE HEAD.
9/22
© 2009 by NEA, Inc.
Peirce

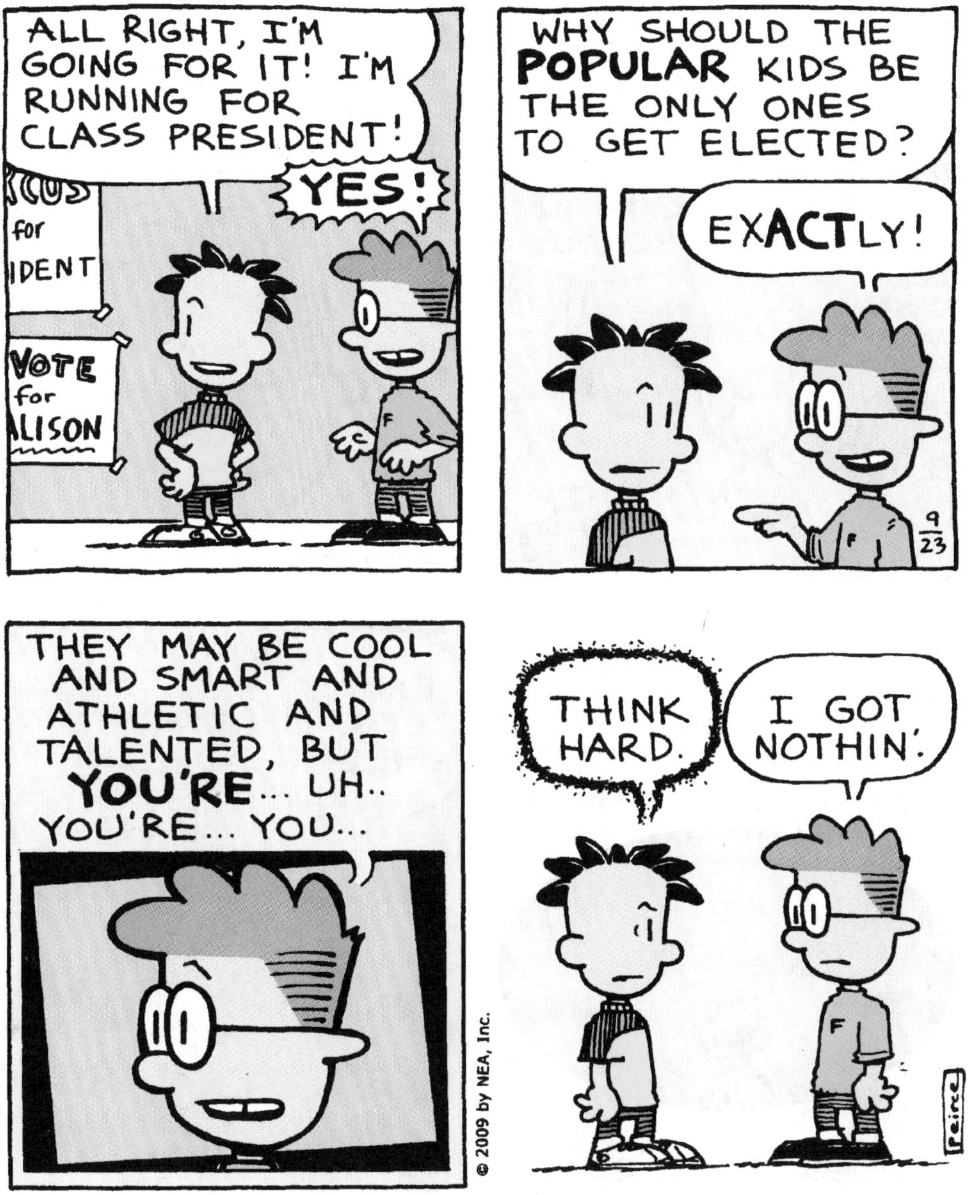
ALL RIGHT, I'M GOING FOR IT! I'M RUNNING FOR CLASS PRESIDENT!
YES!
VOTE for ALISON
WHY SHOULD THE **POPULAR** KIDS BE THE ONLY ONES TO GET ELECTED?
EXACTLY!
9/23
THEY MAY BE COOL AND SMART AND ATHLETIC AND TALENTED, BUT **YOU'RE**... UH.. YOU'RE... YOU...
THINK HARD.
I GOT NOTHIN'.
© 2009 by NEA, Inc.
Peirce

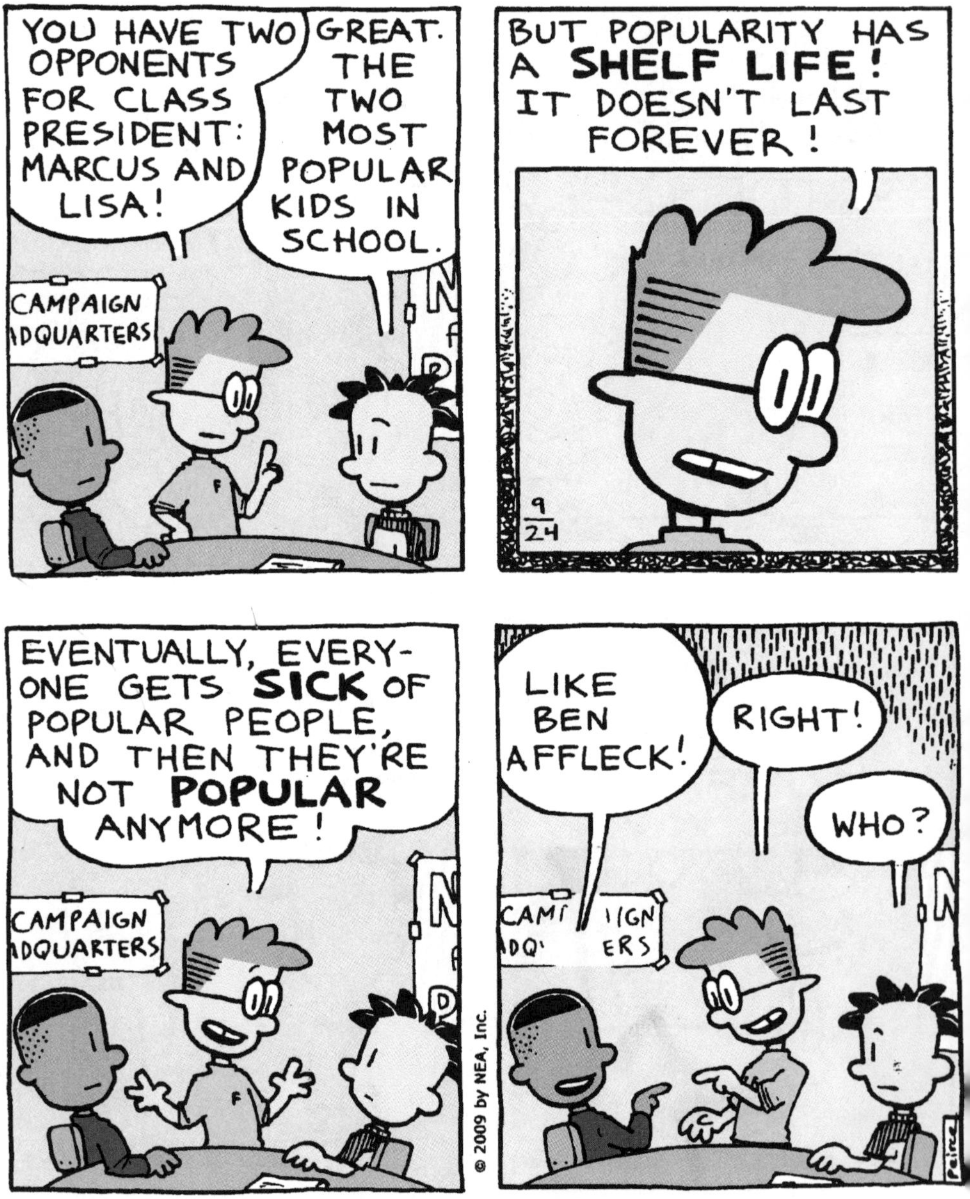
YOU HAVE TWO OPPONENTS FOR CLASS PRESIDENT: MARCUS AND LISA!
GREAT. THE TWO MOST POPULAR KIDS IN SCHOOL.
CAMPAIGN
DQUARTERS
BUT POPULARITY HAS A SHELF LIFE! IT DOESN'T LAST FOREVER!
9/24
EVENTUALLY, EVERYONE GETS SICK OF POPULAR PEOPLE, AND THEN THEY'RE NOT POPULAR ANYMORE!
CAMPAIGN
DQUARTERS
© 2009 by NEA, Inc.
LIKE BEN AFFLECK!
RIGHT!
WHO?
Peirce

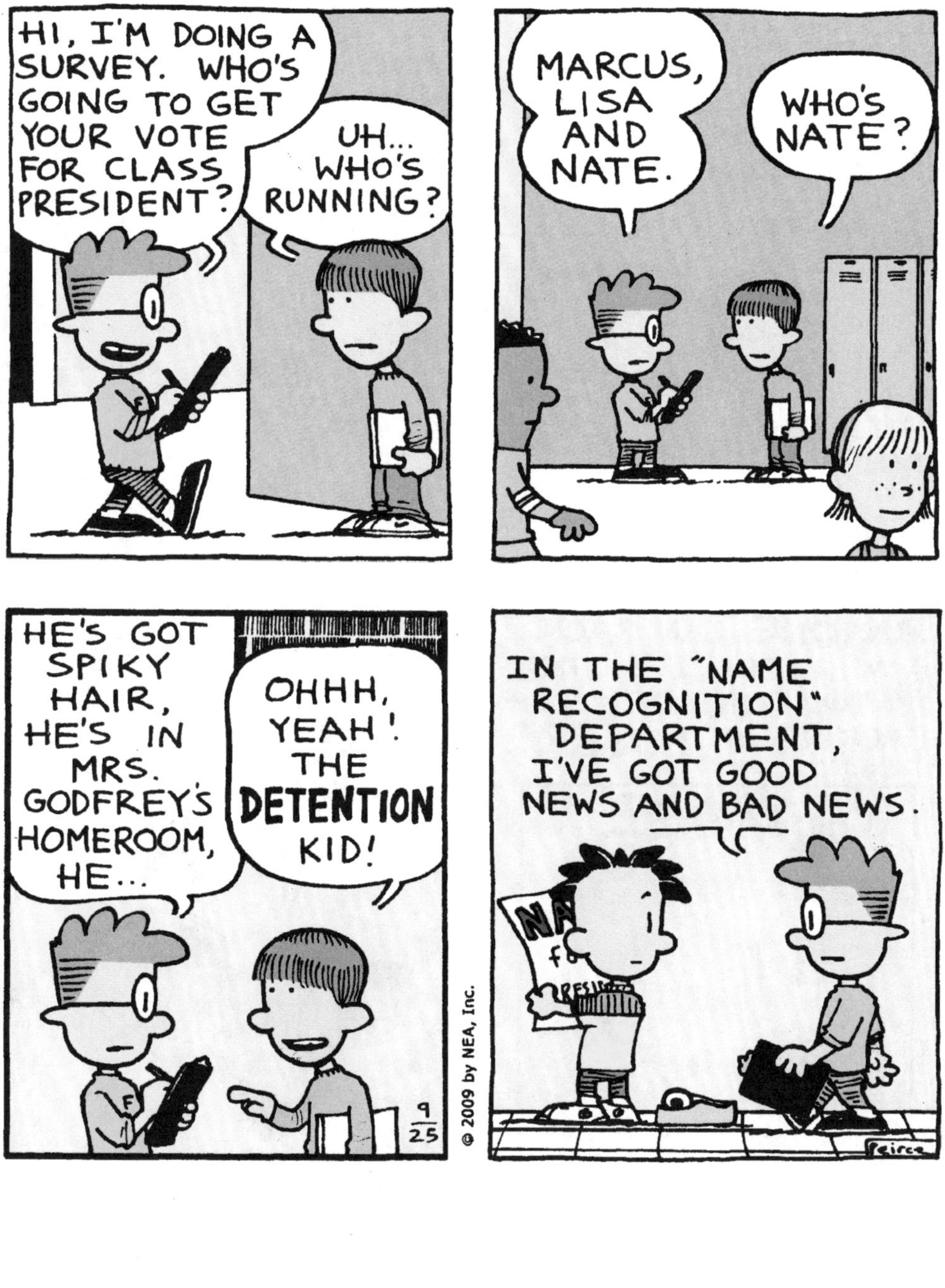
HI, I'M DOING A SURVEY. WHO'S GOING TO GET YOUR VOTE FOR CLASS PRESIDENT?
UH... WHO'S RUNNING?
MARCUS, LISA AND NATE.
WHO'S NATE?
HE'S GOT SPIKY HAIR, HE'S IN MRS. GODFREY'S HOMEROOM, HE...
OHHH, YEAH! THE **DETENTION** KID!
IN THE "NAME RECOGNITION" DEPARTMENT, I'VE GOT GOOD NEWS AND BAD NEWS.
Peirce

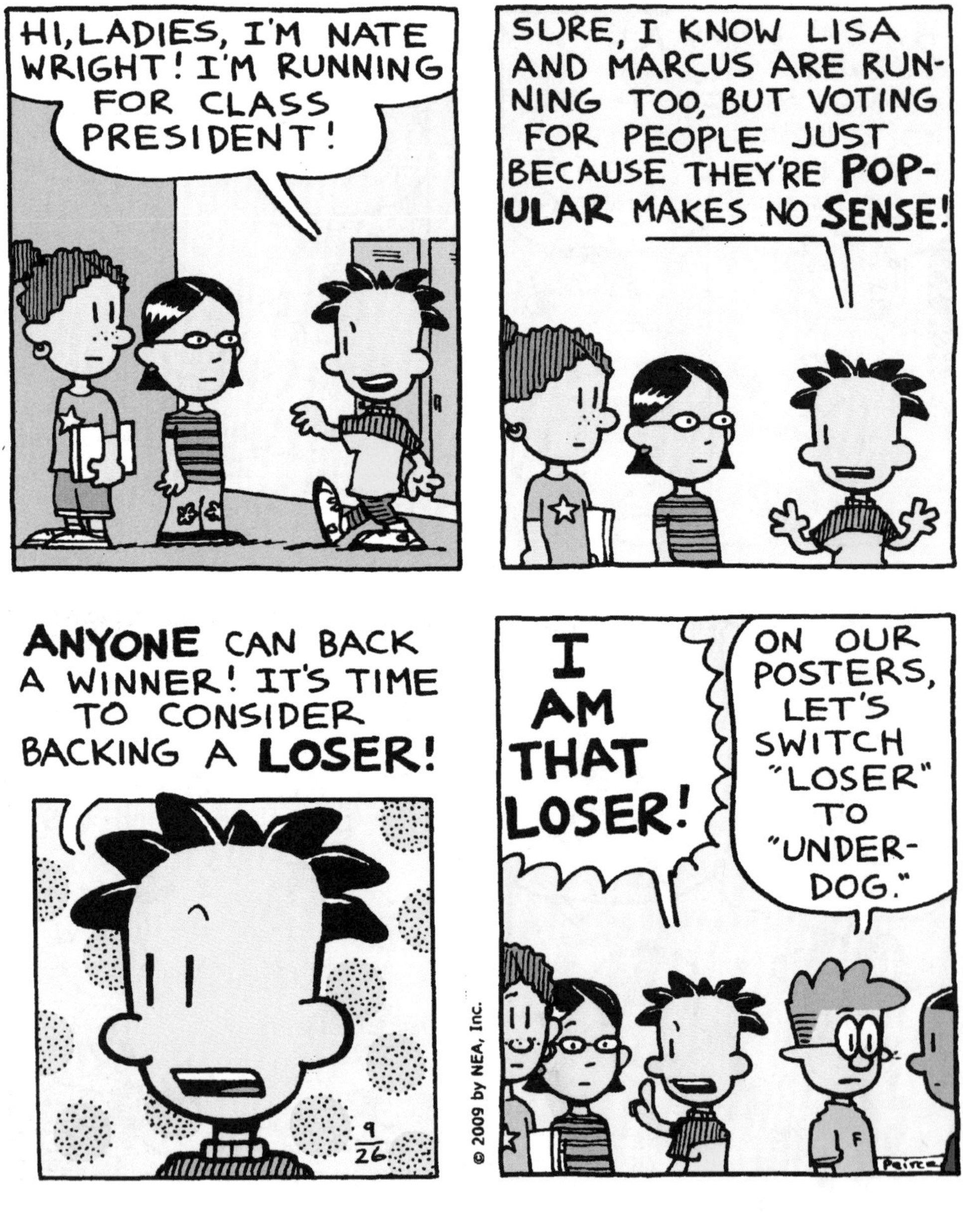
HI, LADIES, I'M NATE WRIGHT! I'M RUNNING FOR CLASS PRESIDENT!
SURE, I KNOW LISA AND MARCUS ARE RUNNING TOO, BUT VOTING FOR PEOPLE JUST BECAUSE THEY'RE POPULAR MAKES NO SENSE!
ANYONE CAN BACK A WINNER! IT'S TIME TO CONSIDER BACKING A LOSER!
9/26
© 2009 by NEA, Inc.
I AM THAT LOSER!
ON OUR POSTERS, LET'S SWITCH "LOSER" TO "UNDERDOG."
PEIRCE

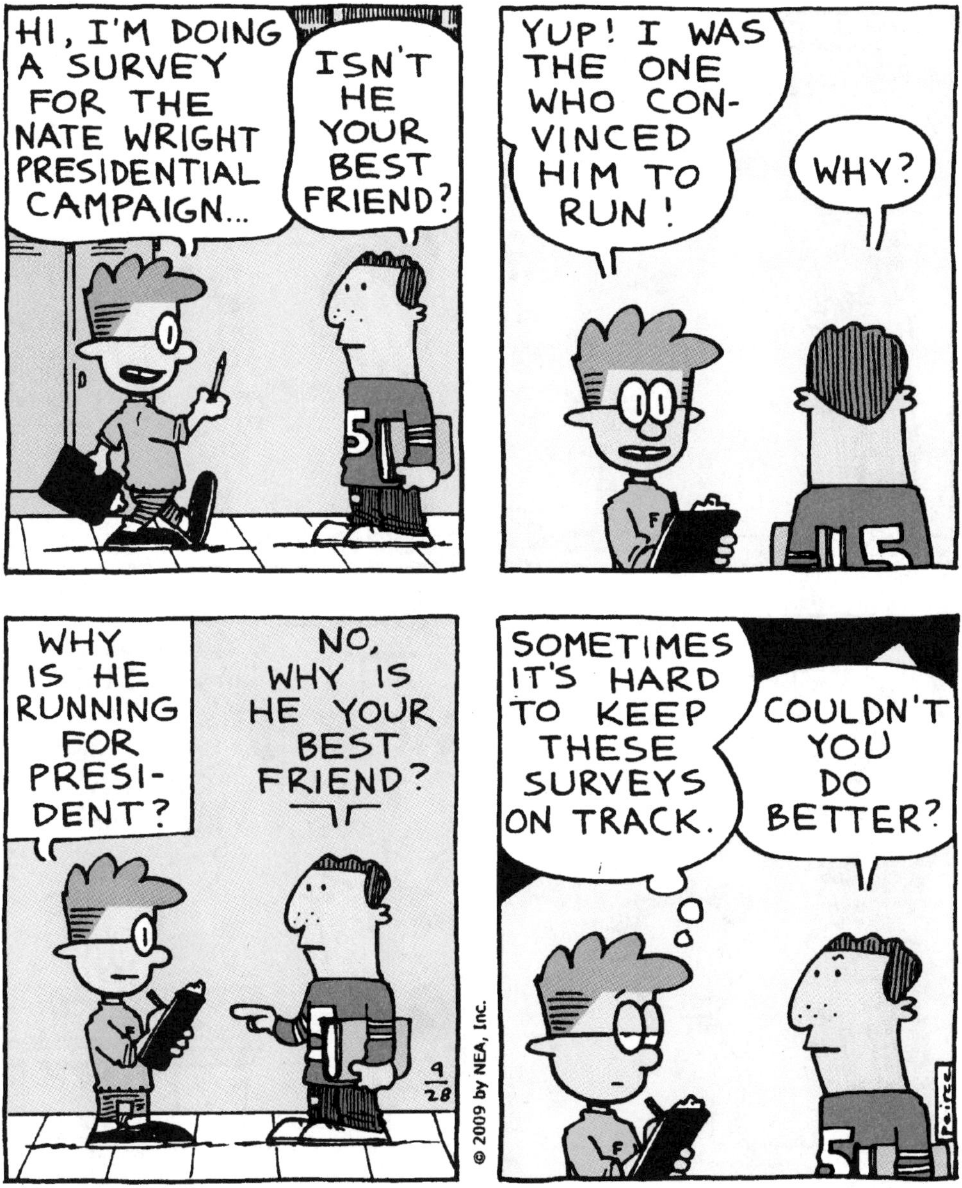
HI, I'M DOING A SURVEY FOR THE NATE WRIGHT PRESIDENTIAL CAMPAIGN...
ISN'T HE YOUR BEST FRIEND?
YUP! I WAS THE ONE WHO CONVINCED HIM TO RUN!
WHY?
WHY IS HE RUNNING FOR PRESIDENT?
NO, WHY IS HE YOUR BEST FRIEND?
9/28
© 2009 by NEA, Inc.
SOMETIMES IT'S HARD TO KEEP THESE SURVEYS ON TRACK.
COULDN'T YOU DO BETTER?
Peirce

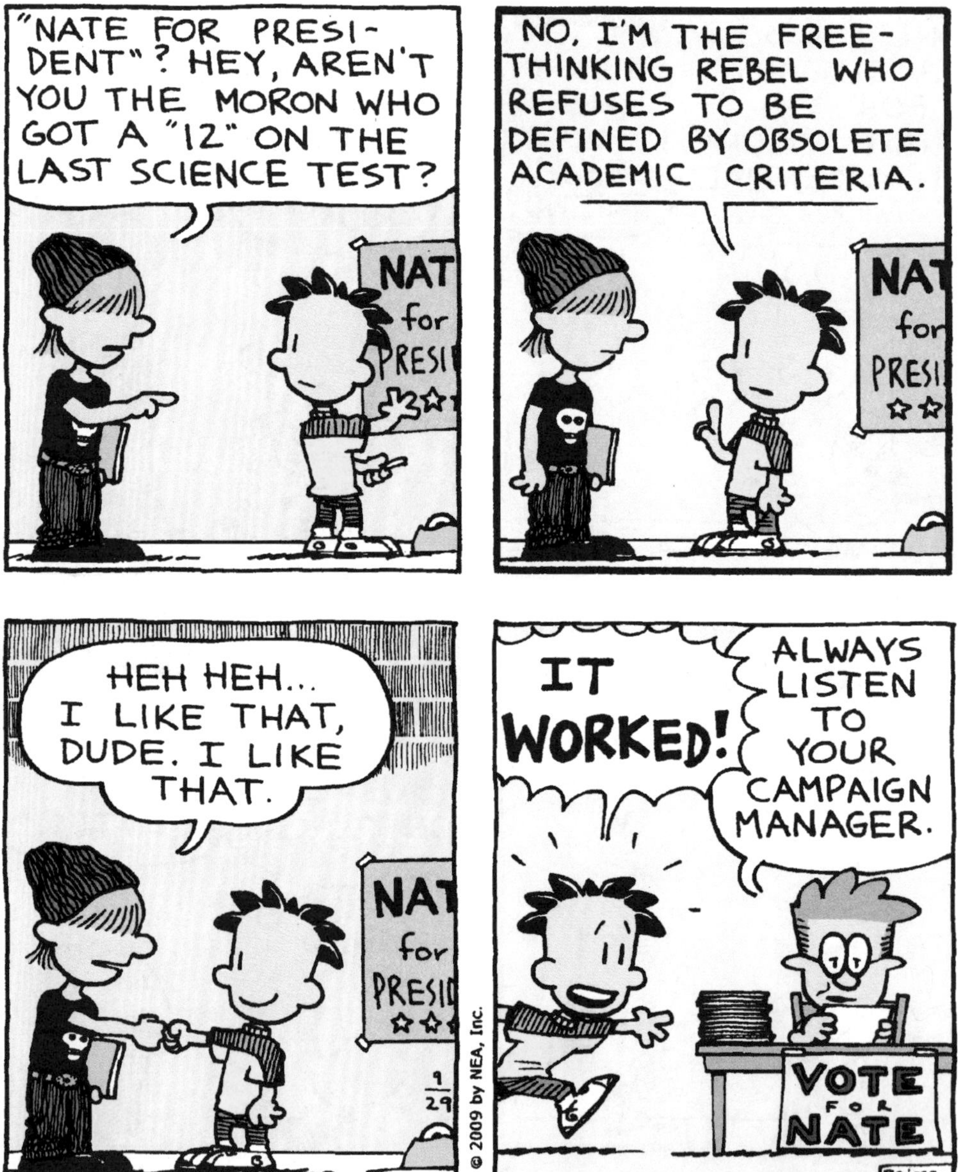
"NATE FOR PRESIDENT"? HEY, AREN'T YOU THE MORON WHO GOT A "12" ON THE LAST SCIENCE TEST?
NATE for PRESI
NO, I'M THE FREE-THINKING REBEL WHO REFUSES TO BE DEFINED BY OBSOLETE ACADEMIC CRITERIA.
HEH HEH... I LIKE THAT, DUDE. I LIKE THAT.
IT WORKED!
ALWAYS LISTEN TO YOUR CAMPAIGN MANAGER.
VOTE FOR NATE
9/29
© 2009 by NEA, Inc.
Peirce

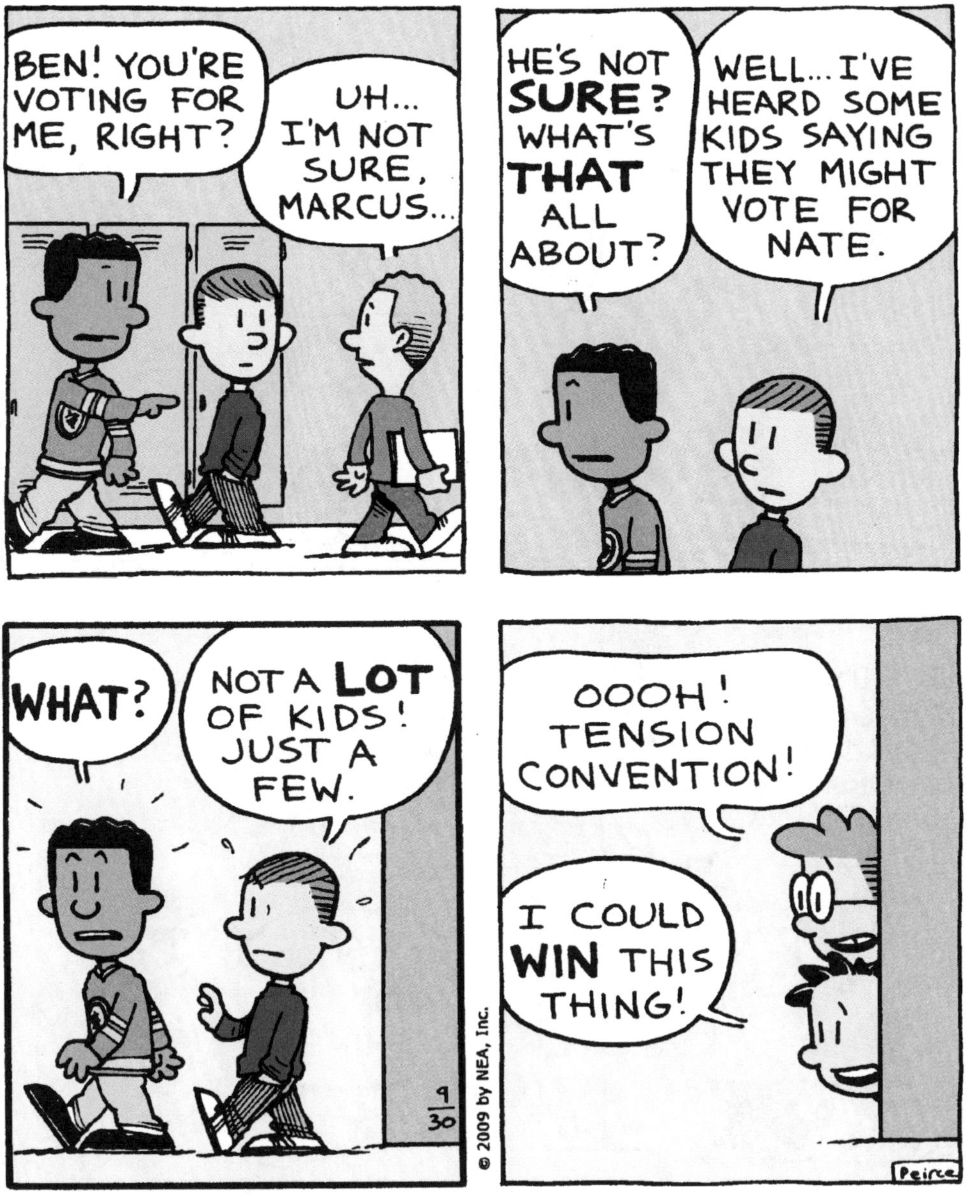
BEN! YOU'RE VOTING FOR ME, RIGHT?
UH... I'M NOT SURE, MARCUS...
HE'S NOT SURE? WHAT'S THAT ALL ABOUT?
WELL... I'VE HEARD SOME KIDS SAYING THEY MIGHT VOTE FOR NATE.
WHAT?
NOT A LOT OF KIDS! JUST A FEW.
9/30
OOOH! TENSION CONVENTION!
I COULD WIN THIS THING!
Peirce

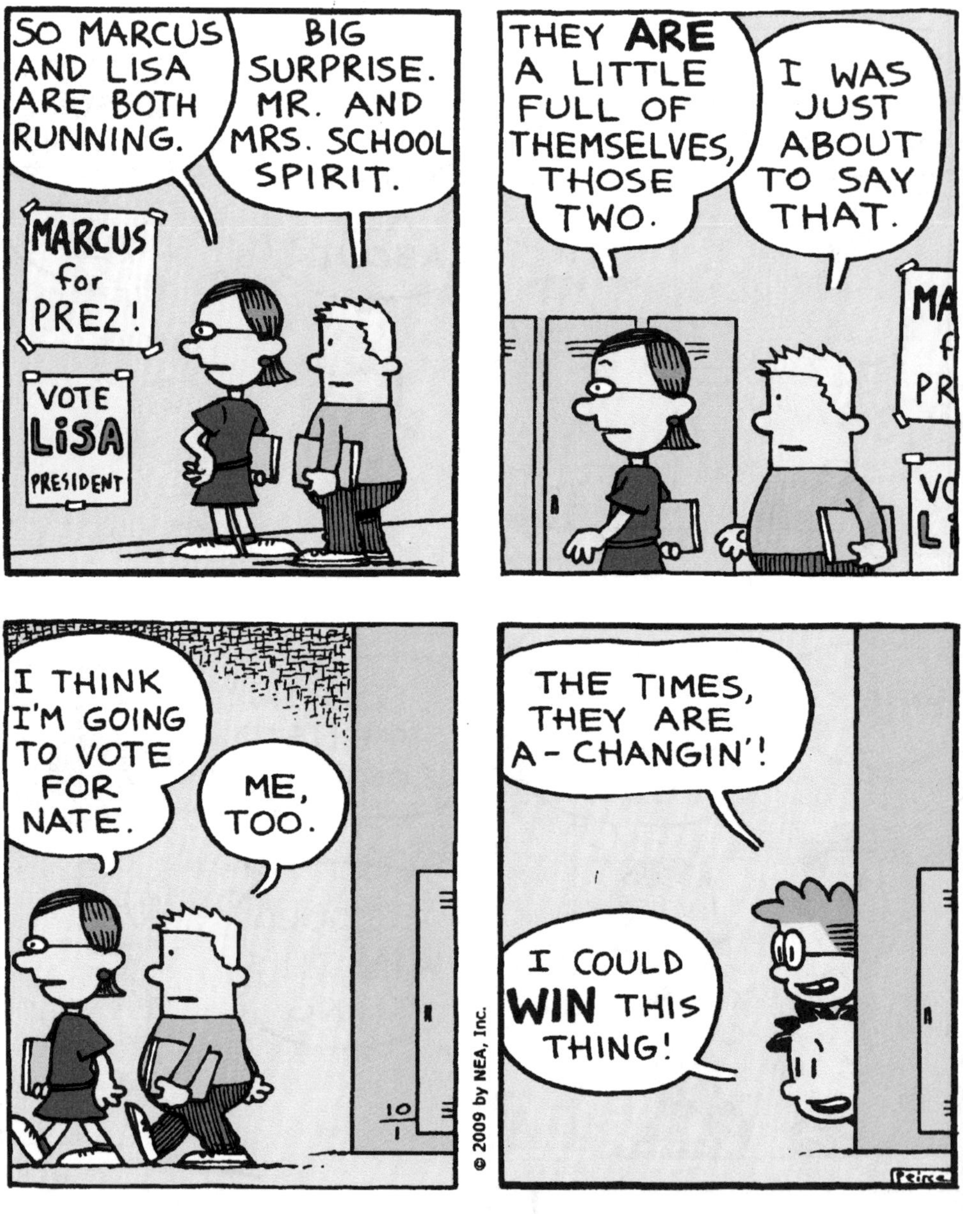
SO MARCUS AND LISA ARE BOTH RUNNING.
BIG SURPRISE. MR. AND MRS. SCHOOL SPIRIT.
MARCUS for PREZ!
VOTE LiSA PRESIDENT
THEY ARE A LITTLE FULL OF THEMSELVES, THOSE TWO.
I WAS JUST ABOUT TO SAY THAT.
I THINK I'M GOING TO VOTE FOR NATE.
ME, TOO.
THE TIMES, THEY ARE A-CHANGIN'!
I COULD WIN THIS THING!

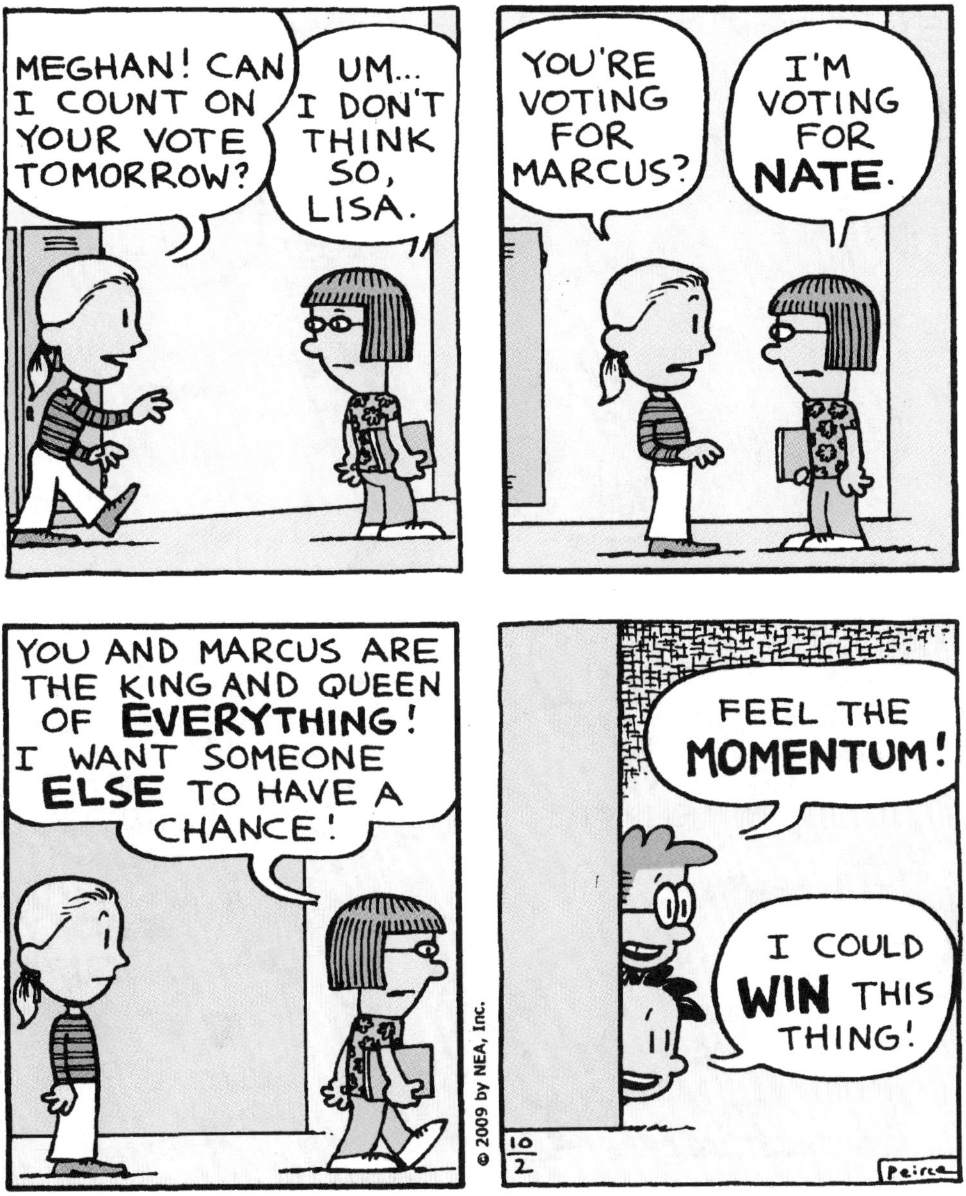
MEGHAN! CAN I COUNT ON YOUR VOTE TOMORROW?
UM... I DON'T THINK SO, LISA.
YOU'RE VOTING FOR MARCUS?
I'M VOTING FOR **NATE**.
YOU AND MARCUS ARE THE KING AND QUEEN OF **EVERYTHING**! I WANT SOMEONE **ELSE** TO HAVE A CHANCE!
FEEL THE **MOMENTUM**!
I COULD **WIN** THIS THING!
© 2009 by NEA, Inc.
10/2
Peirce

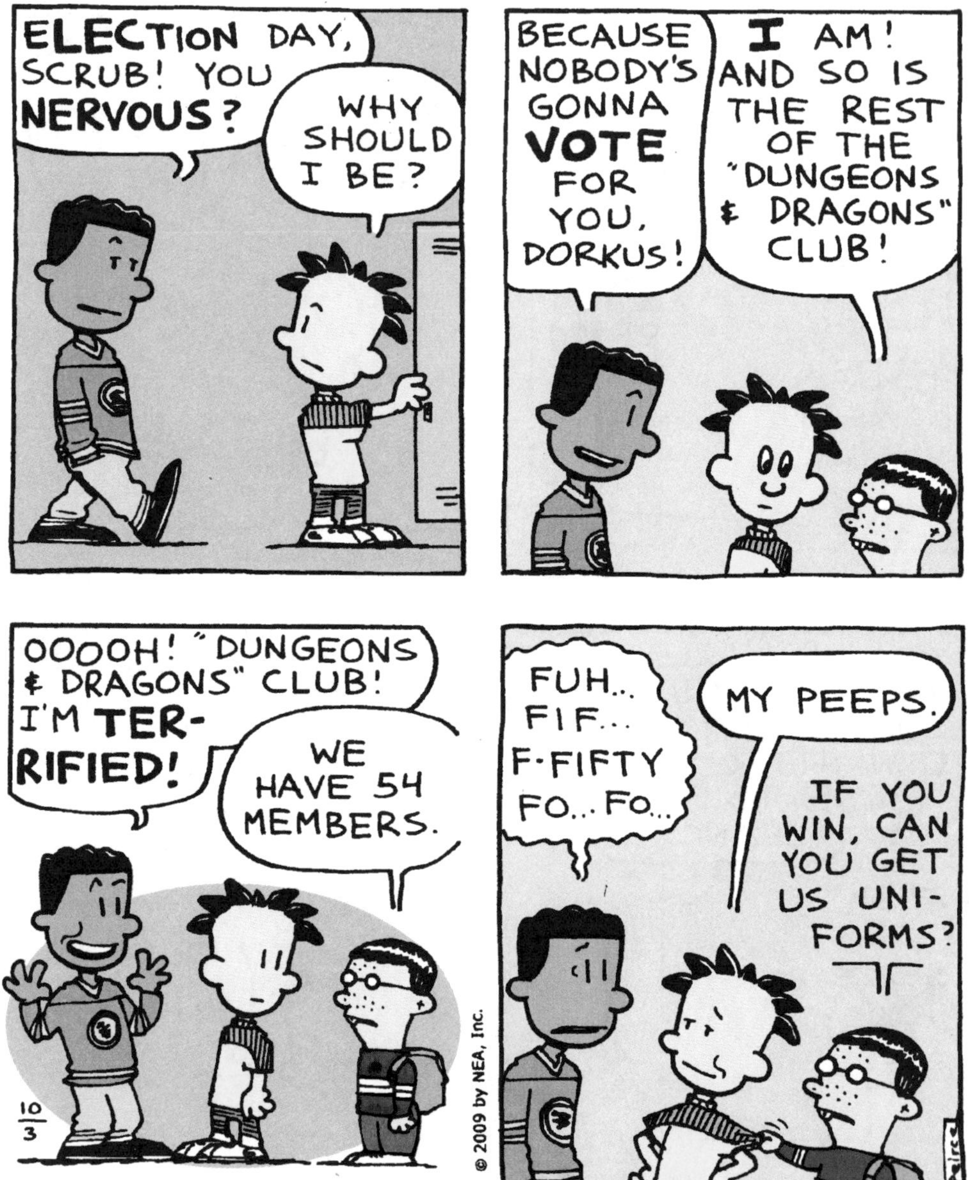
ELECTION DAY, SCRUB! YOU NERVOUS?
WHY SHOULD I BE?
BECAUSE NOBODY'S GONNA VOTE FOR YOU, DORKUS!
I AM! AND SO IS THE REST OF THE "DUNGEONS & DRAGONS" CLUB!
OOOOH! "DUNGEONS & DRAGONS" CLUB! I'M TER-RIFIED!
WE HAVE 54 MEMBERS.
10/3
© 2009 by NEA, Inc.
FUH.. FIF... F-FIFTY FO... FO...
MY PEEPS.
IF YOU WIN, CAN YOU GET US UNI-FORMS?
Peirce

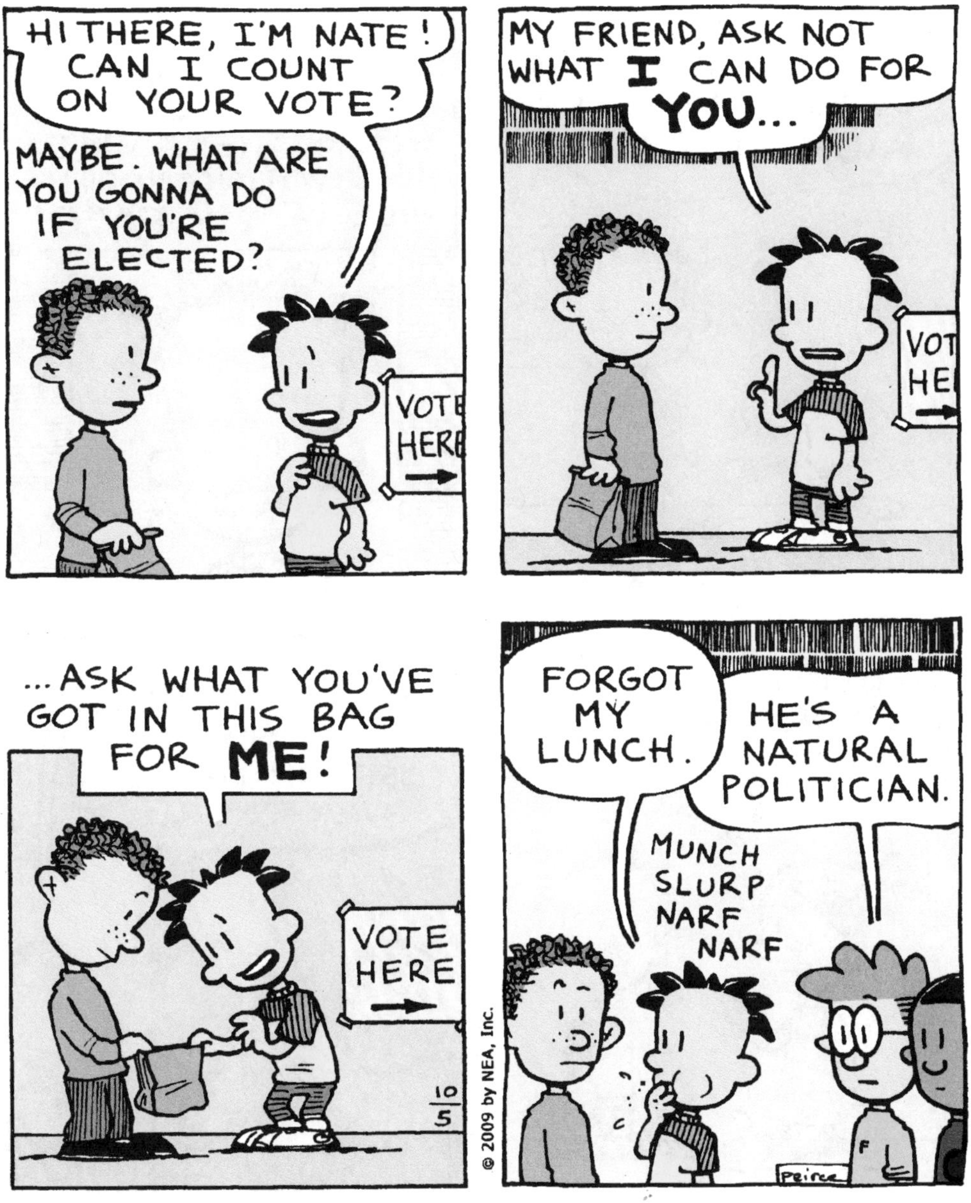
HI THERE, I'M NATE! CAN I COUNT ON YOUR VOTE?
MAYBE. WHAT ARE YOU GONNA DO IF YOU'RE ELECTED?
VOTE HERE
MY FRIEND, ASK NOT WHAT **I** CAN DO FOR **YOU**...
...ASK WHAT YOU'VE GOT IN THIS BAG FOR **ME**!
VOTE HERE
10/5
© 2009 by NEA, Inc.
FORGOT MY LUNCH.
HE'S A NATURAL POLITICIAN.
MUNCH SLURP NARF NARF
Peirce

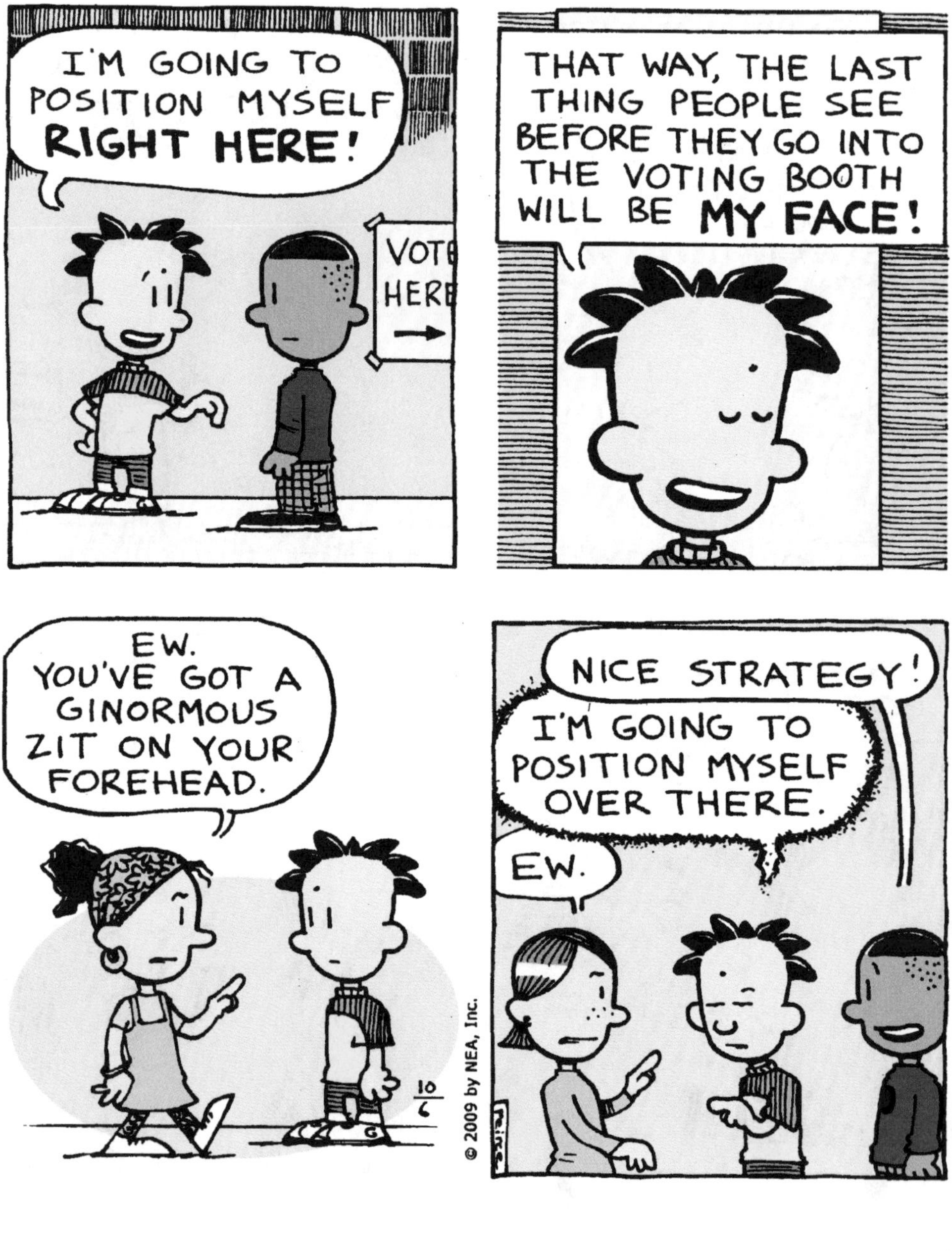
I'M GOING TO POSITION MYSELF RIGHT HERE!
VOTE HERE
THAT WAY, THE LAST THING PEOPLE SEE BEFORE THEY GO INTO THE VOTING BOOTH WILL BE MY FACE!
EW. YOU'VE GOT A GINORMOUS ZIT ON YOUR FOREHEAD.
NICE STRATEGY!
I'M GOING TO POSITION MYSELF OVER THERE.
EW.
© 2009 by NEA, Inc.

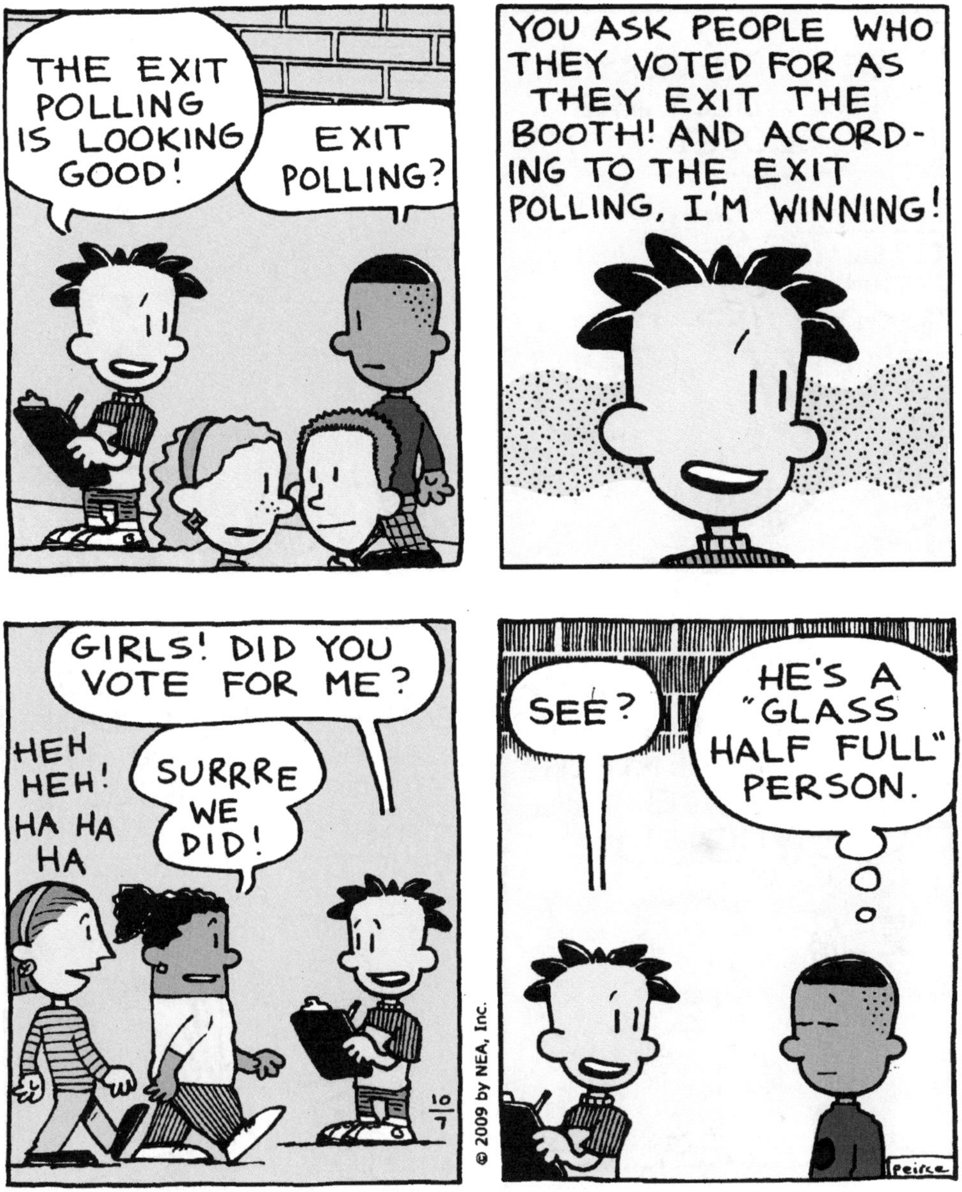
THE EXIT POLLING IS LOOKING GOOD!
EXIT POLLING?
YOU ASK PEOPLE WHO THEY VOTED FOR AS THEY EXIT THE BOOTH! AND ACCORDING TO THE EXIT POLLING, I'M WINNING!
GIRLS! DID YOU VOTE FOR ME?
HEH HEH! HA HA HA
SURRRE WE DID!
SEE?
HE'S A "GLASS HALF FULL" PERSON.
10/7
© 2009 by NEA, Inc.
Peirce

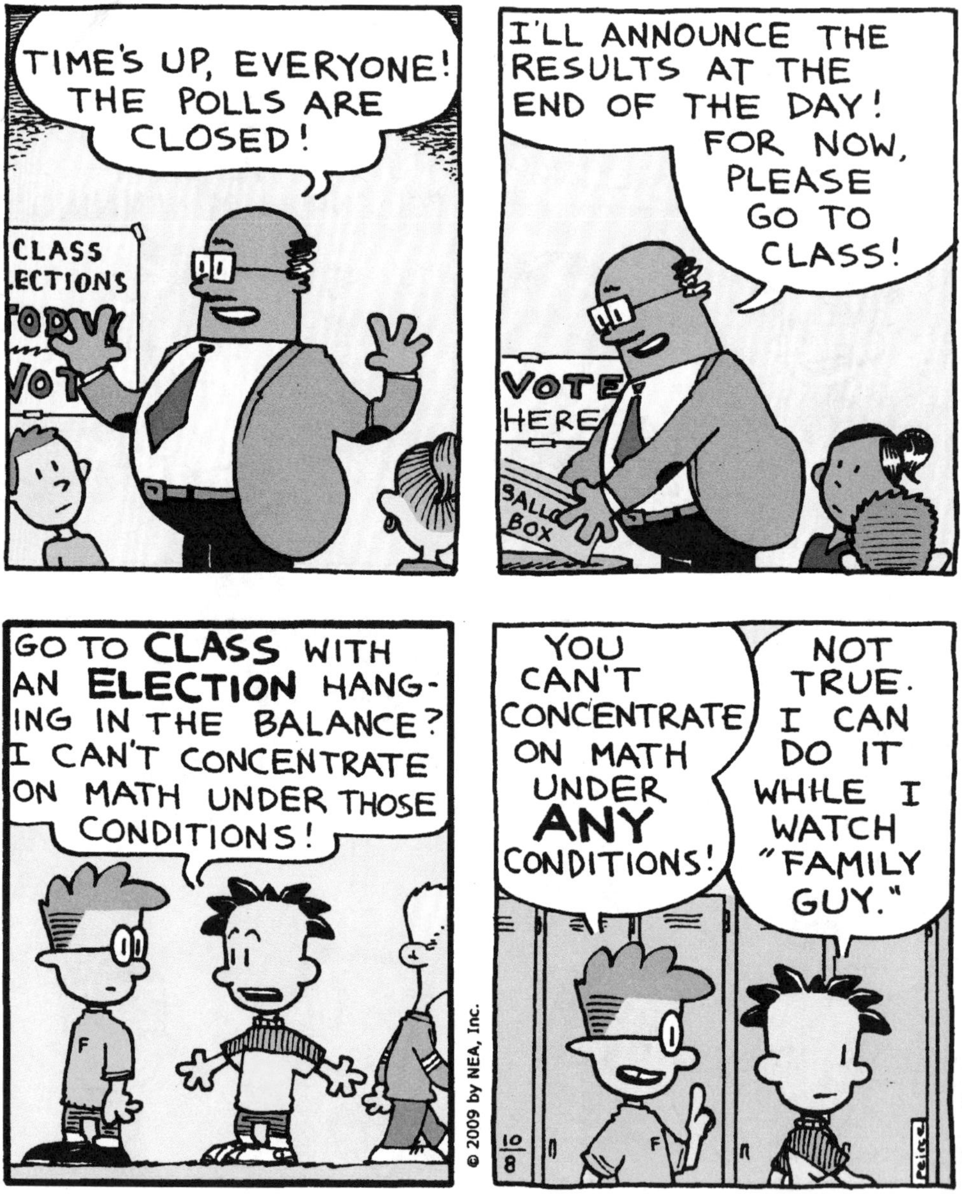
TIME'S UP, EVERYONE! THE POLLS ARE CLOSED!
CLASS ELECTIONS
I'LL ANNOUNCE THE RESULTS AT THE END OF THE DAY! FOR NOW, PLEASE GO TO CLASS!
VOTE HERE
BOX
GO TO CLASS WITH AN ELECTION HANGING IN THE BALANCE? I CAN'T CONCENTRATE ON MATH UNDER THOSE CONDITIONS!
YOU CAN'T CONCENTRATE ON MATH UNDER ANY CONDITIONS!
NOT TRUE. I CAN DO IT WHILE I WATCH "FAMILY GUY."
10/8
Peirce

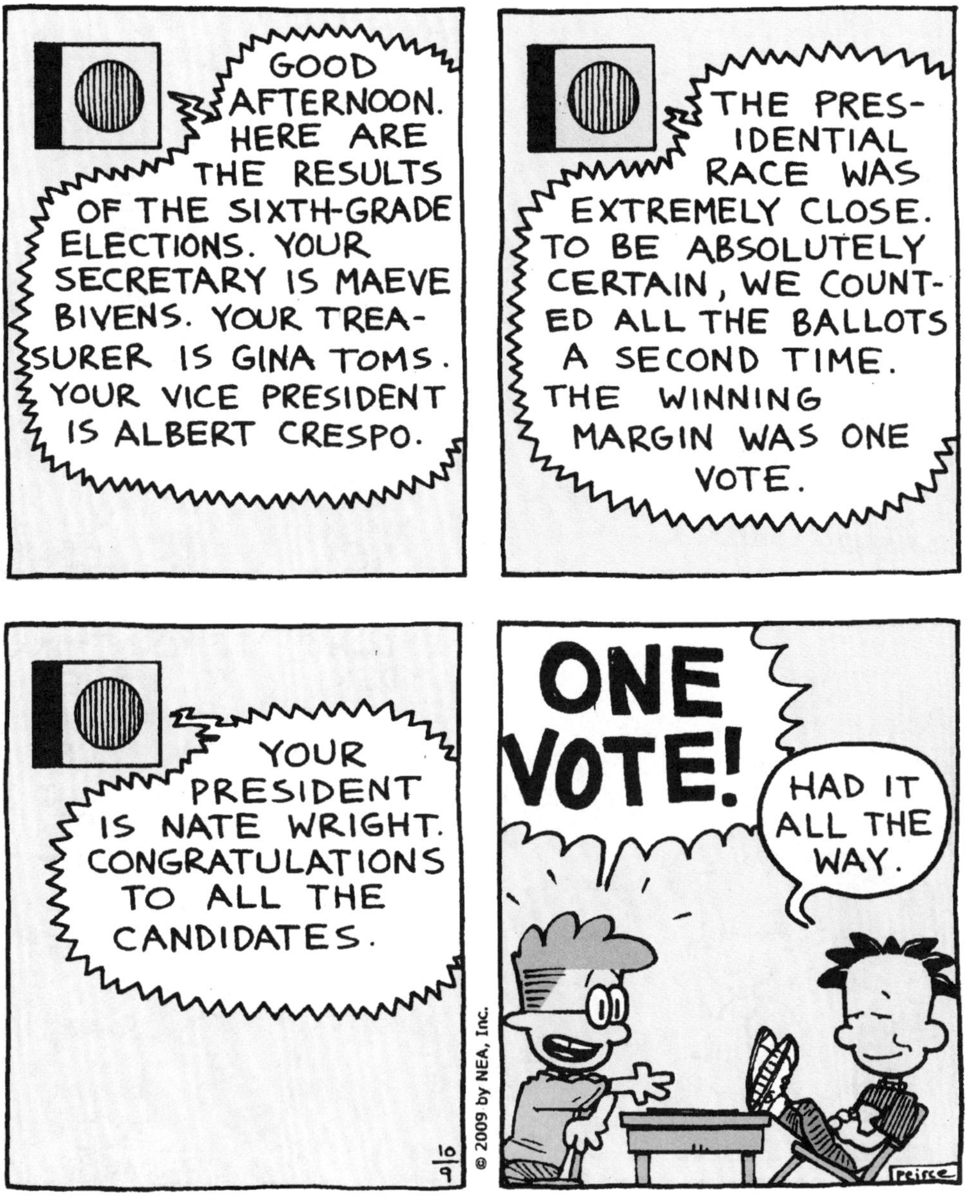
GOOD AFTERNOON. HERE ARE THE RESULTS OF THE SIXTH-GRADE ELECTIONS. YOUR SECRETARY IS MAEVE BIVENS. YOUR TREASURER IS GINA TOMS. YOUR VICE PRESIDENT IS ALBERT CRESPO.
THE PRESIDENTIAL RACE WAS EXTREMELY CLOSE. TO BE ABSOLUTELY CERTAIN, WE COUNTED ALL THE BALLOTS A SECOND TIME. THE WINNING MARGIN WAS ONE VOTE.
YOUR PRESIDENT IS NATE WRIGHT. CONGRATULATIONS TO ALL THE CANDIDATES.
10/9
© 2009 by NEA, Inc.
ONE VOTE!
HAD IT ALL THE WAY.
peirce

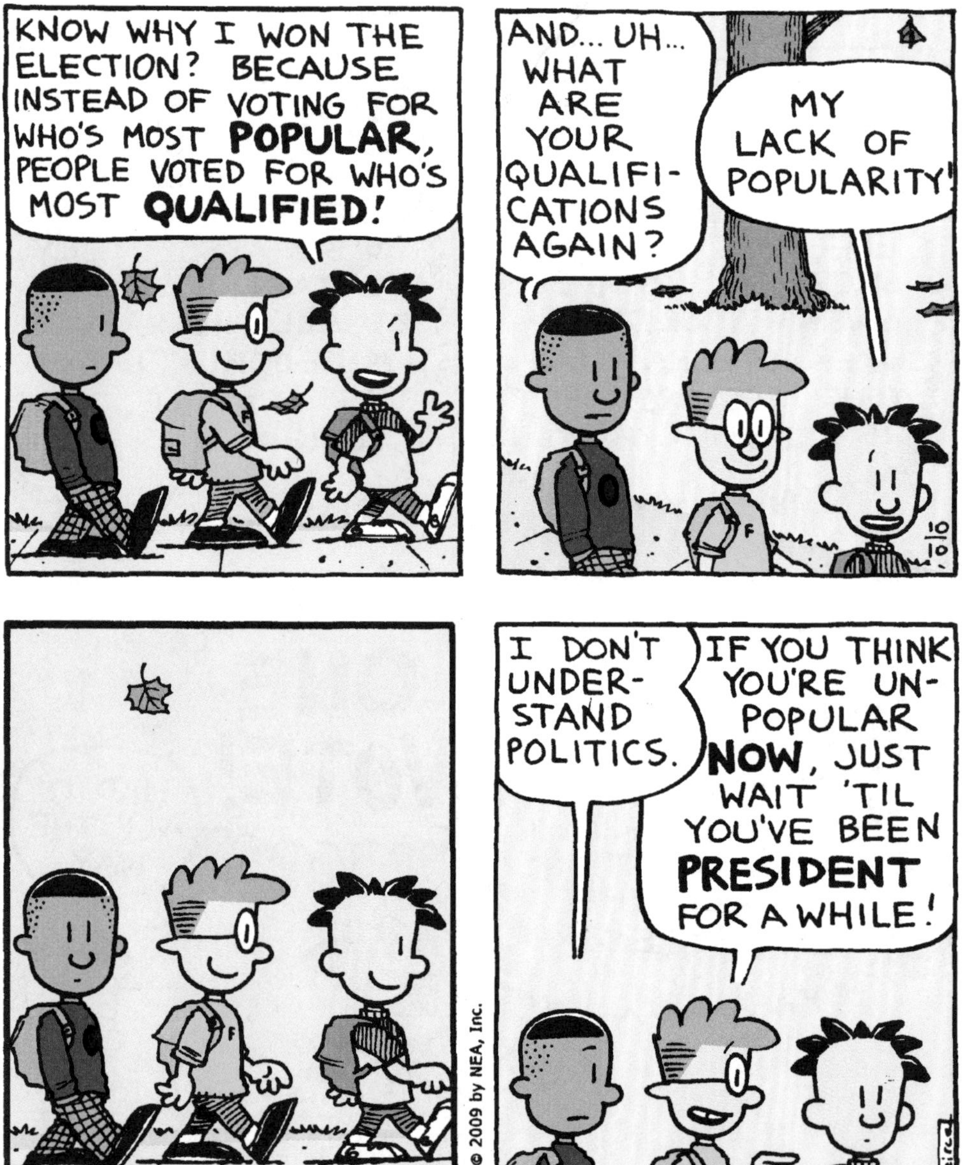
KNOW WHY I WON THE ELECTION? BECAUSE INSTEAD OF VOTING FOR WHO'S MOST POPULAR, PEOPLE VOTED FOR WHO'S MOST QUALIFIED!
AND... UH... WHAT ARE YOUR QUALIFI-CATIONS AGAIN?
MY LACK OF POPULARITY!
10/10
I DON'T UNDER-STAND POLITICS.
IF YOU THINK YOU'RE UN-POPULAR NOW, JUST WAIT 'TIL YOU'VE BEEN PRESIDENT FOR A WHILE!
© 2009 by NEA, Inc.
Peirce

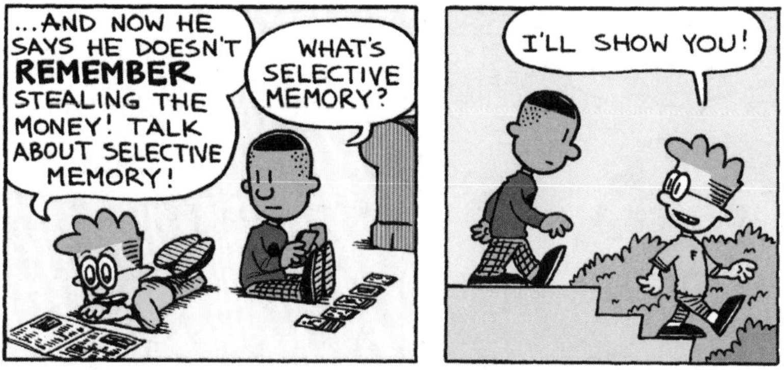
...AND NOW HE SAYS HE DOESN'T **REMEMBER** STEALING THE MONEY! TALK ABOUT SELECTIVE MEMORY!
WHAT'S SELECTIVE MEMORY?
I'LL SHOW YOU!

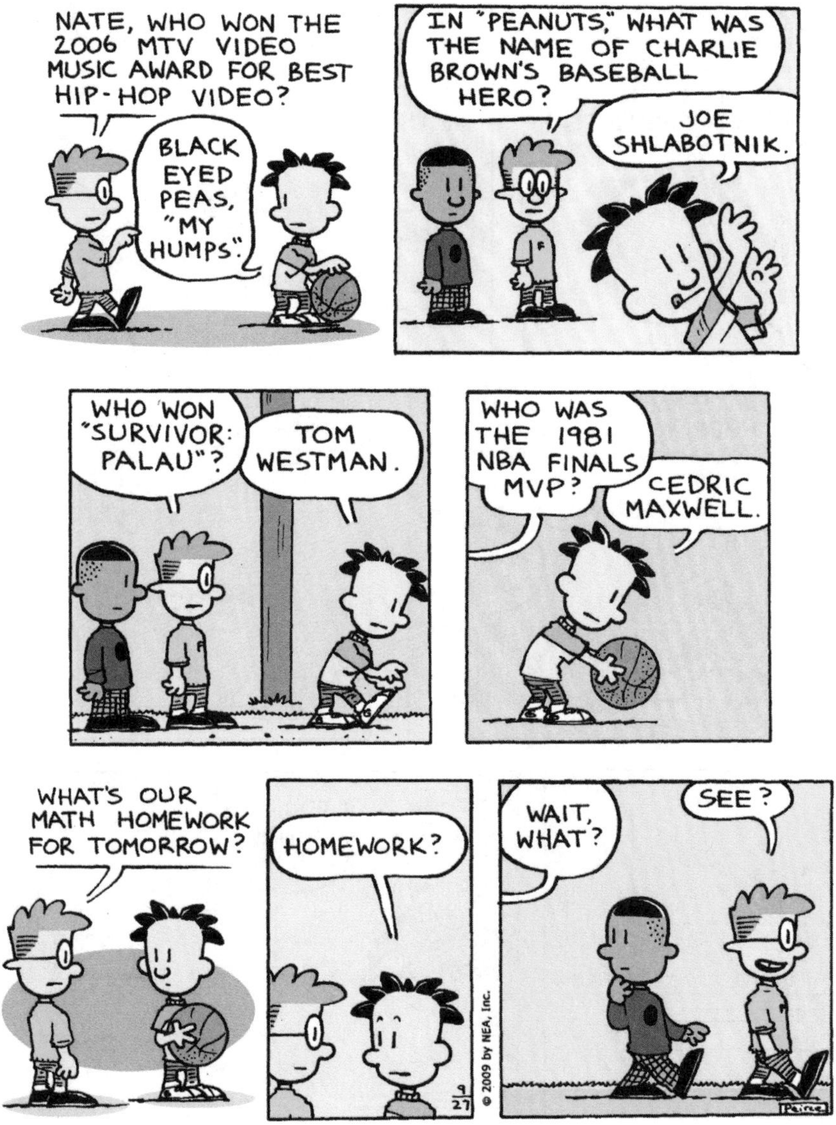
NATE, WHO WON THE 2006 MTV VIDEO MUSIC AWARD FOR BEST HIP-HOP VIDEO?
BLACK EYED PEAS, "MY HUMPS."
IN "PEANUTS," WHAT WAS THE NAME OF CHARLIE BROWN'S BASEBALL HERO?
JOE SHLABOTNIK.
WHO WON "SURVIVOR: PALAU"?
TOM WESTMAN.
WHO WAS THE 1981 NBA FINALS MVP?
CEDRIC MAXWELL.
WHAT'S OUR MATH HOMEWORK FOR TOMORROW?
HOMEWORK?
9/27
© 2009 by NEA, Inc.
WAIT, WHAT?
SEE?
Peirce

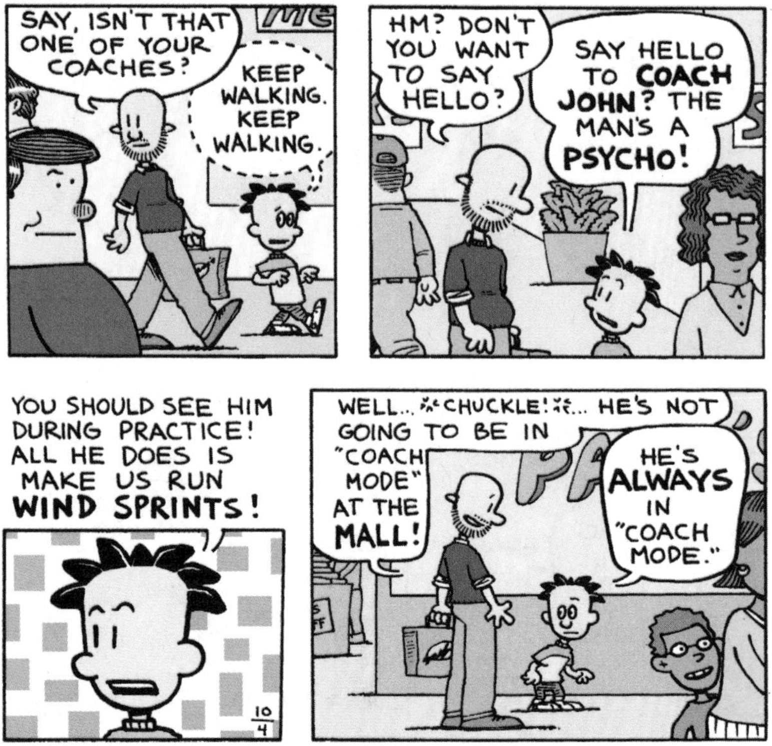
SAY, ISN'T THAT ONE OF YOUR COACHES?
KEEP WALKING. KEEP WALKING.
HM? DON'T YOU WANT TO SAY HELLO?
SAY HELLO TO **COACH JOHN**? THE MAN'S A **PSYCHO**!
YOU SHOULD SEE HIM DURING PRACTICE! ALL HE DOES IS MAKE US RUN **WIND SPRINTS**!
10/4
WELL... *CHUCKLE!*... HE'S NOT GOING TO BE IN "COACH MODE" AT THE **MALL**!
HE'S **ALWAYS** IN "COACH MODE."

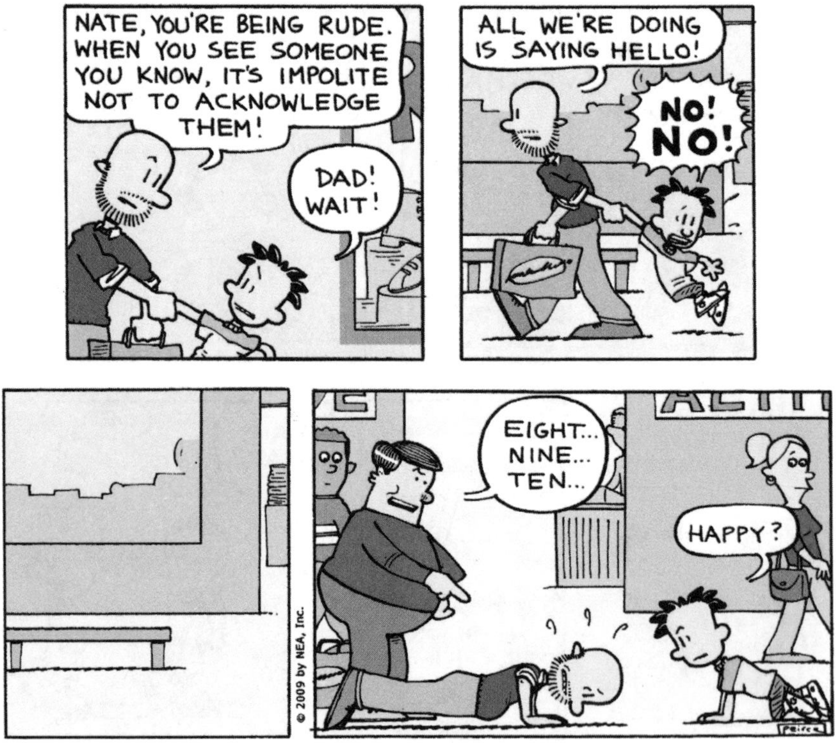
NATE, YOU'RE BEING RUDE. WHEN YOU SEE SOMEONE YOU KNOW, IT'S IMPOLITE NOT TO ACKNOWLEDGE THEM!
DAD! WAIT!
ALL WE'RE DOING IS SAYING HELLO!
NO! NO!
© 2009 by NEA, Inc.
EIGHT... NINE... TEN...
HAPPY?

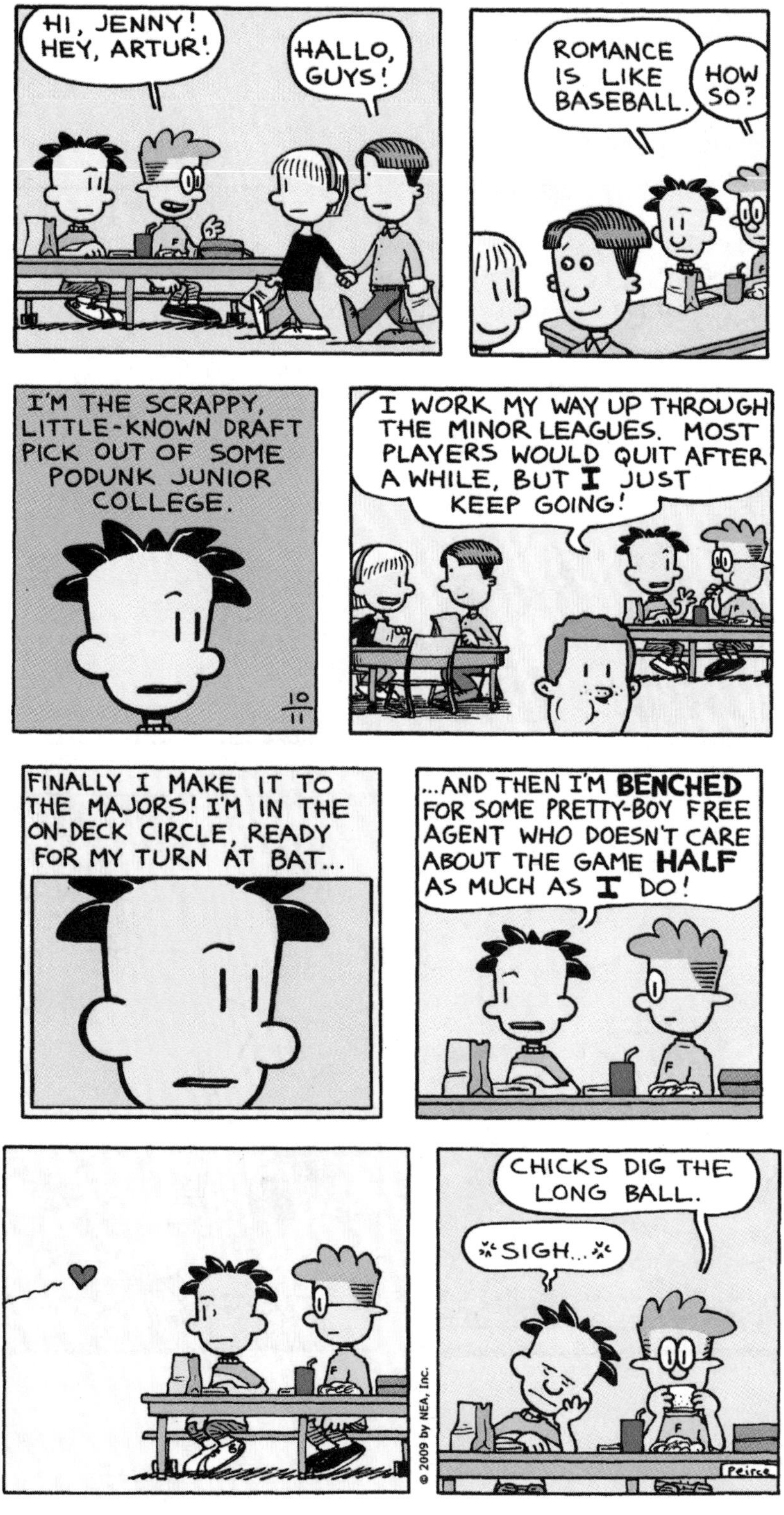
HI, JENNY! HEY, ARTUR!
HALLO, GUYS!
ROMANCE IS LIKE BASEBALL.
HOW SO?
I'M THE SCRAPPY, LITTLE-KNOWN DRAFT PICK OUT OF SOME PODUNK JUNIOR COLLEGE.
10/11
I WORK MY WAY UP THROUGH THE MINOR LEAGUES. MOST PLAYERS WOULD QUIT AFTER A WHILE, BUT I JUST KEEP GOING!
FINALLY I MAKE IT TO THE MAJORS! I'M IN THE ON-DECK CIRCLE, READY FOR MY TURN AT BAT...
...AND THEN I'M BENCHED FOR SOME PRETTY-BOY FREE AGENT WHO DOESN'T CARE ABOUT THE GAME HALF AS MUCH AS I DO!
© 2009 by NEA, Inc.
CHICKS DIG THE LONG BALL.
SIGH...
Peirce

EL PRESIDENTE

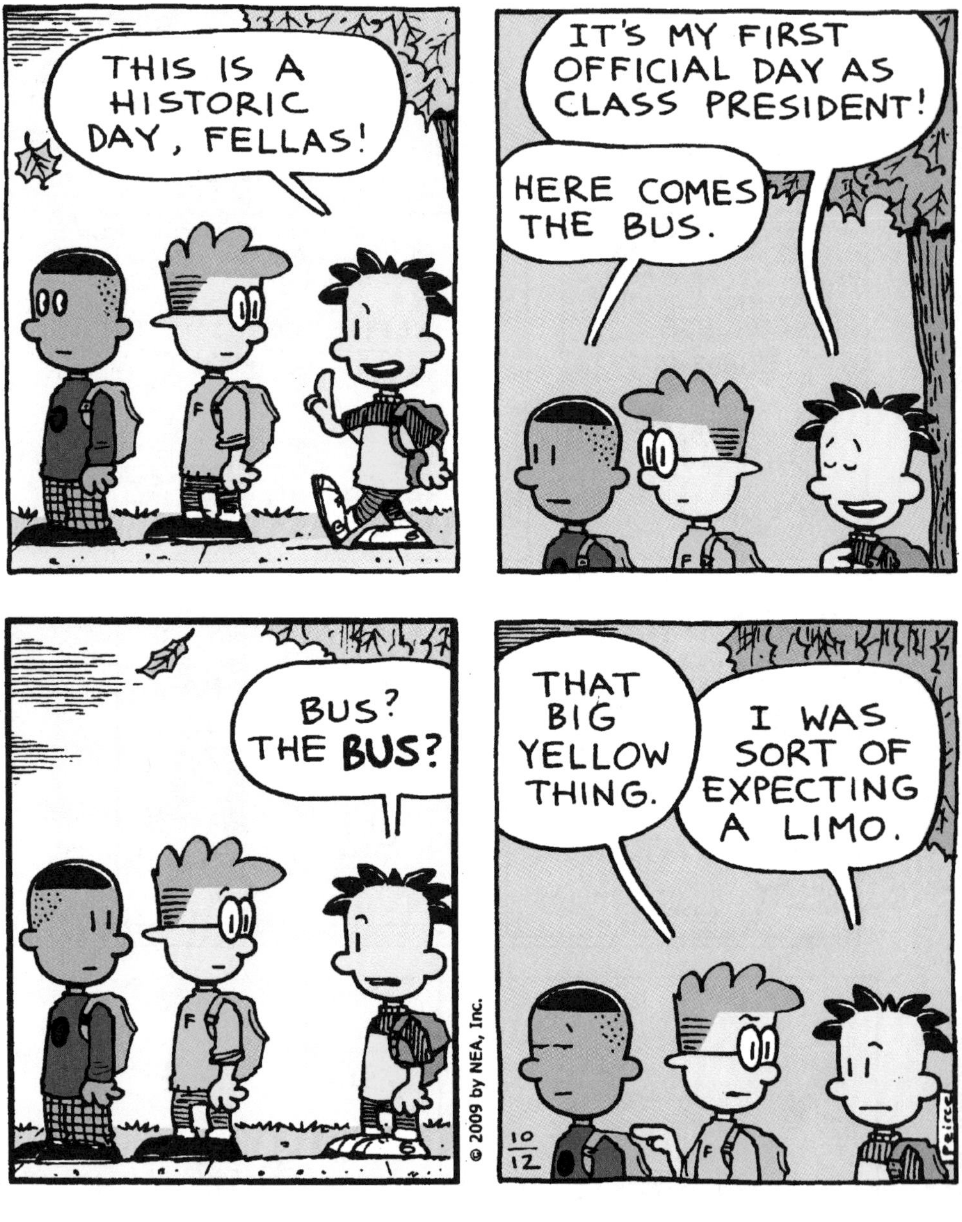

THIS IS A HISTORIC DAY, FELLAS!
IT'S MY FIRST OFFICIAL DAY AS CLASS PRESIDENT!
HERE COMES THE BUS.
BUS? THE **BUS**?
THAT BIG YELLOW THING.
I WAS SORT OF EXPECTING A LIMO.
© 2009 by NEA, Inc.
10/12
Peirce

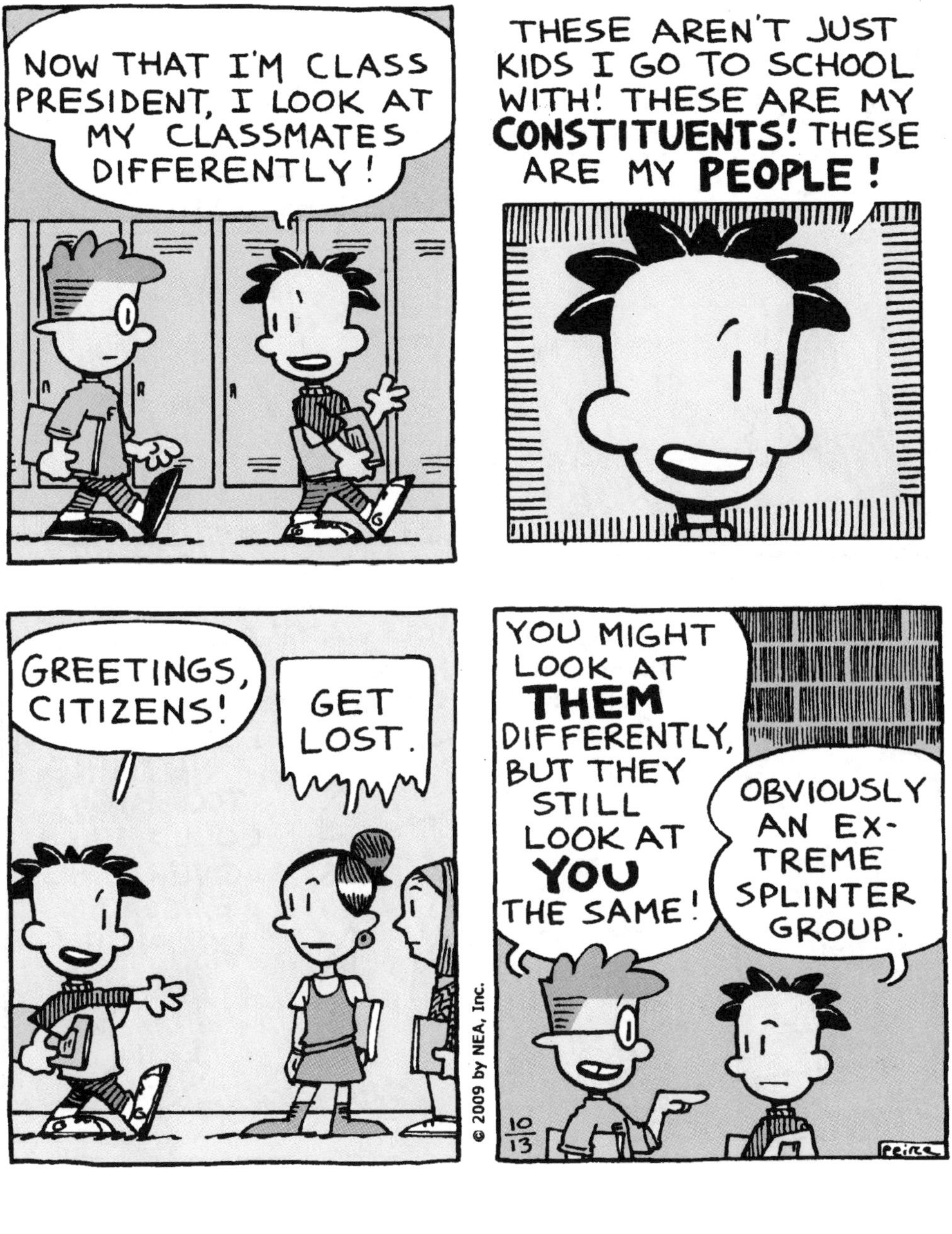
NOW THAT I'M CLASS PRESIDENT, I LOOK AT MY CLASSMATES DIFFERENTLY!
THESE AREN'T JUST KIDS I GO TO SCHOOL WITH! THESE ARE MY CONSTITUENTS! THESE ARE MY PEOPLE!
GREETINGS, CITIZENS!
GET LOST.
YOU MIGHT LOOK AT THEM DIFFERENTLY, BUT THEY STILL LOOK AT YOU THE SAME!
OBVIOUSLY AN EX-TREME SPLINTER GROUP.
© 2009 by NEA, Inc.
10/13
PEIRCE

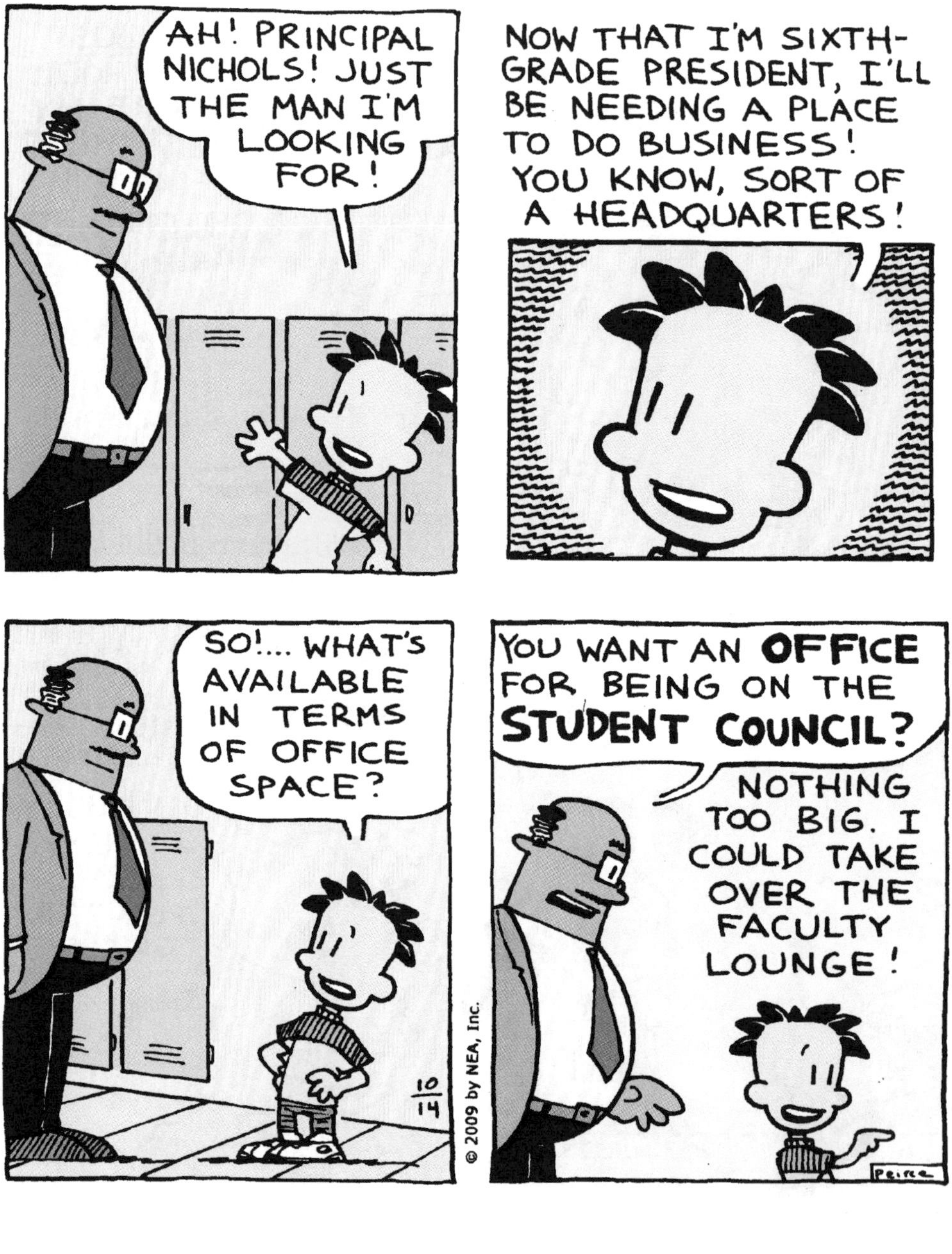

AH! PRINCIPAL NICHOLS! JUST THE MAN I'M LOOKING FOR!
NOW THAT I'M SIXTH-GRADE PRESIDENT, I'LL BE NEEDING A PLACE TO DO BUSINESS! YOU KNOW, SORT OF A HEADQUARTERS!
SO!... WHAT'S AVAILABLE IN TERMS OF OFFICE SPACE?
10/14
© 2009 by NEA, Inc.
YOU WANT AN **OFFICE** FOR BEING ON THE **STUDENT COUNCIL**?
NOTHING TOO BIG. I COULD TAKE OVER THE FACULTY LOUNGE!
PEIRCE

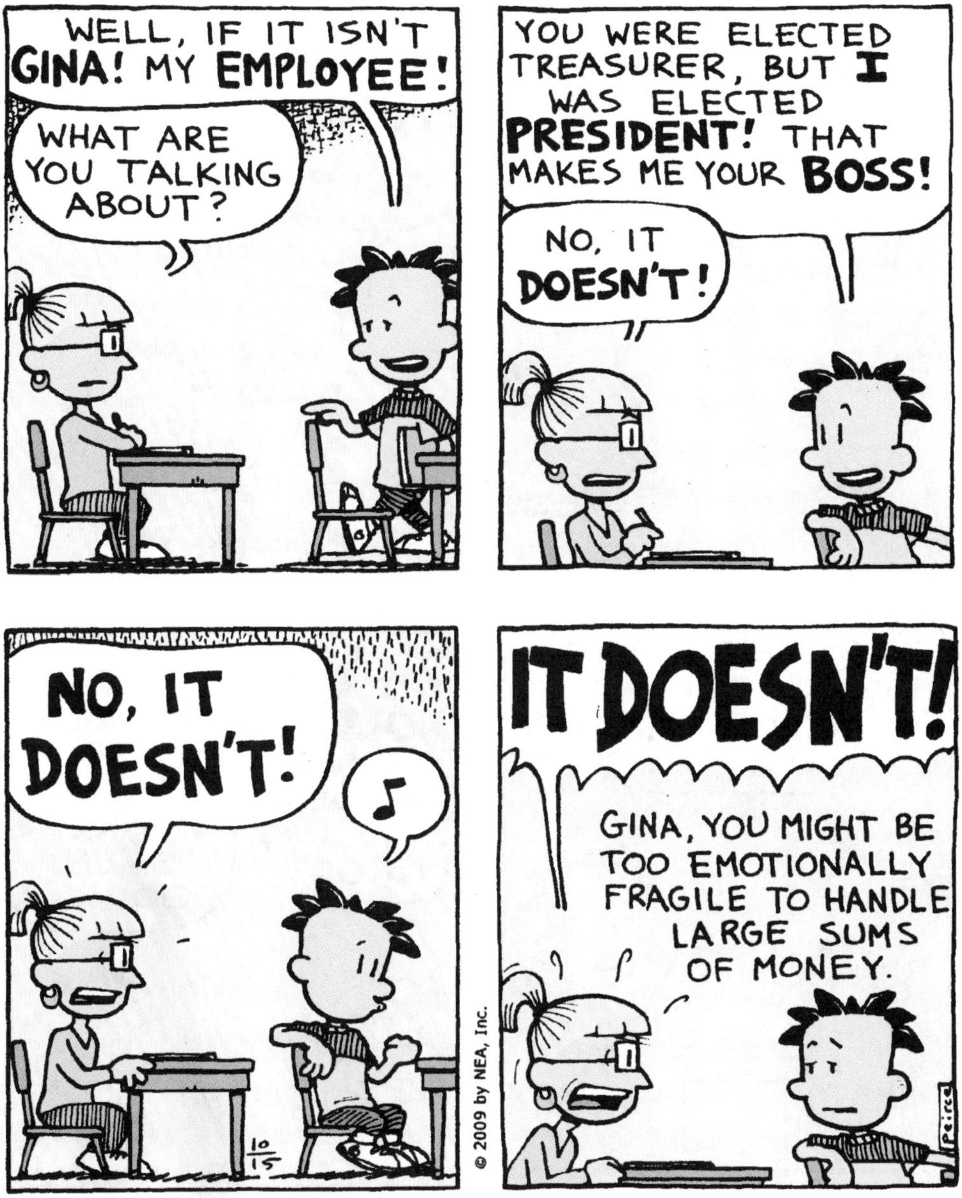
WELL, IF IT ISN'T GINA! MY EMPLOYEE!
WHAT ARE YOU TALKING ABOUT?
YOU WERE ELECTED TREASURER, BUT I WAS ELECTED PRESIDENT! THAT MAKES ME YOUR BOSS!
NO, IT DOESN'T!
NO, IT DOESN'T!
♪
10/15
IT DOESN'T!
GINA, YOU MIGHT BE TOO EMOTIONALLY FRAGILE TO HANDLE LARGE SUMS OF MONEY.
Peirce

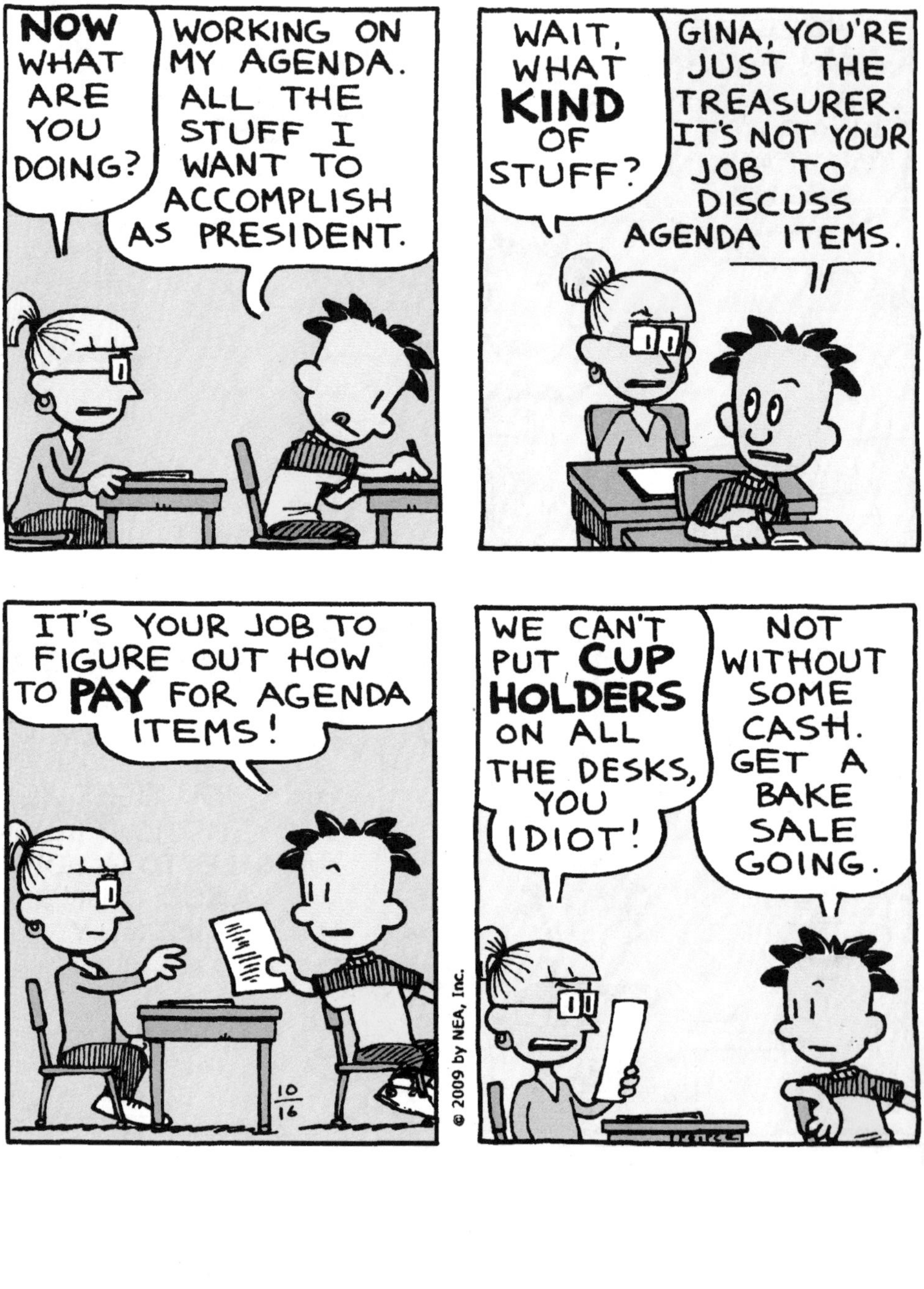
NOW WHAT ARE YOU DOING?
WORKING ON MY AGENDA. ALL THE STUFF I WANT TO ACCOMPLISH AS PRESIDENT.
WAIT, WHAT KIND OF STUFF?
GINA, YOU'RE JUST THE TREASURER. IT'S NOT YOUR JOB TO DISCUSS AGENDA ITEMS.
IT'S YOUR JOB TO FIGURE OUT HOW TO PAY FOR AGENDA ITEMS!
WE CAN'T PUT CUP HOLDERS ON ALL THE DESKS, YOU IDIOT!
NOT WITHOUT SOME CASH. GET A BAKE SALE GOING.
10/16
© 2009 by NEA, Inc.

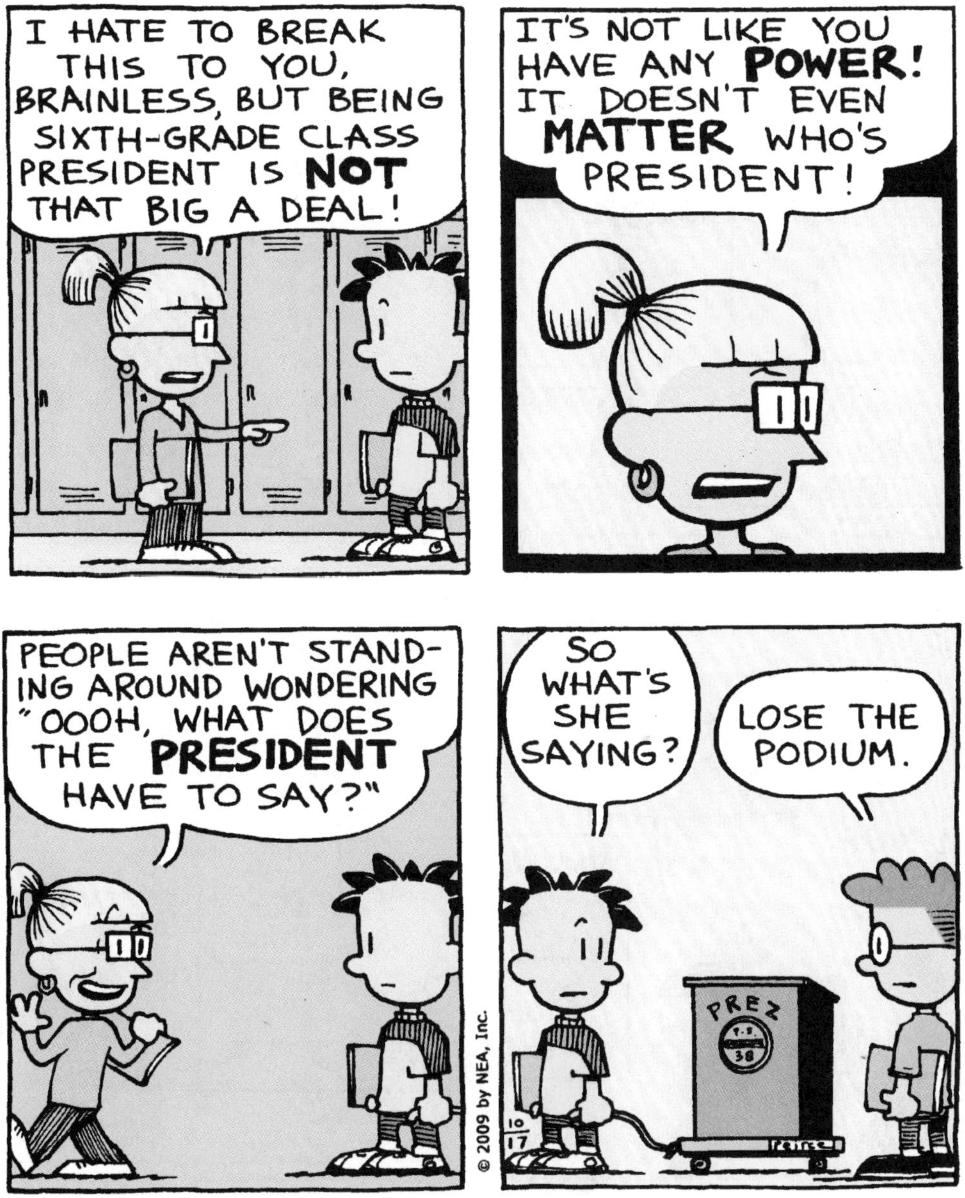
I HATE TO BREAK THIS TO YOU, BRAINLESS, BUT BEING SIXTH-GRADE CLASS PRESIDENT IS NOT THAT BIG A DEAL!
IT'S NOT LIKE YOU HAVE ANY POWER! IT DOESN'T EVEN MATTER WHO'S PRESIDENT!
PEOPLE AREN'T STANDING AROUND WONDERING "OOOH, WHAT DOES THE PRESIDENT HAVE TO SAY?"
SO WHAT'S SHE SAYING?
LOSE THE PODIUM.
PREZ
© 2009 by NEA, Inc.
10/17

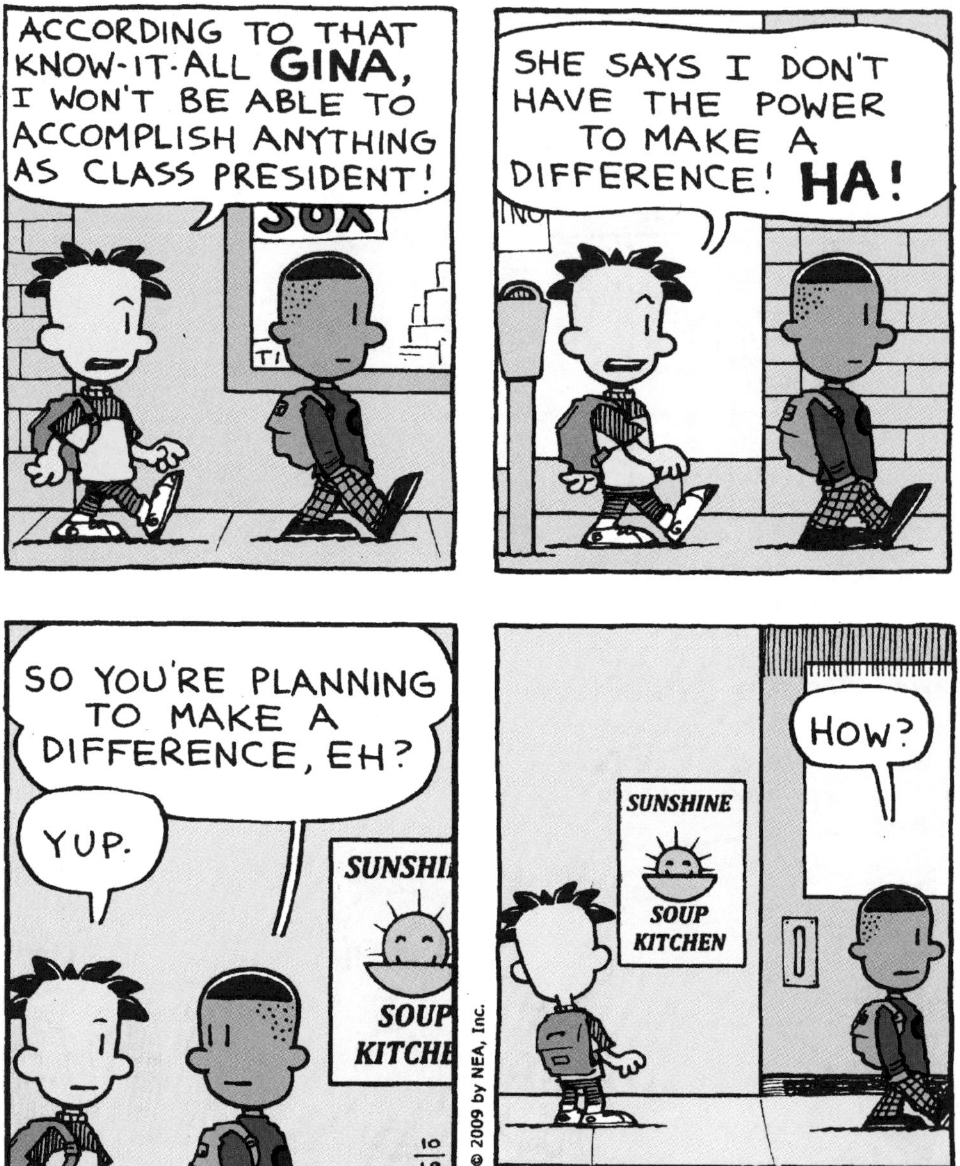
ACCORDING TO THAT KNOW-IT-ALL **GINA**, I WON'T BE ABLE TO ACCOMPLISH ANYTHING AS CLASS PRESIDENT!
SHE SAYS I DON'T HAVE THE POWER TO MAKE A DIFFERENCE! **HA!**
SO YOU'RE PLANNING TO MAKE A DIFFERENCE, EH?
YUP.
SUNSHINE SOUP KITCHEN
HOW?
10/19
© 2009 by NEA, Inc.
Peirce

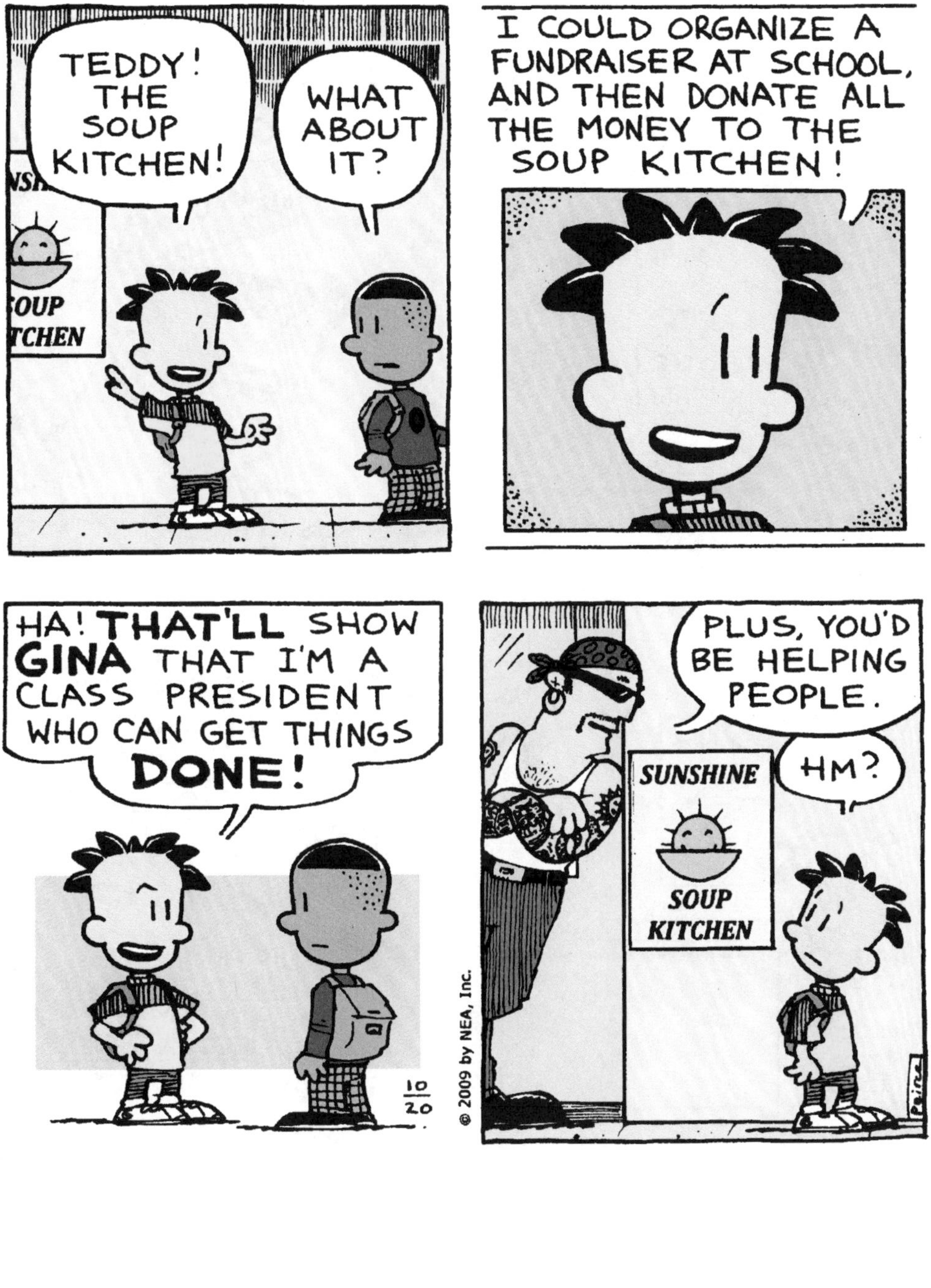
TEDDY! THE SOUP KITCHEN!
WHAT ABOUT IT?
I COULD ORGANIZE A FUNDRAISER AT SCHOOL, AND THEN DONATE ALL THE MONEY TO THE SOUP KITCHEN!
HA! THAT'LL SHOW GINA THAT I'M A CLASS PRESIDENT WHO CAN GET THINGS DONE!
10/20
© 2009 by NEA, Inc.
PLUS, YOU'D BE HELPING PEOPLE.
SUNSHINE SOUP KITCHEN
HM?
Peirce

© 2009 by NEA, Inc.

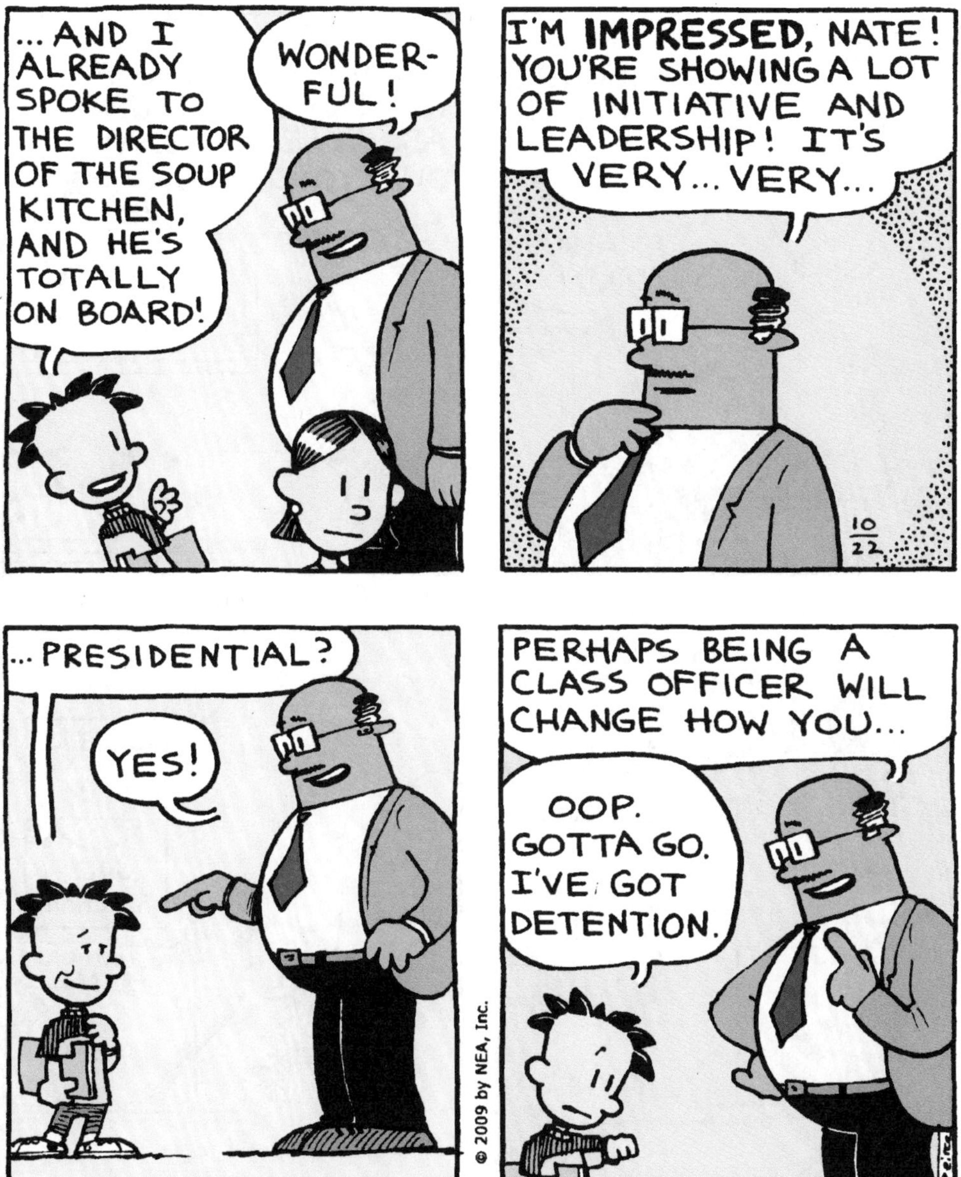
...AND I ALREADY SPOKE TO THE DIRECTOR OF THE SOUP KITCHEN, AND HE'S TOTALLY ON BOARD!
WONDER-FUL!
I'M **IMPRESSED**, NATE! YOU'RE SHOWING A LOT OF INITIATIVE AND LEADERSHIP! IT'S VERY... VERY...
10
22
...PRESIDENTIAL?
YES!
PERHAPS BEING A CLASS OFFICER WILL CHANGE HOW YOU...
OOP. GOTTA GO. I'VE GOT DETENTION.

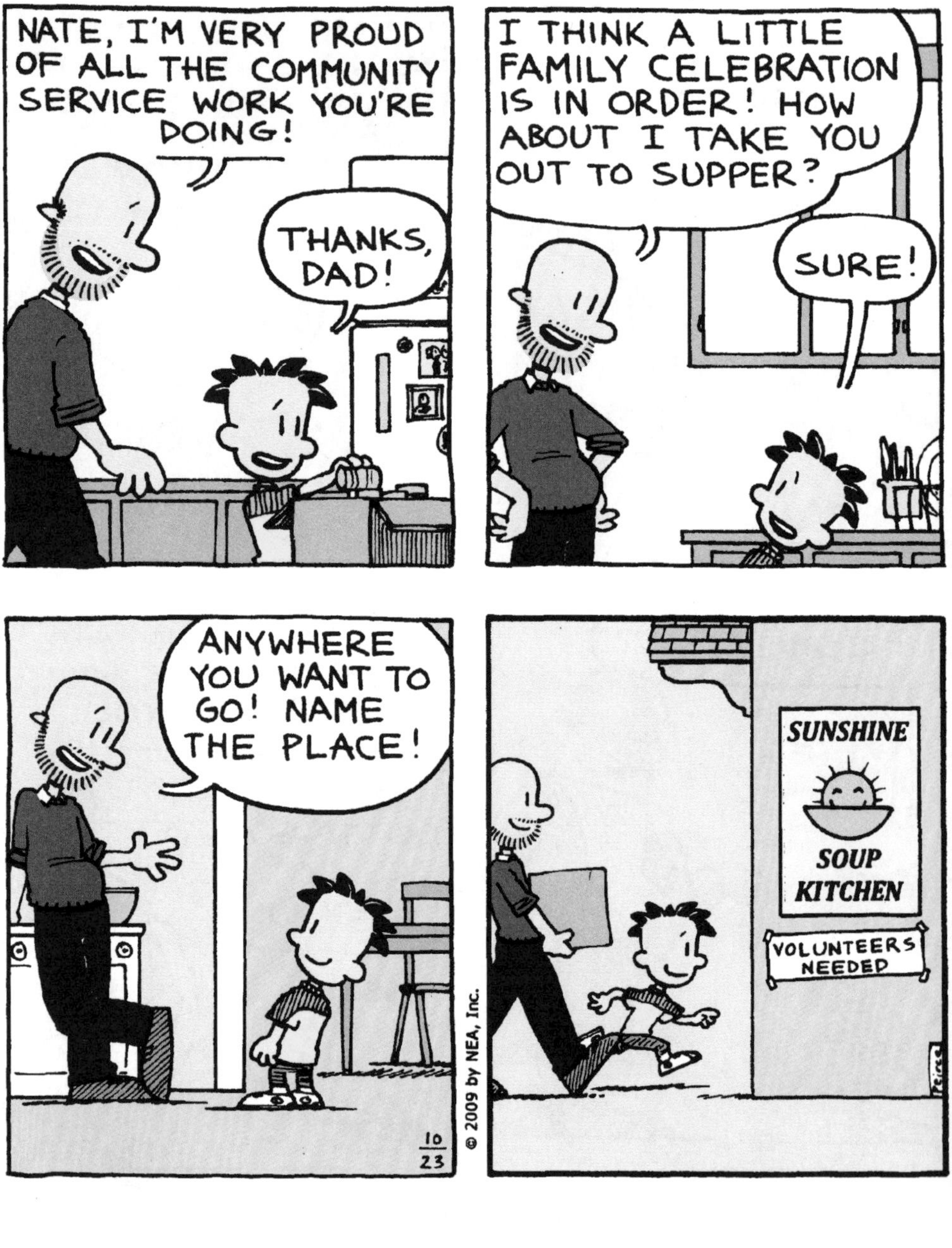
NATE, I'M VERY PROUD OF ALL THE COMMUNITY SERVICE WORK YOU'RE DOING!
THANKS, DAD!
I THINK A LITTLE FAMILY CELEBRATION IS IN ORDER! HOW ABOUT I TAKE YOU OUT TO SUPPER?
SURE!
ANYWHERE YOU WANT TO GO! NAME THE PLACE!
10
23
© 2009 by NEA, Inc.
SUNSHINE
SOUP KITCHEN
VOLUNTEERS NEEDED

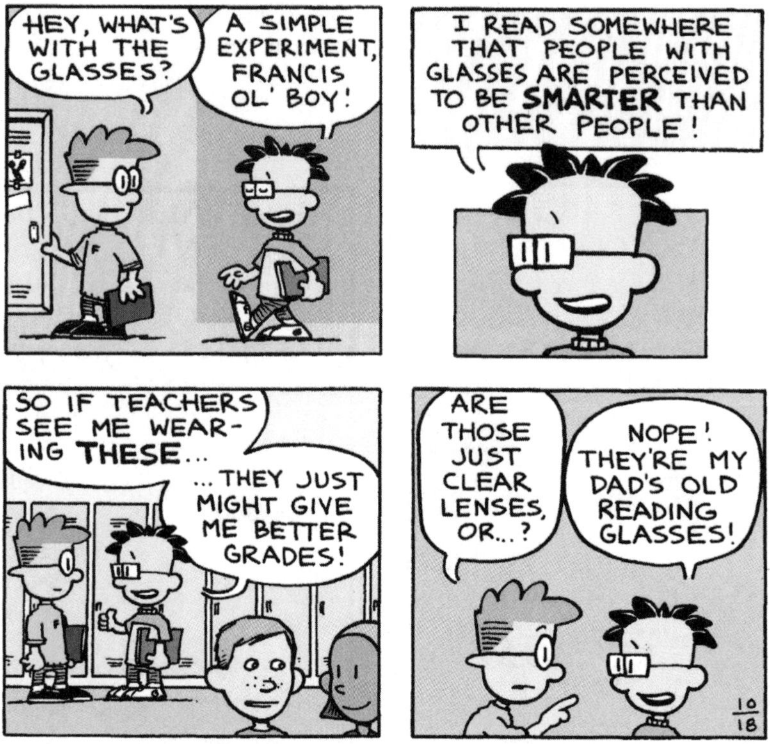
HEY, WHAT'S WITH THE GLASSES?
A SIMPLE EXPERIMENT, FRANCIS OL' BOY!
I READ SOMEWHERE THAT PEOPLE WITH GLASSES ARE PERCEIVED TO BE **SMARTER** THAN OTHER PEOPLE!
SO IF TEACHERS SEE ME WEARING **THESE**...
...THEY JUST MIGHT GIVE ME BETTER GRADES!
ARE THOSE JUST CLEAR LENSES, OR...?
NOPE! THEY'RE MY DAD'S OLD READING GLASSES!
10/18

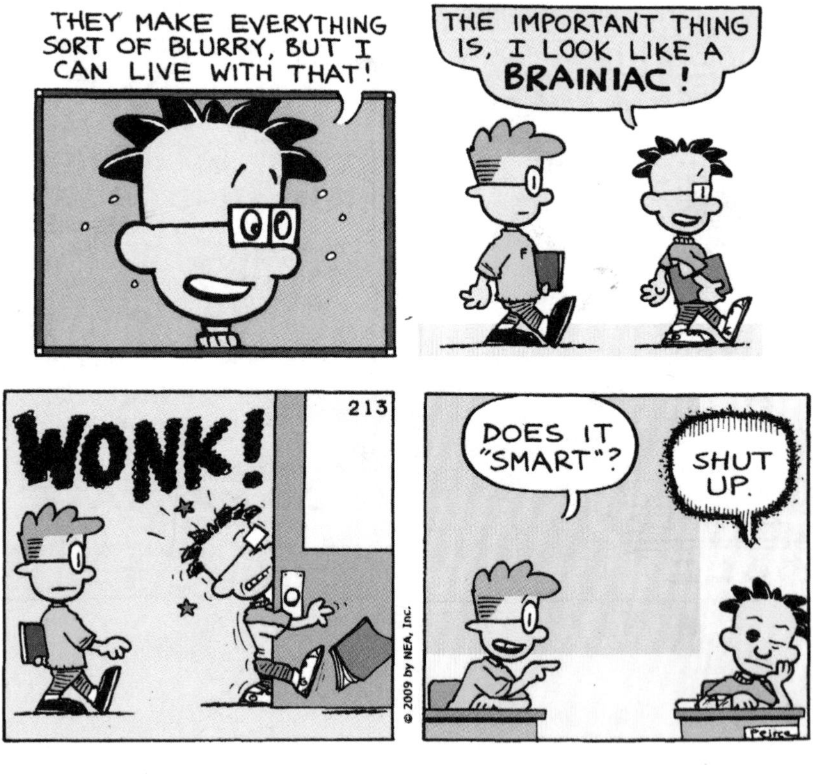
THEY MAKE EVERYTHING SORT OF BLURRY, BUT I CAN LIVE WITH THAT!
THE IMPORTANT THING IS, I LOOK LIKE A **BRAINIAC**!
213
WONK!
© 2009 by NEA, Inc.
DOES IT "SMART"?
SHUT UP.
Peirce

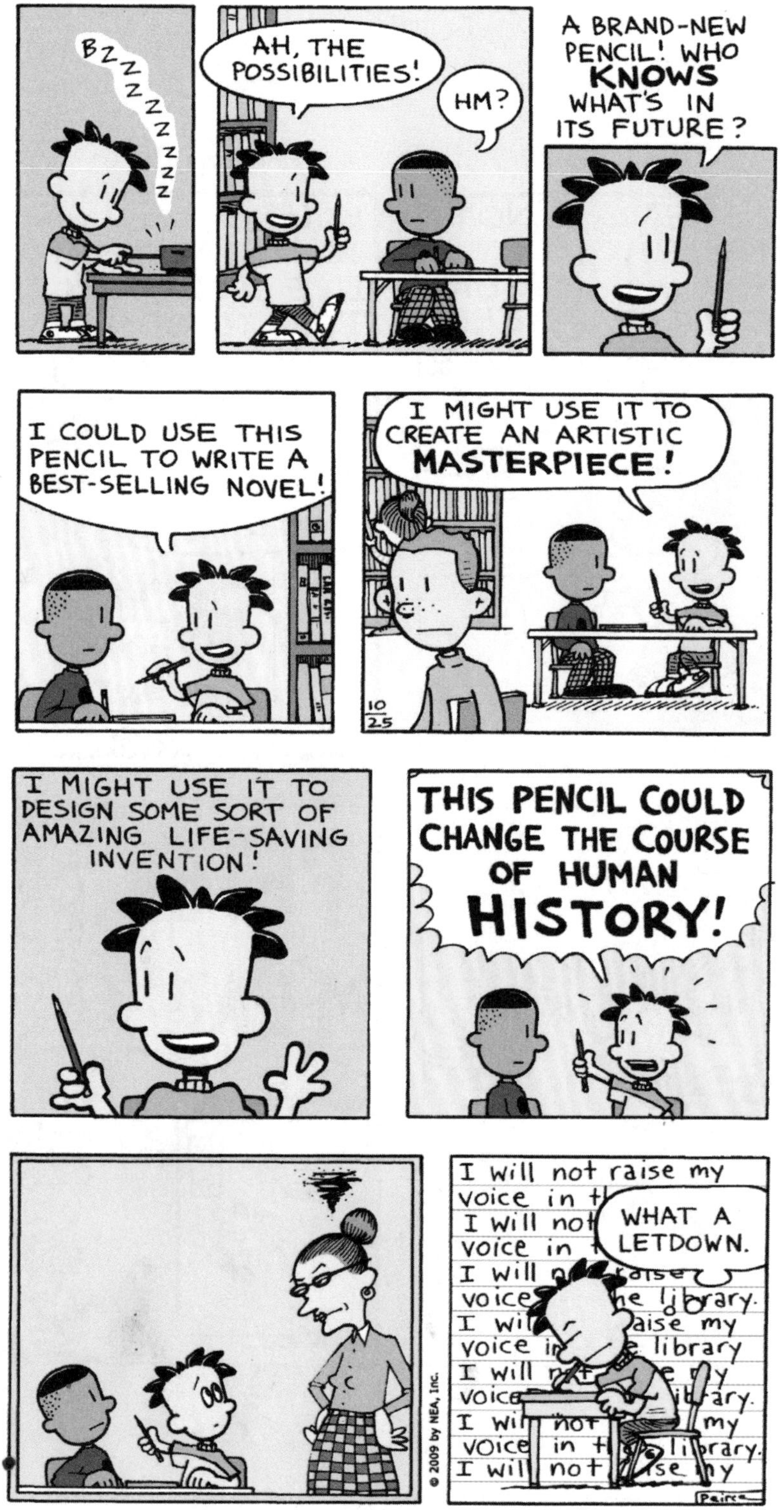
BZZZZZZZZZ
AH, THE POSSIBILITIES!
HM?
A BRAND-NEW PENCIL! WHO KNOWS WHAT'S IN ITS FUTURE?
I COULD USE THIS PENCIL TO WRITE A BEST-SELLING NOVEL!
I MIGHT USE IT TO CREATE AN ARTISTIC MASTERPIECE!
10
25
I MIGHT USE IT TO DESIGN SOME SORT OF AMAZING LIFE-SAVING INVENTION!
THIS PENCIL COULD CHANGE THE COURSE OF HUMAN HISTORY!
© 2009 by NEA, Inc.
WHAT A LETDOWN.
Peirce

TRICKED OUT

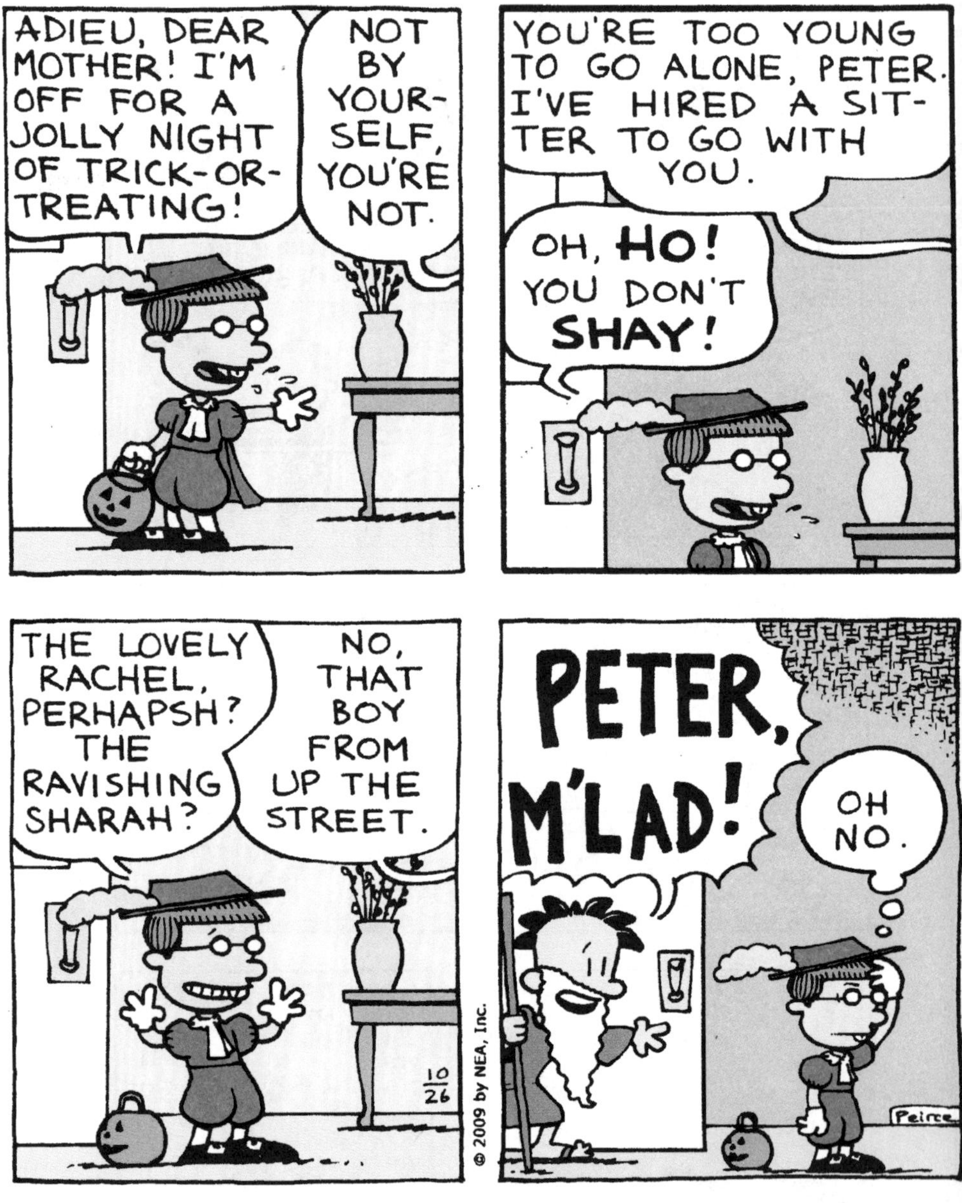
ADIEU, DEAR MOTHER! I'M OFF FOR A JOLLY NIGHT OF TRICK-OR-TREATING!
NOT BY YOURSELF, YOU'RE NOT.
YOU'RE TOO YOUNG TO GO ALONE, PETER. I'VE HIRED A SITTER TO GO WITH YOU.
OH, HO! YOU DON'T SHAY!
THE LOVELY RACHEL, PERHAPSH? THE RAVISHING SHARAH?
NO, THAT BOY FROM UP THE STREET.
10/26
© 2009 by NEA, Inc.
PETER, M'LAD!
OH NO.
Peirce

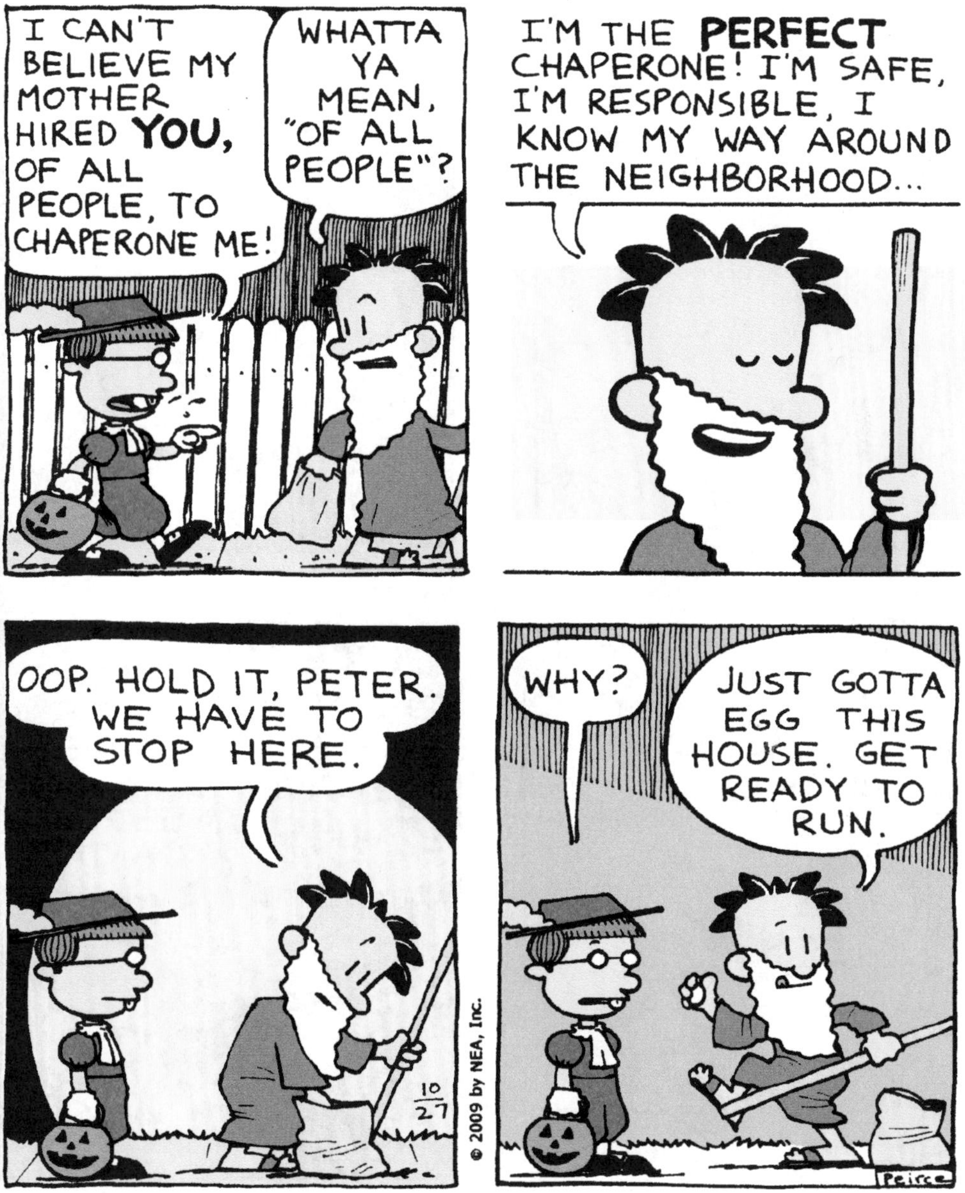
I CAN'T BELIEVE MY MOTHER HIRED YOU, OF ALL PEOPLE, TO CHAPERONE ME!
WHATTA YA MEAN, "OF ALL PEOPLE"?
I'M THE PERFECT CHAPERONE! I'M SAFE, I'M RESPONSIBLE, I KNOW MY WAY AROUND THE NEIGHBORHOOD...
OOP. HOLD IT, PETER. WE HAVE TO STOP HERE.
10/27
© 2009 by NEA, Inc.
WHY?
JUST GOTTA EGG THIS HOUSE. GET READY TO RUN.
Peirce

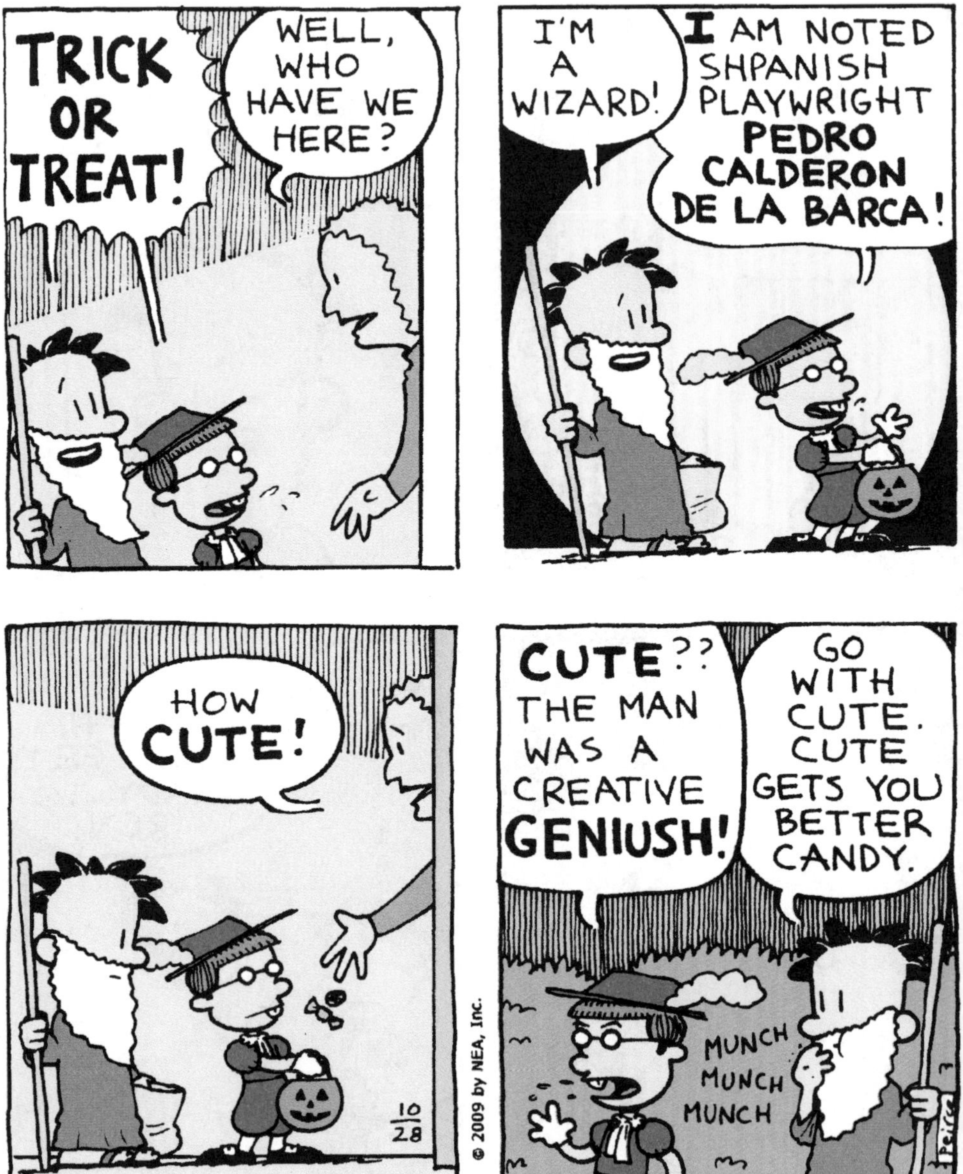
TRICK OR TREAT!
WELL, WHO HAVE WE HERE?
I'M A WIZARD!
I AM NOTED SHPANISH PLAYWRIGHT PEDRO CALDERON DE LA BARCA!
HOW CUTE!
10/28
CUTE?? THE MAN WAS A CREATIVE GENIUSH!
GO WITH CUTE. CUTE GETS YOU BETTER CANDY.
MUNCH MUNCH MUNCH
PEIRCE

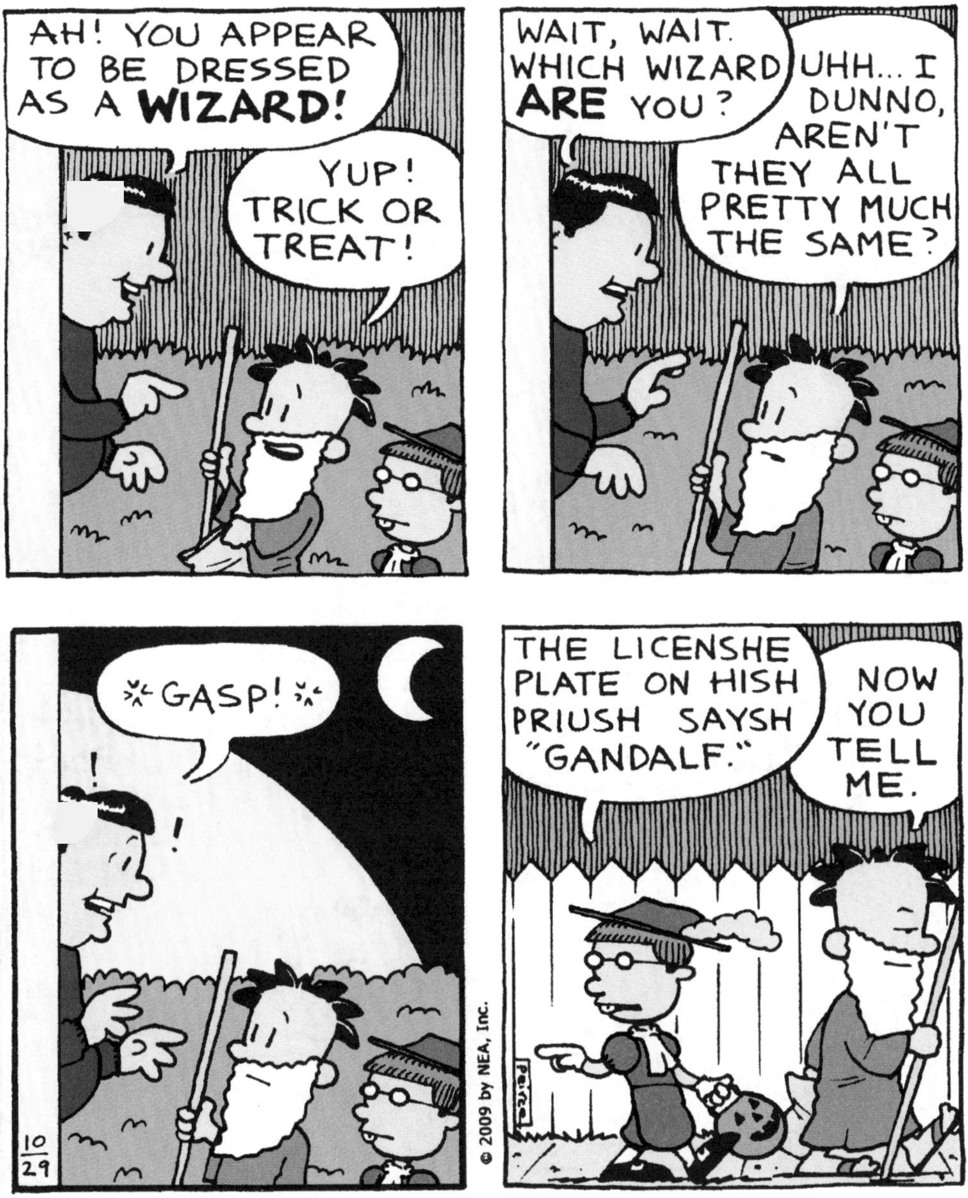
AH! YOU APPEAR TO BE DRESSED AS A **WIZARD**!
YUP! TRICK OR TREAT!
WAIT, WAIT. WHICH WIZARD **ARE** YOU?
UHH... I DUNNO, AREN'T THEY ALL PRETTY MUCH THE SAME?
GASP!
!
!
10/29
THE LICENSHE PLATE ON HISH PRIUSH SAYSH "GANDALF."
NOW YOU TELL ME.
Peirce
© 2009 by NEA, Inc.

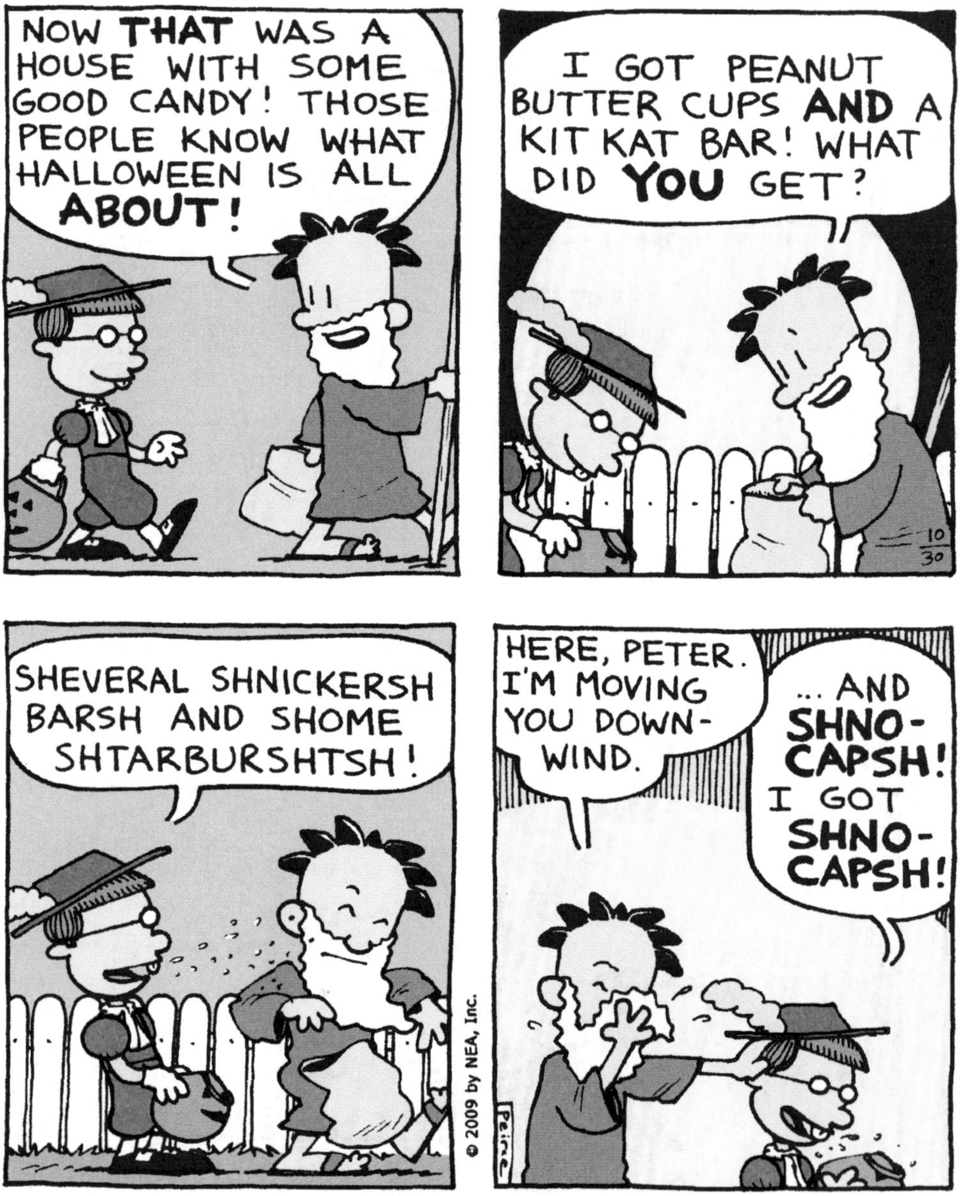
NOW THAT WAS A HOUSE WITH SOME GOOD CANDY! THOSE PEOPLE KNOW WHAT HALLOWEEN IS ALL ABOUT!
I GOT PEANUT BUTTER CUPS AND A KIT KAT BAR! WHAT DID YOU GET?
10/30
SHEVERAL SHNICKERSH BARSH AND SHOME SHTARBURSHTSH!
HERE, PETER. I'M MOVING YOU DOWN-WIND.
... AND SHNO-CAPSH! I GOT SHNO-CAPSH!
© 2009 by NEA, Inc.
Peirce

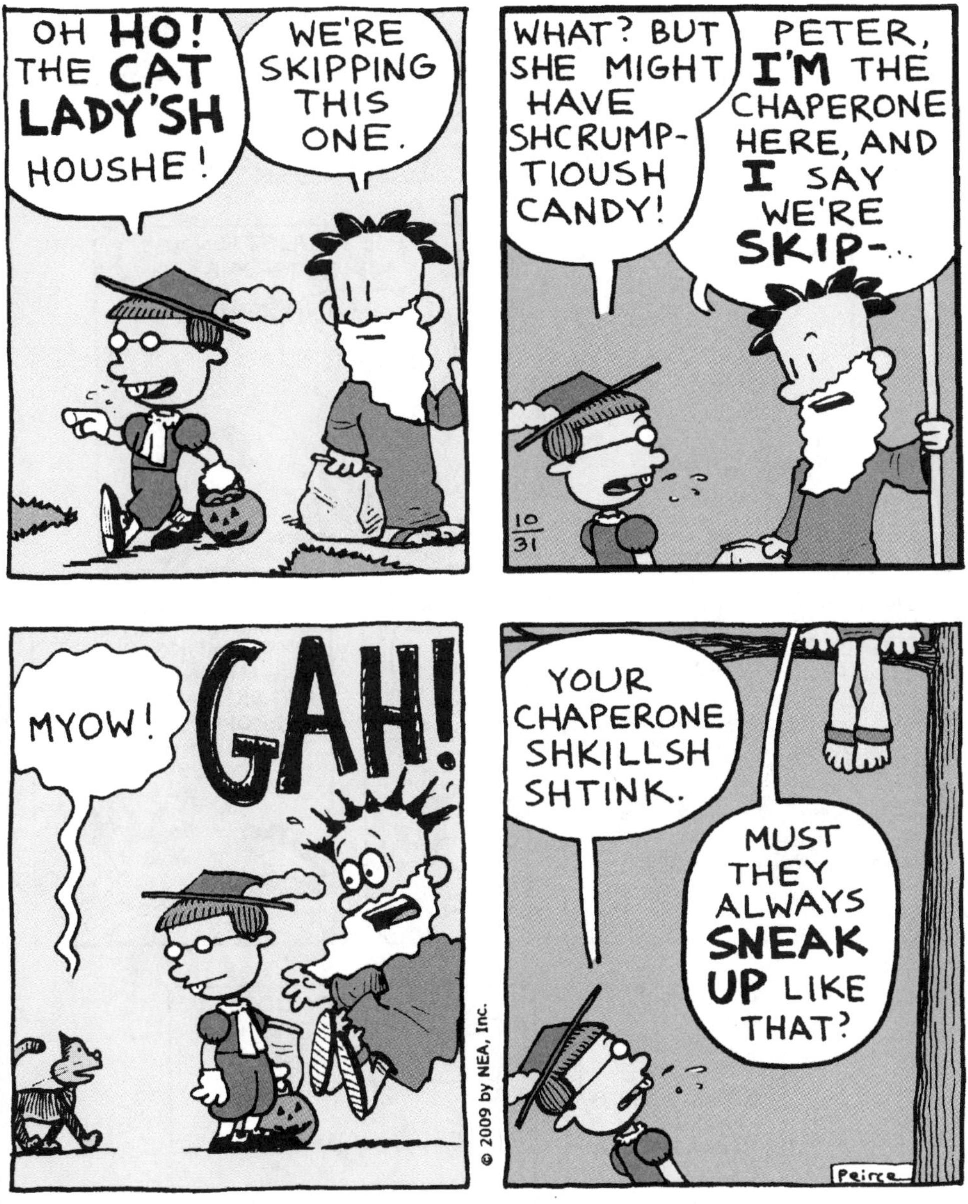
OH HO! THE CAT LADY'SH HOUSHE!
WE'RE SKIPPING THIS ONE.
WHAT? BUT SHE MIGHT HAVE SHCRUMP-TIOUSH CANDY!
PETER, I'M THE CHAPERONE HERE, AND I SAY WE'RE SKIP-...
10/31
MYOW!
GAH!
© 2009 by NEA, Inc.
YOUR CHAPERONE SHKILLSH SHTINK.
MUST THEY ALWAYS SNEAK UP LIKE THAT?
Peirce

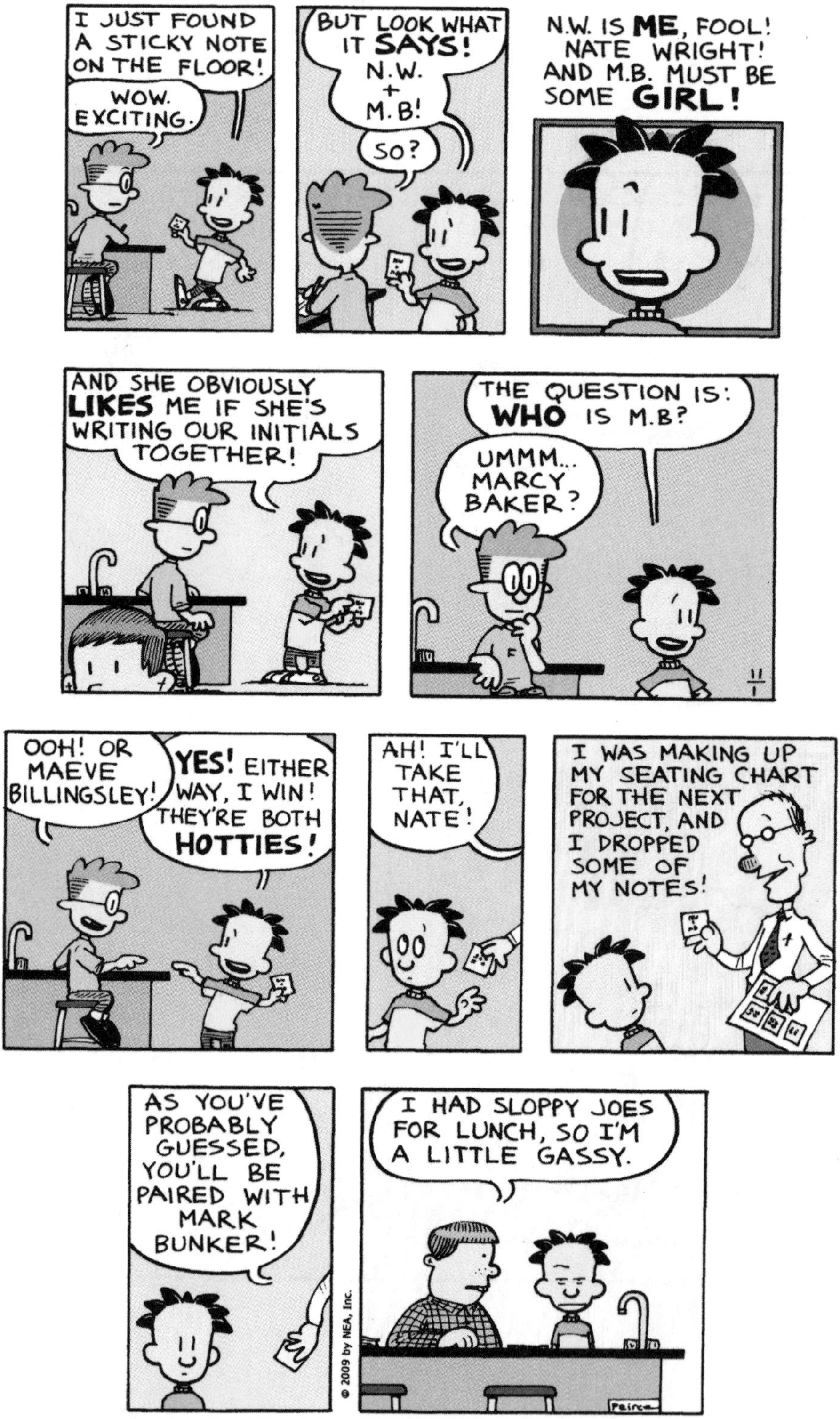
I JUST FOUND A STICKY NOTE ON THE FLOOR!
WOW. EXCITING.
BUT LOOK WHAT IT SAYS! N.W. + M.B!
SO?
N.W. IS ME, FOOL! NATE WRIGHT! AND M.B. MUST BE SOME GIRL!
AND SHE OBVIOUSLY LIKES ME IF SHE'S WRITING OUR INITIALS TOGETHER!
THE QUESTION IS: WHO IS M.B?
UMMM... MARCY BAKER?
OOH! OR MAEVE BILLINGSLEY!
YES! EITHER WAY, I WIN! THEY'RE BOTH HOTTIES!
AH! I'LL TAKE THAT, NATE!
I WAS MAKING UP MY SEATING CHART FOR THE NEXT PROJECT, AND I DROPPED SOME OF MY NOTES!
AS YOU'VE PROBABLY GUESSED, YOU'LL BE PAIRED WITH MARK BUNKER!
I HAD SLOPPY JOES FOR LUNCH, SO I'M A LITTLE GASSY.
© 2009 by NEA, Inc.
Peirce

MR. FANCY-PANTS

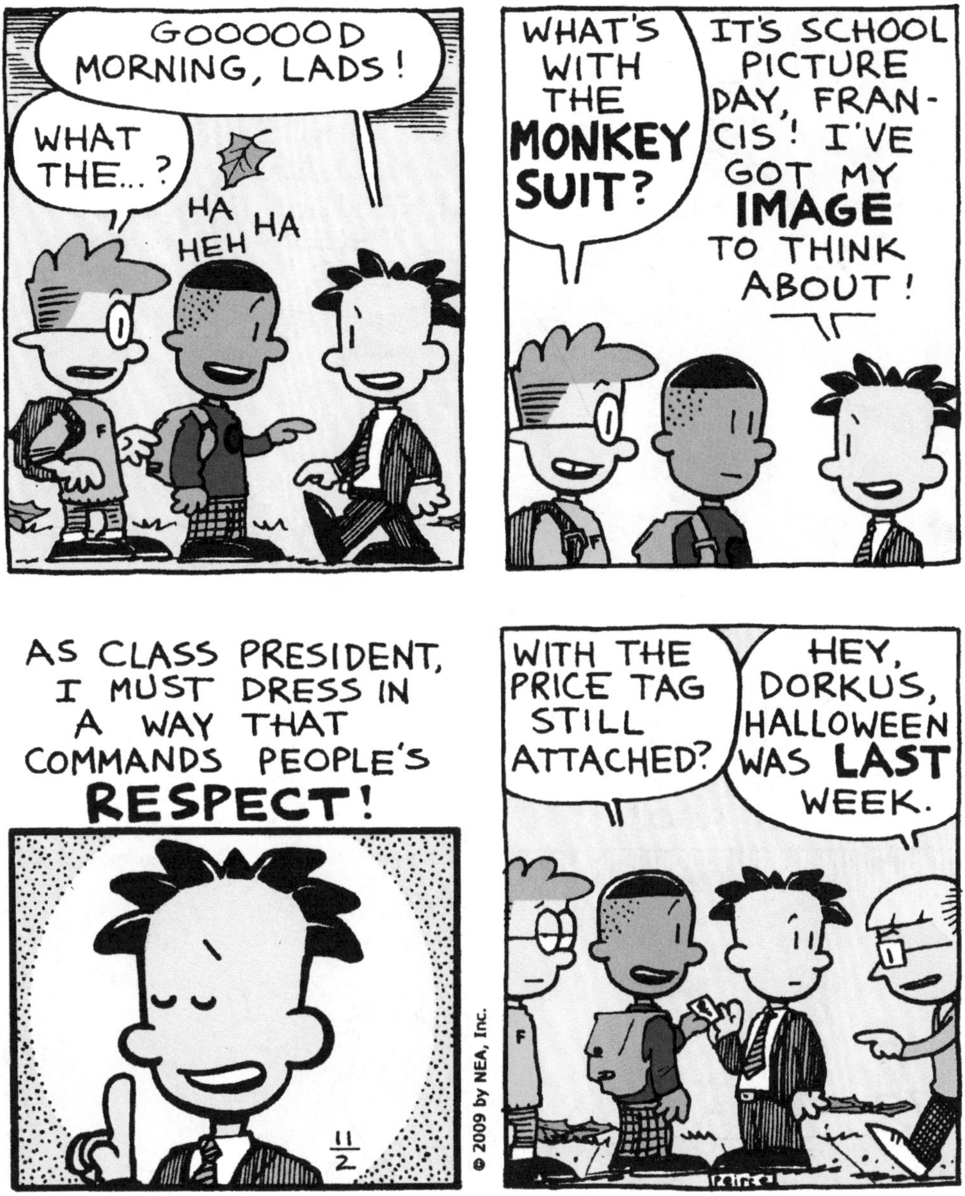
GOOOOOD MORNING, LADS!
WHAT THE...?
HA HEH HA
WHAT'S WITH THE MONKEY SUIT?
IT'S SCHOOL PICTURE DAY, FRANCIS! I'VE GOT MY IMAGE TO THINK ABOUT!
AS CLASS PRESIDENT, I MUST DRESS IN A WAY THAT COMMANDS PEOPLE'S RESPECT!
11 2
© 2009 by NEA, Inc.
WITH THE PRICE TAG STILL ATTACHED?
HEY, DORKUS, HALLOWEEN WAS LAST WEEK.

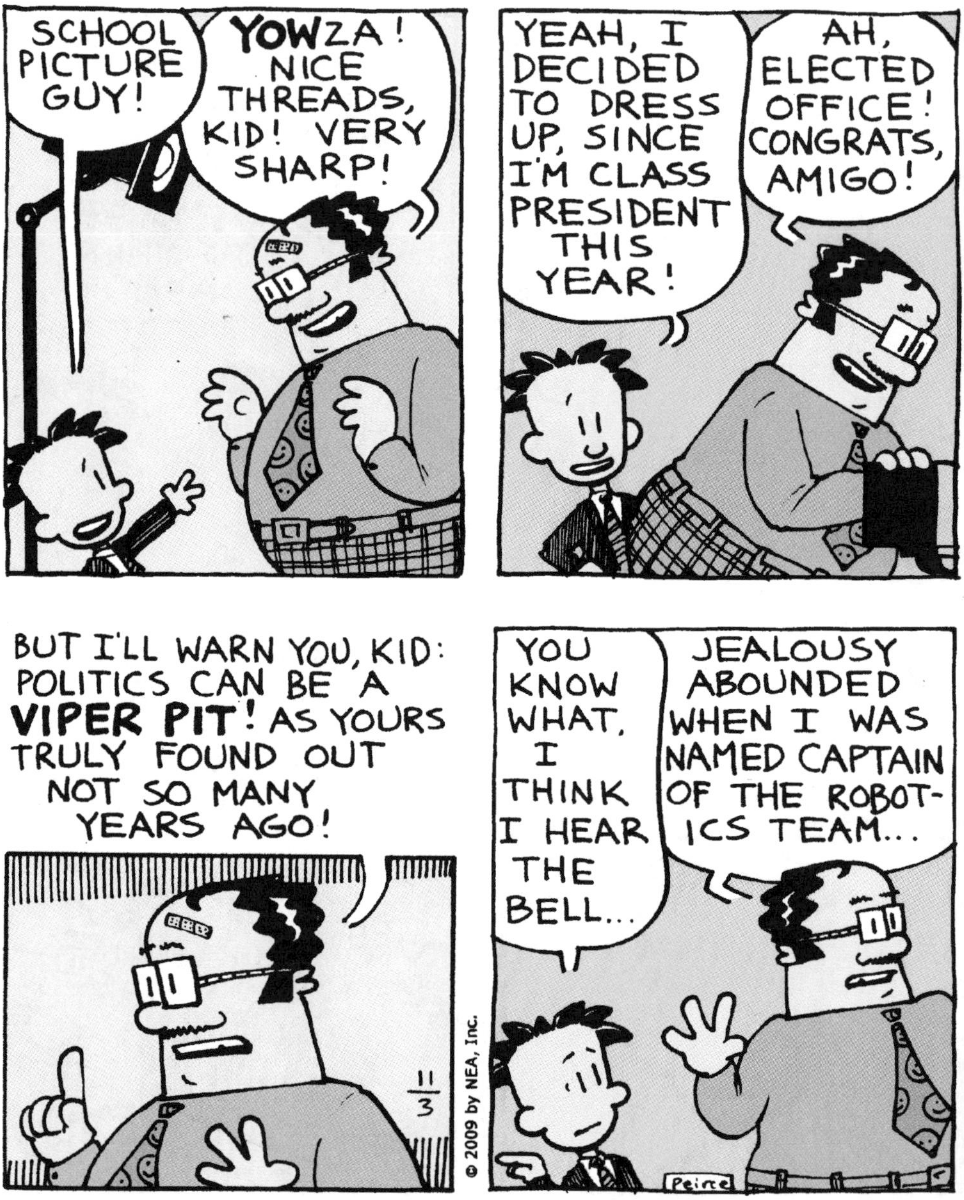
SCHOOL PICTURE GUY!
YOWZA! NICE THREADS, KID! VERY SHARP!
YEAH, I DECIDED TO DRESS UP, SINCE I'M CLASS PRESIDENT THIS YEAR!
AH, ELECTED OFFICE! CONGRATS, AMIGO!
BUT I'LL WARN YOU, KID: POLITICS CAN BE A VIPER PIT! AS YOURS TRULY FOUND OUT NOT SO MANY YEARS AGO!
11/3
© 2009 by NEA, Inc.
JEALOUSY ABOUNDED WHEN I WAS NAMED CAPTAIN OF THE ROBOTICS TEAM...
YOU KNOW WHAT, I THINK I HEAR THE BELL...
Peirce

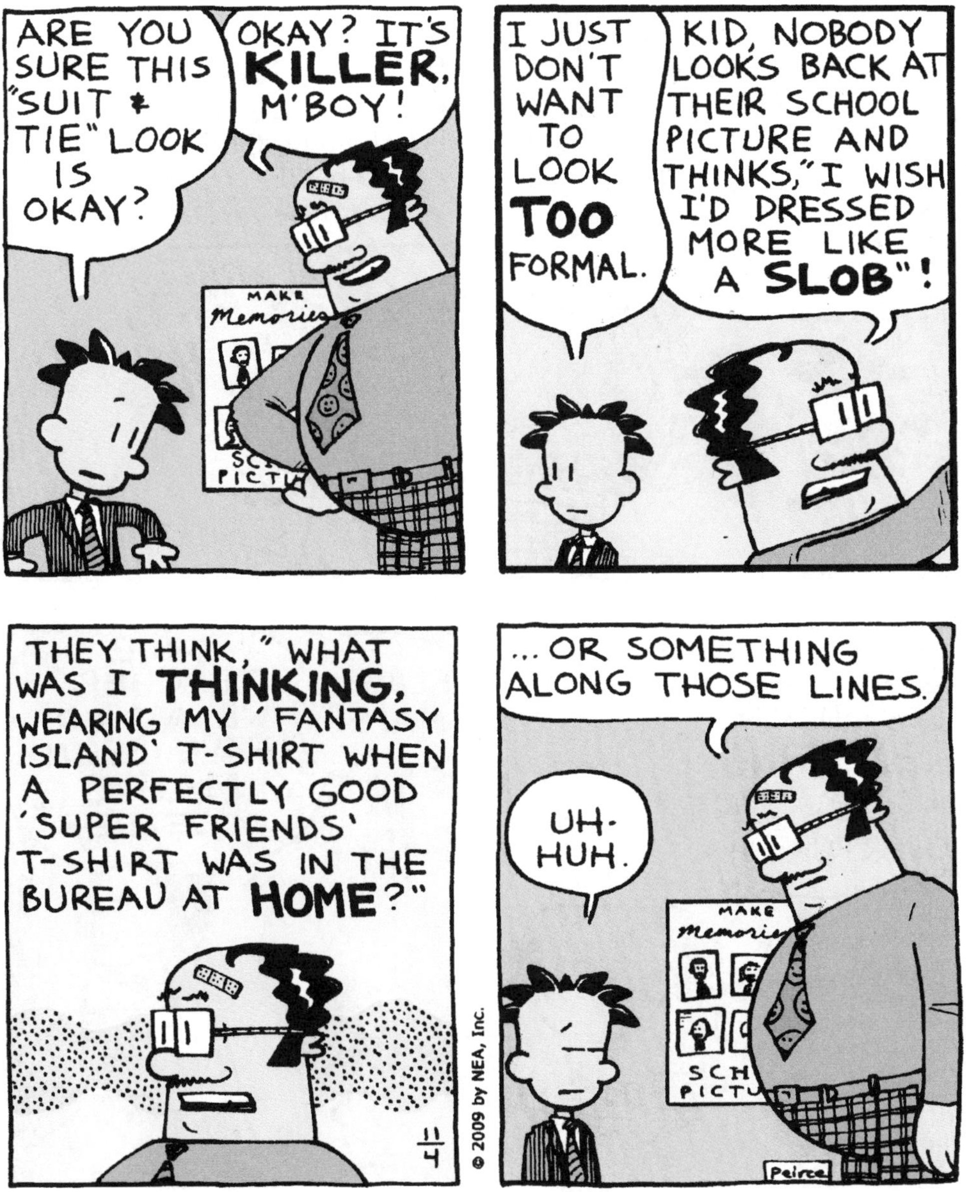
ARE YOU SURE THIS "SUIT & TIE" LOOK IS OKAY?
OKAY? IT'S **KILLER**, M'BOY!
I JUST DON'T WANT TO LOOK **TOO** FORMAL.
KID, NOBODY LOOKS BACK AT THEIR SCHOOL PICTURE AND THINKS, "I WISH I'D DRESSED MORE LIKE A **SLOB**"!
THEY THINK, "WHAT WAS I **THINKING**, WEARING MY 'FANTASY ISLAND' T-SHIRT WHEN A PERFECTLY GOOD 'SUPER FRIENDS' T-SHIRT WAS IN THE BUREAU AT **HOME**?"
...OR SOMETHING ALONG THOSE LINES.
UH-HUH.
MAKE Memories
11/4
© 2009 by NEA, Inc.
Peirce

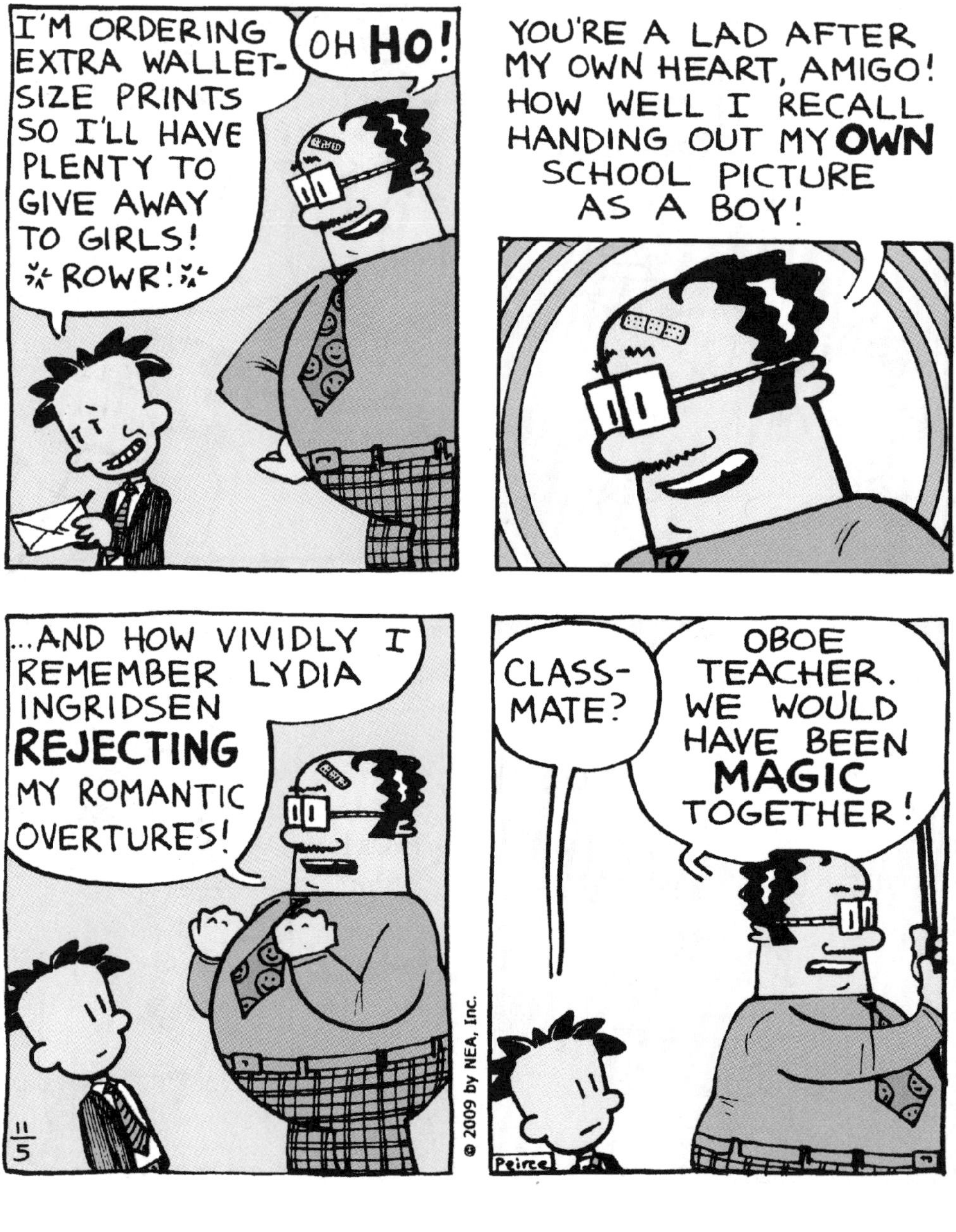
I'M ORDERING EXTRA WALLET-SIZE PRINTS SO I'LL HAVE PLENTY TO GIVE AWAY TO GIRLS! ROWR!
OH HO!
YOU'RE A LAD AFTER MY OWN HEART, AMIGO! HOW WELL I RECALL HANDING OUT MY OWN SCHOOL PICTURE AS A BOY!
...AND HOW VIVIDLY I REMEMBER LYDIA INGRIDSEN REJECTING MY ROMANTIC OVERTURES!
CLASS-MATE?
OBOE TEACHER. WE WOULD HAVE BEEN MAGIC TOGETHER!
11/5
© 2009 by NEA, Inc.
Peirce

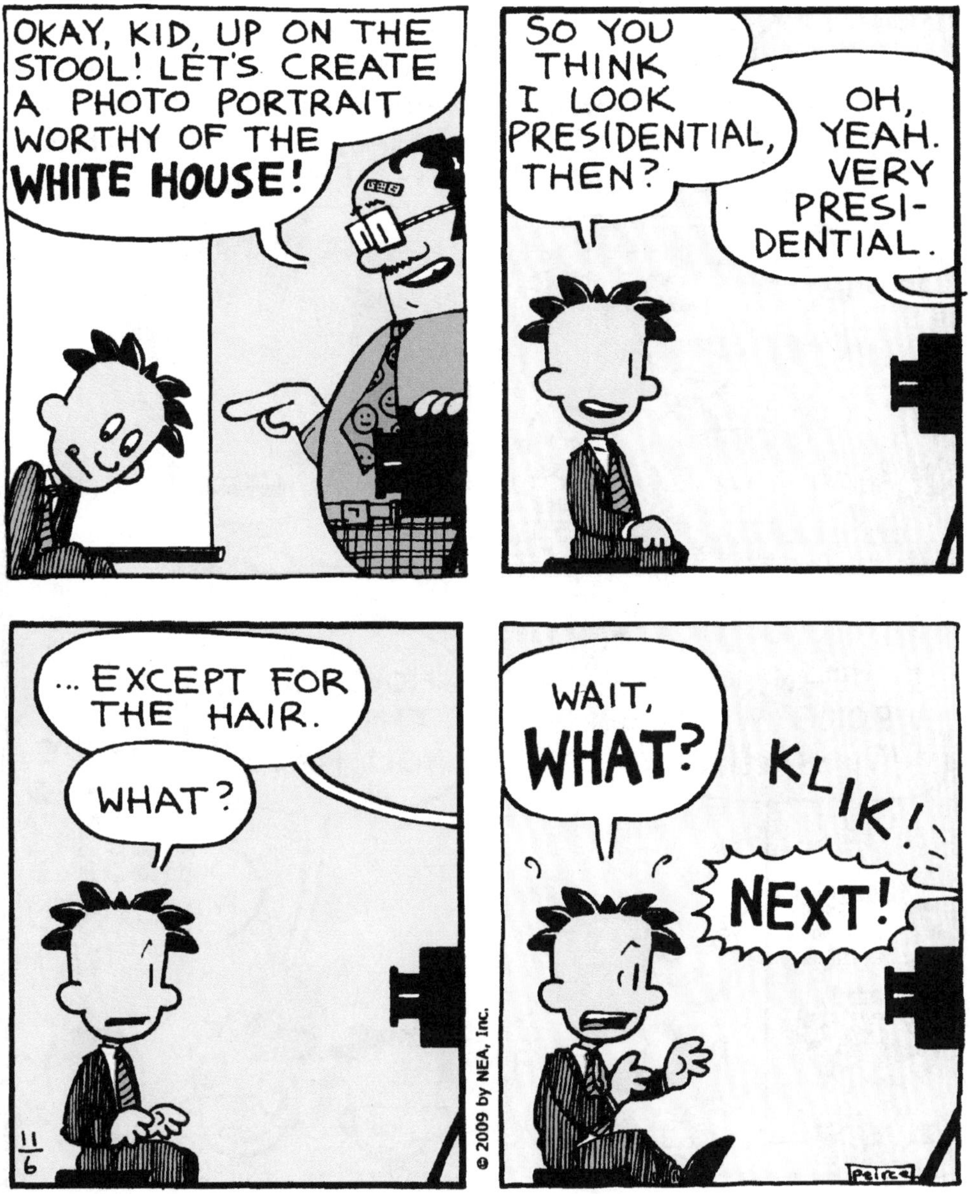
OKAY, KID, UP ON THE STOOL! LET'S CREATE A PHOTO PORTRAIT WORTHY OF THE WHITE HOUSE!
SO YOU THINK I LOOK PRESIDENTIAL, THEN?
OH, YEAH. VERY PRESI-DENTIAL.
... EXCEPT FOR THE HAIR.
WHAT?
11/6
© 2009 by NEA, Inc.
WAIT, WHAT?
KLIK!
NEXT!
PEIRCE

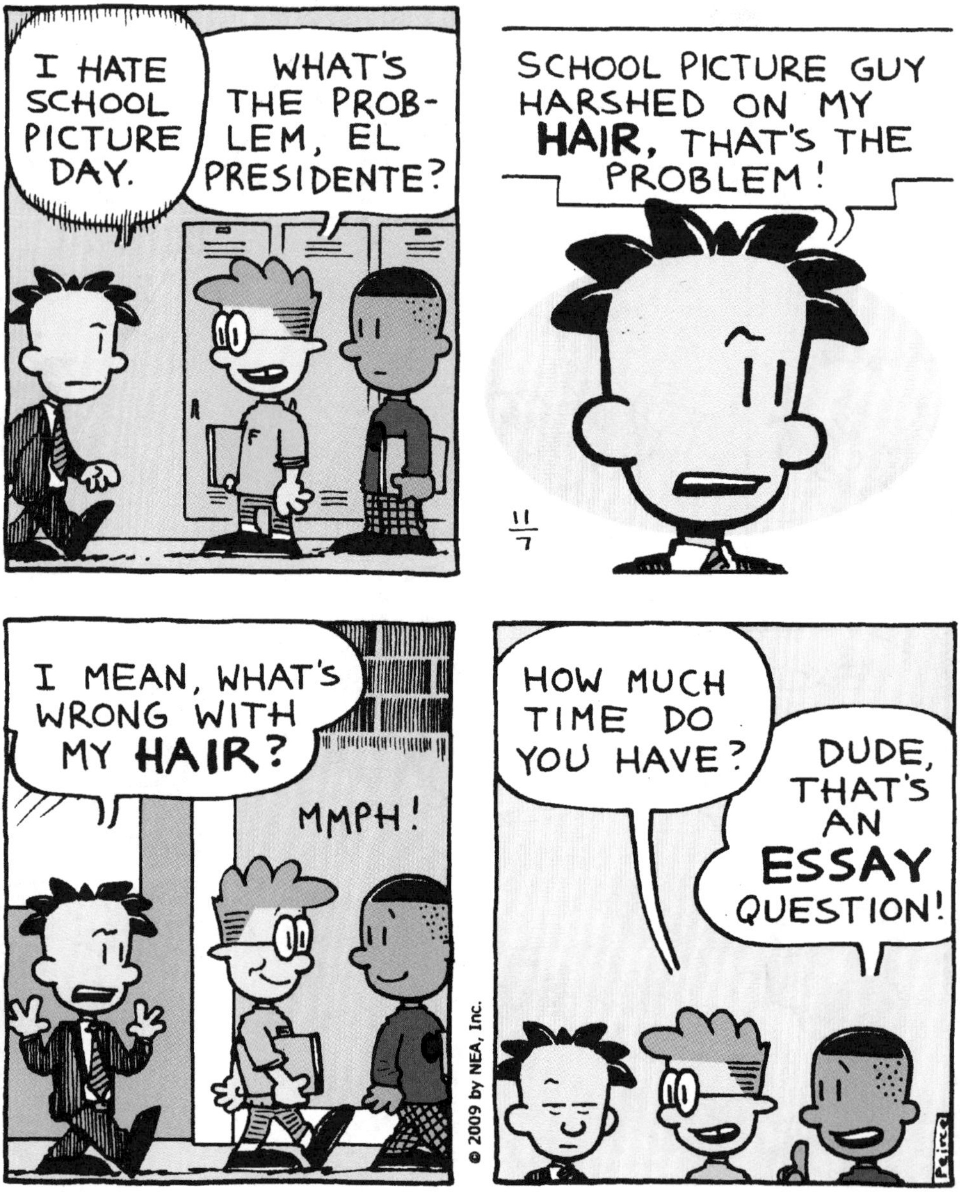
I HATE SCHOOL PICTURE DAY.
WHAT'S THE PROBLEM, EL PRESIDENTE?
SCHOOL PICTURE GUY HARSHED ON MY **HAIR**, THAT'S THE PROBLEM!
11/7
I MEAN, WHAT'S WRONG WITH MY **HAIR**?
MMPH!
© 2009 by NEA, Inc.
HOW MUCH TIME DO YOU HAVE?
DUDE, THAT'S AN **ESSAY** QUESTION!
Peirce

NO-MAN'S-LAND

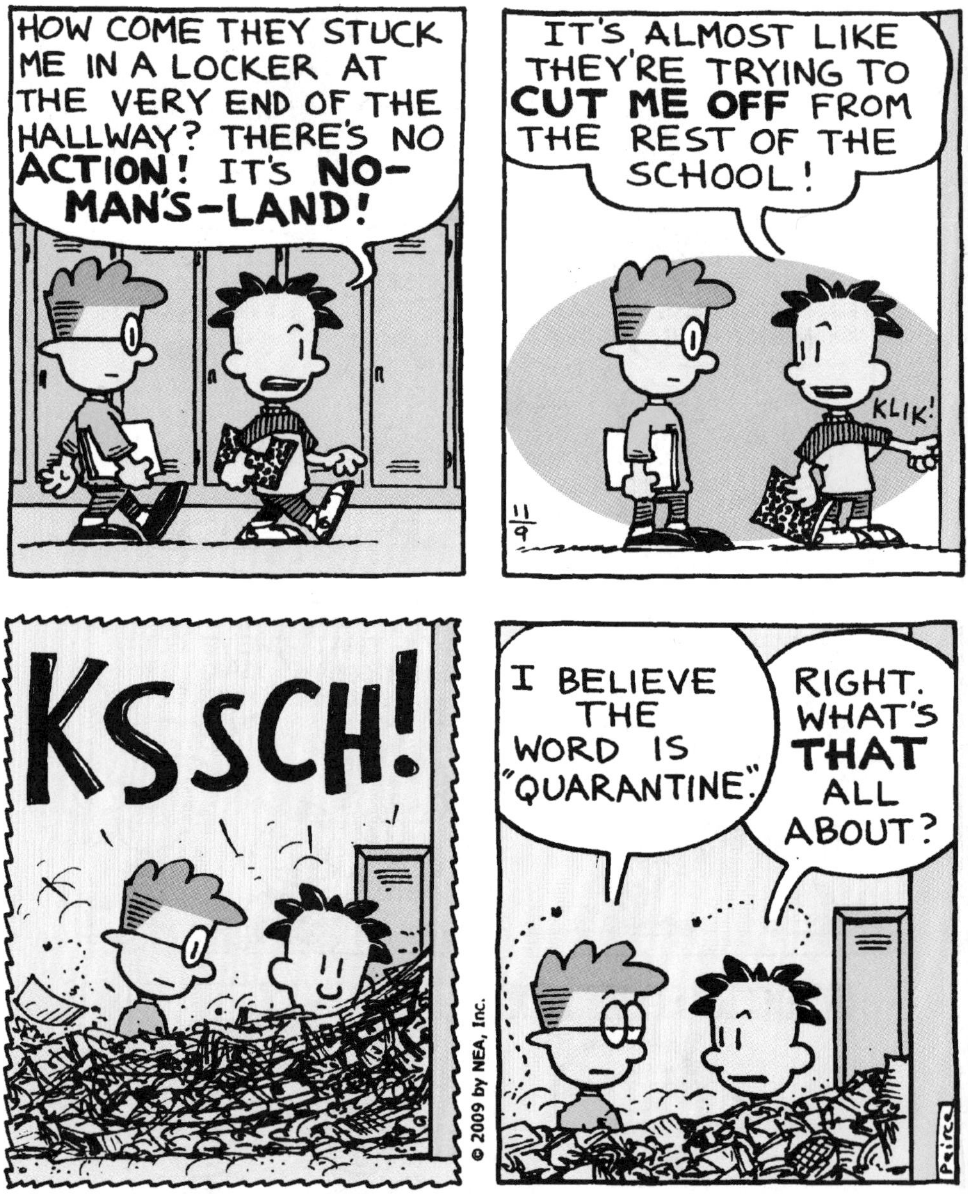
HOW COME THEY STUCK ME IN A LOCKER AT THE VERY END OF THE HALLWAY? THERE'S NO **ACTION**! IT'S **NO-MAN'S-LAND!**
IT'S ALMOST LIKE THEY'RE TRYING TO **CUT ME OFF** FROM THE REST OF THE SCHOOL!
KLIK!
11/9
KSSCH!
I BELIEVE THE WORD IS "QUARANTINE."
RIGHT. WHAT'S **THAT** ALL ABOUT?
© 2009 by NEA, Inc.
Peirce

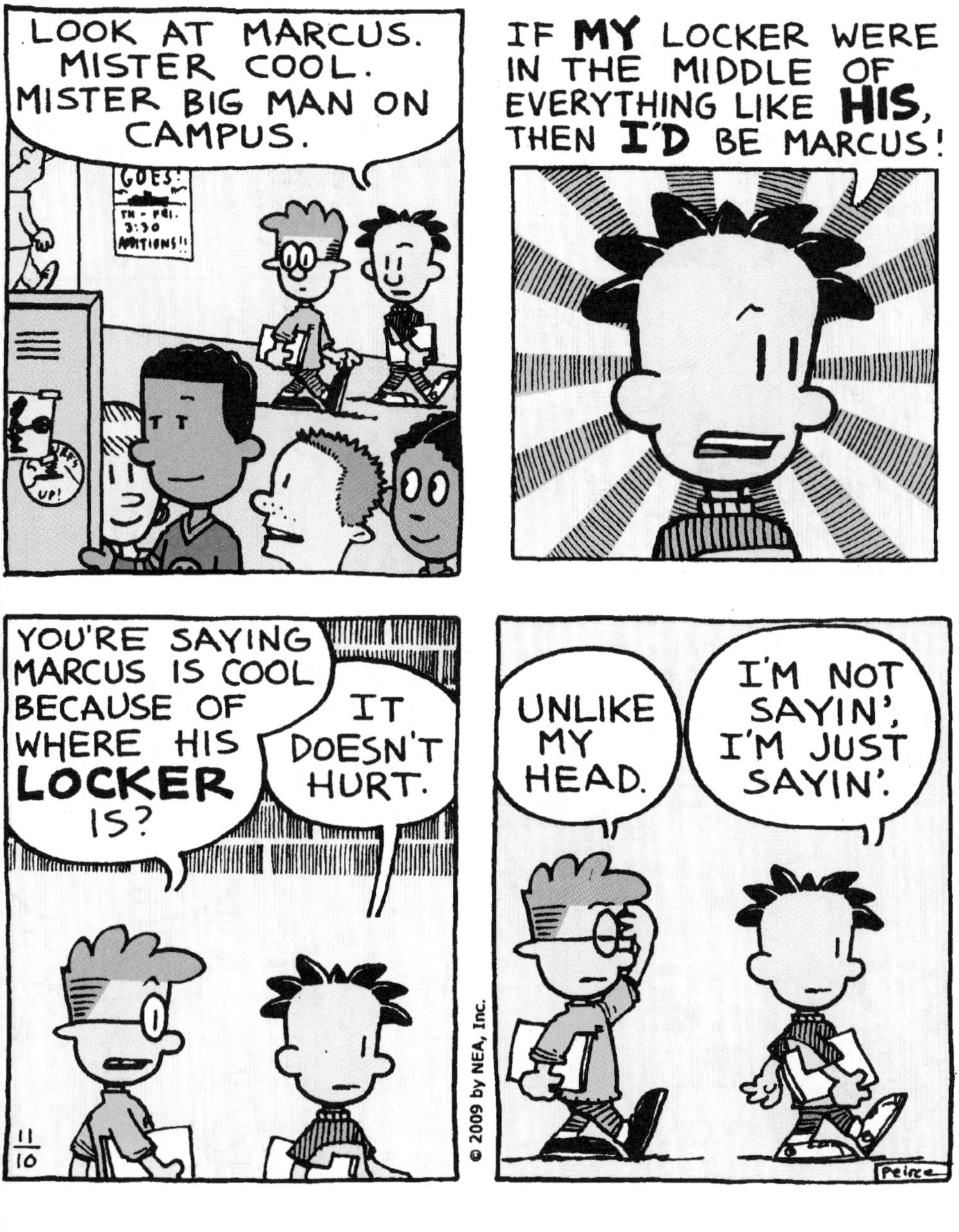
LOOK AT MARCUS. MISTER COOL. MISTER BIG MAN ON CAMPUS.
GOES!
TH - FRI. 3:30
AUDITIONS!!
UP!
IF MY LOCKER WERE IN THE MIDDLE OF EVERYTHING LIKE HIS, THEN I'D BE MARCUS!
YOU'RE SAYING MARCUS IS COOL BECAUSE OF WHERE HIS LOCKER IS?
IT DOESN'T HURT.
11/10
© 2009 by NEA, Inc.
UNLIKE MY HEAD.
I'M NOT SAYIN', I'M JUST SAYIN'.
Peirce

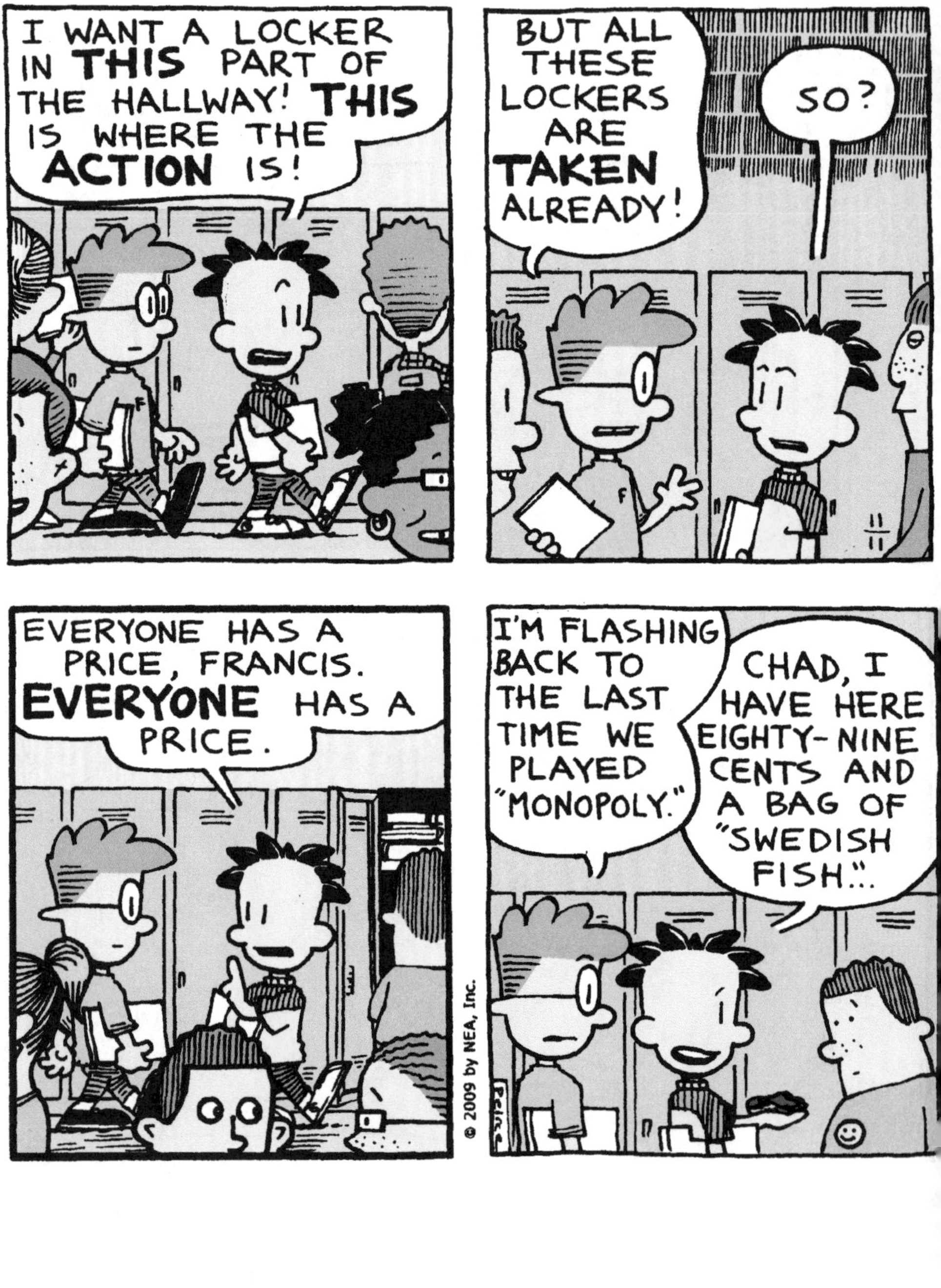
I WANT A LOCKER IN THIS PART OF THE HALLWAY! THIS IS WHERE THE ACTION IS!
BUT ALL THESE LOCKERS ARE TAKEN ALREADY!
SO?
EVERYONE HAS A PRICE, FRANCIS. EVERYONE HAS A PRICE.
I'M FLASHING BACK TO THE LAST TIME WE PLAYED "MONOPOLY."
CHAD, I HAVE HERE EIGHTY-NINE CENTS AND A BAG OF "SWEDISH FISH."
© 2009 by NEA, Inc.

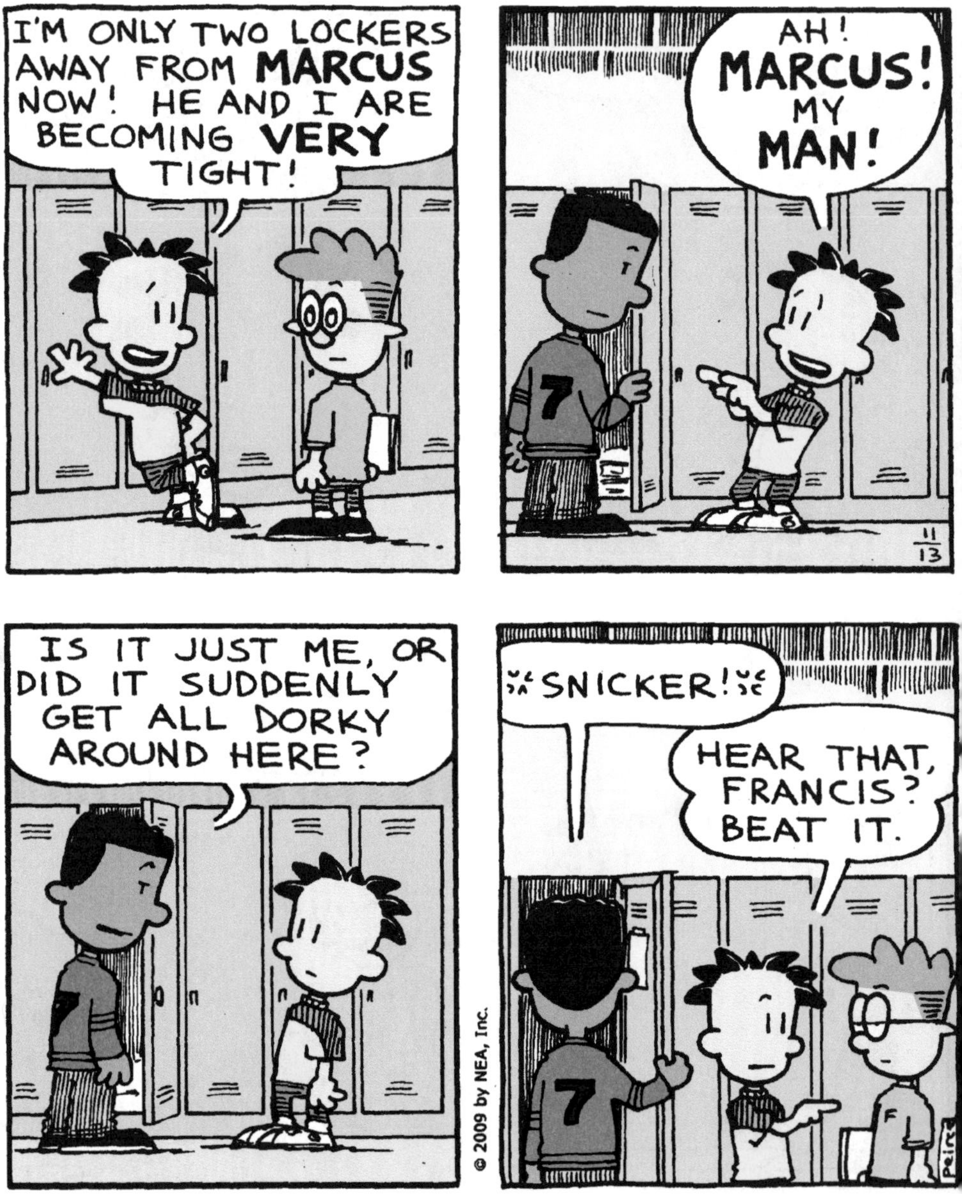
I'M ONLY TWO LOCKERS AWAY FROM **MARCUS** NOW! HE AND I ARE BECOMING **VERY** TIGHT!
AH! **MARCUS!** MY **MAN!**
11/13
IS IT JUST ME, OR DID IT SUDDENLY GET ALL DORKY AROUND HERE?
SNICKER!
HEAR THAT, FRANCIS? BEAT IT.
Peirce

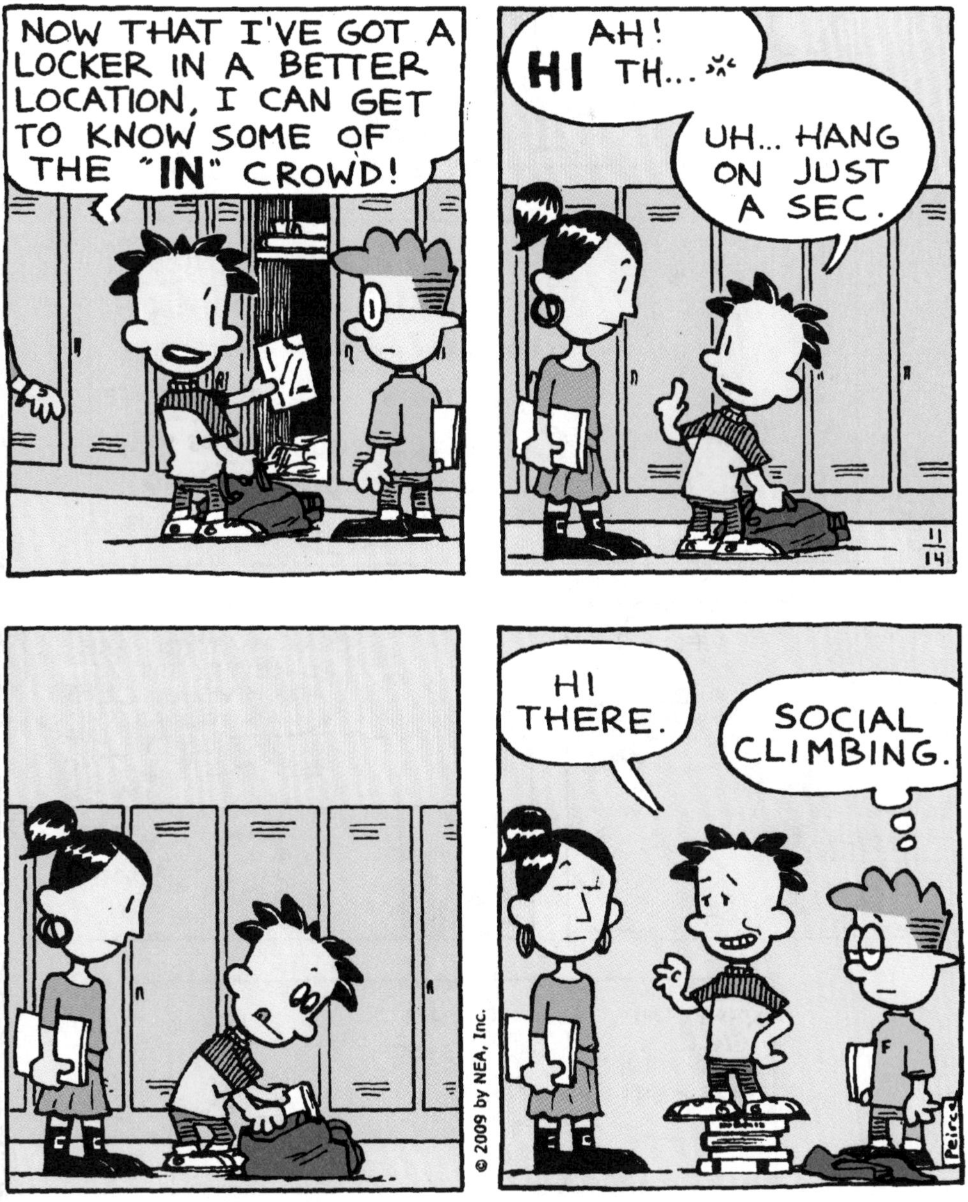
NOW THAT I'VE GOT A LOCKER IN A BETTER LOCATION, I CAN GET TO KNOW SOME OF THE "IN" CROWD!
AH! HI TH...
UH... HANG ON JUST A SEC.
11/14
HI THERE.
SOCIAL CLIMBING.
Peirce
© 2009 by NEA, Inc.

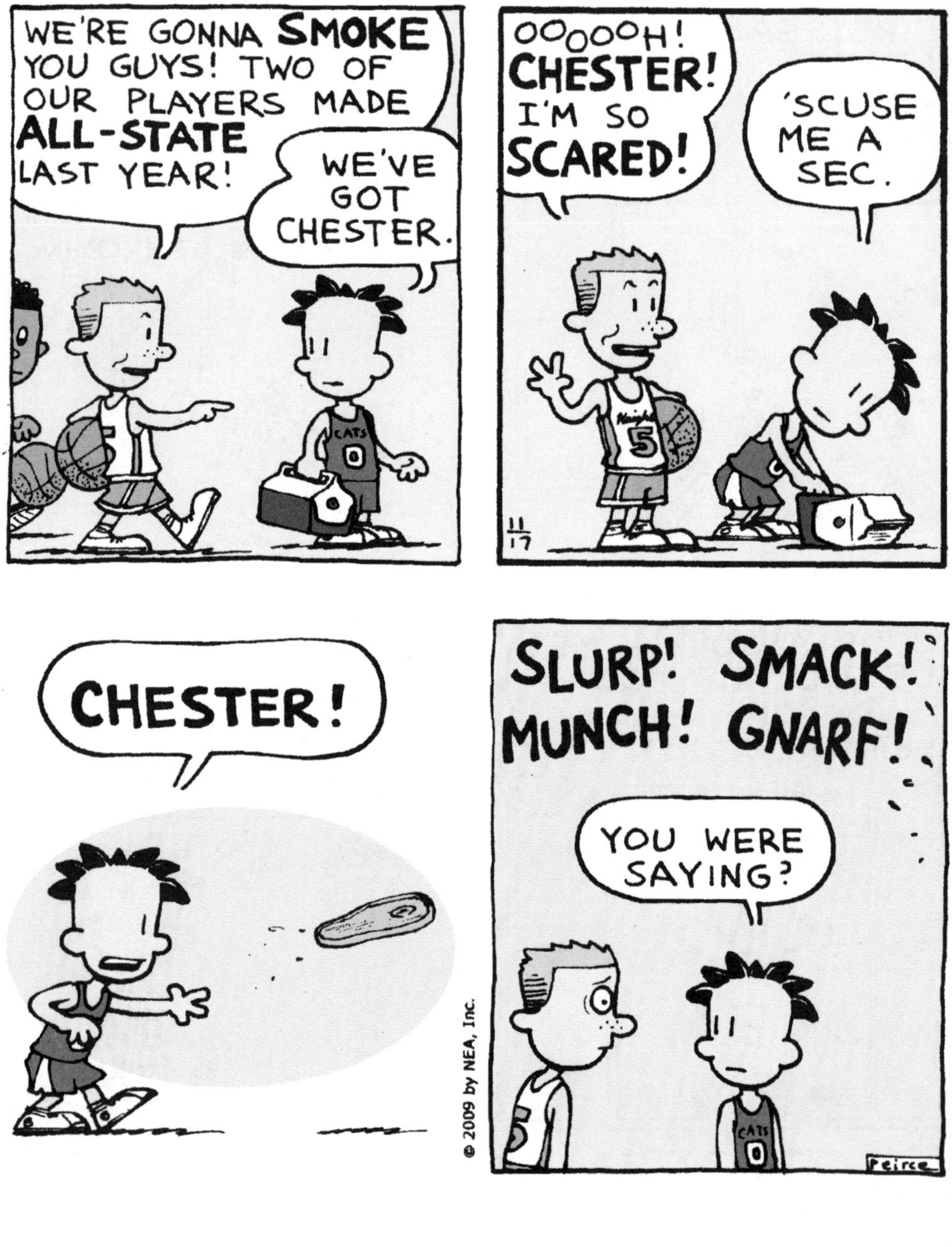
WE'RE GONNA SMOKE YOU GUYS! TWO OF OUR PLAYERS MADE ALL-STATE LAST YEAR!
WE'VE GOT CHESTER.
OOOOOOH! CHESTER! I'M SO SCARED!
'SCUSE ME A SEC.
11
17
CHESTER!
SLURP! SMACK! MUNCH! GNARF!
YOU WERE SAYING?
© 2009 by NEA, Inc.
Peirce

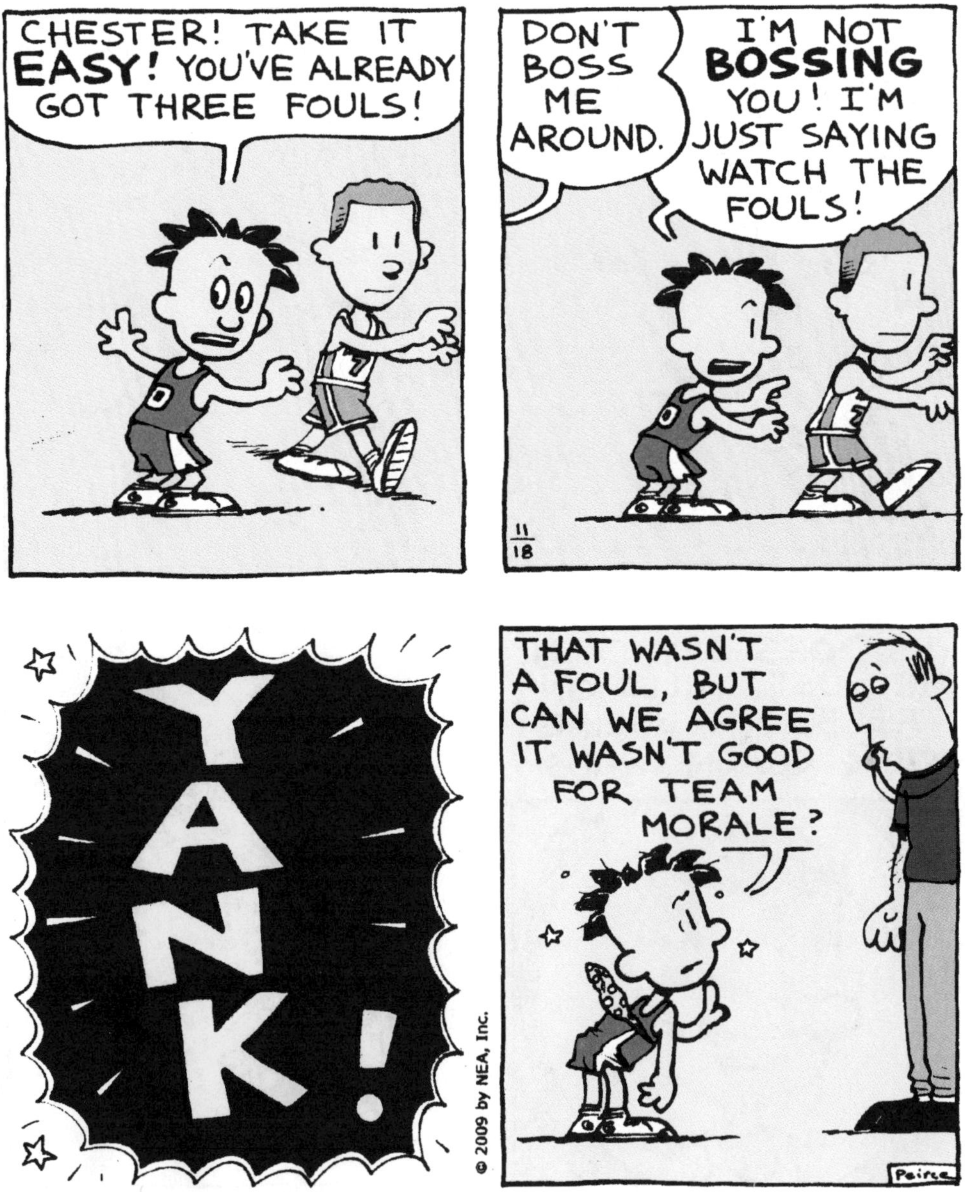
CHESTER! TAKE IT **EASY**! YOU'VE ALREADY GOT THREE FOULS!
DON'T BOSS ME AROUND.
I'M NOT **BOSSING** YOU! I'M JUST SAYING WATCH THE FOULS!
11/18
YANK!
THAT WASN'T A FOUL, BUT CAN WE AGREE IT WASN'T GOOD FOR TEAM MORALE?
Peirce

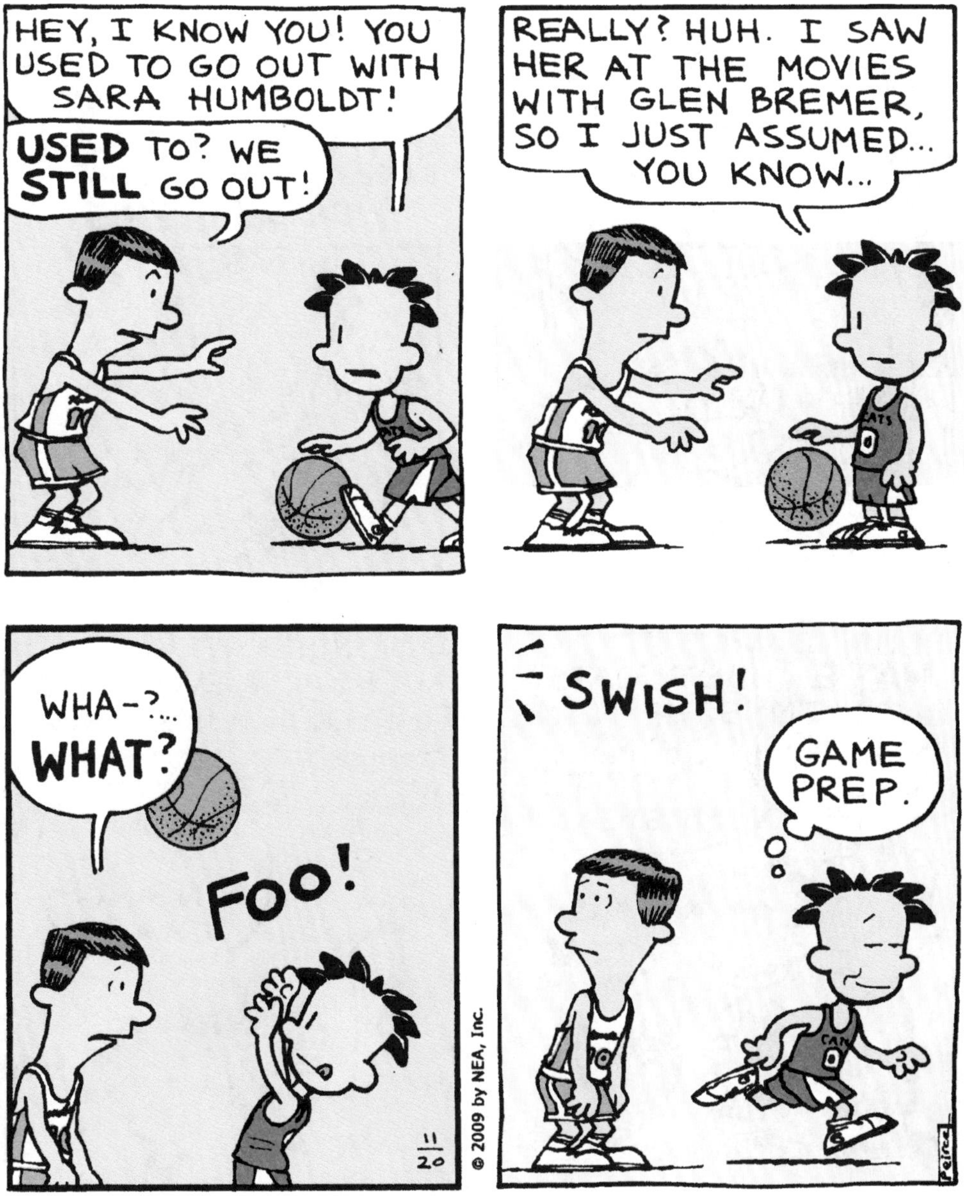
HEY, I KNOW YOU! YOU USED TO GO OUT WITH SARA HUMBOLDT!
USED TO? WE STILL GO OUT!
REALLY? HUH. I SAW HER AT THE MOVIES WITH GLEN BREMER, SO I JUST ASSUMED... YOU KNOW...
WHA-?... WHAT?
FOO!
11/20
© 2009 by NEA, Inc.
SWISH!
GAME PREP.
Peirce

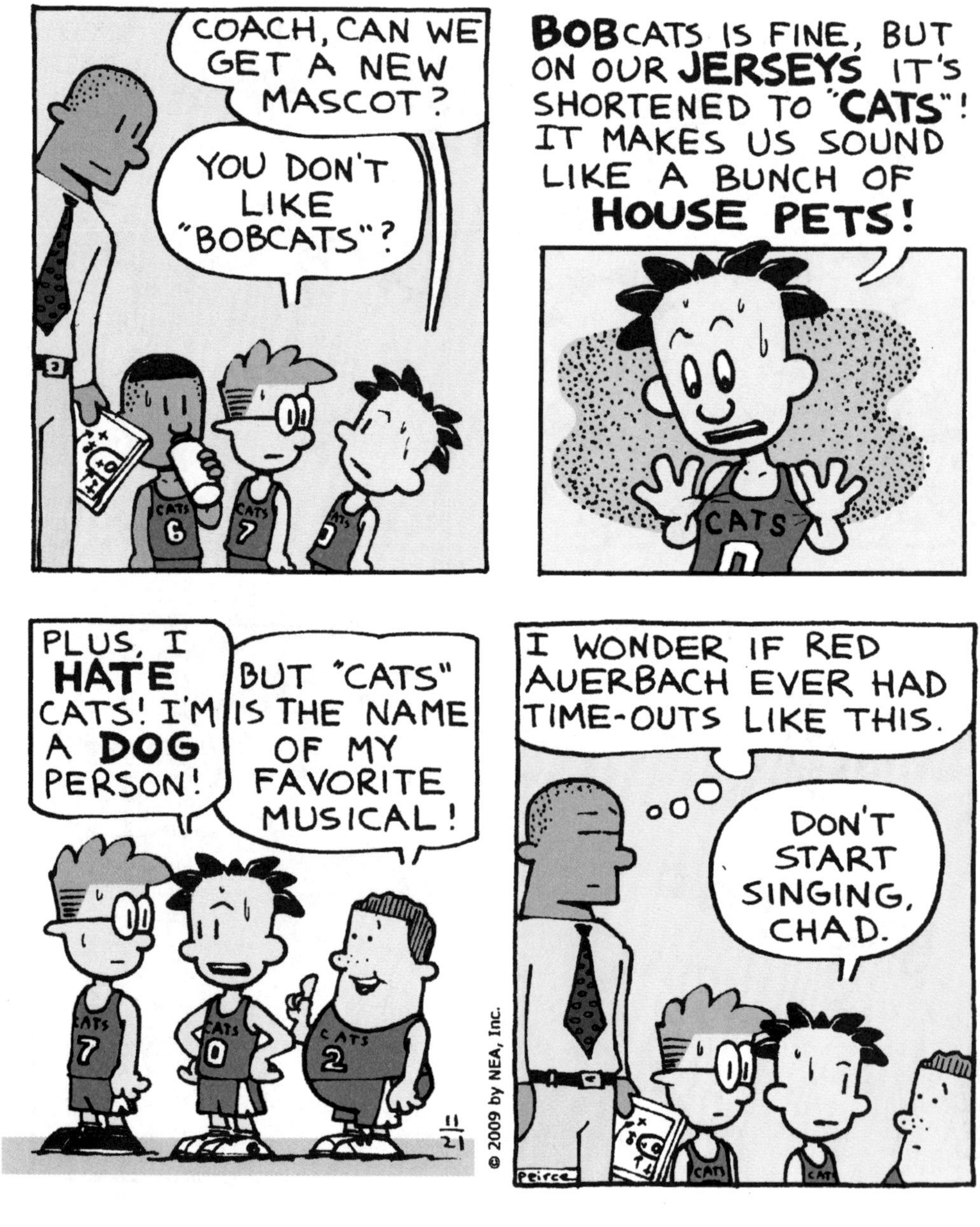
COACH, CAN WE GET A NEW MASCOT?
YOU DON'T LIKE "BOBCATS"?
CATS 6
CATS 7
BOBCATS IS FINE, BUT ON OUR JERSEYS IT'S SHORTENED TO "CATS"! IT MAKES US SOUND LIKE A BUNCH OF HOUSE PETS!
CATS
PLUS, I HATE CATS! I'M A DOG PERSON!
BUT "CATS" IS THE NAME OF MY FAVORITE MUSICAL!
CATS 7
CATS 0
CATS 2
11/21
© 2009 by NEA, Inc.
I WONDER IF RED AUERBACH EVER HAD TIME-OUTS LIKE THIS.
DON'T START SINGING, CHAD.
Peirce

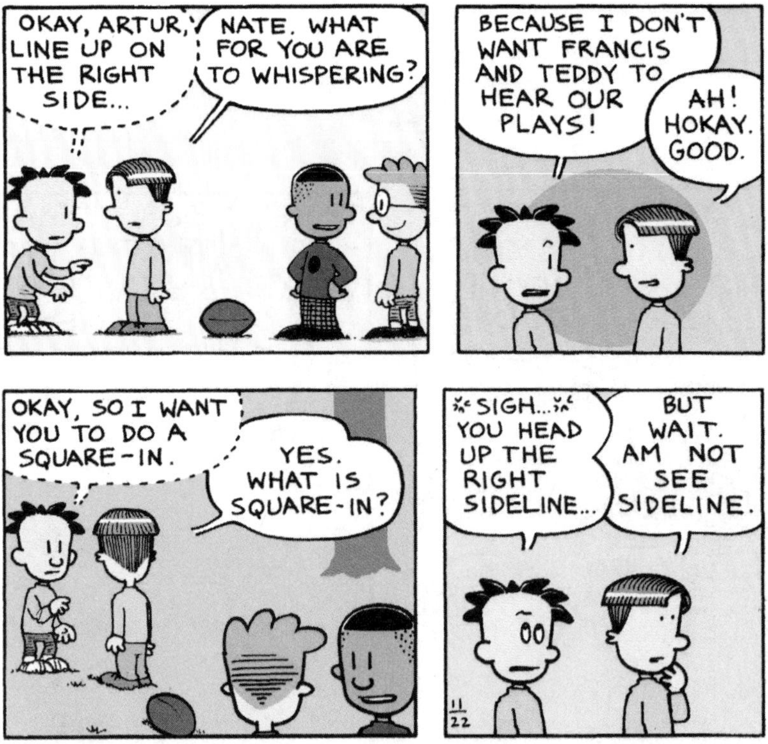
OKAY, ARTUR, LINE UP ON THE RIGHT SIDE...
NATE. WHAT FOR YOU ARE TO WHISPERING?
BECAUSE I DON'T WANT FRANCIS AND TEDDY TO HEAR OUR PLAYS!
AH! HOKAY. GOOD.
OKAY, SO I WANT YOU TO DO A SQUARE-IN.
YES. WHAT IS SQUARE-IN?
SIGH... YOU HEAD UP THE RIGHT SIDELINE...
BUT WAIT. AM NOT SEE SIDELINE.
11 22

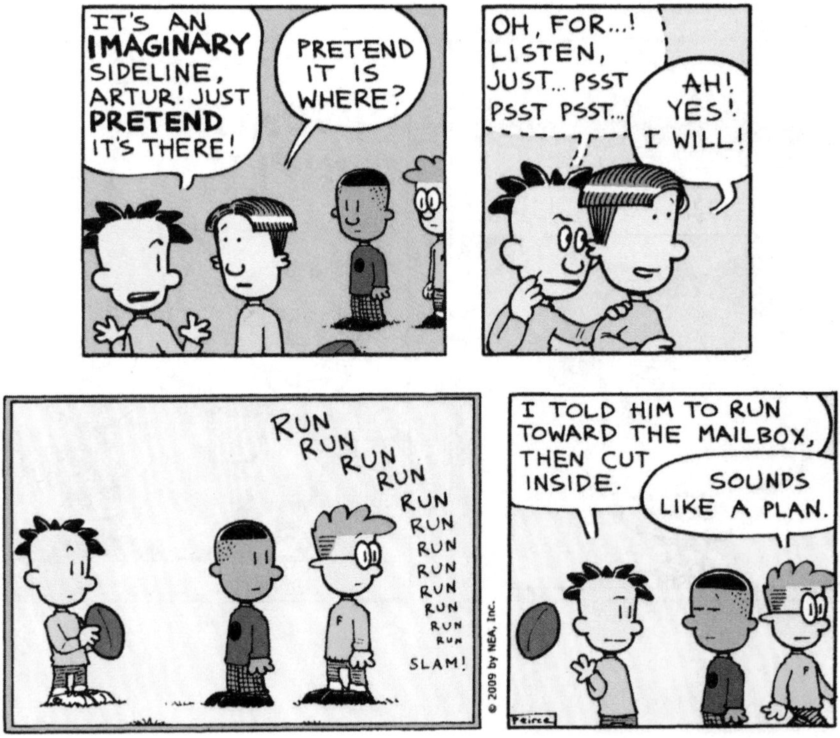
IT'S AN **IMAGINARY** SIDELINE, ARTUR! JUST **PRETEND** IT'S THERE!
PRETEND IT IS WHERE?
OH, FOR...! LISTEN, JUST... PSST PSST PSST...
AH! YES! I WILL!
RUN RUN RUN RUN RUN RUN RUN RUN RUN RUN RUN RUN
SLAM!
© 2009 by NEA, Inc.
I TOLD HIM TO RUN TOWARD THE MAILBOX, THEN CUT INSIDE.
SOUNDS LIKE A PLAN.
Peirce

P.D.A.

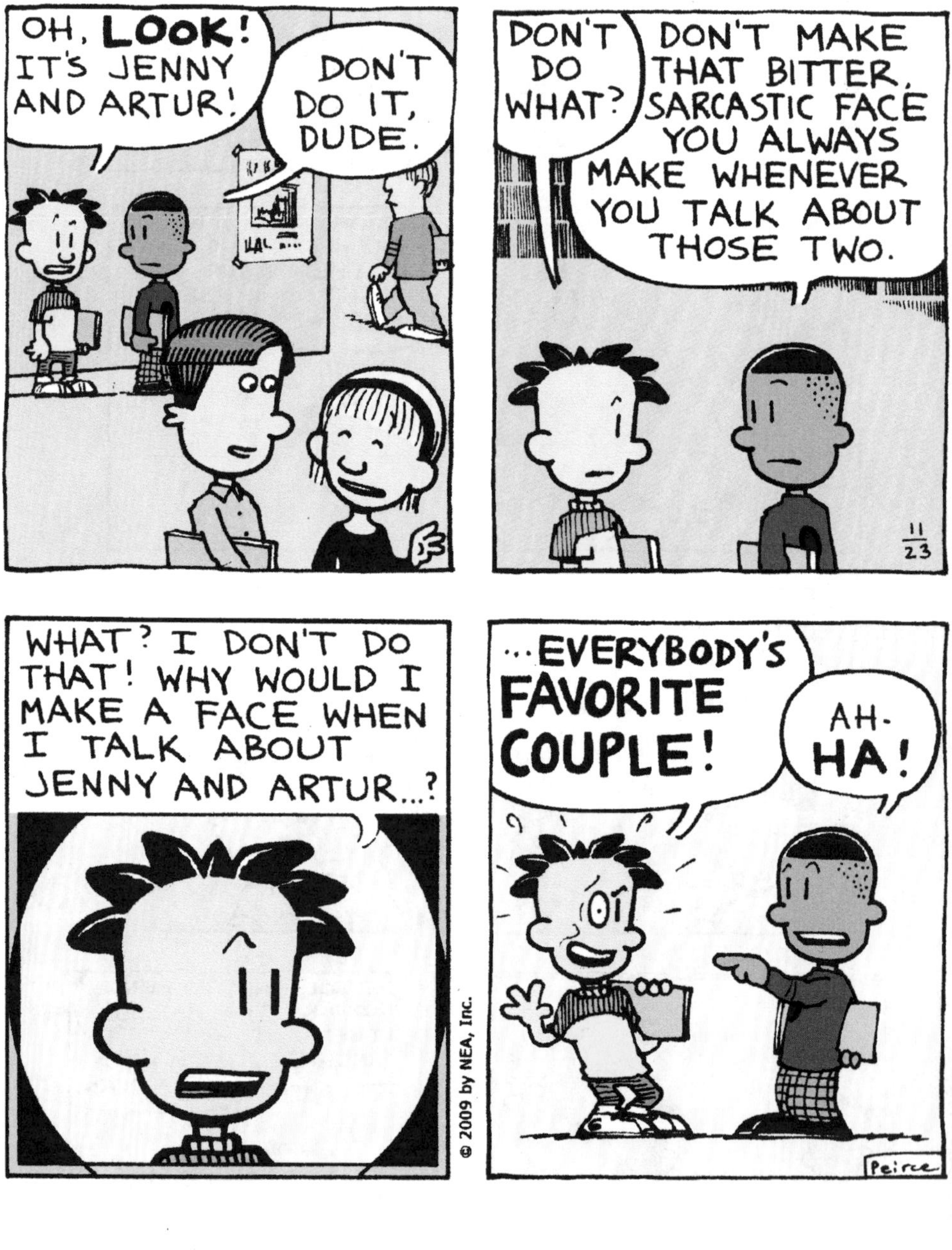

OH, **LOOK!** IT'S JENNY AND ARTUR!
DON'T DO IT, DUDE.
DON'T DO WHAT?
DON'T MAKE THAT BITTER, SARCASTIC FACE YOU ALWAYS MAKE WHENEVER YOU TALK ABOUT THOSE TWO.
11/23
WHAT? I DON'T DO THAT! WHY WOULD I MAKE A FACE WHEN I TALK ABOUT JENNY AND ARTUR...?
© 2009 by NEA, Inc.
...EVERYBODY'S **FAVORITE COUPLE!**
AH-**HA!**
Peirce

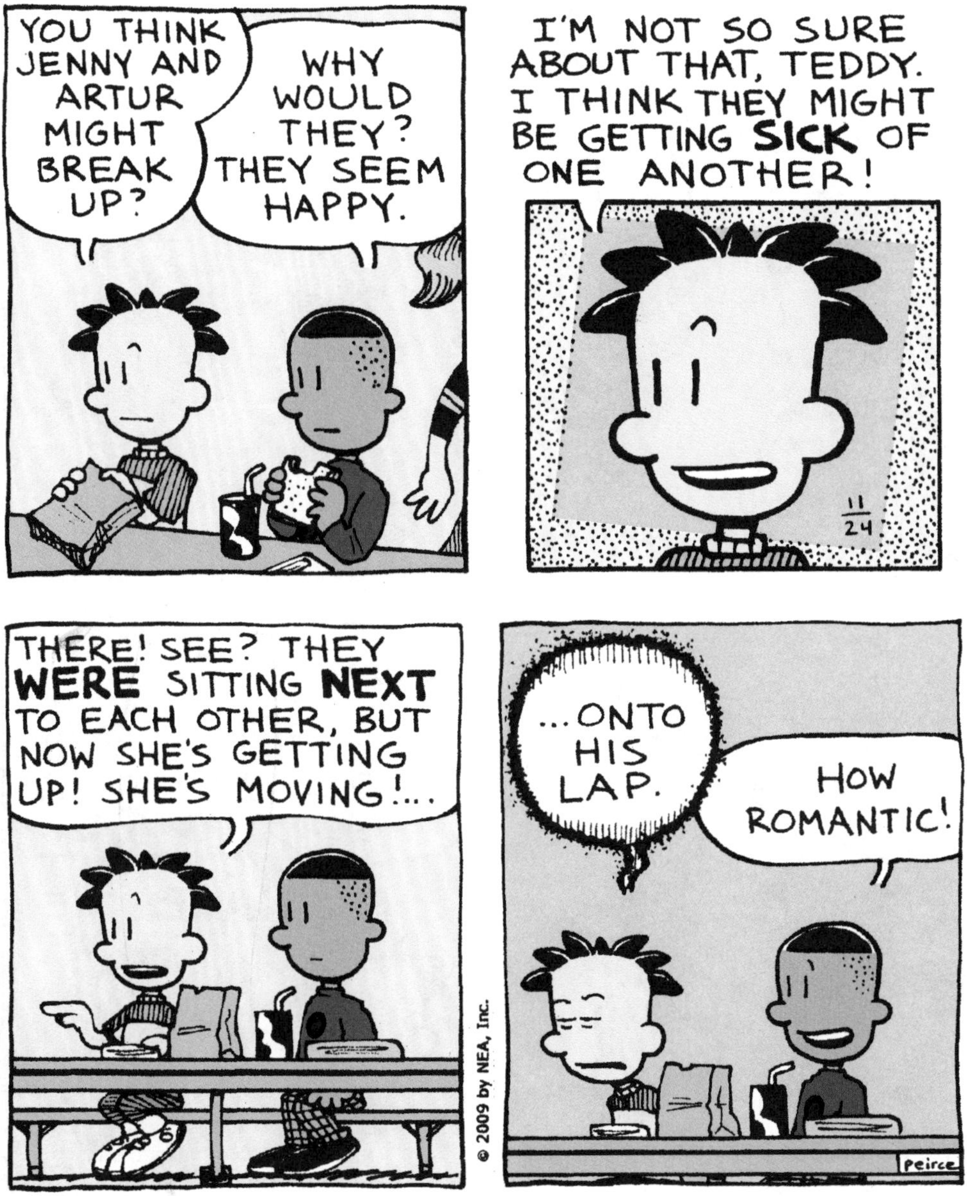
YOU THINK JENNY AND ARTUR MIGHT BREAK UP?
WHY WOULD THEY? THEY SEEM HAPPY.
I'M NOT SO SURE ABOUT THAT, TEDDY. I THINK THEY MIGHT BE GETTING **SICK** OF ONE ANOTHER!
11/24
THERE! SEE? THEY **WERE** SITTING **NEXT** TO EACH OTHER, BUT NOW SHE'S GETTING UP! SHE'S MOVING!...
...ONTO HIS LAP.
HOW ROMANTIC!
peirce

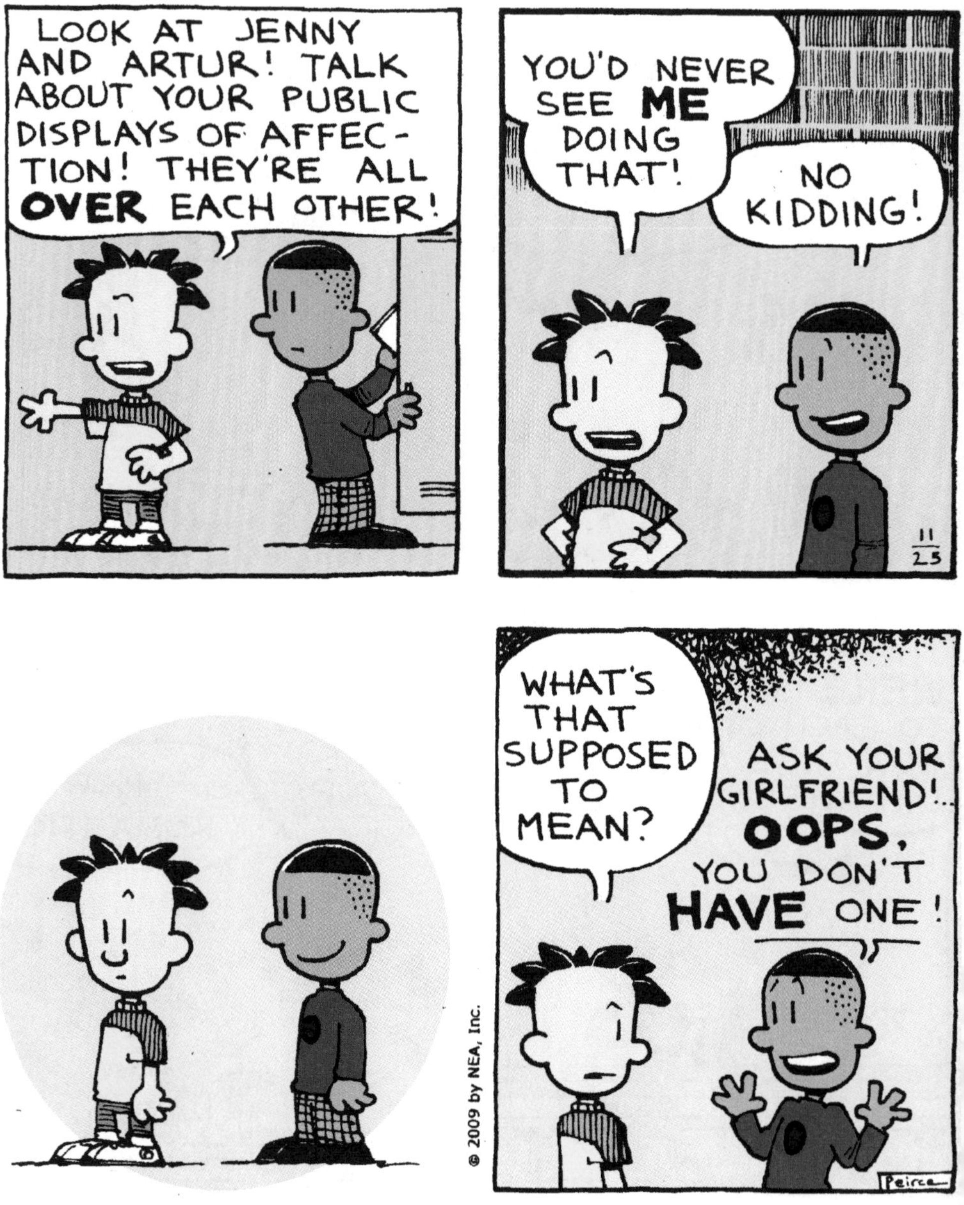

LOOK AT JENNY AND ARTUR! TALK ABOUT YOUR PUBLIC DISPLAYS OF AFFECTION! THEY'RE ALL **OVER** EACH OTHER!
YOU'D NEVER SEE **ME** DOING THAT!
NO KIDDING!
11/25
WHAT'S THAT SUPPOSED TO MEAN?
ASK YOUR GIRLFRIEND!.. **OOPS**, YOU DON'T **HAVE** ONE!
Peirce

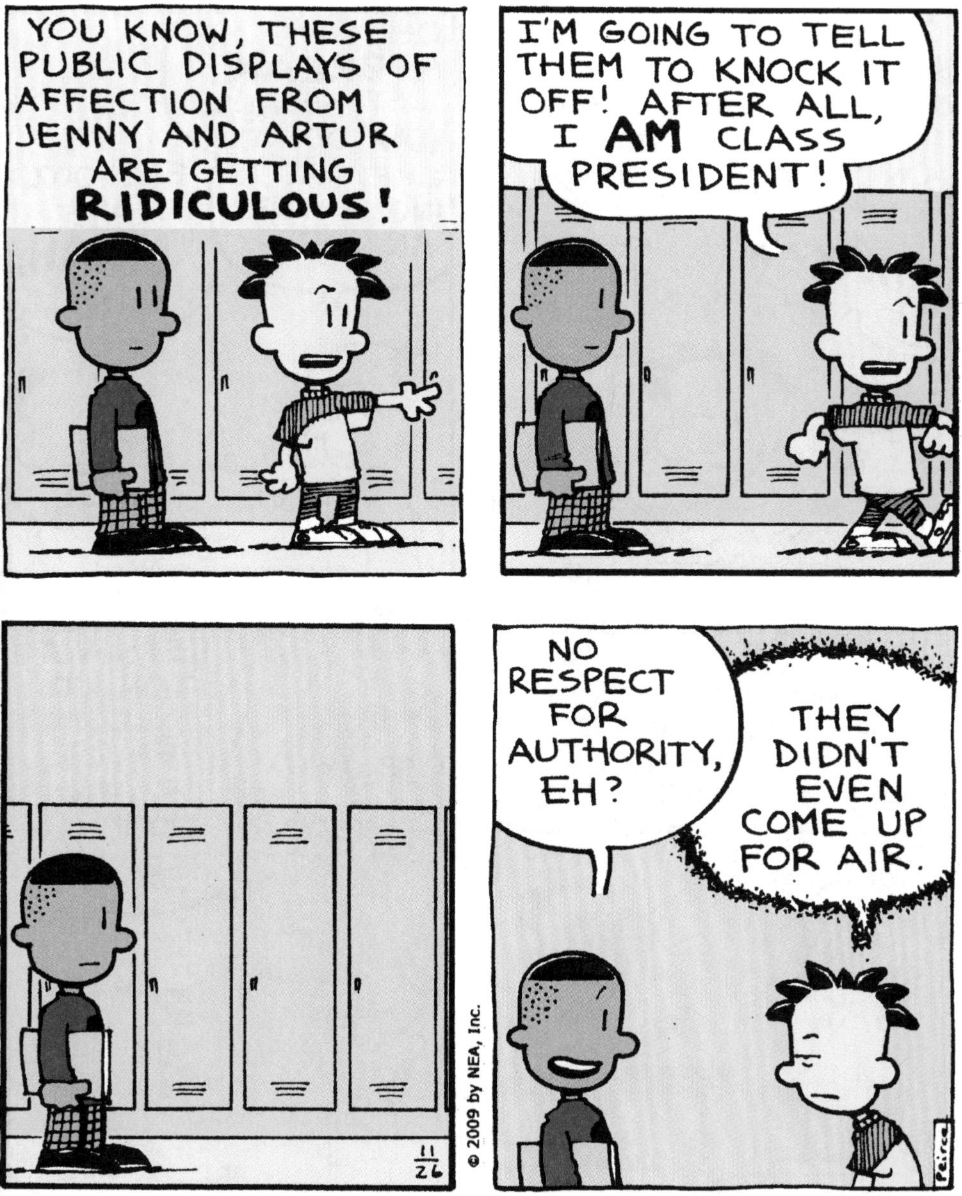
YOU KNOW, THESE PUBLIC DISPLAYS OF AFFECTION FROM JENNY AND ARTUR ARE GETTING **RIDICULOUS!**
I'M GOING TO TELL THEM TO KNOCK IT OFF! AFTER ALL, I **AM** CLASS PRESIDENT!
NO RESPECT FOR AUTHORITY, EH?
THEY DIDN'T EVEN COME UP FOR AIR.
© 2009 by NEA, Inc.

BON VOYAGE!

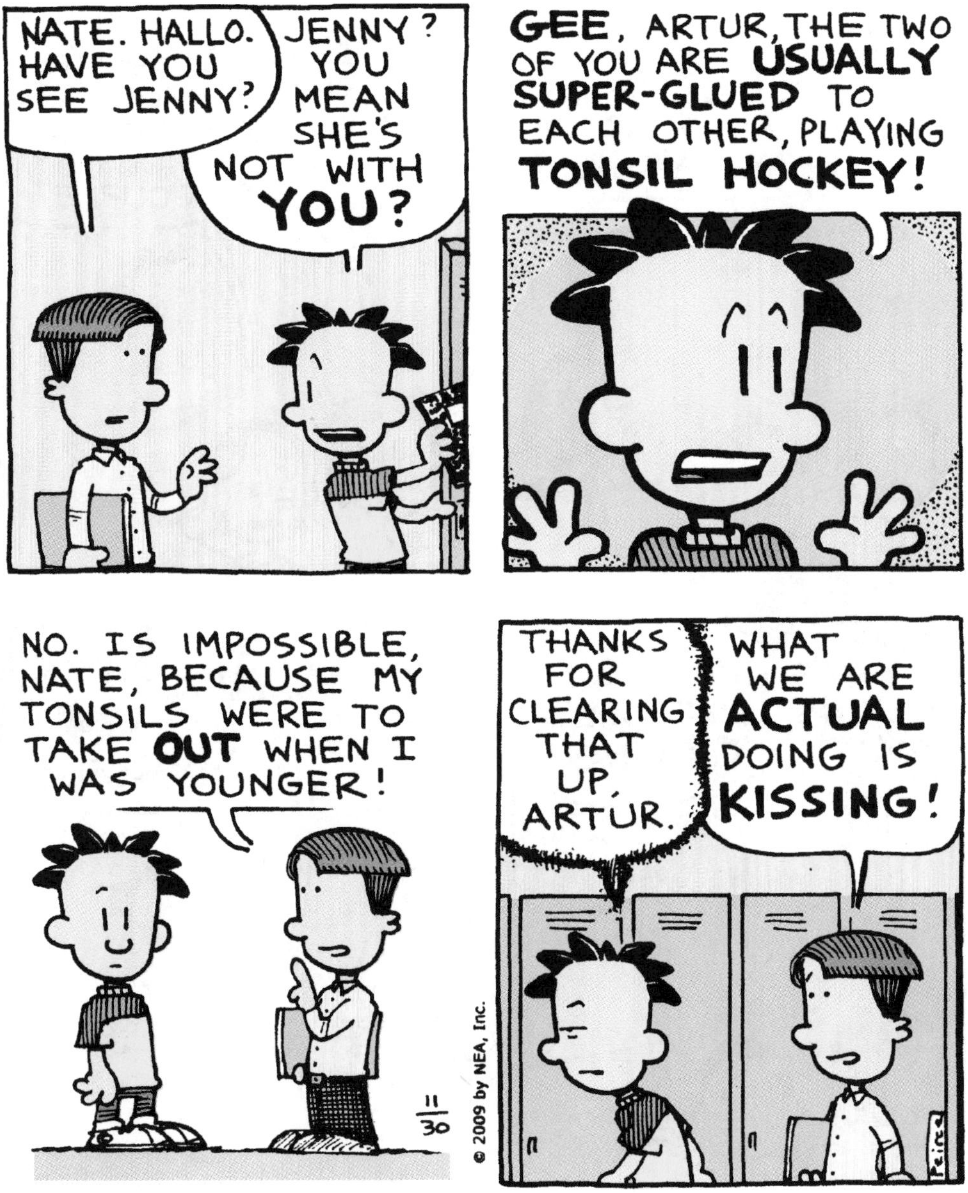
NATE. HALLO. HAVE YOU SEE JENNY?
JENNY? YOU MEAN SHE'S NOT WITH **YOU**?
GEE, ARTUR, THE TWO OF YOU ARE **USUALLY SUPER-GLUED** TO EACH OTHER, PLAYING **TONSIL HOCKEY**!
NO. IS IMPOSSIBLE, NATE, BECAUSE MY TONSILS WERE TO TAKE **OUT** WHEN I WAS YOUNGER!
11/30
© 2009 by NEA, Inc.
THANKS FOR CLEARING THAT UP, ARTUR.
WHAT WE ARE **ACTUAL** DOING IS **KISSING**!
Peirce

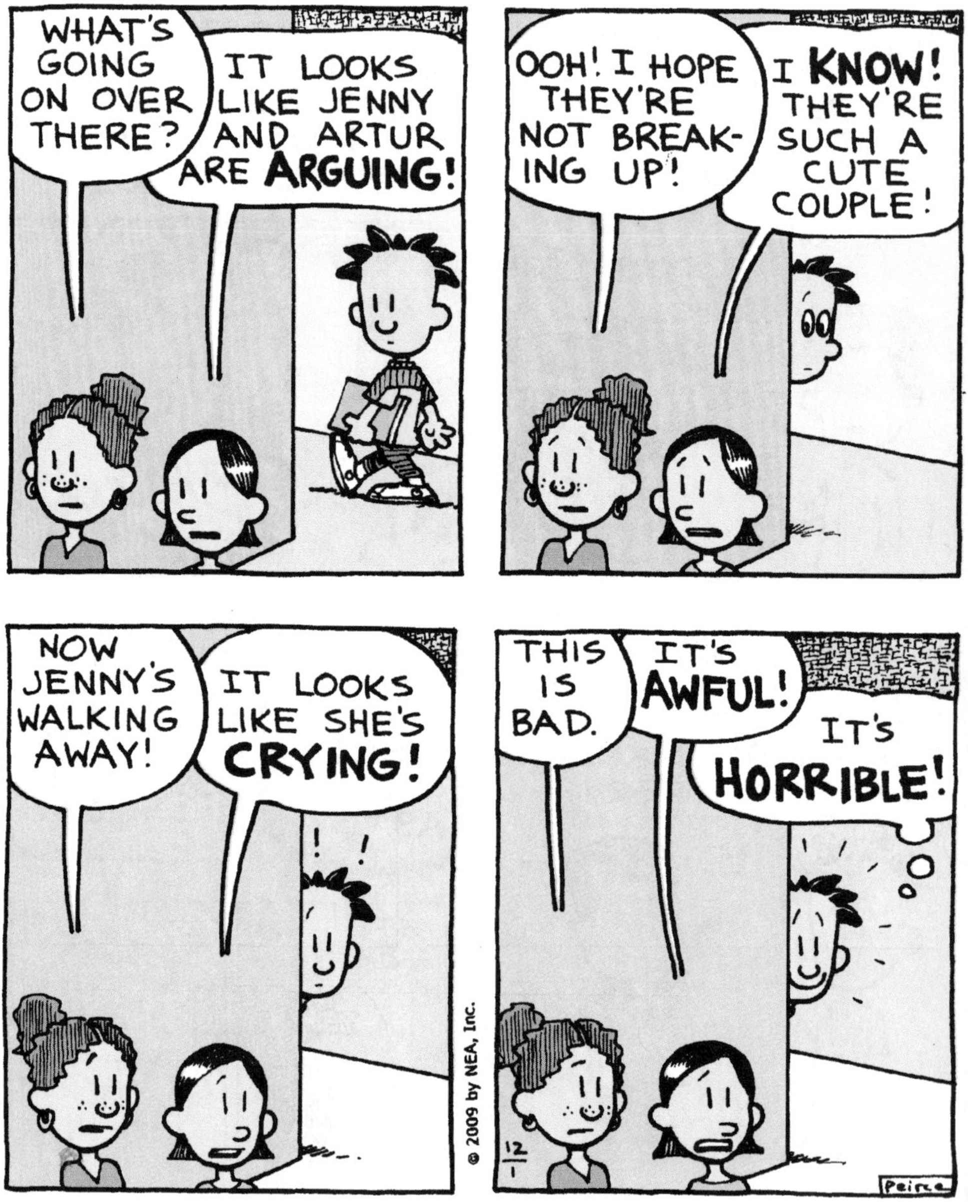
WHAT'S GOING ON OVER THERE?
IT LOOKS LIKE JENNY AND ARTUR ARE ARGUING!
OOH! I HOPE THEY'RE NOT BREAKING UP!
I KNOW! THEY'RE SUCH A CUTE COUPLE!
NOW JENNY'S WALKING AWAY!
IT LOOKS LIKE SHE'S CRYING!
! !
THIS IS BAD.
IT'S AWFUL!
IT'S HORRIBLE!
© 2009 by NEA, Inc.
12/1
Peirce

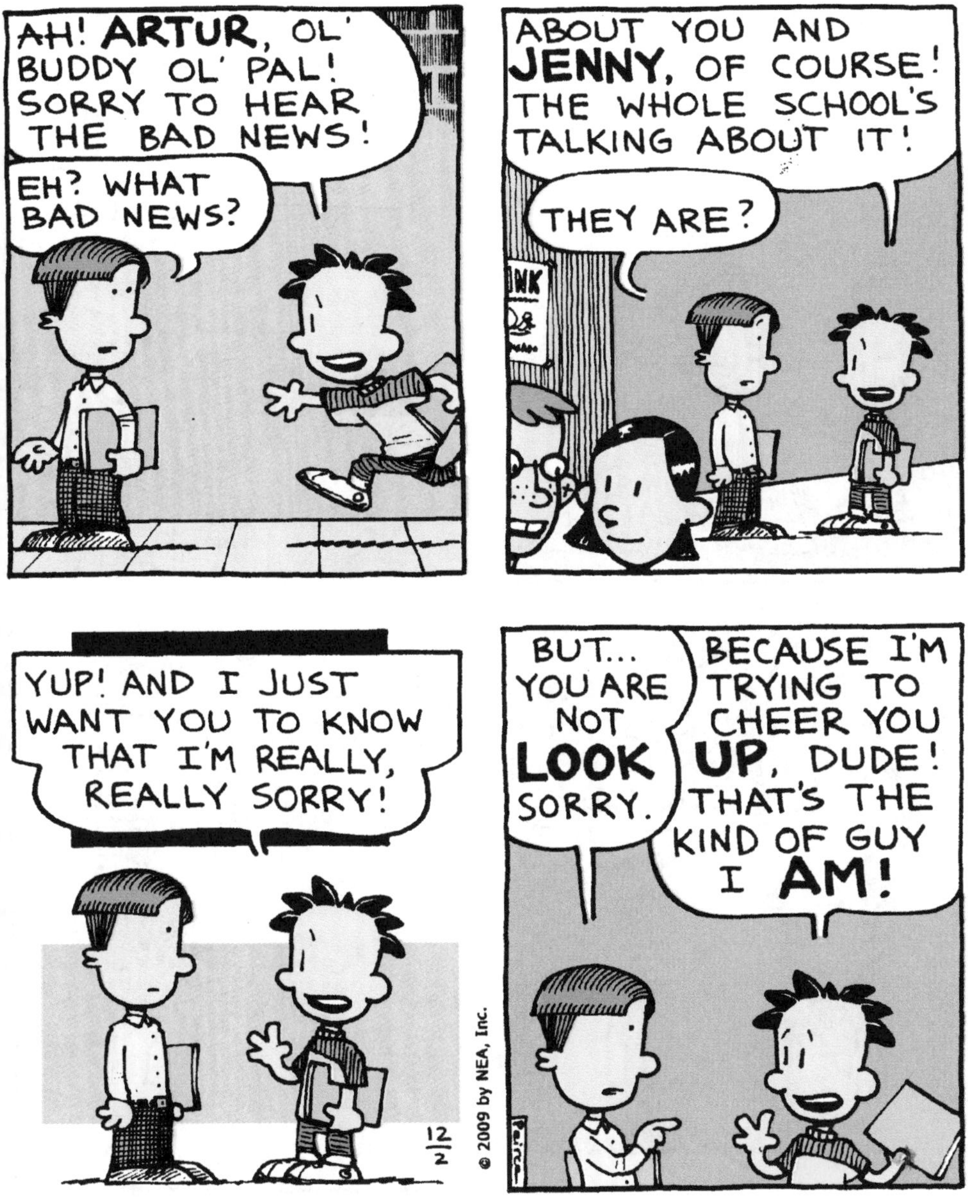
AH! ARTUR, OL' BUDDY OL' PAL! SORRY TO HEAR THE BAD NEWS!
EH? WHAT BAD NEWS?
ABOUT YOU AND JENNY, OF COURSE! THE WHOLE SCHOOL'S TALKING ABOUT IT!
THEY ARE?
YUP! AND I JUST WANT YOU TO KNOW THAT I'M REALLY, REALLY SORRY!
12/2
© 2009 by NEA, Inc.
BUT... YOU ARE NOT LOOK SORRY.
BECAUSE I'M TRYING TO CHEER YOU UP, DUDE! THAT'S THE KIND OF GUY I AM!

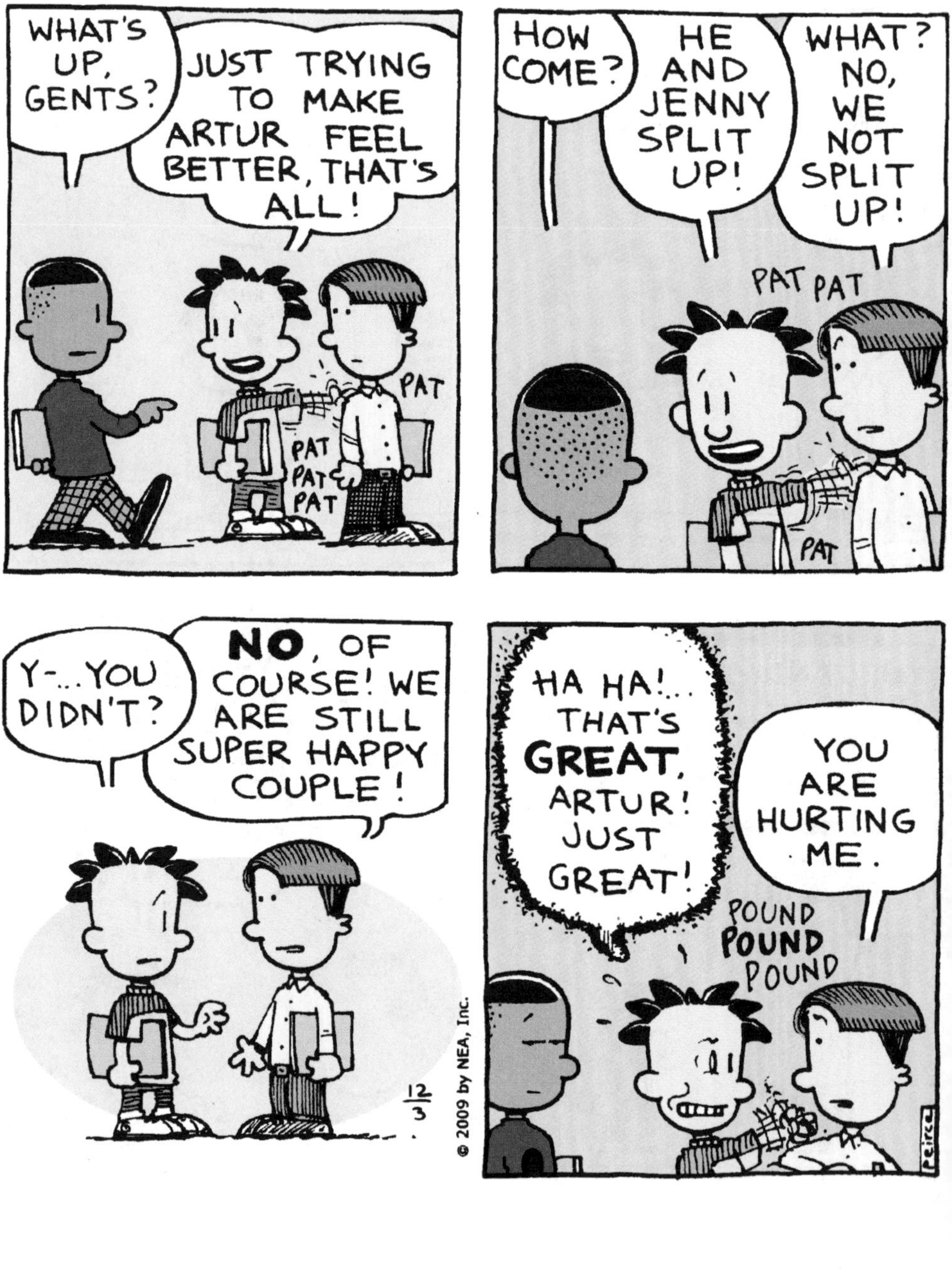
WHAT'S UP, GENTS?
JUST TRYING TO MAKE ARTUR FEEL BETTER, THAT'S ALL!
PAT
PAT PAT PAT
HOW COME?
HE AND JENNY SPLIT UP!
WHAT? NO, WE NOT SPLIT UP!
PAT PAT
PAT
Y-... YOU DIDN'T?
NO, OF COURSE! WE ARE STILL SUPER HAPPY COUPLE!
HA HA!... THAT'S GREAT, ARTUR! JUST GREAT!
YOU ARE HURTING ME.
POUND POUND POUND
12/3
© 2009 by NEA, Inc.
Peirce

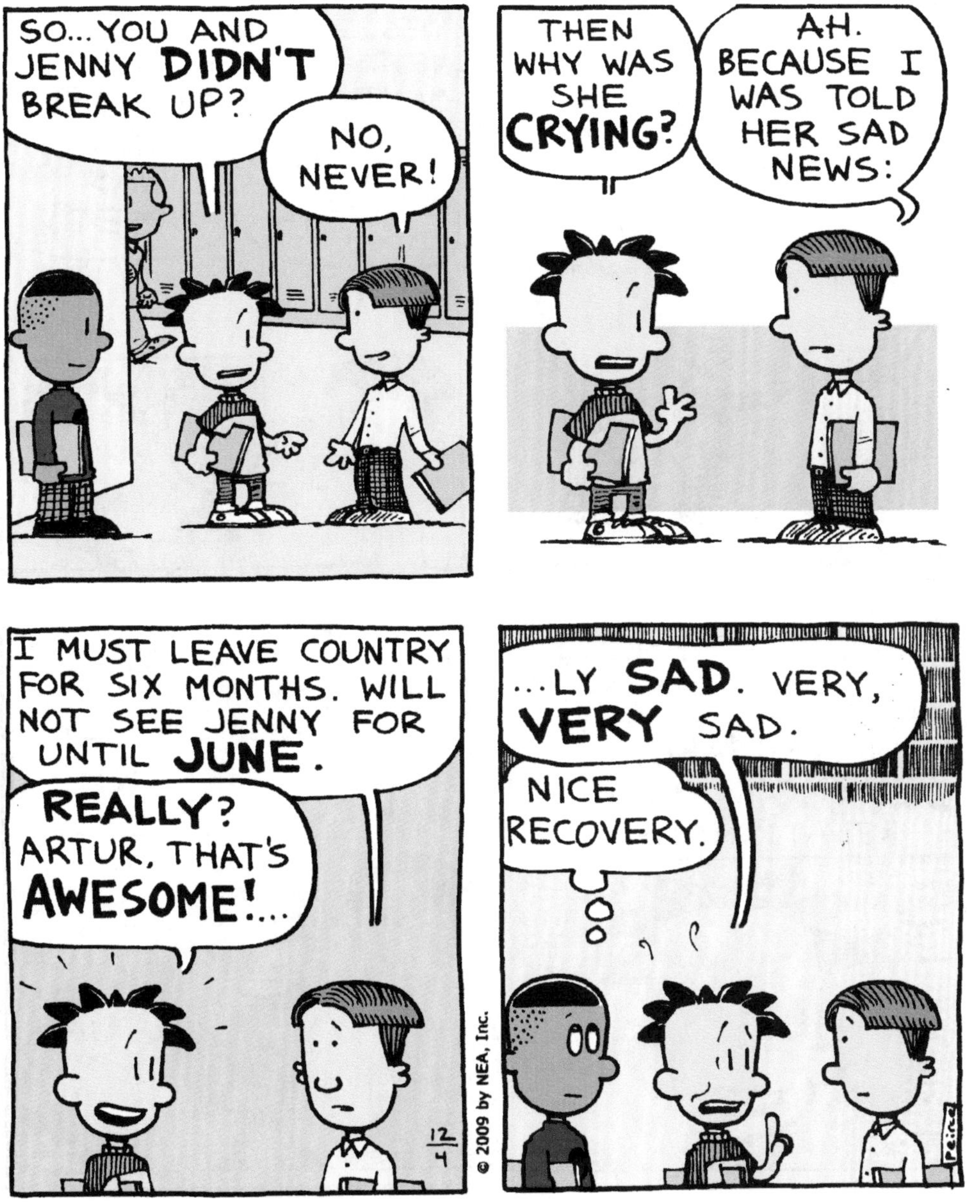
SO... YOU AND JENNY DIDN'T BREAK UP?
NO, NEVER!
THEN WHY WAS SHE CRYING?
AH. BECAUSE I WAS TOLD HER SAD NEWS:
I MUST LEAVE COUNTRY FOR SIX MONTHS. WILL NOT SEE JENNY FOR UNTIL JUNE.
REALLY? ARTUR, THAT'S AWESOME!...
...LY SAD. VERY, VERY SAD.
NICE RECOVERY.
12
4
© 2009 by NEA, Inc.
Peirce

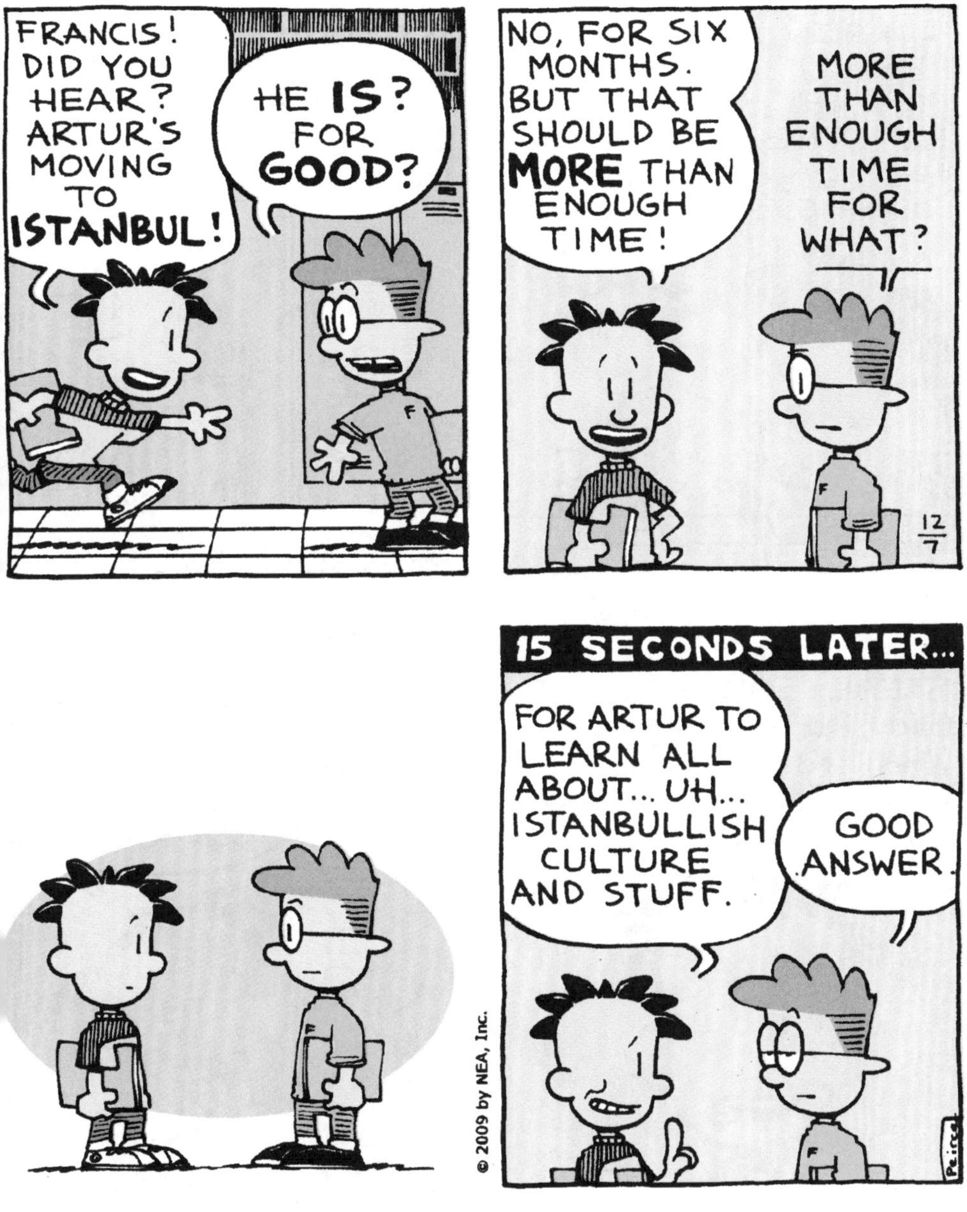
FRANCIS! DID YOU HEAR? ARTUR'S MOVING TO **ISTANBUL**!
HE **IS**? FOR **GOOD**?
NO, FOR SIX MONTHS. BUT THAT SHOULD BE **MORE** THAN ENOUGH TIME!
MORE THAN ENOUGH TIME FOR WHAT?
15 SECONDS LATER...
FOR ARTUR TO LEARN ALL ABOUT... UH... ISTANBULLISH CULTURE AND STUFF.
GOOD ANSWER.

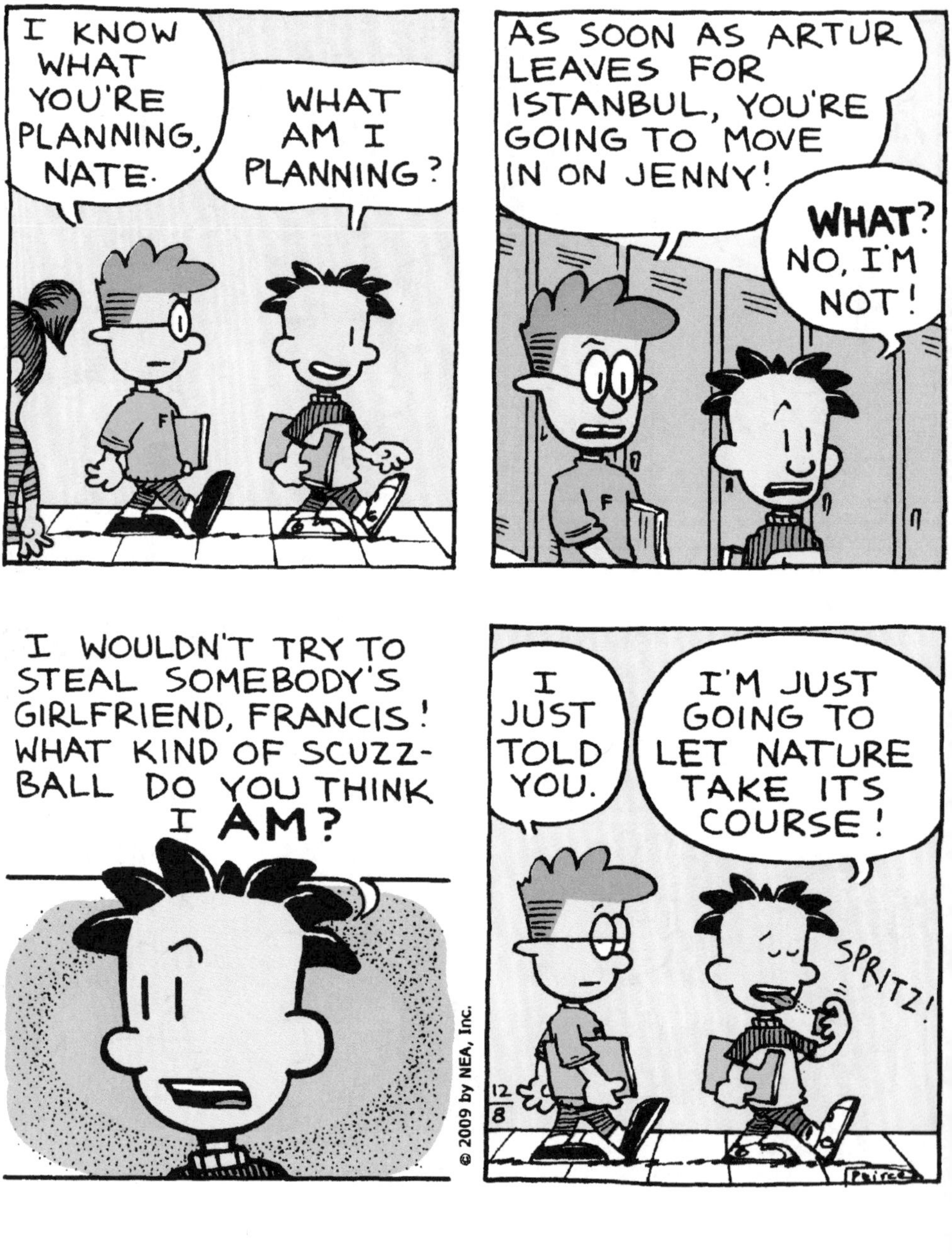
I KNOW WHAT YOU'RE PLANNING, NATE.
WHAT AM I PLANNING?
AS SOON AS ARTUR LEAVES FOR ISTANBUL, YOU'RE GOING TO MOVE IN ON JENNY!
WHAT? NO, I'M NOT!
I WOULDN'T TRY TO STEAL SOMEBODY'S GIRLFRIEND, FRANCIS! WHAT KIND OF SCUZZ-BALL DO YOU THINK I AM?
I JUST TOLD YOU.
I'M JUST GOING TO LET NATURE TAKE ITS COURSE!
SPRITZ!
12 8
PEIRCE

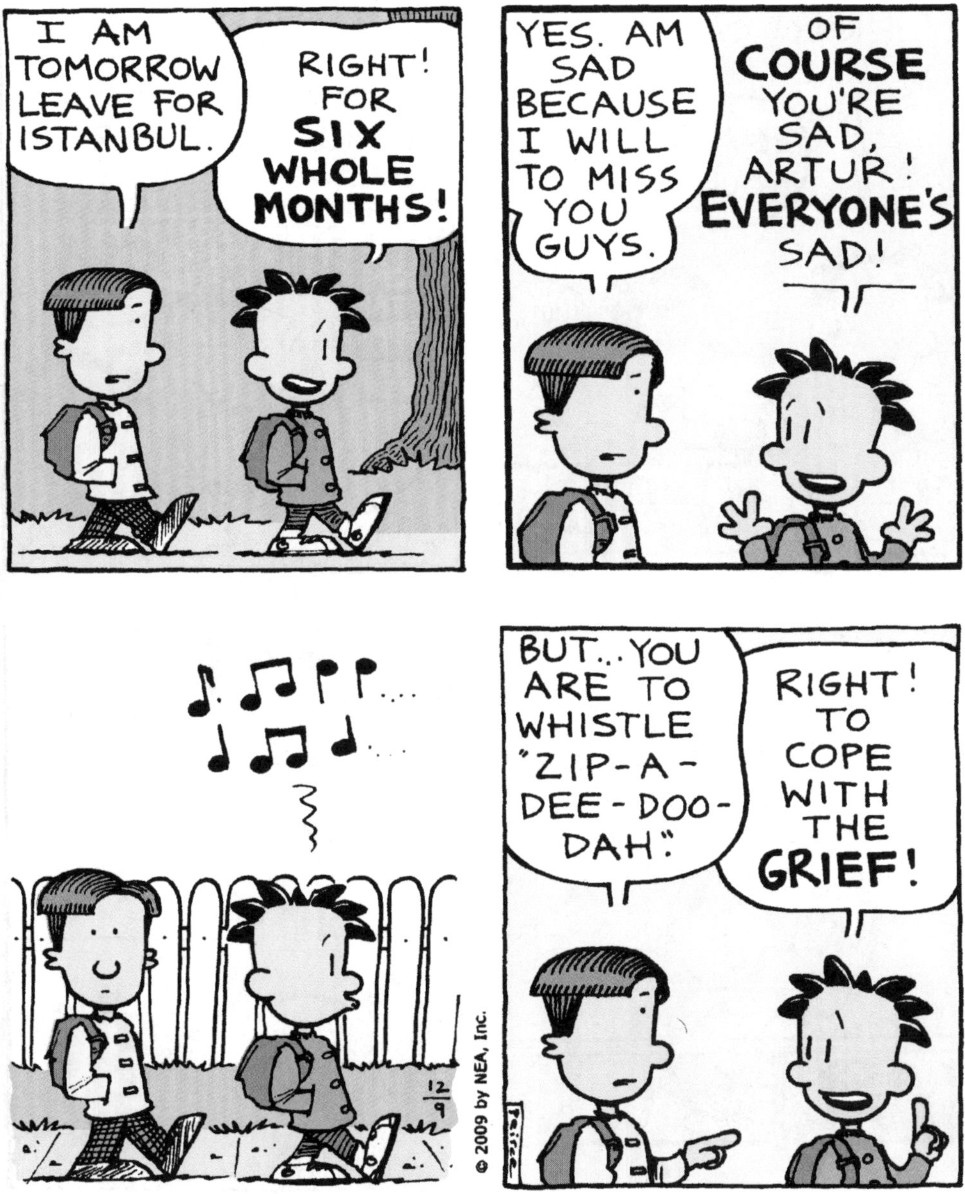
I AM TOMORROW LEAVE FOR ISTANBUL.
RIGHT! FOR **SIX WHOLE MONTHS!**
YES. AM SAD BECAUSE I WILL TO MISS YOU GUYS.
OF **COURSE** YOU'RE SAD, ARTUR! **EVERYONE'S** SAD!
© 2009 by NEA, Inc.
12/9
BUT... YOU ARE TO WHISTLE "ZIP-A-DEE-DOO-DAH".
RIGHT! TO COPE WITH THE **GRIEF!**

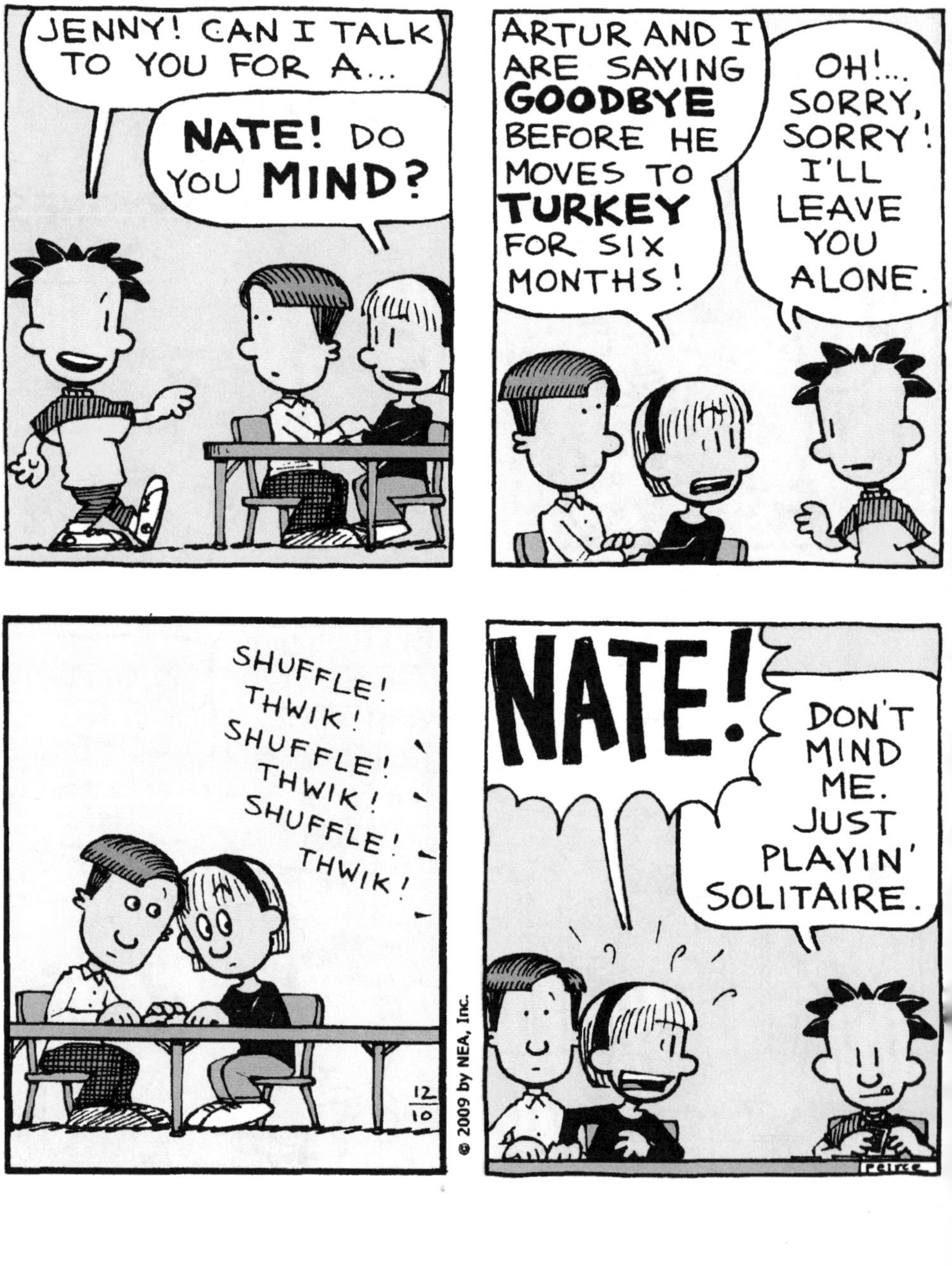
JENNY! CAN I TALK TO YOU FOR A...
NATE! DO YOU MIND?
ARTUR AND I ARE SAYING GOODBYE BEFORE HE MOVES TO TURKEY FOR SIX MONTHS!
OH!... SORRY, SORRY! I'LL LEAVE YOU ALONE.
SHUFFLE! THWIK! SHUFFLE! THWIK! SHUFFLE! THWIK!
12/10
© 2009 by NEA, Inc.
NATE!
DON'T MIND ME. JUST PLAYIN' SOLITAIRE.
Peirce

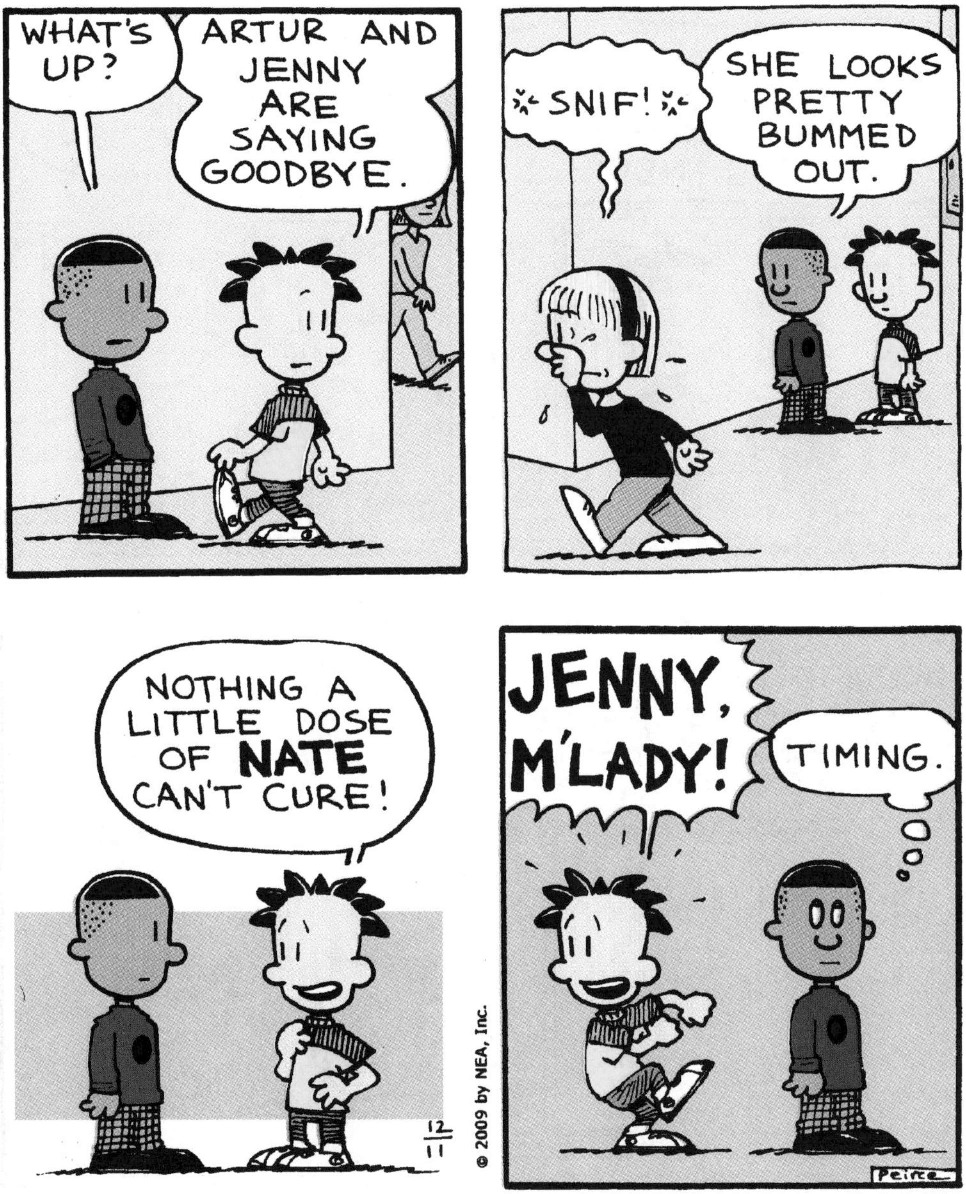
WHAT'S UP?
ARTUR AND JENNY ARE SAYING GOODBYE.
SNIF!
SHE LOOKS PRETTY BUMMED OUT.
NOTHING A LITTLE DOSE OF **NATE** CAN'T CURE!
12/11
© 2009 by NEA, Inc.
JENNY, M'LADY!
TIMING.
Peirce

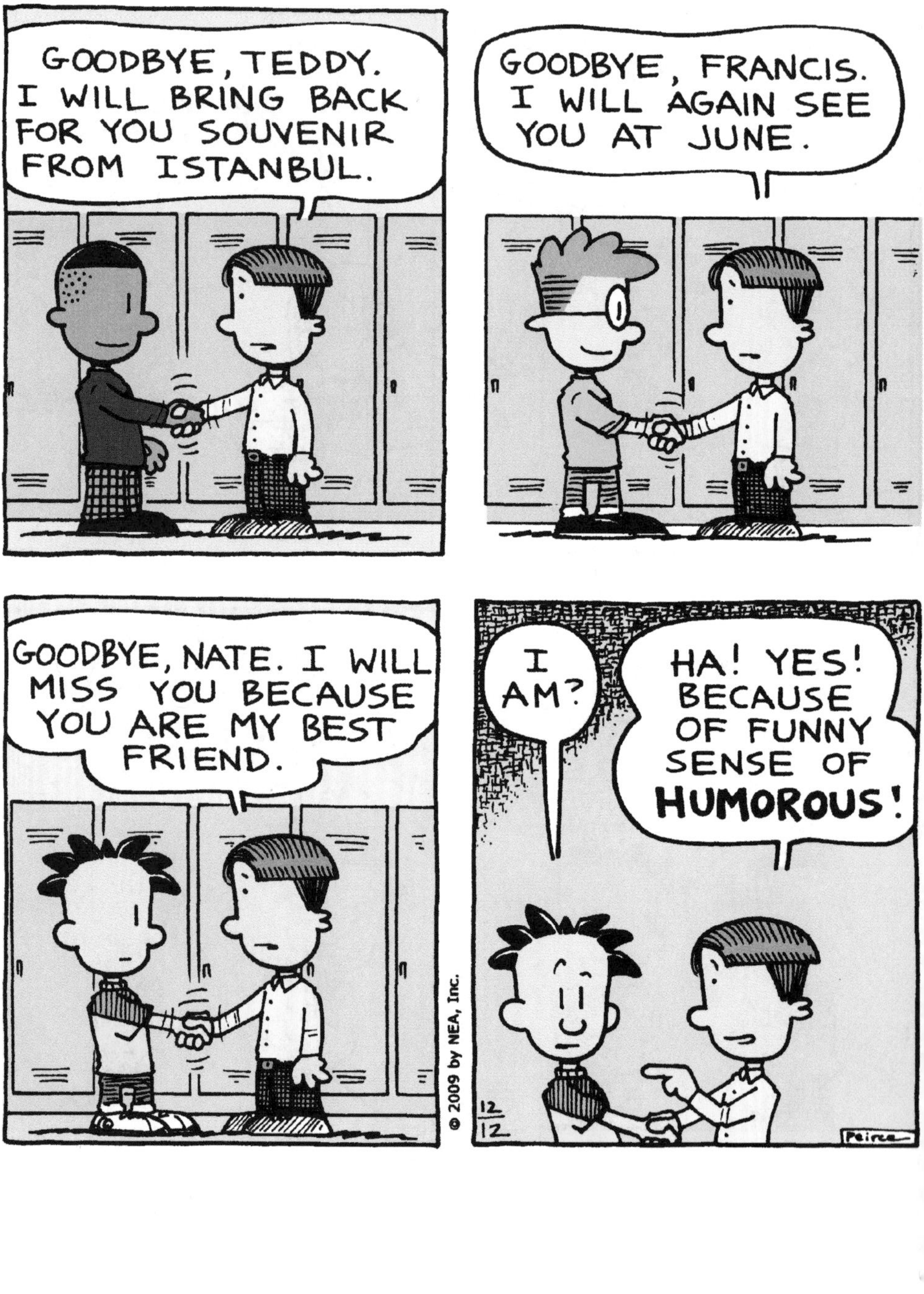
GOODBYE, TEDDY. I WILL BRING BACK FOR YOU SOUVENIR FROM ISTANBUL.
GOODBYE, FRANCIS. I WILL AGAIN SEE YOU AT JUNE.
GOODBYE, NATE. I WILL MISS YOU BECAUSE YOU ARE MY BEST FRIEND.
I AM?
HA! YES! BECAUSE OF FUNNY SENSE OF **HUMOROUS**!
12/12
Peirce

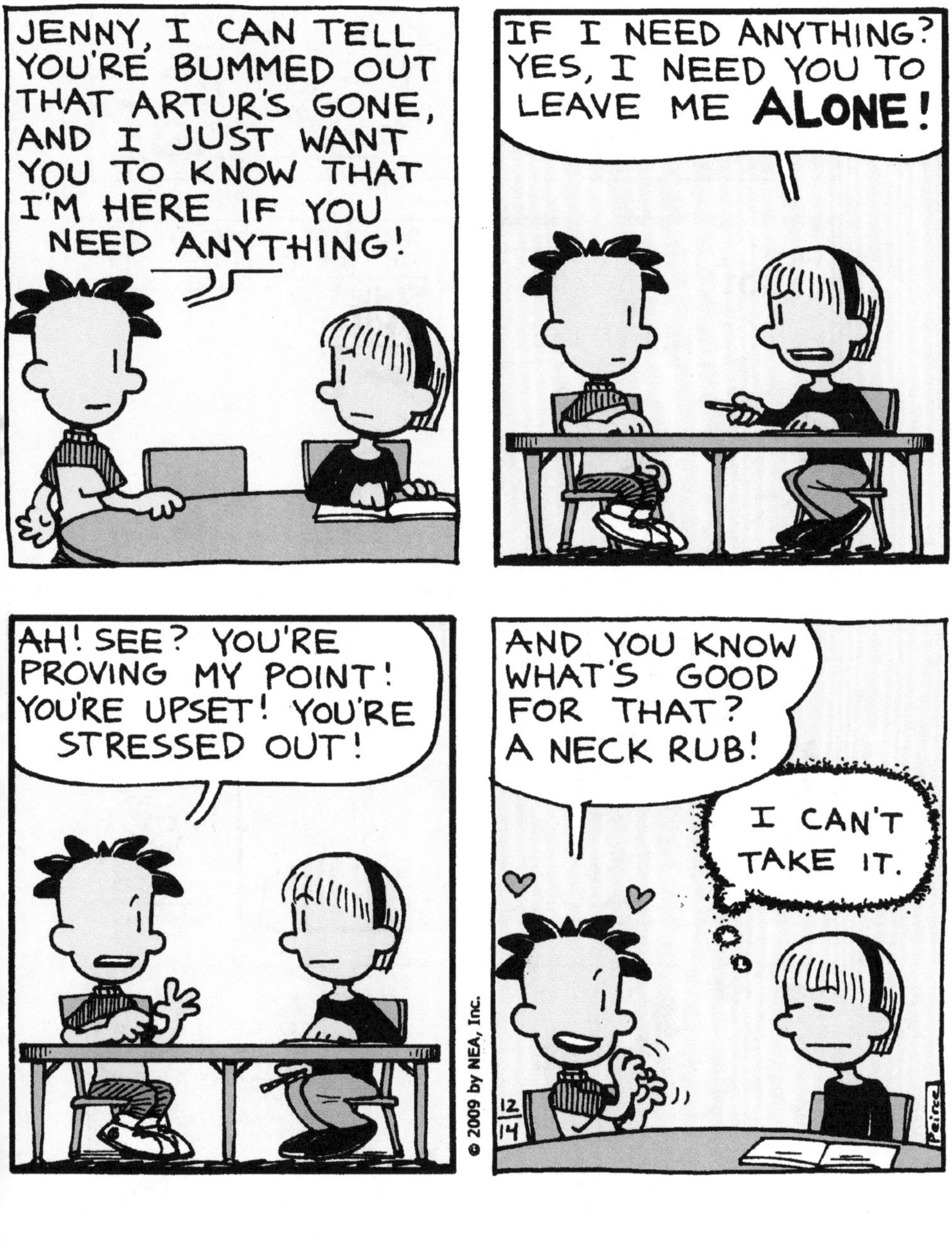
JENNY, I CAN TELL YOU'RE BUMMED OUT THAT ARTUR'S GONE, AND I JUST WANT YOU TO KNOW THAT I'M HERE IF YOU NEED ANYTHING!
IF I NEED ANYTHING? YES, I NEED YOU TO LEAVE ME ALONE!
AH! SEE? YOU'RE PROVING MY POINT! YOU'RE UPSET! YOU'RE STRESSED OUT!
AND YOU KNOW WHAT'S GOOD FOR THAT? A NECK RUB!
I CAN'T TAKE IT.
© 2009 by NEA, Inc.
12/14
Peirce

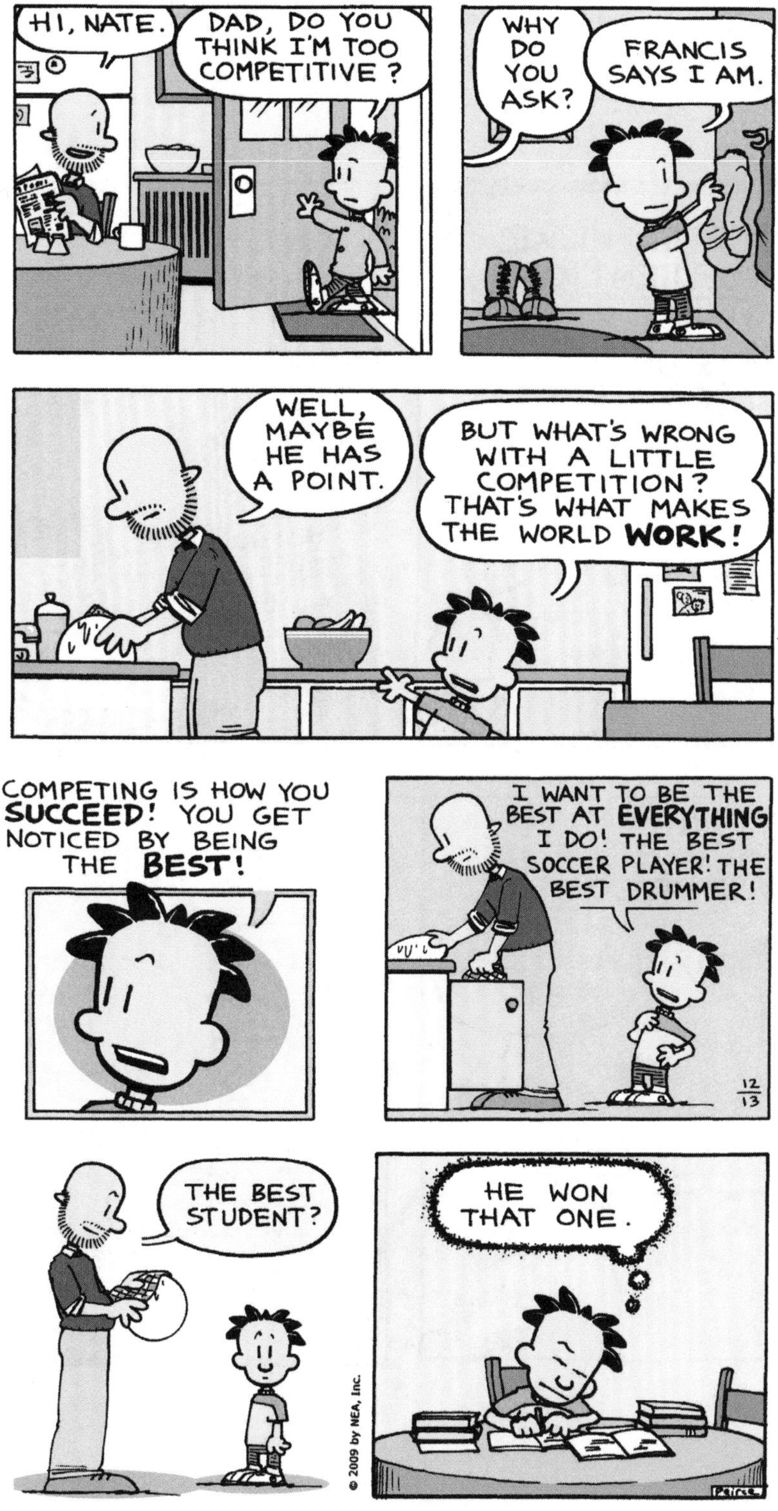
HI, NATE.
DAD, DO YOU THINK I'M TOO COMPETITIVE?
WHY DO YOU ASK?
FRANCIS SAYS I AM.
WELL, MAYBE HE HAS A POINT.
BUT WHAT'S WRONG WITH A LITTLE COMPETITION? THAT'S WHAT MAKES THE WORLD **WORK**!
COMPETING IS HOW YOU **SUCCEED**! YOU GET NOTICED BY BEING THE **BEST**!
I WANT TO BE THE BEST AT **EVERYTHING** I DO! THE BEST SOCCER PLAYER! THE BEST DRUMMER!
12/13
THE BEST STUDENT?
HE WON THAT ONE.
© 2009 by NEA, Inc.
Peirce

DATE WITH DETENTION

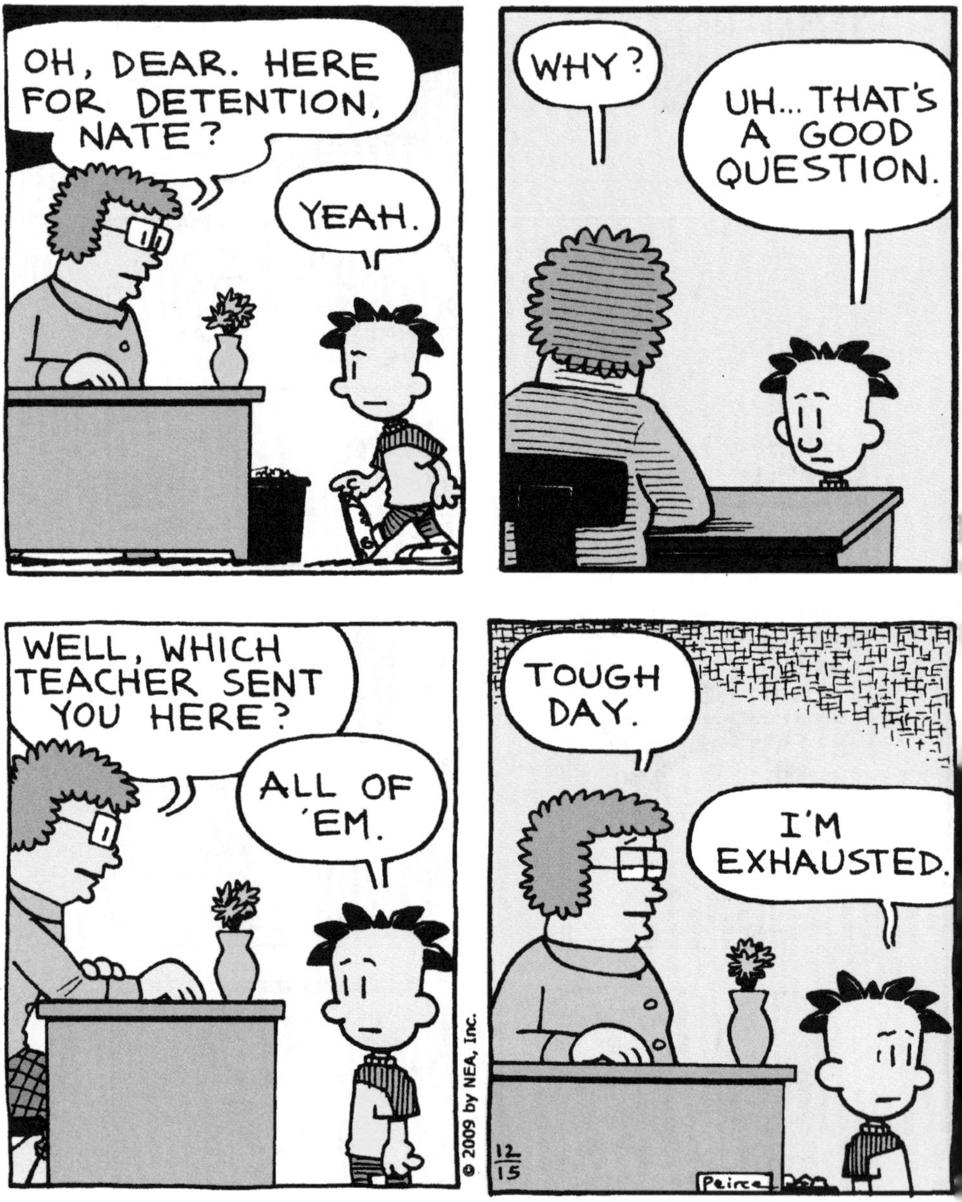

OH, DEAR. HERE FOR DETENTION, NATE?
YEAH.
WHY?
UH... THAT'S A GOOD QUESTION.
WELL, WHICH TEACHER SENT YOU HERE?
ALL OF 'EM.
TOUGH DAY.
I'M EXHAUSTED.
© 2009 by NEA, Inc.
12/15
Peirce

IT'S PRACTICALLY CHRISTMAS AND WE HAVEN'T HAD A SINGLE SNOWFLAKE! THIS IS TOTALLY UNACCEPTABLE!

I'M GOING TO CALL THE TV WEATHER GUY AND GIVE HIM A PIECE OF MY MIND!

BOOP BEEP BOOP BEEP

BUT IS MISDIRECTED ANGER IN KEEPING WITH THE HOLIDAY SPIRIT?

WHAT'S **THAT** SUPPOSED TO MEAN?

© 2009 by NEA, Inc.

NEVER MIND.

THEY'RE PLAYING "LET IT SNOW" WHILE I'M ON HOLD! OH, THAT'S **HILARIOUS!**

Peirce

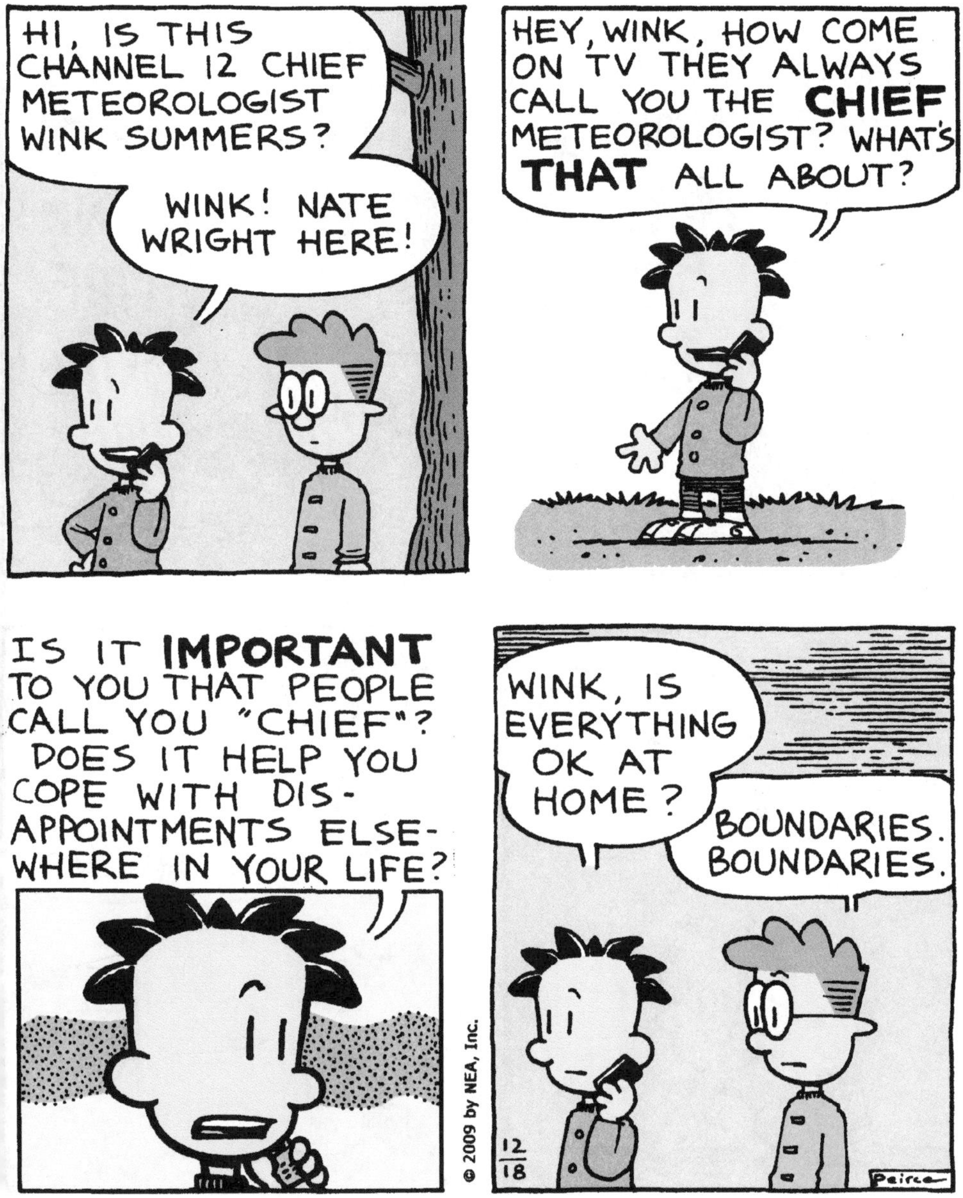
HI, IS THIS CHANNEL 12 CHIEF METEOROLOGIST WINK SUMMERS?
WINK! NATE WRIGHT HERE!
HEY, WINK, HOW COME ON TV THEY ALWAYS CALL YOU THE **CHIEF** METEOROLOGIST? WHAT'S **THAT** ALL ABOUT?
IS IT **IMPORTANT** TO YOU THAT PEOPLE CALL YOU "CHIEF"? DOES IT HELP YOU COPE WITH DIS-APPOINTMENTS ELSE-WHERE IN YOUR LIFE?
© 2009 by NEA, Inc.
WINK, IS EVERYTHING OK AT HOME?
BOUNDARIES. BOUNDARIES.
12/18
Peirce

12/20

© 2009 by NEA, Inc.

Peirce

133

REALITY BITES

'TWAS THE NATE
BEFORE CHRISTMAS

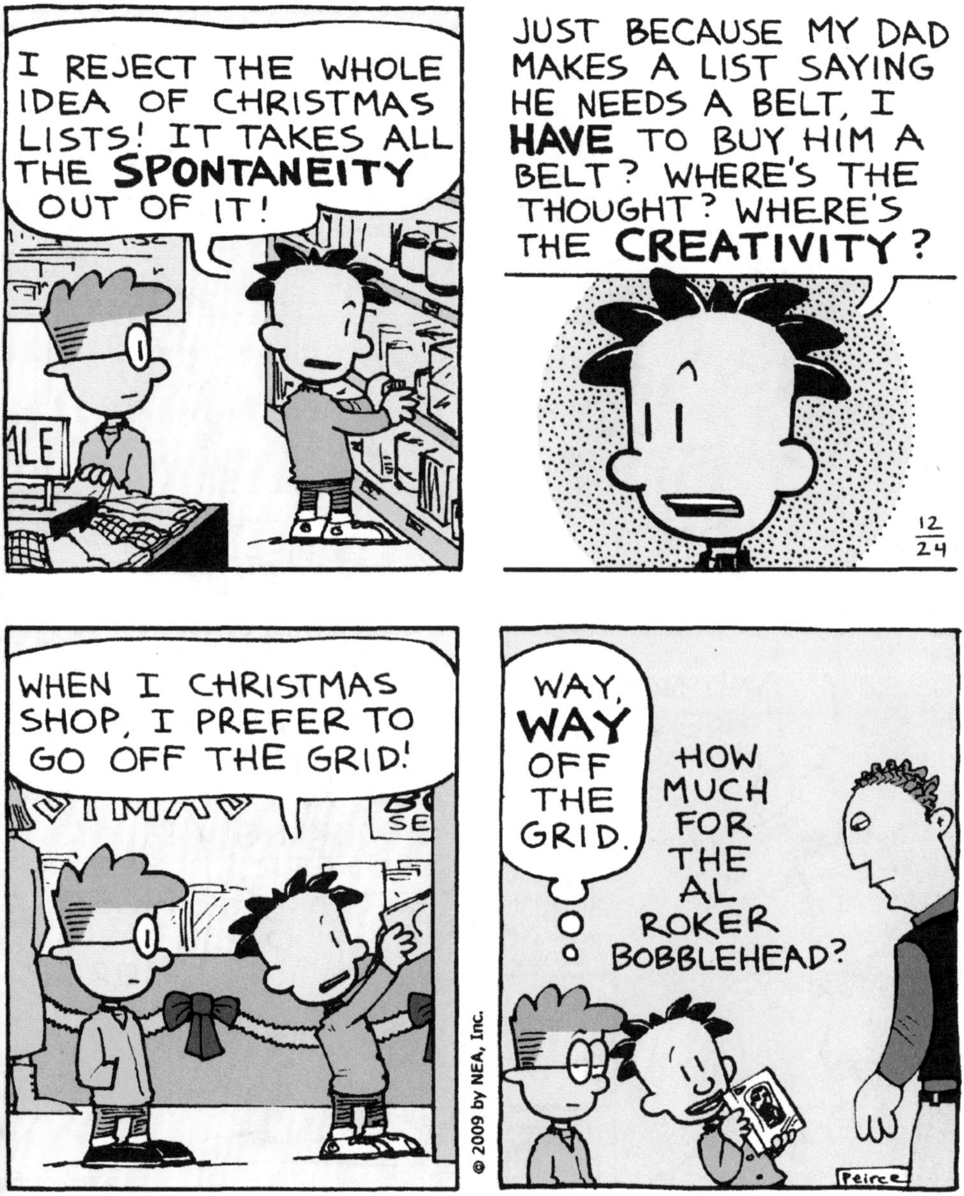
I REJECT THE WHOLE IDEA OF CHRISTMAS LISTS! IT TAKES ALL THE SPONTANEITY OUT OF IT!
JUST BECAUSE MY DAD MAKES A LIST SAYING HE NEEDS A BELT, I HAVE TO BUY HIM A BELT? WHERE'S THE THOUGHT? WHERE'S THE CREATIVITY?
12/24
WHEN I CHRISTMAS SHOP, I PREFER TO GO OFF THE GRID!
WAY, WAY OFF THE GRID.
HOW MUCH FOR THE AL ROKER BOBBLEHEAD?
Peirce
© 2009 by NEA, Inc.

SNOW BUSINESS

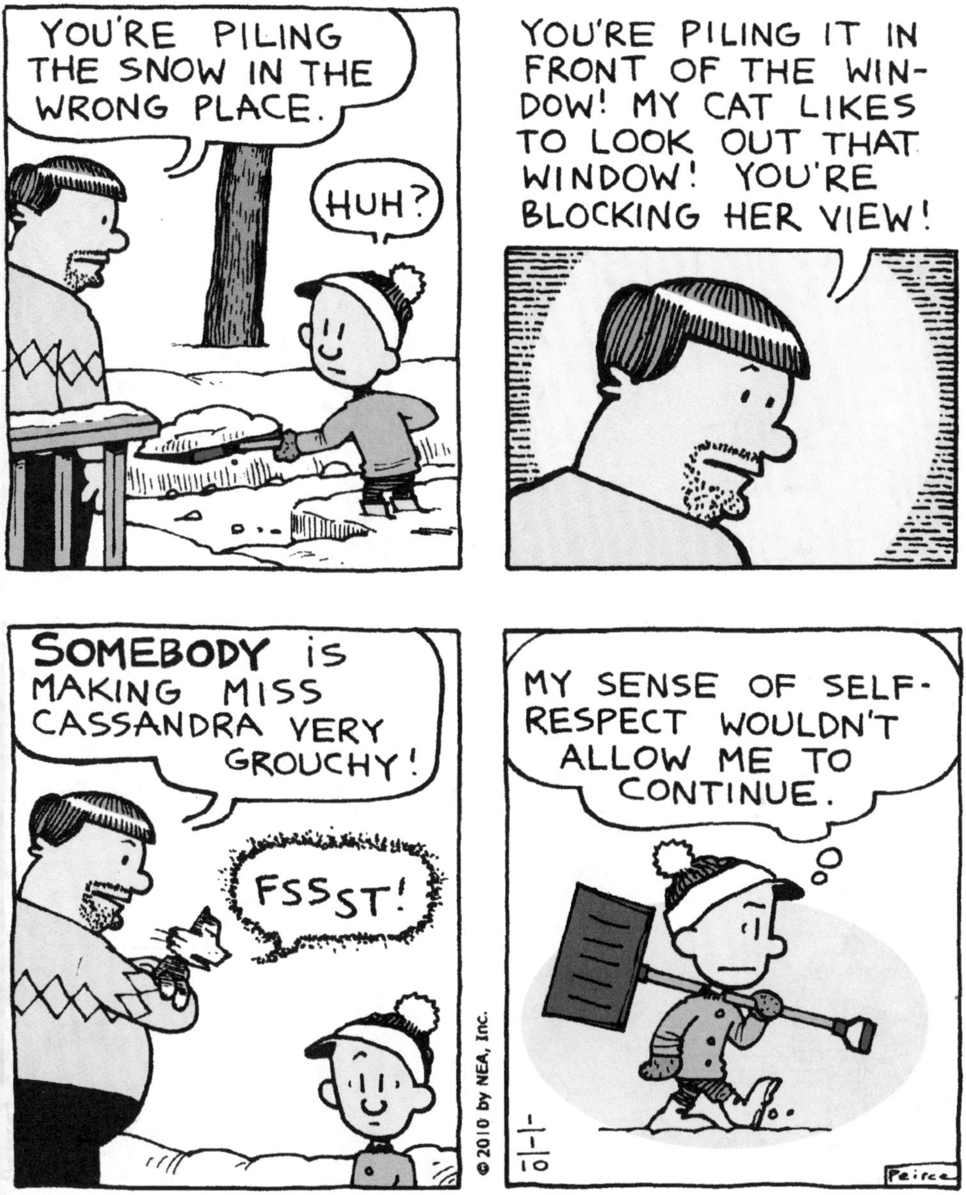

YOU'RE PILING THE SNOW IN THE WRONG PLACE.
HUH?
YOU'RE PILING IT IN FRONT OF THE WIN-DOW! MY CAT LIKES TO LOOK OUT THAT WINDOW! YOU'RE BLOCKING HER VIEW!
SOMEBODY is MAKING MISS CASSANDRA VERY GROUCHY!
FSSST!
MY SENSE OF SELF-RESPECT WOULDN'T ALLOW ME TO CONTINUE.
©2010 by NEA, Inc.
1-1-10
Peirce

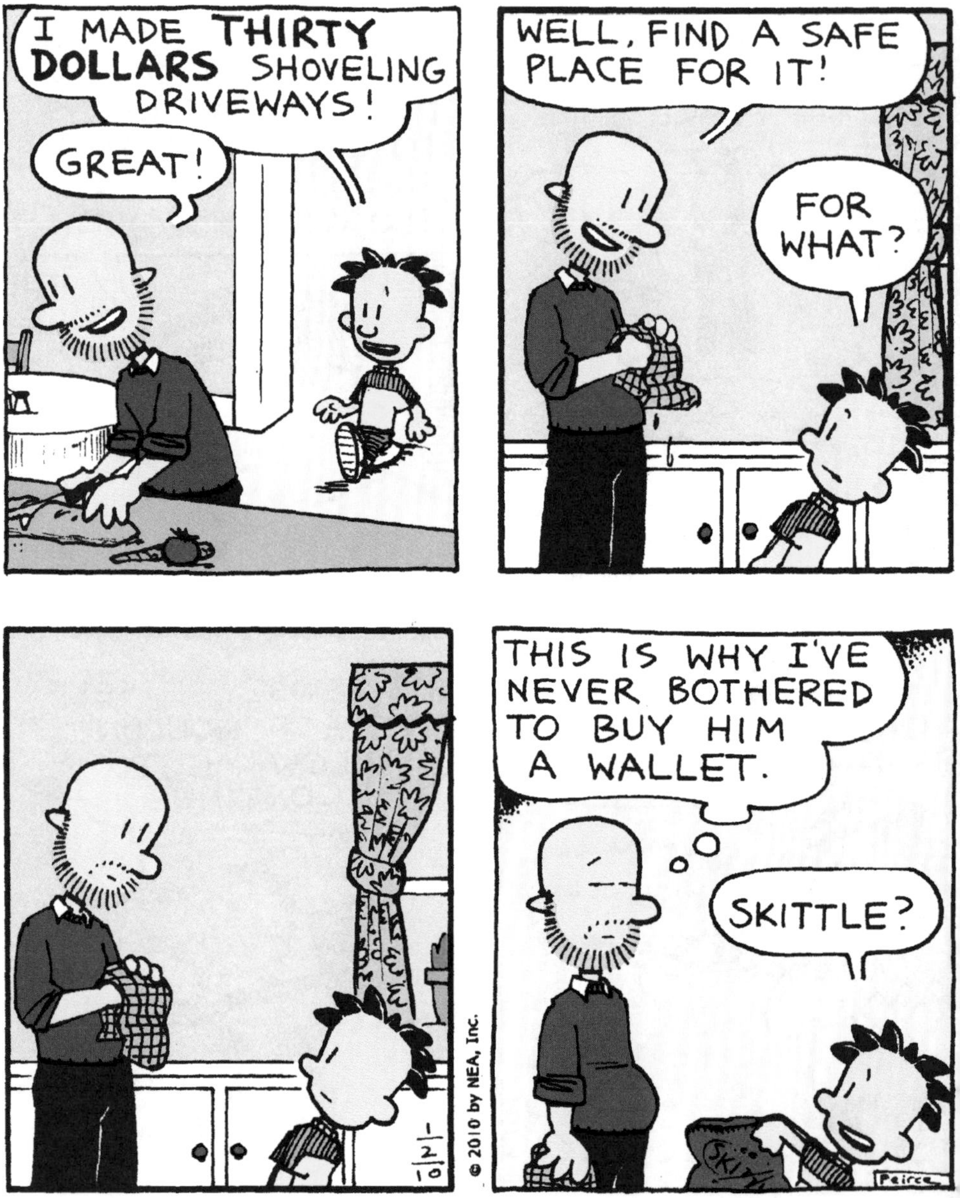
I MADE **THIRTY DOLLARS** SHOVELING DRIVEWAYS!
GREAT!
WELL, FIND A SAFE PLACE FOR IT!
FOR WHAT?
THIS IS WHY I'VE NEVER BOTHERED TO BUY HIM A WALLET.
SKITTLE?
1/2/10
© 2010 by NEA, Inc.
Peirce

© 2010 UFS, Inc.

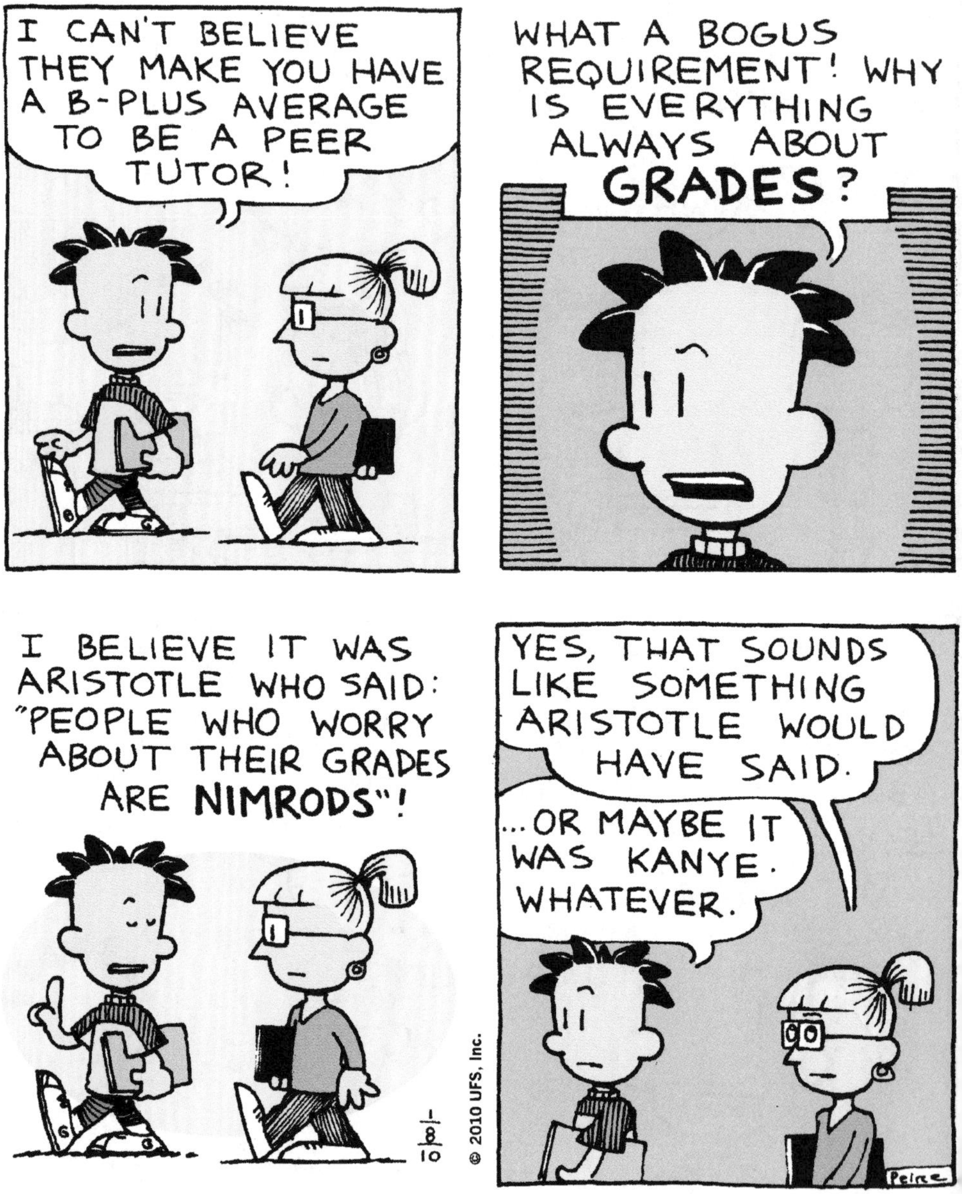
I CAN'T BELIEVE THEY MAKE YOU HAVE A B-PLUS AVERAGE TO BE A PEER TUTOR!
WHAT A BOGUS REQUIREMENT! WHY IS EVERYTHING ALWAYS ABOUT **GRADES**?
I BELIEVE IT WAS ARISTOTLE WHO SAID: "PEOPLE WHO WORRY ABOUT THEIR GRADES ARE **NIMRODS**"!
1/8/10
© 2010 UFS, Inc.
YES, THAT SOUNDS LIKE SOMETHING ARISTOTLE WOULD HAVE SAID.
...OR MAYBE IT WAS KANYE. WHATEVER.
Peirce

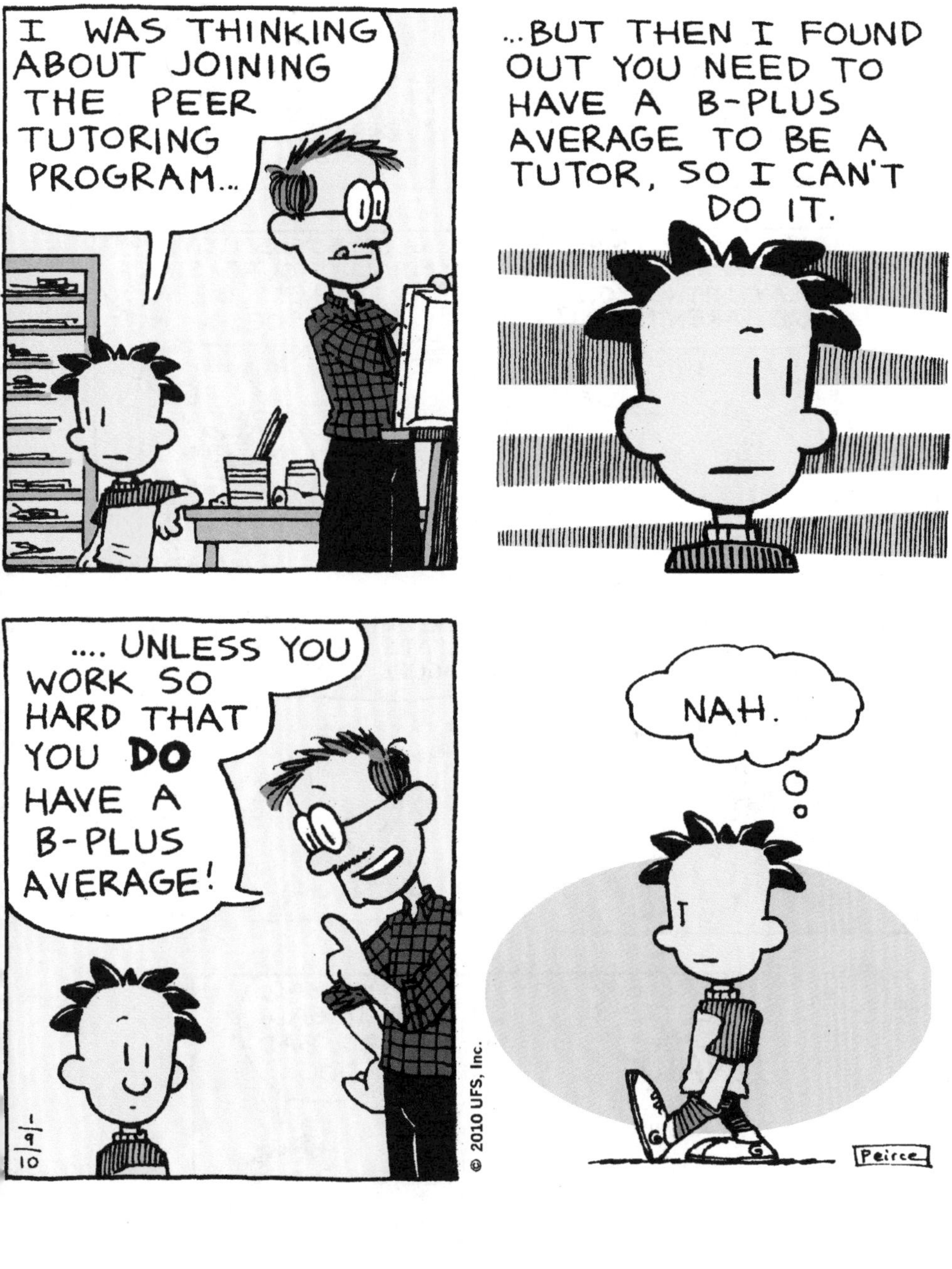
I WAS THINKING ABOUT JOINING THE PEER TUTORING PROGRAM...
...BUT THEN I FOUND OUT YOU NEED TO HAVE A B-PLUS AVERAGE TO BE A TUTOR, SO I CAN'T DO IT.
.... UNLESS YOU WORK SO HARD THAT YOU **DO** HAVE A B-PLUS AVERAGE!
NAH.
1/9/10
© 2010 UFS, Inc.
Peirce

NATE WRIGHT, VIBE CONSULTANT

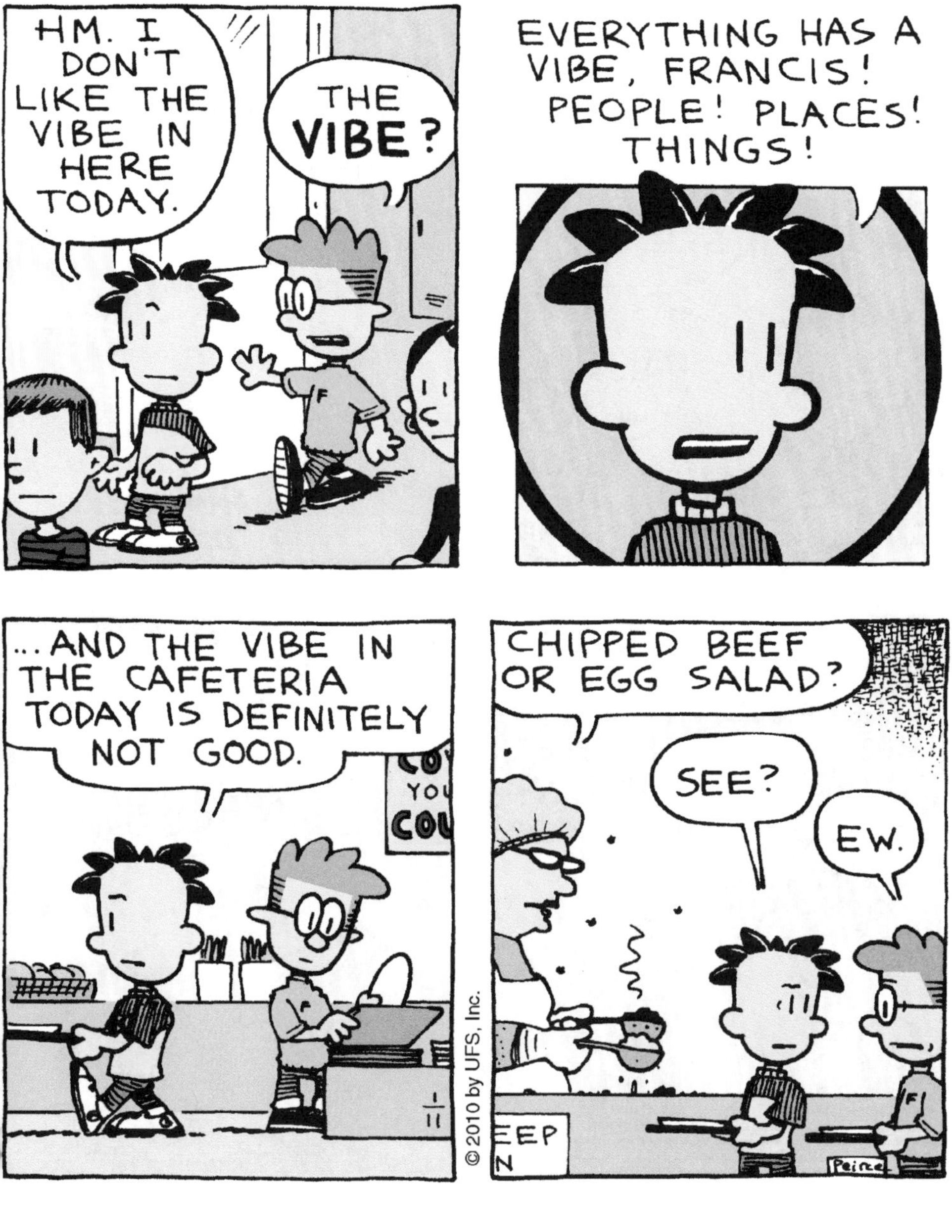
HM. I DON'T LIKE THE VIBE IN HERE TODAY.
THE VIBE?
EVERYTHING HAS A VIBE, FRANCIS! PEOPLE! PLACES! THINGS!
...AND THE VIBE IN THE CAFETERIA TODAY IS DEFINITELY NOT GOOD.
CHIPPED BEEF OR EGG SALAD?
SEE?
EW.
© 2010 by UFS, Inc.
Peirce

© 2010 by UFS, Inc.

1/13

© 2010 by UFS, Inc.

THOMAS JEFFERSON, FOUNDING FATHER
By Nate Wright

Thomas Jefferson, a great American, was born on the historic day of April 13, 1743 in the sleepy little village of Shadwell, Virginia. Tom's dad was named Peter and his mom was Jane. When Tom was fourteen years old, his dad (Peter) died, so from then on Tom was in charge because his father was dead. Tom decided he wanted to go to college, but apparently there weren't many colleges around back then because the only one he could find had the very strange name of William and Mary. But he went there anyway. Also, during this time he learned how to play the violin. After college Tom got married. His wife was named Martha, which by coincidence was also the name of George Washington's wife Martha.

Anyway, married life must have been kind of boring, because Tom decided to get into politics. He was in the Virginia House of Burgesses and also was a member of the second Continental Congress. Tom drafted (which is a fancy word for "wrote") the Declaration of Independence, which was when the colonial guys told the British to give them their freedom. Writing the Declaration of Independence was the reason Tom was one of the founding fathers, which is why I called this essay "Thomas Jefferson, Founding Father." During the whole American Revolution thing, Tom was elected governor of Virginia. Then his wife died. What she died from, I have no idea. But obviously Tom got on with his life, because pretty soon after that he became a congressman. Then he became minister to France, so he spent a lot of time hanging around in Paris. And then George Washington, who was president at the time, hired Tom to be the secretary of state.

Tom ran for president in 1796, but he lost the election to John Adams, so he became vice president instead. Then in 1800 Tom ran again, and this time he won. So then he was president. He was the third president in United States history. Some of his major accomplishments that he did while he was president were the Louisiana Purchase and the Embargo Act. He also invented the University of Virginia.

After that, Tom just hung out and got old, and he died on July 4th, 1826, which is an amazing coincidence because that was the 50th anniversary of the Declaration of Independence, which Tom wrote as we all remember so well. So, to sum up the life and career of Thomas Jefferson, founding father (which is also the title of this essay): he was a congressman, a governor, a secretary of state, a vice president, and a president. Wow, that is truly incredible. Oh, and also Tom's picture is on a nickel. Thomas Jefferson will never be forgotten. It is so, so, so, so, so, so, so, so, so, so, so, so, so important that today's American citizens understand how very, very, very, very, very, very important he was.

THE END

MOUSE!

© 2010 by UFS, Inc.

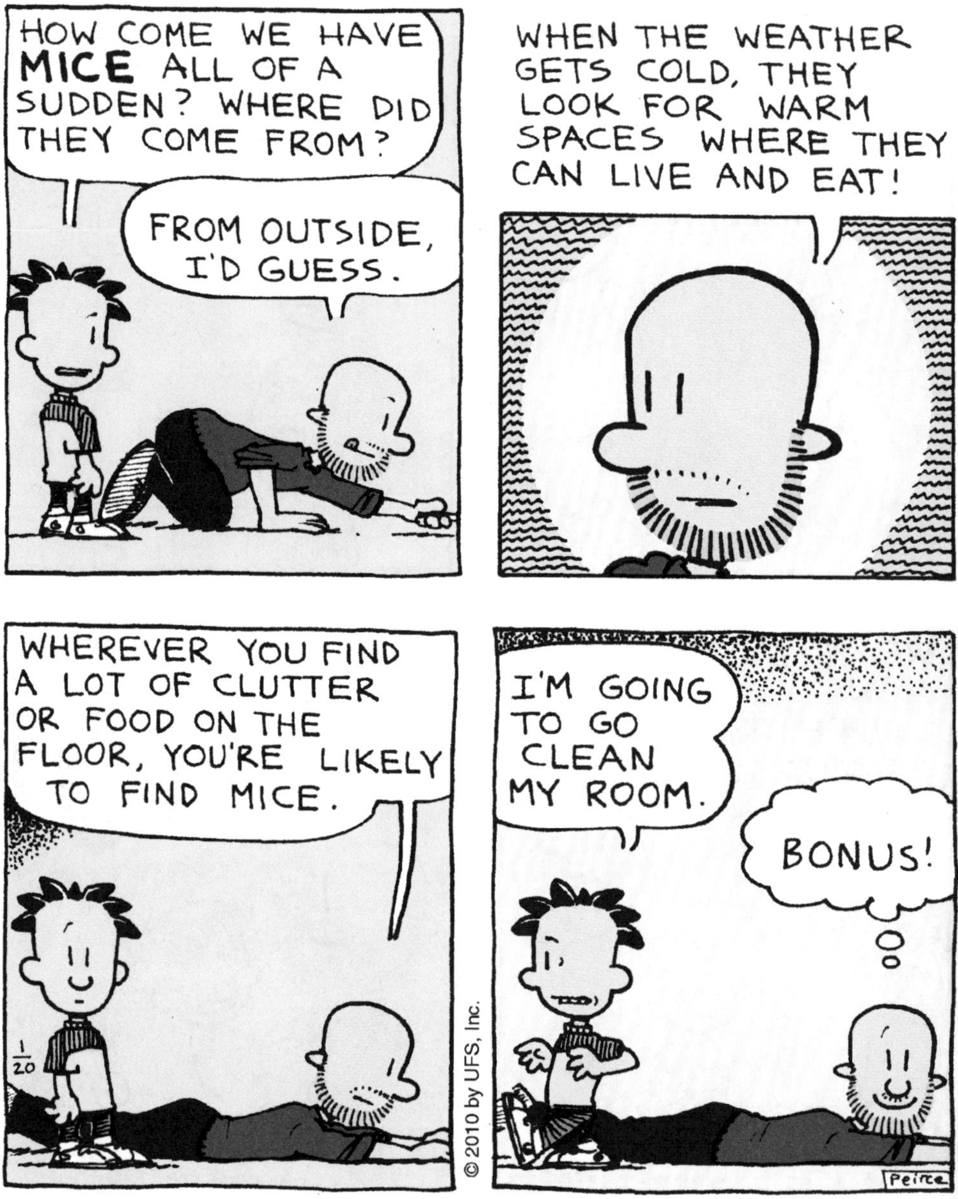
HOW COME WE HAVE **MICE** ALL OF A SUDDEN? WHERE DID THEY COME FROM?
FROM OUTSIDE, I'D GUESS.
WHEN THE WEATHER GETS COLD, THEY LOOK FOR WARM SPACES WHERE THEY CAN LIVE AND EAT!
WHEREVER YOU FIND A LOT OF CLUTTER OR FOOD ON THE FLOOR, YOU'RE LIKELY TO FIND MICE.
1/20
© 2010 by UFS, Inc.
I'M GOING TO GO CLEAN MY ROOM.
BONUS!
Peirce

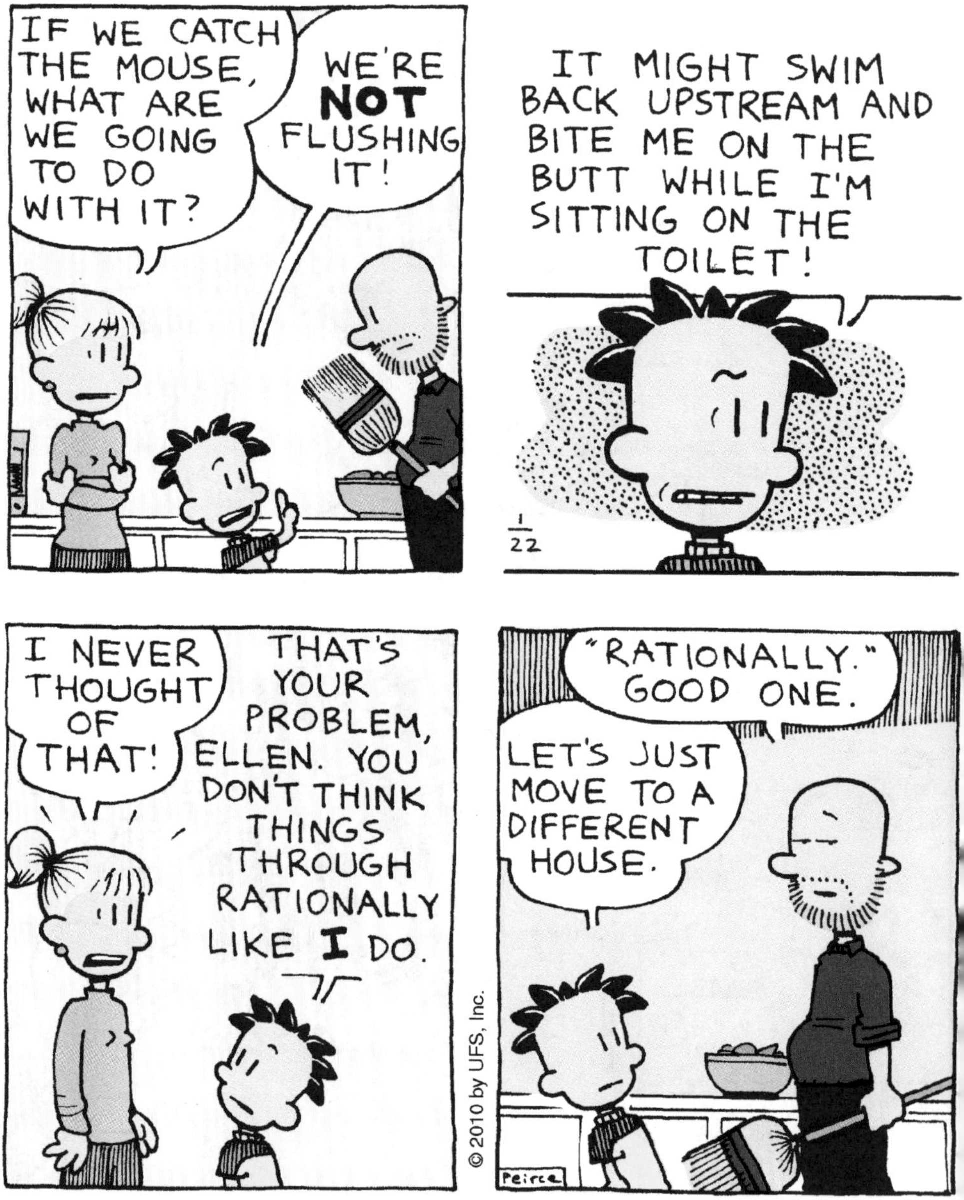
IF WE CATCH THE MOUSE, WHAT ARE WE GOING TO DO WITH IT?
WE'RE **NOT** FLUSHING IT!
IT MIGHT SWIM BACK UPSTREAM AND BITE ME ON THE BUTT WHILE I'M SITTING ON THE TOILET!
1/22
I NEVER THOUGHT OF THAT!
THAT'S YOUR PROBLEM, ELLEN. YOU DON'T THINK THINGS THROUGH RATIONALLY LIKE **I** DO.
"RATIONALLY." GOOD ONE.
LET'S JUST MOVE TO A DIFFERENT HOUSE.
Peirce

WOW!

© 2010 by UFS, Inc.

$\frac{1}{24}$

© 2010 by UFS, Inc.

WHAT WOULD YOU LIKE TO TALK ABOUT, NATE?

WAIT, WE'RE NOT GONNA TALK IN THESE **CHAIRS**, ARE WE?

TEDDY SAID THAT WHEN **HE** WAS HERE, YOU TOOK OFF YOUR SHOES AND DID DEEP BREATHING EXERCISES!

AH! OKAY!

IF YOU'D LIKE TO TAKE OFF YOUR SHOES, GO RIGHT AHEAD!

© 2010 by UFS, Inc.

...ALTHOUGH I MIGHT SKIP THE DEEP BREATHING.

GOT ANY FOOD?

SO WHAT'S ON YOUR MIND, NATE?

ARTUR KEEPS SHOWING UP IN MY DREAMS.

MM-HM. AND WHO'S ARTUR?

HE'S A KID IN MY CLASS.

BUT OF COURSE **YOU** DON'T **KNOW** HIM, BECAUSE **MISTER PERFECT** NEVER **NEEDS** TO SEE THE SCHOOL COUNSELOR!

2/2

© 2010 by UFS, Inc.

HM. THAT'S INTERESTING.

BUT NOT AS INTERESTING AS ARTUR! HE'S **FASCINATING!**

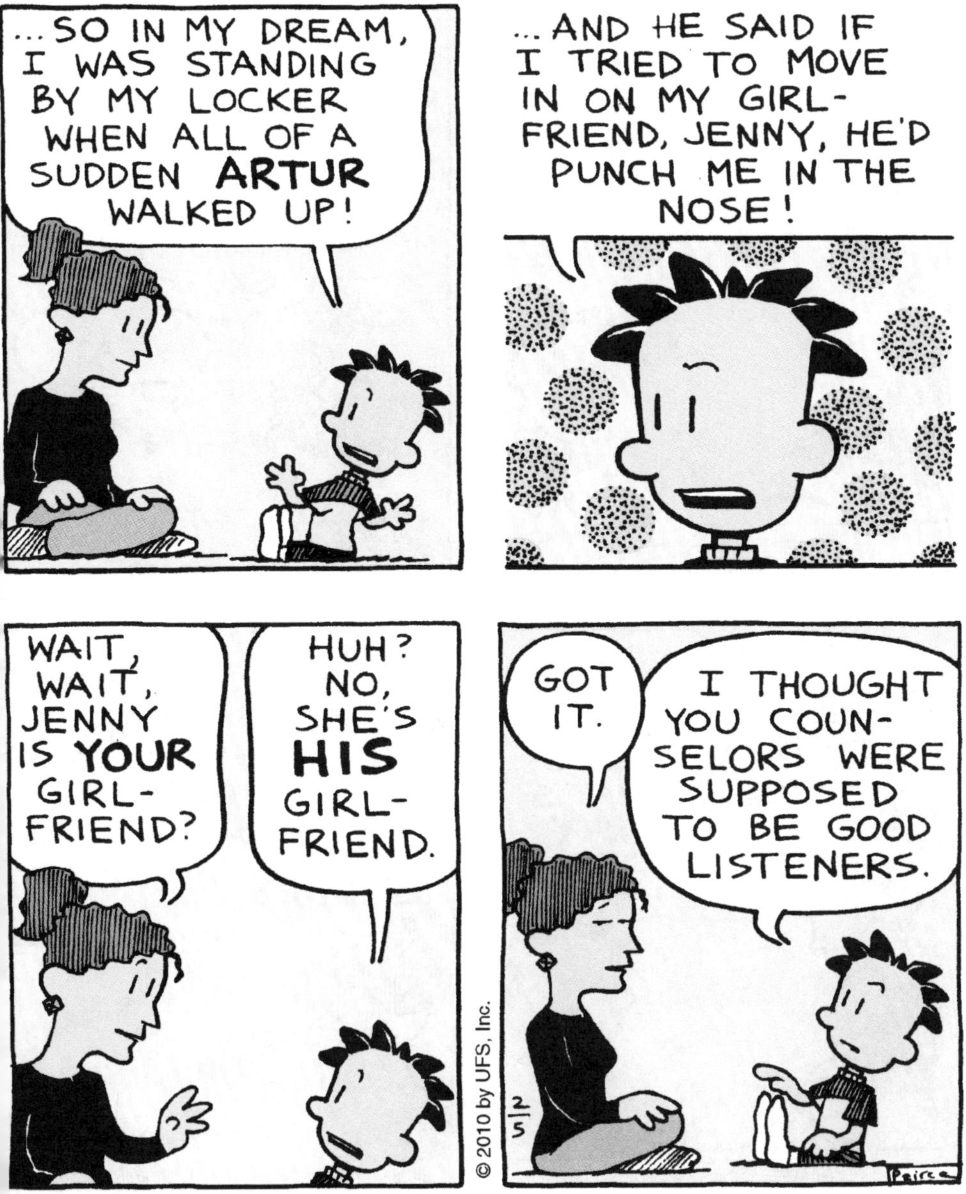
...SO IN MY DREAM, I WAS STANDING BY MY LOCKER WHEN ALL OF A SUDDEN ARTUR WALKED UP!
...AND HE SAID IF I TRIED TO MOVE IN ON MY GIRL-FRIEND, JENNY, HE'D PUNCH ME IN THE NOSE!
WAIT, WAIT, JENNY IS YOUR GIRL-FRIEND?
HUH? NO, SHE'S HIS GIRL-FRIEND.
GOT IT.
I THOUGHT YOU COUN-SELORS WERE SUPPOSED TO BE GOOD LISTENERS.
© 2010 by UFS, Inc.
2/5
Peirce

OKAY, NATE, LET'S SEE IF I'VE GOT THIS STRAIGHT...

YOU'RE FRIENDLY WITH ARTUR, BUT YOU ALSO RESENT HIS POPULARITY AND DON'T LIKE THE FACT THAT HE'S GOING OUT WITH A GIRL YOU HAVE A LONG-STANDING CRUSH ON.

WHAT?

NO. NO, THAT'S TOTALLY WRONG. THAT'S **WAY** OFF.

$\frac{2}{6}$

WELL, I THOUGHT IT MIGHT BE.

WHERE'S ALL THE STUFF I TOLD YOU ABOUT HOW **ANNOYING** ARTUR IS?

MAYBE THE SCHOOL COUNSELOR WAS RIGHT. SHE SAID I SHOULD STOP CHASING AFTER JENNY.

YES! FINALLY!!

SO YOU'RE ACTUALLY GOING TO ACCEPT THE FACT THAT JENNY AND ARTUR ARE A COUPLE?

YEAH, I THINK I'LL STEP ASIDE. IT'S THE RIGHT THING TO DO.

IT MEANS I'M PUTTING **JENNY'S** HAPPINESS AHEAD OF MY **OWN!** IT'S A VERY UNSELFISH MOVE ON MY PART! VERY NOBLE!

...AND MAYBE JENNY WILL **SEE** HOW NOBLE I AM, AND THEN SHE'LL FALL MADLY IN LOVE WITH ME AND DUMP ARTUR AND YAK YAK YAK YAK HK YAK YAK YAK YAK

JUST SHOOT ME.

OKAY, JENNY, IT'S DECIDED! I'M OFFICIALLY NOT PURSUING YOU ROMANTICALLY ANYMORE!

HALLE-LUJAH.

FROM NOW ON WE'RE JUST FRIENDS! RIGHT?

RIGHT. JUST FRIENDS.

... AND WHAT **IS** A FRIEND?

WHAT?

2/11

A FRIEND IS SOMEONE YOU SPEND **TIME** WITH, RIGHT?

UH-OH.

© 2010 by UFS, Inc.

Peirce

I THINK IT'S GOOD THAT MY CRUSH ON JENNY IS OFFICIALLY OVER!

NOW SHE AND I CAN FOCUS ON HAVING A **FRIENDSHIP** INSTEAD OF A **ROMANCE!**

2/13

RIGHT, JENNY? A **FRIENDSHIP!**

LEAVE ME ALONE, YOU ▬

GOTCHA! WE'LL CHAT LATER!

YOUR FRIENDSHIP IS TAKING ON WATER.

Peirce

189

BE SEATED

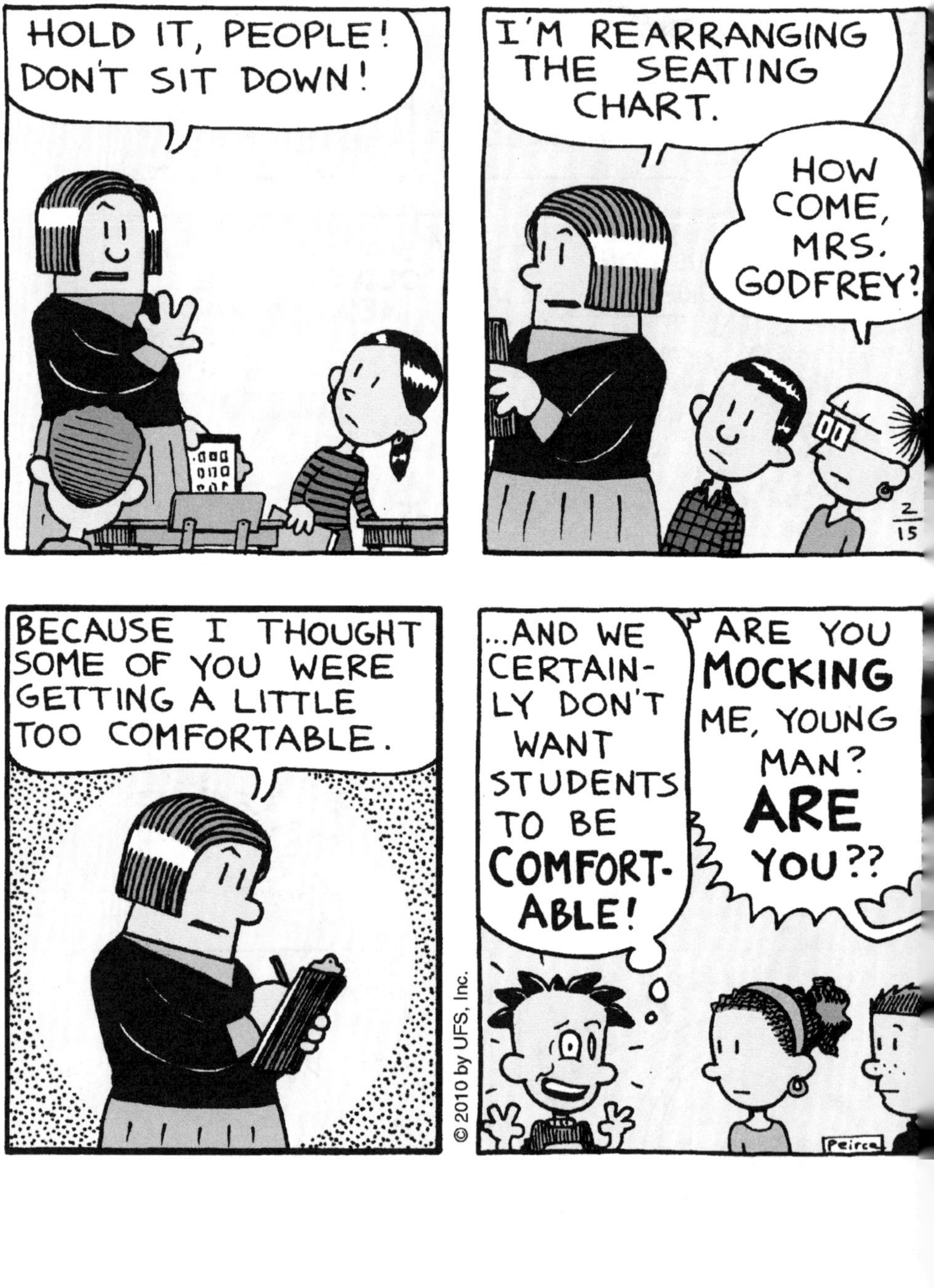

HOLD IT, PEOPLE! DON'T SIT DOWN!
I'M REARRANGING THE SEATING CHART.
HOW COME, MRS. GODFREY?
2/15
BECAUSE I THOUGHT SOME OF YOU WERE GETTING A LITTLE TOO COMFORTABLE.
...AND WE CERTAINLY DON'T WANT STUDENTS TO BE COMFORTABLE!
ARE YOU MOCKING ME, YOUNG MAN? ARE YOU??
Peirce

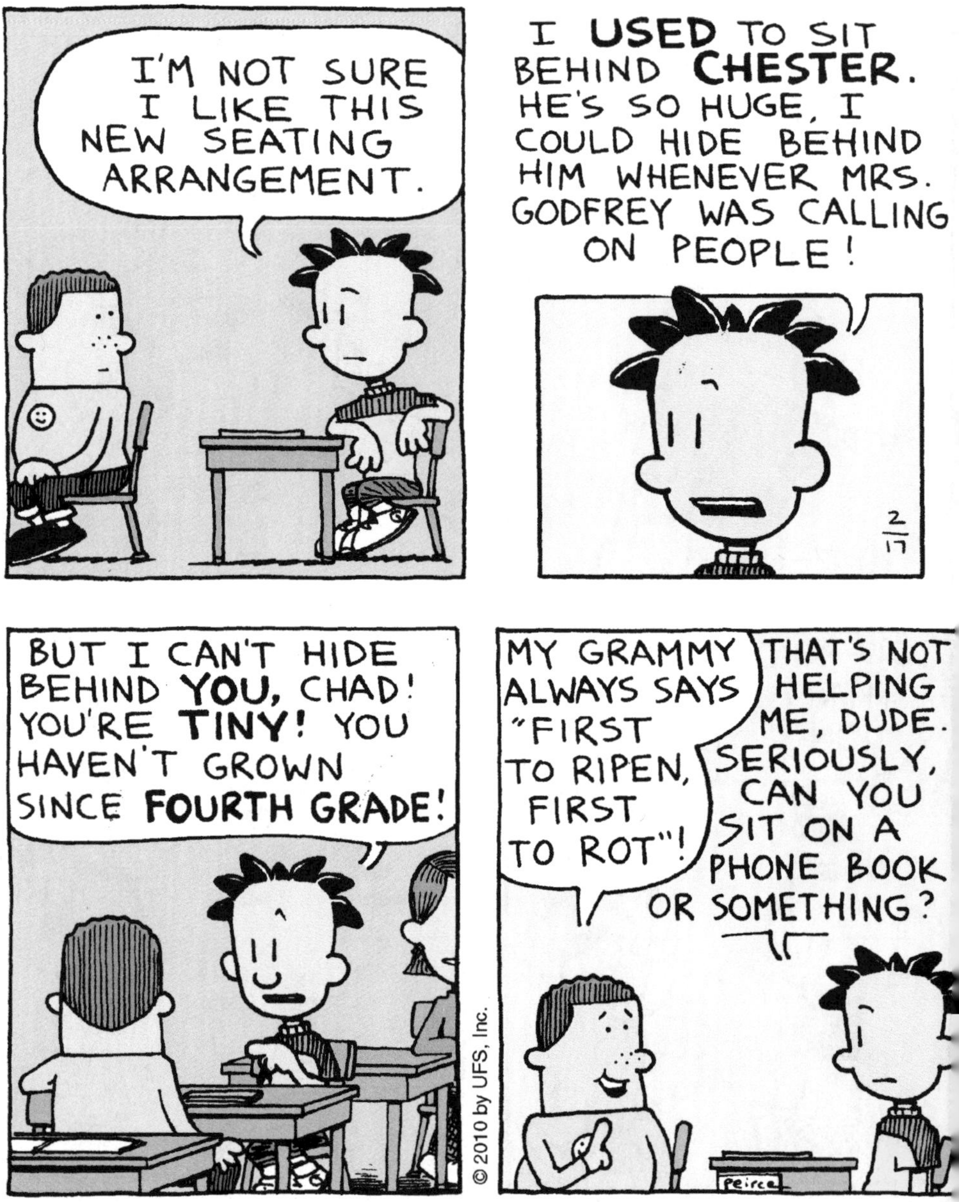
I'M NOT SURE I LIKE THIS NEW SEATING ARRANGEMENT.
I USED TO SIT BEHIND CHESTER. HE'S SO HUGE, I COULD HIDE BEHIND HIM WHENEVER MRS. GODFREY WAS CALLING ON PEOPLE!
2/17
BUT I CAN'T HIDE BEHIND YOU, CHAD! YOU'RE TINY! YOU HAVEN'T GROWN SINCE FOURTH GRADE!
MY GRAMMY ALWAYS SAYS "FIRST TO RIPEN, FIRST TO ROT"!
THAT'S NOT HELPING ME, DUDE. SERIOUSLY, CAN YOU SIT ON A PHONE BOOK OR SOMETHING?
Peirce

WHAT'S YOUR POINT?

© 2010 by UFS, Inc.

WHY ARE YOU CARRYING THAT THING AROUND?

THIS "**THING**," FRANCIS, IS MY PRESIDENTIAL **GAVEL**!

IT'S A **SYMBOL** OF THE RESPECT I COMMAND AS CLASS PRESIDENT!

HEY, WHO'S THE DORK WITH THE DOLL HAMMER?

HA HA HA HA HA

IT'S ALSO GOOD FOR HITTING PEOPLE.

© 2010 by UFS, Inc.

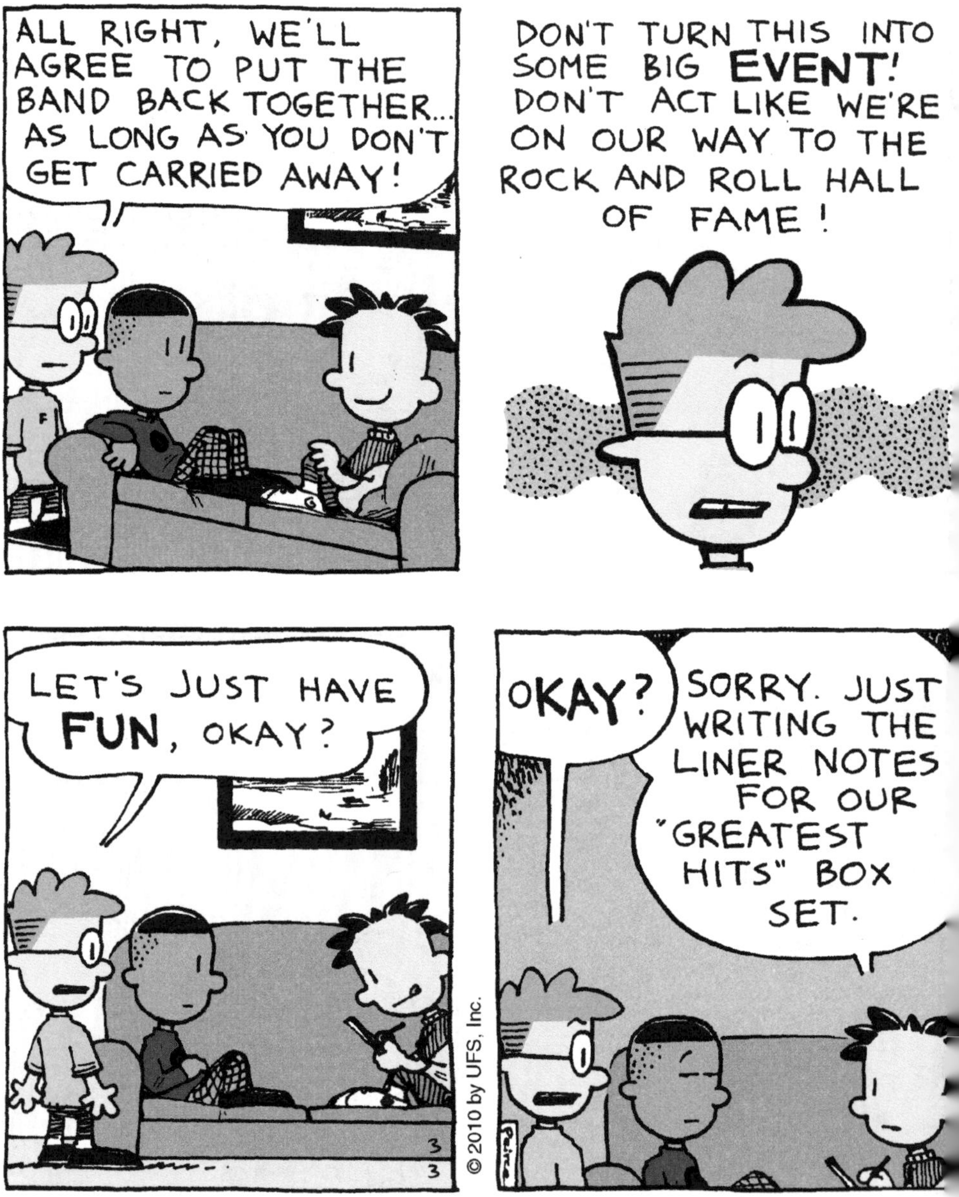
ALL RIGHT, WE'LL AGREE TO PUT THE BAND BACK TOGETHER... AS LONG AS YOU DON'T GET CARRIED AWAY!
DON'T TURN THIS INTO SOME BIG EVENT! DON'T ACT LIKE WE'RE ON OUR WAY TO THE ROCK AND ROLL HALL OF FAME!
LET'S JUST HAVE FUN, OKAY?
OKAY?
SORRY. JUST WRITING THE LINER NOTES FOR OUR "GREATEST HITS" BOX SET.
3
3
© 2010 by UFS, Inc.

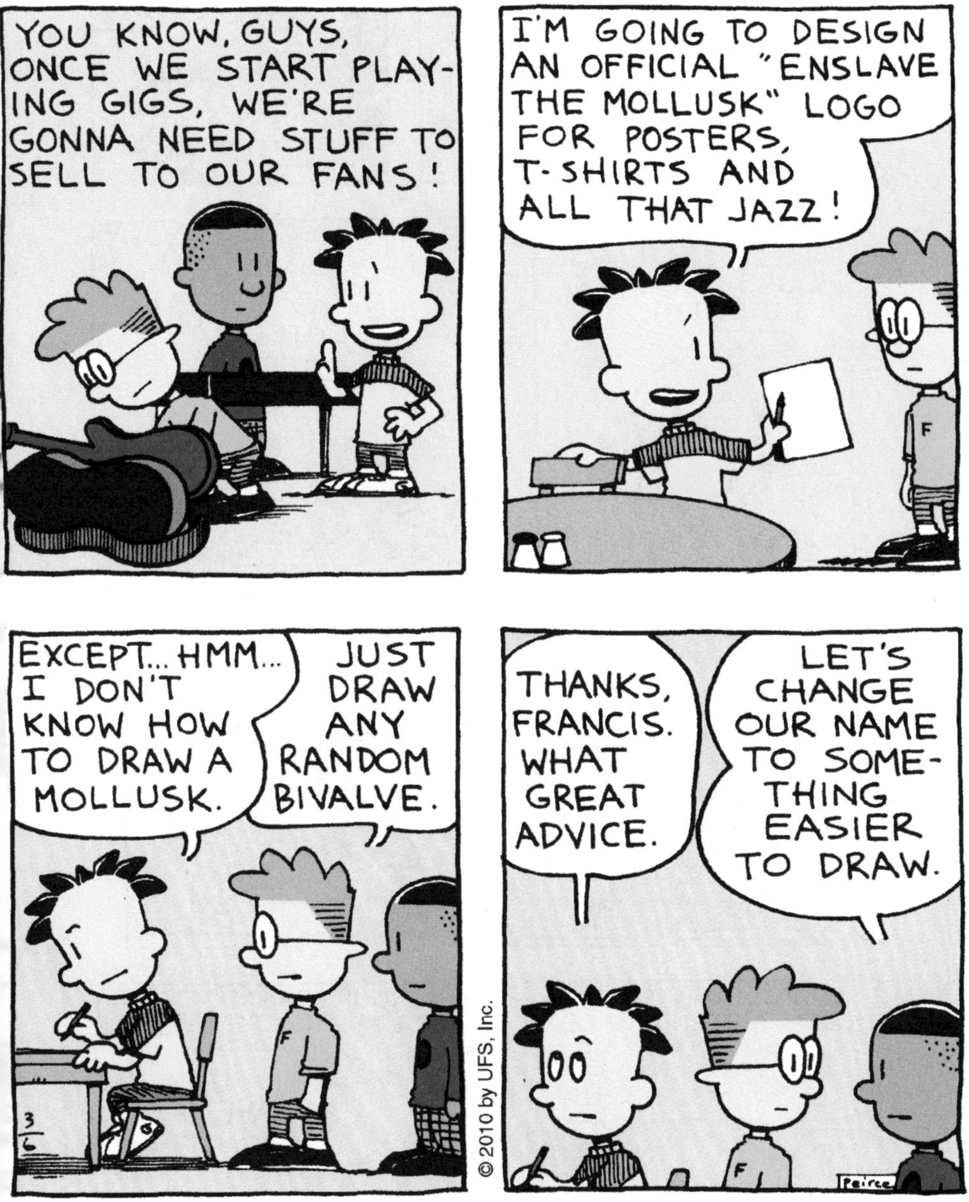
YOU KNOW, GUYS, ONCE WE START PLAYING GIGS, WE'RE GONNA NEED STUFF TO SELL TO OUR FANS!
I'M GOING TO DESIGN AN OFFICIAL "ENSLAVE THE MOLLUSK" LOGO FOR POSTERS, T-SHIRTS AND ALL THAT JAZZ!
EXCEPT... HMM... I DON'T KNOW HOW TO DRAW A MOLLUSK.
JUST DRAW ANY RANDOM BIVALVE.
THANKS, FRANCIS. WHAT GREAT ADVICE.
LET'S CHANGE OUR NAME TO SOMETHING EASIER TO DRAW.
3/6
© 2010 by UFS, Inc.
Peirce

STUCK ON NATE

BONUS ACTIVITIES TO CRACK YOU UP!

CAPTION ACTION

Ready, set, write! Come up with cool captions for Nate's sketches.

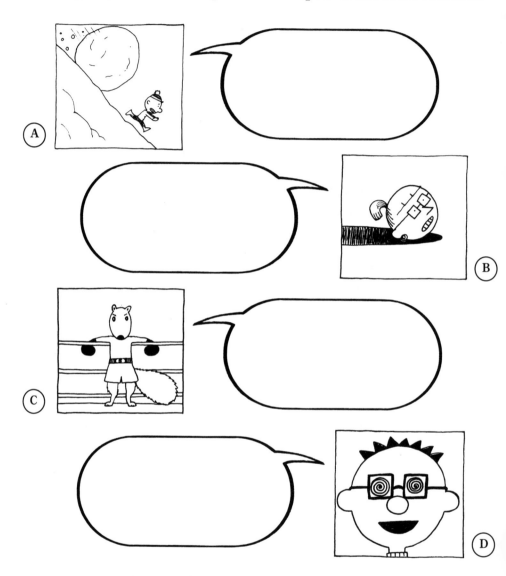

EXTRA CREDIT! Match each sketch to the original comic.

Comic A goes on page _____.

Comic B goes on page _____.

Comic C goes on page _____.

Comic D goes on page _____.

FAST FORWARD

What's going to happen next? It's up to you!

Bonus: Can you match each sketch to its Sunday strip?

Comic A goes on page _____.

Comic B goes on page _____.

Comic C goes on page _____.

ALL ABOUT YOU!

Nate loves sports, Spitsy (most of the time), and Jenny.
How about you?

NATE

YOU

Favorite sport

Favorite animal

Favorite friend (or crush!)

BRAIN BOWL

Nate's brain is
filled with trivia!

Now write down all the things running through *your* brain.

LIVIN' LARGE!

P.S. 38 is pretty small. Everyone knows everyone else. So whenever a new kid shows up, it's a major event. Especially when he's got a name like **THIS**:

Anyway, Principal Nichols asked me to be the kid's "buddy," so it's my job to help him make friends...

... and to show him around the school, which is falling apart. That's what happens when a building is one hundred years old.

Lincoln Peirce

(pronounced "purse") is a cartoonist/writer and *New York Times* bestselling author of the hilarious Big Nate book series (www.bignatebooks.com), now published in twenty-five countries worldwide and available as ebooks and audiobooks and as an app, Big Nate: Comix by U! He is also the creator of the comic strip *Big Nate*. It appears in over three hundred U.S. newspapers and online daily at www.gocomics.com/bignate. Lincoln's boyhood idol was Charles Schulz of *Peanuts* fame, but his main inspiration for Big Nate has always been his own experience as a sixth grader. Just like Nate, Lincoln loves comics, ice hockey, and Cheez Doodles (and dislikes cats, figure skating, and egg salad). His Big Nate books have been featured on *Good Morning America* and in the *Boston Globe*, the *Los Angeles Times*, *USA Today*, and the *Washington Post*. He has also written for Cartoon Network and Nickelodeon. Lincoln lives with his wife and two children in Portland, Maine.

BiG NATE

SUPER FAN SWEEPSTAKES

Enter the Big Nate Super Fan Sweepstakes for a chance to appear in Big Nate's next book!

Official rules and entry on www.bignatebooks.com

One Grand Prize Winner:
Will appear in the next
Big Nate book,
Big Nate Lives It Up

Ten Runner-up Prize Winners:
Copies of *Big Nate: In the Zone*,
Big Nate: Mr. Popularity, and
Big Nate Laugh-O-Rama

READ ALL THE BOOKS TODAY!

Big Nate art © UFS, Inc. Big Nate ®

TEDDY RATES ALL THE BiG NATE BOOKS!

Grade: A

Comments: My fortune cookie says Nate is destined for detention!

Grade: A

Comments: Nate and Gina are partners? Even I couldn't come up with something that funny!

Grade: A

Comments: Better than a bag of Cheez Doodles!

Grade: A

Comments: I get warm fuzzies thinking about our Timber Scout fund-raiser. Ha!

Grade: A

Comments: P.S. 38 is ready to put an end to Jefferson's seven-year winning streak! We rock!